THE ANGEL OF MARYE'S HEIGHTS:

The True Story of Richard Kirkland

A NOVEL

Anthony J Ziebol

First Printing, 2015
ISBN 978-1-329-64280-5
Ruckus Wind Publishing
Minneapolis, MN

FOR MY INCREDIBLY SUPPORTIVE PARENTS

Prologue

DECEMBER 14, 1975
FREDERICKSBURG, VIRGINIA

With stiff legs they walked silently past the remnants of the historic stone wall.

Nine-year-old Jeremy Pratt looked over at his father, who was curiously nervous and distant, which seemed to manifest the instant they stepped out of the family car.

Edward had kept his son in suspense on the drive down from Central New York in their wrinkled and panting Ford Falcon sedan, and now the reverence and awe of what he considered sacred ground had overtaken his usual affable demeanor. Many a night he lay awake thinking of this day, ever since his son came wailing into this world.

Would I be able to convey the enormity of this lesson and with the same eloquence as my dad? Will Jeremy embrace my words and continue the unbroken chain of the family legacy?

Edward was well aware that his son was not very mature, even for his age. Jeremy was more of a free spirit, like his mother, a trait that Edward both admired and feared in equal measures. And as they left the parking lot of the Fredericksburg Battlefield Visitor Center, the lingering doubts had reappeared.

Was he ready for this moment?

After all, a lesson learned often does not come without visiting its treacherous cousin.

While this particular story was one of tremendous beauty and hope, to find this oak of truth, one must navigate through fields of blood.

Of course, Edward could have waited another year or two. But his son had reached the age of tradition three months ago and he had decided to follow the rite of passage.

The previous evening, at Jeremy's normal bedtime, the boy found himself in the backseat of his father's car, cradled by the worn backseat and his grandmother's crocheted afghan. Behind the driver, on the floor, a single white rose had been placed in a cardboard box. Edward did not tell him where they were going, and Jeremy was too tired to argue about the strangeness of the night journey. Before the first song of the Marshal Tucker Band 8-track was over, he was asleep.

For eight hours, stopping only for food and bathroom breaks, father and son drove in silence, the bouncing hum of the road keeping Jeremy sedated. At one point, after pulling over for fuel and a snack, Jeremy finally rubbed his eyes, looked out the window and asked his father THE question.

"Are we running away, dad?"

Edward giggled inside, but he kept his composure, wanting to retain an air of mystery that would hold his son's often wayward attention.

"No, son," he said. "We'll be back tomorrow."

"Where are we going?"

"You'll see."

For an exhausted pre-teen who trusted his parents implicitly, that was enough, and he went back to sleep. His father had wanted to roll in to Fredericksburg as close to dawn as possible, before the tourists arrived for the anniversary events, so they would be alone. As they arrived for the familial birthright, 113 years in the making, they had found the parking lot of their destination empty, much to Edward's relief. Jeremy, always the inquisitive one amongst the family of four, was now wide awake, and increasingly curious. Yet his questions were again pushed aside with short, evasive answers.

"You'll see."

"It won't be long now."

And then the maddening:

"Because I said so."

As they left the parking lot, they turned onto a path leading through a wall of carefully placed stones. The boy was about to break the silence with another query, but the intense, almost uncomfortable look on his father's face made him hesitate. And so, nary a word, with his hands buried deep in his winter coat pockets, he followed his father's determined gait on the centuries-old sunken road, where generations of wagons had torn away at its surface.

Held delicately by Edward's left hand, the single rose matched in color the frosted exhales of the two pilgrims on the chilled, eerily-hushed morning.

Patches of winter incarnate adorned the steep hill to their left as if covering long-forgotten, but still emanating stains on the land. At the summit of the hill, a grand, four-pillared mansion, Brompton, stood watch above the town, which had crept much closer to its perch in the last century.

To their right they came to a large, coffee-colored, wooden well, complete with a simple platform and pointed roof. Behind the wellhouse was the location where the Martha Stevens House once knelt between piles of corpses, the foundation now humbly marked by a layer of stone.

A short distance further, a small, whitewashed dwelling known as the Innis House stood wounded, riddled with bullet holes, yet still looming in defiance.

At last, beyond the halting stone wall, a large statue came into the anxious view.

Jeremy had not thought it possible, but the moment it struck his father's gaze, his countenance shifted to another level of solemnity. For a moment, the vision arrested Edward's feet and he stood there frozen, as if in the presence of the Holy. But as quickly as the paralysis occurred, it passed, and he found his long stride again.

Following his father directly to the front of the poignant sculpture created by renowned artist Felix de Weldon in the year of Jeremy's birth, the boy took it in: a Civil War soldier raising up another in his arms and helping the fallen soldier to a drink from his canteen.

Still muted, Edward waited while his son read part of the inscription.

In Memorium
Richard Rowland Kirkland
Co. G, 2nd South Carolina Volunteers
C. S. A.

Finally, the mysterious silence was broken.

"I bring you here today because now you are old enough to understand," Edward said in a light but firm tone, choosing his words carefully. "My father brought me here to this battlefield when I was your age, and I will bring your sister here when she is old enough."

He paused and Jeremy still could not fathom what his father was talking about.

"I know I've told you that our ancestor, my Great-Great Grandfather, my namesake, fought in the Civil War, in the 57th New York Infantry," Edward continued. "He fought here at Fredericksburg, and nearly died charging the very wall we just passed."

Handing the rose to his son, he motioned for Jeremy to place it before the memorial. Sensing the weight of the moment, but unsure of its significance, Jeremy obeyed.

"You see that name there?"

Jeremy looked at the inscription.

"Richard Kirkland. Never heard of him," said the boy with indifference.

His father put his hand on his young son's shoulder, and looked directly into his eyes.

"You must never, in all your days, forget his name. Our family, and the generations that have preceded us, owe everything to him. For without this man so honored before you, this family would never have existed."

Chapter 1

December 20, 1860

FLAT ROCK, SOUTH CAROLINA

The crash of hooves into Little Flat Rock Creek sent up a spray of kindled orange clay.

With reckless thrust, two bobbing Hackney stallions, controlled by novice men but adept riders, dove into the shallow waterway that bowed its way between tall, elderly pines and under a yawning, cherry sky.

The staggering trail, that when in season, nuzzled fields of cotton in orderly bench terraces on the hills and elongated rows of Indian corn where the slopes gradually leveled, had long been pummeled of anything green. It was as if the grass and soil had caught fire, turned a lasting red by the dueling hooves.

Although the riders were the best of friends, when it came to racing horses, the competitive desire postponed all affections. As soon as the preliminary handshake dropped to a three-count start, it was war.

Richard Rowland Kirkland, average in height and weight, but nothing else, was no stranger to the equine, and was a gifted rider. Unusually mature for a boy of seventeen, with balanced shoulders extending to his mind, his tranquil brown eyes hid anchors of ferocious purpose and healthy ambition. Physically, he was not an imposing specimen. Despite a healthy appetite, he was, by even the modest of descriptors, quite skinny.

While attractive above the neighbor-norm, he was not a candidate for sculpture. A long, bird-realm neck made him appear taller than he was, but it was a telling trait, as if God wanted extra separation between his chivalrous head and a lowly, terrestrial body.

Despite being only moderately educated in a rural church classroom, Kirkland's mind was continually studious, rummaging the farm lanes for truth and wisdom. He was practical, however, with a mental posture streamlined in a layer below the clouds.

On a near opposite of the personality and physical spectrum was Joseph Duncan.

A capable horseman himself, his eternal optimism never wavered, even in the glare of bleak circumstances. The difference was in his toes' position, often far removed from the pragmatic clay. Joe was always the audacious one, ready to leap from the ground and drift among the wispy cirrus forms. To him, life was a hedonistic playground, meant to be enjoyed at every turn. Tall, chiseled and strong, a year older than Kirkland but in no hurry to dismiss a few adolescent charms, Joe was light-hearted and charismatic, able to knock the drapes from a room with his casual grace or natural smile. Of course, these qualities endeared him to the order of eligible daughters and were known to even put a belle's parents under his spell. As a result, a weekend invitation to social events among the local middle class was as common as his buoyant grin.

Kirkland benefitted from Joe's popularity as well, for it was known that inviting Joe meant setting the table for an additional pal. It was not as if Kirkland was merely a tag along, however. For his steady bearing and humble confidence garnered widespread respect and admiration, which did not go unnoticed by the Kershaw District belles nor by fathers seeking a worthy mate for their daughter.

It was an interesting dynamic, as local planters immensely enjoyed the duo's company, yet feared for their progenies' splintered hearts. Many in the rural community questioned how it was possible these seemingly opposites were so inseparable of friends. Even Kirkland and Joe had discussed the absurdity, but only far enough to toss a shrug and rib-poking joke. They left the "why" to their pocket philosopher friend, Alexander Morrison, and they urged him on just to see what elaborate language would arrow from his contemplative tongue.

★   ★   ★

With a near whiplash-inducing jolt, Kirkland and his mount Brimstone flung to a slight lead over his pursuing friend: up a steep hill and alongside a pile of boulders, around a longbow curve lined by Sassafras trees, through a gawking cover of long-leaf pines, and finally north to the quarter-mile victory stretch that widened with each hoof-digging rush.

The enormous red oak tree that marked the finish line came tumbling into view, with Joe's horse scratching at Brimstone's rear. Kirkland, feeling his horse had one more burst in him, turned with a confident look at his opposition, dug in and shot a full length and a half ahead past the victory tree.

Side by side they slowed their horses to a trot, Joe shaking his head, but with a glossy smile on his face. Nearing the stables, a short and stocky boy, muscular beyond his age, walked up between the two horses and grabbed the reins.

"Beat you again, huh Joe?" said the dark-skinned boy playfully, as the two riders dismounted.

"Well, you must know," said Joe, still grinning. "I wanted his head to grow a little more."

The three laughed easily, having long-since ignored the normal conduct and etiquette between servant and served. Kirkland and Joe had developed a fondness for the now sixteen-year-old boy, Tom, having grown up together.

"What does that make it? Four in a row? I'd say it was the horse, but since I used yours last week…" Kirkland teased.

Joe: "Look, his head is growing as we speak."

"Naw," Kirkland said, feigning arrogance, and stroking Brimstone's sweat-lathered neck. "I can't help being good."

Tom smiled and shook his head, walking the horses toward the stables.

"I think you's right, Joe. Right soon he'll be a stick with a watermelon head."

★   ★   ★

The Kirkland Plantation consisted of three large tracts of land: Flat Rock, White Oak, and Gun Swamp, the latter two now overseen by Richard's two older brothers, James and Daniel. Located about fifteen miles north of the isolated, prosperous town of Camden and sixty miles south of Charlotte, NC, the farms had been in the family's possession for more than a century, with each generation improving upon its prosperity in the wild Carolina midlands.

Through wise business dealings and ever-growing crop proceeds, the current generations enjoyed the simple luxuries of a comfortable, high-yeoman living.

A close-knit family of seven on the Flat Rock stead of 600 acres, the four youngest children had been nurtured by their widowed father, John, and older siblings. Richard's sister Caroline and brother Jesse had both recently married, leaving three in the roost. William, who everyone called Billy, was 21, and the youngest, though by no means the pushed-aside runt, was Sam, 15, who spent the first few years of his life with his grandparents after his mother died propelling him into the world.

Father John was a docile and tolerant old gentleman, yet had no patience for poor manners or careless misdeeds. While he had slowed down some, allowing his sons to take much of the control in the family business, he hadn't fully relinquished the reigns, keeping a hawk's eye on the plantation's books and daily operations.

If he disapproved of something, the sons knew about it, and immediately. Acknowledging his experience and fairness, however, the disagreements between father and sons were few and were usually washed down the creek by the next morning's breakfast.

Taking good care of John was the elderly house servant/cook Mayberry, who in the absence of a mother, helped raise the Kirkland children as her own in the two-storied brick and heartpine farmhouse on a gentle plateau. When in season, the house stood sentinel over quivering puff clouds of short-staple cotton.

The comfortable home was modest and sensible, but with an atmosphere of engaging warmth. Like the pines that gave it birth, it was rooted and fused with the land, almost as if it was an extension of it. Adding to this connection were two large chimneys embracing its sides, their smoky-red bricks a mirror image of the surrounding clay of which they were formed. These mortared giants climbed to converse with the tree tops and towered over the detached kitchen behind the house. Imbued with a raised porch that ran the entire length of the house, its slanting roof was supported by six detached, cream columns devoid of classical ornateness.

Although the lifestyle was a far cry from the extravagance of the elite planter class in Camden, the Kirklands had no cause for complaint, and they knew it. The passed-down stories of family struggle kept their feet firmly planted on the ground and father John would never let his offspring forget the rugged backbones of their forebears.

Within shouting distance of the main residence were three small cabins, where Tom and his parents, Seth and Mary, lived with six other field hands and their children. While the hands tended to the fields, the Kirklands were accustomed to manual labor and dirt finding haven beneath jagged fingernails.

Cotton and corn brought a comfortable living, but to save money, they grew most of their own food with several acres of gardens devoted to beans, squash, cow peas, collards, turnips and whatever else they could purge from the soil. For additional needs and to feed the small numbers of cows, hogs and sheep which roamed free in the wooded area and small pastures, wheat, oats and rye were also planted.

While on prosperity's edge, an uneasiness reigned, for Mother Nature's volatile and unforgiving presence left little room for error or misfortune. The slightest frost or punching hail, high winds or burning drought, could mean replanting a field several times over or worse—a complete loss of income and sustenance. Summers were unbearably hot, where even a moonlit stroll could be agonizing under August's oppression. The cool

13

mountain air of the west was entirely absent and the ocean breeze to the east was scorched before reaching the Carolina midlands.

While cotton was hard on the land and fields had to be constantly rotated to preserve the rich layer of black topsoil, the results were hard to ignore. But there was increasing evidence that the soil was being eroded, the red clay surfacing for breath.

And the forested areas had enemies as well. Twisting, strangling briars and thorns abhorred their clearing, and were always waiting in ambush to reclaim their territory among the pines. They hated being interrupted, and any dalliance from maintaining the land would ensure their revival. While the pines ruled, many others found their niches at corner lairs, roots defiant against the evergreen oppression.

Kirkland's favorites were the gums—sweet and black, especially in autumn, when they danced in gold, orange and fiery scarlet. In the summer, the intoxicating fruit of the shaggy mulberry was the enemy of a white cotton shirt, but a blissful treat to a skipping boy.

And like the hickory, Kirkland grew to be strong and resilient, yet it was a place of limited dreaming, where sons replaced fathers who in turn, had replaced their fathers. Aspirations for anything different were for the city folk, for the Camden elite. No, in rural Kershaw District, there were two options: farming and learning a trade that supported farming. To his credit, Kirkland had at least aligned himself as a prodigy to a local surveyor, earning enough money to purchase farming equipment for his future inheritance. The land was what he knew, and what he loved. Its burrows and hollows, snaking creeks and forested valleys were a sanctuary from an early age.

Whether happening upon a muskrat ambling clumsily between waterways or catching the tail of a beaver crashing into the brush on a rounding trail, these were cherished moments, far from trivial. They were placed in a mason jar with a vented cover, allowing the memories to breathe the air and whisper for years to come.

And he had no desire to live anywhere else.

★   ★   ★

On the porch, the tender horsemen warmed themselves by sipping coffee while resting on spartan chairs, cut and whittled by the guiding hands of the inventive Daniel, who was adept at birthing the useful out of discarded wood scraps. Lost in a lavender sunset, Kirkland was only mildly paying attention to the usual animated ramblings of Joe.

"If I happen to cross paths with that degenerate Virgil Ratcliff... Someone took a shot at one of my cousin's hogs. Took off one of his ears. I know it was him. Who else but Ratcliff and his half-wit partner Wesley Hux would do such a thing? They need a proper talkin' to. And prob'ly a lot more. Not that it would do any good. Men like that have cotton for brains. They just don't..."

"Hold on," said Kirkland, who stood up and cut his friend off with a wave of his hand.

The sound of a rapidly approaching horse was just within earshot.

"Now who would be calling at this late hour?" asked Joe.

They could see the outline of a rider and horse in full gallop heading towards them from the south. In seconds he was upon them, stopping directly in front of the curious stares. They greeted their long-absent friend, who quickly dismounted.

"Hello, Alex," said Joe, who along with Kirkland sprang to his feet to greet their intellectual friend. "How are the Morrisons?"

"Uh... splendid," said Alex, out of breathe and obviously anxious to speak of other matters. "But enough about that. I bring important news from Camden. They actually did it."

Kirkland and Joe looked at each other in confusion.

"What are you speaking of?" said Joe, impatiently.

"A telegraph came in from Charleston. The South Carolina General Assembly has passed an ordinance of secession. We are withdrawing from the Union."

By chance, the young Morrison had been returning home for Christmas from South Carolina College in Columbia when he heard the news in Camden.

This was not entirely unexpected. The fire-eaters in the newspapers had proclaimed for months that it was a foregone conclusion, yet in the rural backbone of Kershaw District, level-headed folks had taken a wait-and-see stance. But it was by far the number one topic of conversation, equally among radical elements and cautioning scribes. No matter on what side of the fence a person stood, the proposition of leaving the Union was both a terrifying doorway and seductive allure.

"My God," said Kirkland softly.

"That's great news!" exclaimed Joe. "'Bout time someone stood up to them Yankees. It might as well be us."

"With the election of Lincoln, the writing was on the wall," said Kirkland. "Now we'll show them what South Carolinians are made of."

Alex, finally having caught his breath, patted his charcoal horse's mane.

"You should see Camden. The whole place is in an uproar. People crowding the streets. Bands are playing. Someone fired an old cannon. You'd think it was the Fourth of July."

That comment struck a sober chord in the three buddies. Although during the past few years, Independence Day celebrations had shrunk to mere passive nods, they remembered when it meant something, even as naïve children. All three had ancestors who had fought during the Revolution. Turning their back on a flag that once meant so much to their families wasn't to be made without a shiver in their shoulders.

"It's time for a new Revolution," said Joe, ending the brief silence. "And maybe this time states' rights will be respected. Do you think there'll be a war, Alex?"

"I don't know. But I tend to think there will be. There's too much pride on all sides. Peace never lasts, even in a Republic. War is in our nature."

"The philosopher speaks."

Joe smiled at his friend.

But Kirkland was in no mood for casual jesting. He turned to Alex.

"Has the governor called for troops?"

"Not that I'm aware of."

16

"If he does, I'm going to enlist."

Joe let out an enthusiastic shriek.

"Think of the excitement," he said. "All of the ladies will call on us. Our names will be etched forever as heroes of Carolina."

With eyebrow's raised, both Joe and Kirkland gave a questioning look to their academic friend.

"Well?" Joe said impatiently.

"Why not? Someone has to look after you unenlightened ones."

Joe rushed forward and thrust his arms around Alex's waist, lifting him over his shoulders.

"God have mercy on Washington," he yelled. "Dixie has spoken."

Chapter 2

The governor had made the call, and years of smoldering rhetoric had finally sparked into a runaway fire.

Growing outrage over Federal troops taking over and then refusing to leave Fort Sumter in Charleston had caused a hurricane of military spirit that swept the embers west to gather all available arms in its path. Men and boys converged in a massive, fevered migration to towns all over the Palmetto state to enlist, fearful of missing what was thought to become a short conflict, if anything. But if battle were to rage, few wanted to let the opportunity pass by like a regretful wind, to deny their name from being presented in bold letters joining the likes of Carolina soldier-legends such as Francis Marion and Thomas Sumter. The possibility of their friends returning to glory and prestige, while they remained locked inside a farmer's story, would be a fate worse than death.

Richard, Joe and Alex had stopped near Camden the previous night, sleeping under the stars and campfire dreams, on Kirkland lands at Gum Swamp.

They had politely declined an invitation to sleep indoors, figuring they might as well get used to the soldier's life. And while not spoken of, all were distinctly aware that they were resting their heads on hallowed ground. Here, Patriots had made a stand against the British in the battle of Camden. While it was a terrible defeat that August day in 1780, their ancestors had been there, defiant in the face of tyranny. Richard had gone to sleep with his great-grandfather's name forged between his temples. Daniel Kirkland had made a stand, here, and so would he eighty years later, along with his pals.

They had come to enlist, with their families' blessings, and were determined to catch a ride to wherever fate might take them. Tom had accompanied them, in case they were ordered to leave immediately. If that were to happen, Tom would return home with their horses.

It had been a cold night, and each had woken up several times to add wood to the fire before rejoining the snoring neophytes of winter bivouac.

★   ★   ★

Kirkland stood up, his thumb and forefinger stroking his well-groomed mustache.

Joe and Alex were already up, feasting on corn bread that they hastily packed before rushing south from Flat Rock. They handed some to Kirkland and Tom, who was pouring water over the whimpering orange glow. Having never cooked for themselves before, they had hoped to grab a meal somewhere in town, and didn't bother to bring much to fill their eager stomachs. In their haste, all they had packed was an extra set of clothes and their crude, outdated hunting weapons.

The fire having been put out, the foursome mounted and rode swiftly until reaching Camden's city limits where they slowed to a casual gait, taking in the whitewashed and stunning houses on Broad Street and beyond. Equally as lavish as the neoclassical mansions were the impeccably groomed lawns and gardens, waiting for the touch of spring to explode in color.

Nearing the business district of South Carolina's oldest inland city, it was readily apparent that the transient population had exploded overnight. The streets were filled with hopeful recruits, from all corners of the district, who walked with defiant eyes and puffed up stares. Ladies in their foremost Paris fashions huddled in groups, flirting with the wannabe recruits, and thoroughly enjoying the spectacle. Local shopkeepers had put on their finest frock coats and tried to take advantage of the gathering, encouraging all to sample their goods. Kirkland and his friends ignored them all, but it was a false avoidance. For in truth, they noticed every detail, storing them away for future memoirs and rocking-chair tales.

Reaching the edge of the business district, they continued past the courthouse, designed by Robert Mills, the architect of the Washington Monument.

They didn't bother to ask for directions, knowing that there was only one suitable place for mustering. Soon they could see at a distance the crowd in front of the dominating Cornwallis House. Seized by Lord Charles Cornwallis for his headquarters in 1780 during the Revolution and held by the British for eleven months, it was ground zero for the southern campaign against the Patriots. Ever since, to the people of Kershaw District, it had been revered as a symbol of independence and a reminder of the sacrifice their forebears made against tyranny. And it was the district's namesake, Joseph Kershaw, an outspoken advocate of going to war with Britain, who had built the noble home.

A set of tables had been arranged in the front yard, dwarfed by the classic Georgian mansion's twelve white-washed pillars fronting a two-storied portico. Men stood in long lines to make their mark for one-year enlistments.

With starry eyes, Kirkland was admiring the grand residence when he spotted some familiar faces among the strangers ambling by.

"William," Kirkland called out.

A robust teen—about his age—with a ruffled goatee turned around.

"Richard, how goes it friend? Joe. Alex. How're ya'll?"

They exchanged greetings with William Truesdel, whose family was prevalent in the Flat Rock area and intertwined with the Kirklands. Over the years, several marriages had occurred within the two families and two of Richard's siblings, Caroline and Jesse, had wed William's brother and sister.

"We're fixin' to enlist, ready to hoof it," said Kirkland.

"You know me. Can't miss out on any high jinks," added Joe.

"Well, you might have to wait, I'm afraid," said William. "They are only forming one company presently. Mainly Camden men. I hear they are to form a Flat Rock company, but at a later date."

"Just think on it Richard," exclaimed Joe. "A whole company from Flat Rock. Maybe not entirely, but certainly we could gather enough men from the district who would cast their lot with us."

"Without a doubt," said Alex. "Every youthful eye clouded by prospects of glory. I'm sure if given the choice they would prefer farming."

"That must be what they call sarcasm," said Joe in a childlike voice, smiling, pretending to raise a hand to Alex's face.

Kirkland had been strangely silent, and the others noticed him deep in contemplation.

"What is it, Richard?" asked Joe.

Kirkland surveyed the large open land in front of the Cornwallis house, having heard stories of the British unceremoniously dumping the bodies of hundreds of American patriots in long trenches there. He imagined the Redcoats with debasing sneers taking great pleasure in the macabre work, piling bodies four deep and kicking at the lifeless limbs to make them fit into a puzzle of rebellious flesh.

Kirkland gritted his teeth.

The time for a new Revolution has dawned.

"I came here to enlist and that's what I'm going to do."

"What? Why? You *must* wait. There ain't men better than those from Flat Rock. Why join up with strangers who you can't trust? You don't know their mettle."

"Joe's right, for once, Richard," said Alex. "If I'm going into battle, I want men who have handled a pitchfork by my side. Though it's hard to

21

predict what a man will do when fired upon, I'd rather throw in with those I'm familiar with."

"That may be so. But the war could be over in a week, and I'm not going to miss it. No, my mind is made up."

Joe looked over at Alex in a wordless plea to get him to change their friend's mind. But Alex knew it was no use. When Kirkland had a course, either latch on for the ride or let him pass. The decision was now for the remainder, to break the trio or follow their friend against their own wishes. Joe continued to wait for Alex to say something and the deafening silence was beginning to unravel his usual carefree disposition.

It was William, however, who spoke up first.

"Gentlemen, I'm going home to see how this thing shakes out with the Flat Rock outfit. Richard, best of luck to you. Godspeed."

He shook Kirkland's hand, turned, and walked away to catch up with his other friends who were preparing to ride home.

"Richard," Joe said. "Forgive me. I respect your wishes, but these city boys... I'd much rather fight with my country folk."

"City boys or not," said Alex. "I'm not in that big of a hurry to get myself killed. These problems with Congress and the Yankees could go on longer than anyone knows. Yes, I can wait."

Incredulous, Kirkland threw up his hands.

"I can't believe you two. We've got the three of us together. We can watch each other's backs. Look over there."

He pointed to the ragtag line of men: laborers, clerks, merchants, students, farmers and mechanics, among others.

"They are signing up for the greatest adventure of their lives and you are going to just pass that up? Go home, then. Back to the farm. I'll see ya'll when I get back."

"Rich...," Joe attempted to reason with him.

But Kirkland was already gone, anger propelling him forward almost as much as his bullish resolve. And he placed himself in line to add his signature to the war effort, however brief or enduring it may be.

★　　　★　　　★

22

April 8, 1861

Believing that the company, now known as the Camden Volunteers, would be sent into active service within a week or two, Kirkland became disheartened as three months passed without a hint of troop movement. In Camden, the newly formed company did little preparation for war except to elect its officers and drill twice a day on the very field where hundreds of patriot martyrs slept beneath their cumbersome feet, unmarked and without proper reverence. Initially disturbed, Kirkland reasoned that these anonymous men would be proud of the new breed of patriots standing up to a government overstepping its bounds.

"At ease, men," said Captain John Doby Kennedy to his breathless troops, assembled in a long line on the parade ground in front of the Cornwallis house.

His voice was a deep rumble, far more cavernous and seasoned than such a young man should possess. While some would say the 21-year-old budding lawyer was the epitome of an upper crust, southern gentleman, this label was only partially accurate. Unlike many of his status whose public appearance hid many defects of character, Kennedy was genuine, with no contempt for those on lower rungs, and generous, almost to a fault. As a leader, he was relaxed in his ways, seldom raising his voice in anger, and was fair with his punishments. These traits endeared the captain to his men, and it hadn't taken long to gain the soldiers' respect and loyalty. Even though many of his troops were his elder by several years, they had quickly noticed the "old soul" in him.

A courier handed a message to Kennedy yet no one was looking at their youthful leader. All were hushed, focused like eagles on paper prey. With a similar appetite, Kirkland wanted to rush up and snatch the order from Kennedy's grasp.

For three months, Kirkland had been going back and forth from Camden, each time hoping not to return to Flat Rock. Each time he had been disappointed.

The only positive was receiving that first uniform, a militia outfit—light blue pants with a white stripe and a navy jacket with gold buttons and cuffs—which he wore with pride. When he first put on this uniform, his whole body tingled in recognition. He was indeed a soldier now.

In the meantime, to his dismay, the Flat Rock Guards, as they came to be called, were organized only eight days after his friends left him in Camden. Joe and Alex had enlisted in this company, as did William Truesdel and many others Kirkland knew well.

Saluting the messenger, Kennedy perused the note, while a hundred heads craned, inching closer. After what seemed like an eternity, the captain said a few words to the courier, out of earshot to his troops, and dismissed him. Turning to face his impatient crowd, he surveyed the troops from left to right, and smiled slightly.

Finally, after judging that his men were about ready to topple forward, he spoke.

"Gentlemen, tonight you must say goodbye to your wives and sweethearts, because tomorrow we leave for Charleston."

In an instant, the sky was filled with spinning hats and manic-chested roars. So loud was the collective burst that Kirkland was sure the Yankees in Charleston were alerted to their presence. As the men shook hands with an overdose of ivory, Kennedy waited for the ruckus to settle.

"I expect you to be at the train station by dawn as we will wait for no stragglers. I cannot promise you any action, but we will be there in the event hostilities do take place. Men, do what you must to get ready, and I will greet you in the morning. Dismissed."

★   ★   ★

The planter looked at his son as only a father can, interpreting Richard's face to reveal the expected news.

Maneuvering another pine log into the popping orange hues, Richard's father returned to his rocking chair, moving with the steady rhythm of paternal thought. Richard and his brothers, Billy and Jesse, knew a story

24

was brewing under that old riding hat that he rarely removed from his balding head.

Eventually, John cleared his throat and the tale began.

"When I was a young man, my father took me well back into the woods to a large swamp. We walked around until my father found what he was after. He snapped off a tree branch and stepped between a large cottonmouth and the water. The snake formed an aggressive, coiled posture, reared its triangular head, opened its mouth wide and showed its fangs. My father kept his distance and so did the snake. After a short standoff, he approached the snake and held out the branch. In an instant the snake struck before recoiling and striking again. My father dropped the branch and we cautiously backed away.

"When we were out of danger, he said to me, 'Son, did you see how perfect a weapon that snake was? Even though I was a towering giant in his world, he held his ground and waited for the precise moment to strike. He was patient and kept his head focused. If you are ever cornered by someone bigger than you or if you ever find yourself threatened and outnumbered, remember the cottonmouth.'"

John stood up and walked over to the novice soldier.

"Richard, my father was trying to tell me that in a brawl, the strongest won't necessarily win. The one that remains calm and takes what his opponent gives him, will always come out ahead. God go with you, son."

They embraced briefly, and John, never one to show much emotion, went back to his habitual rocking.

Moved and desiring eloquence, Richard wanted to respond with a declaration of love and admiration toward a father and teacher, but the words got stuck in a masculine thicket. "Goodbye, father," was all that came through, and his father just lifted a palm from the grip of his haven chair.

Billy followed a dry-throated Richard to the porch.

Once outside, Richard threw back his head and sucked in the cool air, partially restoring his equilibrium.

"If there's a war, Dan and I won't be far behind you," said Billy, adjusting his derby hat. "Though I'd much rather be on a horse, than tramping through all creation on foot."

"Wouldn't it be something to meet on the same field, in a distant land?"

"I don't believe it will come to that. But if it does, there's no one else I'd rather fight alongside than my own little brother. Take care of yourself, Rich."

They shook hands, and as Richard descended the steps, he encountered Sam running toward him.

Stopping in front of his brother, Sam put his hands on his knees, trying to catch his breath.

"Rich," said Sam, gasping for air. "Are you off this time… to fight the Yankees?"

"We leave tomorrow."

"I'm coming with you."

Being of closest age to Richard, Sam had always looked up to him, and Richard had always kept a watchful eye on his younger sibling, as his brothers had done for him.

Instead of applying a harassment normally given to one of dew-drenched ears, Richard treated Sam like a respected apprentice. He had kept Sam in line, encouraging him when necessary and scolding him when proper.

Maybe it was the absence of a mother that brought on this added responsibility and maturity, or perhaps Richard had simply hopped over the age of sibling terrorism. Whatever the reason, the curious tether between the two youngest Kirklands was cast iron and inseparable, and neither brother seemed to mind the dynamic. This had made the decision to enlist especially hard on Richard, knowing his brother was too young to follow him. Of course, this wasn't the first instance Sam had thrown out intentions to join the war effort. From the moment Richard had announced his ambition, Sam was determined to cling to his brother's heels. Though he had tried in vain to delicately remove the notion from Sam's overzealous head, it had little effect. He was too much like his brother.

26

"Sam," said Richard in a father-like tone. "I know you want to go with me, but pa needs you here to help with the farm. I need you to watch over him. As you know, he's not getting any younger. This is an important responsibility. Besides, they wouldn't take someone your age."

"But I'm stronger than most two years older than me."

"Yes, you are. The more reason for you to stay and work the farm. Jesse can't do it all by his lonesome. They need you here. Listen, brother."

He put his hands on Sam's shoulders.

"I won't be gone long. I'll be back chasing down possums with you before time has a chance to grow whiskers."

Disgusted, Sam ran into the house, nearly slamming into Jesse coming out the front door. Sidestepping him at the last moment, Jesse gave Richard a quizzical look.

"What did you say to *him*?" said Jesse.

"Aw, he wants to follow me all the way to Washington. He won't listen. Stubborn as a mule."

"I'm not surprised. He'd argue with a fence post. Takes after someone else I know."

He winked at Richard and sighed.

"I'd go with you too if present duties allowed."

"You be sure to watch over Sam as well."

"You know I will, Richard."

The two embraced.

"Tell Caroline I will write."

Richard was confident in his replacement for looking after Sam, as Jesse was the one who had taught him just about everything he knew. It was Jesse who had instructed Richard how to shoot and ride.

"Before you go..." Jesse walked inside the house briefly before returning with arms full.

"Here, take this with you. At least until you get something better."

Jesse handed him his gun, an old .50 caliber flintlock converted to percussion cap, the most powerful weapon in the family's arsenal.

"Thank you," said Richard, the drought-mouth rearing again.

27

Not wanting to show his affliction, he bowed and turned tail to pack the weapons on his horse at the hitching post. Throwing his leg over the saddle, he tipped his cap to his brother while avoiding his eyes, and quickly trotted Brimstone over to the entrance of the path leading to his mother.

★   ★   ★

As he rode, Richard tried to levitate a vision of her in his mind. He barely remembered his mother, who died when he was only two years old. Even the scant memories he had Richard questioned whether they were products of his father's stories or true recollections.

John spoke of his dearly departed wife often, wanting to keep her memory alive, especially with their youngest children, who never had a chance to know her warm smile and gentle spirit. As he grew older, Richard latched on to his father's every mention of her. More than the words, Richard saw the spark ignite in his father's eyes when he described even the most commonplace events they shared together. And when the embers in his eyes faded to cool impressions of loneliness, Richard had felt ashamed to encourage the pain.

With the stories, Richard felt an ever-strengthening bond with the woman described as the peacekeeper. She was the one with the uncanny ability to dissolve all family disputes or sibling quarrels with tranquilizing words and a firm but loving eye-potion—one look and the finger pointers relaxed in amnesia, forgetting what the fuss was all about.

A rabbit, surprised by the horse and rider, dashed in front to its next hiding place, interrupting Richard's struggling reflections. Halting his mount, he watched the puffy round tail disappear into the underbrush before a gentle kick moved them on past the small peach orchard to the hill with a view. Before reaching the family cemetery, he dismounted and plucked a few starry white flowers growing wild at the trailside. Tying Brimstone to a tree, he continued on foot.

A handful of simple wooden markers stuck out of the ground at odd angles, having long since shifted from their initial placement by grieving hands. The family had chosen the hill with the highest elevation and most pleasant view to place their loved ones at eternal rest. At the other side of the cemetery was a wild jigsaw puzzle of treetops in a jagged valley, untouched by the plow. Unsuitable for farming, the Kirkland family left this "unimproved land" the way nature had intended. Richard had often explored its lair, and many a weekend he and his brothers went hunting rabbits, raccoons, possums, an occasional deer or whatever else they could bring home for extra meat.

Before the freshest marker with the initials MVK, Richard dismounted and knelt in reverence. Placing the pinxter-flower bouquet before it, he settled in to a one-way conversation with his mother. The words struggled to form at his lips but he soon cast aside the initial blockage. When he found his voice, unrehearsed and with naked truth, it imitated the breeze kissing his back.

"Mother… I'm sorry it's been so long since I last visited. Pa and your children are all well and God has blessed us."

Richard put a hand through his dark hair.

"I came here to say goodbye. Not forever, God willing, but I don't know when I'll be back. There may be a war comin' and comin' soon. I have enlisted in the defense of our state and I leave tomorrow for Charleston. If there's any way you can look after pa…"

He paused, listening to the wind speak through the trees.

"Pa misses you fiercely. He needs your angelic hands. Please watch over all our kin." He picked up a lone flower and avoiding the antler-like stamens, buried his nose in it. Its sweet fragrance was calming and he knew his choice for the occasion was sound.

"Well, I must be going now, but I wanted to tell you that I aim to make you proud."

Standing up, Richard put a lingering right hand on the humble marker. With a newfound lightness in his shoulders, he mounted and headed down the trail—there was one last goodbye.

*   *   *

29

Susan Godfrey lived about two miles south of Kirkland. Even if it hadn't been on the way back to Camden, Kirkland would've stopped there last for his final adieu.

Riding along the trail with Tom following, he wished he had left more time for Susan. His familial obligations, though necessary and proper, had shuttered too much daylight. While it pained him to leave his father and brothers behind, the future was beside a southern belle.

The two had been sweethearts for only six months, but had already talked of marriage and children. Like Kirkland, she was only seventeen, but Susan's father had approved of the steady courting with a watchful eye. As both now approached the horizon of adulthood and their eighteenth birthday, Susan's father had lengthened his leash and allowed casual walks on his property.

The match was a proper one, as both came from middle-class plantation families that were friendly with each other, sharing in parties, barbecues and seasonal events. It didn't hurt that these many soirees had given ample evidence to Susan's father that Kirkland was a man of high character and stability and that the Kirkland family was known to be honest and hard-working.

Knowing how easy it was to fall from a father's good graces, he had kept his nose clean. Even the Flat Rock gossip circles, far reaching and unmerciful, threw no stones at his reputation. The tea leaves or crystal ball wasn't needed with this future son-in-law, and Kirkland meant to keep it that way, at home or at war.

He'd been relieved when Susan agreed with his desire to enlist.

Even though, like the Kirklands, the Godfrey family had a military history, he wasn't sure if she would be as agreeable to the proposition as her father.

At last, through a small avenue of bowing oaks draped in frizzled robes of Spanish moss, the small but elegant plantation home appeared in the distance. Slowing his horse to a walk halfway through, Kirkland surrounded himself with a foundation of mental bricks, with extra support for his tingling legs and porous head. The centering exercise was only mildly successful. On dismount, the masonry came crashing down. Walking up the steps to the Godfrey place, Kirkland knocked with a firmness not equaled by his nerves.

The door swung open.

"Hello, Richard," Mr. Godfrey welcomed. "Please come in."

"Thank you, sir. Circumstances don't allow for a proper visit, but I was hoping to have a word with Susan, if I may, sir."

"Certainly. I've heard the news. I know you must be on your way shortly. As you can imagine, my daughter is very precious to me. I couldn't find a better husband for her if I arranged it myself. Please take care of yourself. May God bring you home in good health."

He smiled and held out his hand, which Kirkland took with a solid grip.

"I'll call Susan. She's been waiting for you."

"Thank you, sir."

Hearing Susan's father in the next room calling for her, the nervous air doubled in his chest. Although Kirkland had known this moment was inevitable, he hadn't been quite sure how the colliding emotions would register within.

Keep it under control.

Drawing a long breath, he waited, perspiring from the heat. And then he saw her.

An angel descended the stairs like a Jessamine blossom gliding on a fair wind. It was as if the ceiling had been removed by a Biblical quake, and through this opening, seraphic strobes of honeyed light swirled and encircled her movements. Dressed in a lavish evening gown as if ready to be escorted to a Camden ball, Susan's radiance multiplied with every descending step, jabbing at Kirkland with her sensuous aura. The dress was stunning: lemon taffeta silk, the bodice and overflowing skirt trimmed with black lace. Her glistening shoulders were bare and her auburn hair was pinned up in the back and parted, emphasizing her high cheek bones and serene skin. She wore no jewelry and didn't need to. It would have interfered with perfection, a blemish on a sun-struck window pane. With her feet obscured by the opulently massive box-pleated skirt, even after lifting it slightly with her hands, Susan seemed to glide downward without bothering to touch the mortal treads.

This was more than he expected, much more, and the bewildered Kirkland could do nothing but stare. Stopping at the bottom of the staircase, Susan gave him a winged smile that scattered his backbone. The sweet bludgeoning only increased his diffidence. In the same instant, all the words Kirkland had prepared to say to her vanished like a firefly in the dawn.

"Hello Richard," said Susan, her eyes soft and hypnotic.

Those sparkling blues were the prettiest things he had ever seen, a beacon of shivering warmth.

Whenever in her company, Kirkland had to force himself not to stare into those eyes for too long, for fear of being stupefied and blinded by their spell. He was frightened by the Medusa effect, being turned into stone, incapable of all but blubbering speech. Susan's aura was not to be inhaled void of caution and he was wise enough not to gulp it down. However, such restraint of will was not easy, for from the moment he saw her, he knew she was "the one." And Kirkland, naïve or not, was content to seat her on the mountaintop alone.

Taking in his frozen, parted lips, Susan blushed slightly.

"I wanted to create a lasting image to carry with you. Of course, it's beyond the family's means, but I have a wealthy aunt in Charleston who likes to spoil me on occasion. Although I entertained the notion of having my likeness taken, I thought a memory would be more vivid and lasting."

Suffocated by the visual heat, Kirkland pulled at his collar. Though cognizant of his staring, he was unable to break from the thermal paralysis.

"Thank you," he managed to force out. "I, uh…

Grinning, Susan's father saved him.

"Well, I'll be in the drawing room if you need anything," he joked. "The grounds are yours."

Susan handed Kirkland a knitted shawl, and turned around.

"Won't you be a gentleman?"

"Of, of course," he stammered, holding the shawl up behind her.

Susan made of point of touching his hand as she pulled the shawl over her shoulders. Opening the door for his fair maiden, Kirkland pursued her with aching breast. He had designs on a stroll through the avenue of oaks, but his love interest had other ideas.

"My father has allowed us to wander," said Susan, mischievously. She pointed to a secluded trail through the woods.

"Aren't you a little overdressed?" said Kirkland, only slightly surprised. He knew she was cultured but adventurous. In his eyes, this roughness around the edges only made her more attractive.

"I'll let my mother worry about that later."

"After you."

Kirkland motioned ahead.

As they were about to take to the trail, an elderly black woman surprised them at the entrance. On seeing the young couple, she dropped a large wooden bucket of water heavily to the ground, but without ejecting its contents.

"Mr. Kirkland, Miss Susan," she bowed.

"Hello, Jenna," Susan greeted.

Looking Susan up and down with alarm, Jenna scowled.

"Child, you can't possibly go this way, you'll dirdy dat beautiful dress."

"It's okay, Jenna, we're not going far."

Hesitating, she picked up the water and lurched forward, shaking her head as she left.

"Yous be careful now."

With Kirkland in tow, Susan nearly ran to the threshold of the trees. Once under the canopy, she grabbed his hand. This boldness caught him off guard, as did the sun landing on her cheeks. It was as if the pines could not contain her beauty, and as she walked, the shadows never seemed to obscure her face.

For a while, they walked in silence as if each was unsure of what to say at this fateful occasion. It was not an uncomfortable sleep of speech, however. Hand in hand, Kirkland understood the power of the moment and did not want to ruin it with clumsy smalltalk. He waited for Susan to speak, and finally, she obliged.

"I must admit, I've never been more jealous of anyone as I am right now."

"Jealous of me?"

"Yes, you are standing on the brink of adventure, and will quite possibly witness great events in history."

"I don't know about that."

"Don't be modest, Richard. You must have some inkling that these times are momentous and influential."

"Of course. But we could be gone for a week, or a month or… The pages have not yet been written."

Susan nodded, though was seemingly unimpressed.

"Yes, it is a great unknown. But that's what is so exciting. The entire world will be watching. And good or bad, our own beloved South Carolina has thrust itself in the center of it all."

"Okay, Okay, you read me like a book," Kirkland finally acquiesced. He laughed.

"It is all you say, and more. I'm more than a little anxious, I must admit."

Susan stepped in front of Kirkland, blocking his path.

"My brave soldier, you will make all of us proud. And then you will return to me."

Leaning in, her eyes were soft yet determined. Kirkland held her in his arms, hoping the trembling was only in his head. And then he kissed her. Sweet and tender were her lips, and for a moment, they were an antidote for a mind ravaged by the dread of looming separation. All the brambles and thorns lost their bite and the dagger points smoothed over. He pulled her closer still, holding her halo of warmth as an umbrella against the downpour of regret.

As Kirkland released her, he gripped the new memory tightly, refusing to let the darkness in until he was several miles away.

★　　★　　★

34

APRIL 12, 1861

MORRIS ISLAND OFF CHARLESTON, SC

3 PM

Black plumes of gloomy smoke rose from the fort like dark masses infiltrating heaven. Disappearing into this cloudy darkness were streaking iron missiles launched from batteries ringing the harbor.

Kirkland couldn't imagine how anyone inside the burning fort could still be alive.

Fort Sumter, isolated on a shoal in the middle of the Charleston harbor, was being slowly suffocated and pulverized as if a giant crescent fist was pressing down from above. Only the occasional cannon reply from the lower-tier batteries of the fort showed the attackers that life was yet to be extinguished.

Kirkland's company had arrived by boat on Morris Island south of Sumter a few hours before, having been called into active service on April 9. They were too late for the initial fireworks of war that morning, when batteries on the surrounding islands launched their first attacks well before sunrise. A mammoth banner of 33 bleeding but undaunted stars hovered over Sumter in a majestic cadence. For now the dainty, unfinished fort was all that remained of the Union in one of its original 13 stripes.

While the Palmetto State became the first to call for a second revolution, an entire row on the national standard was in peril of collapsing into vacancy. Mississippi, Florida, Alabama, Georgia, Louisiana and Texas all had voted to leave the Union in a span of less than a month.

Major Robert Anderson, the commanding officer of Union troops at Fort Moultrie in Charleston, had been placed in a treacherous position. Born in Kentucky and with a Georgian wife, Anderson had been sent to Charleston the previous November hoping that his ties to the South would alleviate the political tension. When secession was ratified, however, Anderson was faced with trying to protect national property.

A crumbling and aged fort, Moultrie was no place to offer a defense should the Carolinians attack. Yet it was the only fort in Charleston garrisoned by more than a handful of soldiers.

As a result, on the day after Christmas, Anderson secretly moved his force of 84 soldiers and 43 civilian workers, along with supplies, to Fort Sumter.

Though a work in progress, the pentagonal-shaped Sumter had 60-foot walls. In the center of the corridor leading to and from the harbor, it was the one fort capable of being defended.

It was a logical maneuver, but only exacerbated the already tense situation. Many in Charleston believed than an invasion was imminent and that Sumter's guns would be soon pointed at the city.

In the months that followed Anderson's chess move, South Carolina prepared itself for just such an event, moving powerful guns and manpower in an arc that surrounded the fort.

On January 9, the *Star of the West*, a steamship carrying reinforcements and supplies to Sumter, had been fired upon and denied access to the fort by cadets from the Citadel Academy.

War now appeared unavoidable.

Yet Major Anderson had showed restraint and did not return fire.

Neither side was ready to bloody its knuckles.

In the meantime, the Convention of Southern States meeting in Montgomery, Alabama, had adopted a constitution for a provisional government and elected Jefferson Davis as president.

The Confederate government was now the authority in Charleston. It sent Brigadier General P.G.T. Beauregard, a former student under Anderson at West Point, to assume control.

In Washington, Lincoln had taken the oath of office on March 4 and was handed the keys to a nation on the brink of fratricide. Informed that Lincoln was preparing to send a relief expedition to Sumter, Beauregard sent three aides to demand that Anderson surrender the fort.

Anderson refused.

Negotiations broke off at 3:20 AM, as Col. James Chesnut, a former U.S. Senator from Camden, told Anderson to expect war in one hour.

This promise was kept.

One by one, the island batteries encircling Sumter discharged their siege weapons.

By 5 a.m., 43 cannons and mortars were in action, shaking the ground and proclaiming that secession was tangible and irreversible.

A line in the sand had been drawn. America was ripping in half.

For miles around people rushed from their beds to the Charleston waterfront to witness the swirling pyre. However, for the first two and a half hours of the bombardment, Sumter was perplexingly silent and unresponsive. When the fort finally lifted an eyebrow with a single shot towards Morris Island, the sheepish troops on Morris sighed collectively, and cheered with burden-releasing glee.

The reply had been meager at best, though, as manning the heavy guns on the fort's parapet would have been suicidal. The iron rainstorm had forced Anderson's hand, and only the smallest guns that could be fired from relative protection in the lower casemates were employed in the fort's defense.

Although Sumter's batteries were accurate in striking their targets throughout the harbor, the small caliber of the rounds inflicted little damage on the well-fortified positions. The game was on and Kirkland's company had arrived at a rout, in plenty of time for the grand finale. The green recruits were there only in the unlikely event Federal troops landed in the Charleston harbor for a ground attack. Outside the realm of any real danger, though, the troops were content to applaud the one-sided onslaught, mockingly growing louder whenever the enemy launched a half-hearted response.

After crossing the channel from Folly Island, Kirkland and the Camden Volunteers followed the sounds to the far side of Morris Island.

A desolate, wind-beaten land, Morris Island was uninhabited except for the large number of dead rumored to be buried in unmarked graves. Previously it had a more sinister name—Coffin Island—where for more than a century ships unloaded their sick and dying before being allowed to dock in Charleston harbor. A lonely, isolated lighthouse was all that remained of modern occupation. At one end of the island was Cummings Point, only three-fourths of a mile from Fort Sumter, and in plain view.

Hunkered down at the point were several gun crews, including three ten-inch mortars and the Iron Battery, which consisted of three eight-inch Columbiads. Weighing almost a ton each, these behemoth guns could fire a 65-pound solid shot or exploding shell more than two miles. Under roofing of heavy timbers angled downward and plated with railroad iron, the gun crews were well protected. Beneath this cover, only the muzzles of the Columbiads were exposed through port holes with heavy iron shutters, which could be raised and lowered safely from the inside.

It was here that Kirkland witnessed his first brute salvo of war. He had run up behind the battery just as the lanyard of the middle gun was pulled, and the concussion nearly unhitched his bowels. As the gun violently recoiled on its tracks, Kirkland flinched so uncontrollably that he found himself on his back with feet in the air.

Momentarily stunned, he dropped his legs and lifted his head, hoping his virginal reaction had gone unnoticed. While he surveyed for an orbiting choir of laughter, a second shot caught him just as vulnerable and his entire body twitched, hands grasping at air. As his body relaxed, his head hit the sand, but not before a smile wilted his embarrassment.

Supine in the forgiving sand, Kirkland laughed a true bellyful, albeit conscious of his confused and quaking midsection. In mid-giggle, he closed this lighthearted door realizing the next mad rumble could occur at any second. Jumping to his feet, he threw his eyes to the battery, hoping sight would give warning to the next challenge. Sure enough, sponged and loaded, another lanyard was being pulled taught. Gritting his teeth, he took a wide stance and tensed every muscle.

As the Columbiad fired, he shivered yet stood his ground. This improvement failed to satisfy him, and he walked away from the guns in disgust. Sure, Kirkland had witnessed the firing of cannons before at various celebrations, but these were vastly different. Small and outdated field cannons belching nothing but powder was one thing. A heavy siege gun designed to knock out a fort's walls was completely beyond his experience.

He allowed this truth as he walked away, and soon wrestled away the doubt, concluding that time and experience would alleviate the jitters and steel the nerves. Scolding himself for focusing on the negative, he paused his steps, as Sumter materialized before him. As he looked on, a small puff of smoke exhaled from an embrasure of the fort. Before he could even react, the round slammed into the battery's iron roof with an unworldly clamor and bounced harmlessly into the sands behind.

In an instant, the intoxication of visual adventure had returned. Kirkland was like a child at his first visit to the candy store, eyes darting and unable to center, his neck straining to keep up with his rapidly shifting head. After having tasted and swallowed the images of countless rounds sizzling over the walls of the fort in every direction, Kirkland was able to detach himself momentarily to enjoy another novelty—the harbor itself.

The endless pale green was difficult to comprehend, as he had never seen a body of water larger than the Wateree River. The color appeared curiously ominous and soothing at the same time. Storm clouds, bold in the distance, added to the mystique. To Kirkland, the ocean view split into three planes, treacherous above and below, with a small window of utopian calm at the equator. This portal screamed of being mashed between overzealous clouds and a sea proclaiming manifest destiny. It was an uneasy vision, yet he was detached from it and unafraid. Desiring a closer look, he found a secluded spot, where his exploring would go unnoticed.

Removing his socks and shoes, he allowed his toes to breathe in the coolness of the sand and waited, at a safe distance, for the cresting waves to flatline. As the foaming saliva pooled closer, Kirkland retreated at first, away from its salty fangs. After several backpedals, he laughed off his aversion and took residence in the serpent's path. The driving water rushed past and enveloped his feet, the cold sting causing him to shriek. It was much more frigid than he had imagined, but the reactive dancing was shortlived and he allowed his feet to grow accustomed to the temperature. Laughing, he reached down and cupped his hand, quickly bringing the fleeing water to his lips. Swishing the water around in his mouth, he nearly choked before spitting wildly.

That's awful!

But he was smiling in his rebuke. Wiping his mouth with his sleeve, Kirkland stood in the conquered liquid arena, anchored there as a pair of seagulls floated on the wind.

As the hours drifted by like the waves at his numbed feet, he lost all track of time.

It didn't seem real.

As a child, Richard had sat in awe, transfixed as his father and uncles spoke of the family's lineage with war.

While crops dominated conversation at most times of the year, the winter fires sparked wondrous tales of battle and liberal bloodshed.

During these sessions, Kirkland could always be found sprawled in front of the wild hand gestures, elbows locked at attention, with palms at his cheeks. With eyes barely contained in his sockets, he listened to his kin expound on the family's proud tradition of defending their lands and honor.

Kirkland's favorite stories were of his great-grandfather, Daniel Kirkland, the patriot who had dared to fight the British at the Battle of Camden in 1780, and how three Revolutionary War battles were fought within five miles of the Kirkland home.

These thunder-bearing sagas didn't stop there, and Richard welcomed all revelations with fork and spoon.

In disbelief, he learned how the family led a regulator movement to protect local property when plagued by horse thieves and villains after the French and Indian War.

And of course, he salivated at the ancient, passed-down legends of the "old country," a category far removed from Kershaw District and beyond his imagination.

Most precious of these were the yarns involving his ancestors charging with Robert the Bruce against the evil English King Edward at the battle of Bannockburn.

Somewhere across that rolling, gargantuan sea…

A wild cheer sprang up from the Iron Battery and Kirkland scanned the horizon for its cause.

The stars and stripes, louder than the fort itself and more brilliant, despite the thieving clouds and smoke, was in danger.

A shell had severed the halyard, and the standard caught itself at half mast, rejecting submission.

The victorious shouts became intermixed with groans, and the atmosphere was unsettled. Kirkland was unsure if the soldiers' hurrahs were aimed at the flag's demise or an applause to its resiliency.

With the turmoil in his own head, he suspected it was some of both.

Stunned by the flag's power, Kirkland distanced himself from being overly wrapped in its sympathy.

Thus is war.

He stood on the beach, with eyes half shut to the enormity of what he was witnessing, but knowing it was indeed significant.

Will this story rival those of my ancestors?

"Ain't something you see every day, uh, is, is it?"

Kirkland turned around to see who had spoken the understatement of the decade. He eyed a short, rather heavyset man with a bushy beard and spectacles that seemed a couple of sizes too small for his large, round head. The man was obviously several years his senior, but young nevertheless. He spoke with a rapid pace as if his voice had trouble keeping up with his thoughts.

"No, if that don't beat all," Kirkland replied, returning his eyes to the beleaguered fort.

"You have to admire their bravery, mis-, uh, misguided as it is."

"Why don't they just surrender? They must see that the defense is futile."

"Probably cause they're too damn stubborn and too embarrassed to leave with their tails between their legs. Well, they can't sustain this forever. Even with reinforcements."

Kirkland nodded and knew exactly what the last words meant.

Three huge Federal steamers were clearly visible, anchored at the harbor's mouth, yet no attempt had been made to resupply the fort. Instead they treaded water, silent and apparently content to watch the fort and its inhabitants go up in flames.

"My name's, uh, Day-, Davis, Jonathan Davis, but everyone calls me Smith. I've been meaning to introduce myself, as I haven't had the pleasure."

Kirkland, eying his bare feet with a slight abashment, left the water to shake his hand.

"Pleasure to meet you, sir. My name's Kirkland. Why do they call you Smith, if I may be so bold?"

"I'm a blacksmith in Camden. Are you of the Kirklands up Flat Rock way?"

"I am."

"Yes, I believe I've done some work for a James Kirkland."

"He's my brother."

"Ah… he's a good man, good man."

"Thank you, sir. Indeed he is. He helped raise me."

"Then I suppose he's rubbed off on you. Let's hope so. If there's a war ahead, we're going to need some good men."

Smith looked toward the fort and then back to Kirkland.

"Say, you hung-, uh, hungry? I haven't eaten much since we left Camden."

In the excitement, Kirkland had buried thoughts about nourishment, until Smith's remark brought attention to his ignored hunger pains.

"Actually, I'm famished."

"Good, let's change the scene, scenery before our eyeballs are reduced to fire."

42

Finding a dune that partially shielded the wind, they gathered some scrub brush and a few old pieces of driftwood and quickly started a fire. Reaching into his knapsack, Smith produced a miniature frying pan and dropped it into the modest flames.

"I made it specifically for a time like this," said Smith. "It's travel friendly, lightweight and gets hot lickety-split. Of course, it's not meant to feed a company, but in a pinch, it'll serve a man or two right proper."

Smith saw Kirkland watching intently.

"You've never cooked for yourself, have you?"

"No sir."

"Well, it's easy enough. I happen to have a couple of Irish potatoes. Bring a pocket knife?"

"Yes."

"Good." Smith handed Kirkland the potatoes and a tin plate. "Slice these up into chunks. While you're doing that, I'll, uh, I'll get some grease going."

Grabbing some slab bacon that he had set aside on another plate, he tossed it into the pan. Kirkland obeyed, though the end result was various sizes of crude lumps.

"That'll work fine. Don't have to be pretty."

Reaching into a wooden bucket, Smith pulled out a length of salt pork and took a quick glance at the popping grease.

"That should do us well," said Smith. "Once you got some grease, you just place the meat and potatoes in it and it cooks itself. And it'll keep for several days. It may, uh may be a bit salty but the meat has only been soaking a few hours."

In minutes the simple meal was ready, and Smith, using a rag to grip the pan's handle, divied out the steaming portions to each plate.

"It ain't a feast, for sure, but then again, this is no grand dining room. Try it."

Kirkland stabbed at the smallest piece on his plate with his fork and gingerly brought it up to his mouth. While he was certainly familiar with

43

all things pork, he had never been served by a blacksmith, or even a man. Taking a bite, Kirkland winced. It tasted like a mouthful of sea.

Smith giggled at his reaction.

"I warned you. I should have soaked it overnight, but my mind was not on my stomach. Now *that* is a rarity."

Although far removed from gourmet, Kirkland's stomach was pleased to have visitors. Darkness was setting in and he noticed a definite slowing down of Fort Sumter's bombardment.

But still there was no sign of surrender.

A steady rain began to fall as if God Almighty Himself wanted to extinguish Fort Sumter's flames, if only for a night.

Kirkland and his new friend, spotting an old storage shack, ducked inside to escape the downpour. The rundown building was barely large enough for two to stretch out and it leaked from every corner, but it was better than being entirely exposed outside. Spreading out their blankets on the floor, they rested on their backs in silence, listening to the rain caress the wooden canopy, attended by sporadic cannon thunder.

Sleep was attempted, but Kirkland was still in a state of heightened nerves and he reflected on all the sights and sounds of the previous days. Far away from home, at least in his mind, even the train ride into Charleston was a novel delicacy that he resampled throughout the night.

And more than anything, he thought of home, and of sharing his blooming narratives with his brothers. A knot twisted in his belly when he thought of Joe and Alex, wishing they were by his side, witnessing the stunning events together.

The reports of cannon, continued at 15-minute intervals throughout the night, were a constant reminder of where he was and made sleep mostly impossible. While his feet had explored new territories, his baptism into the fraternity of war was unfulfilled. Kirkland was well aware that his experience as of yet was nothing more than that of a newspaper correspondent—an observer.

Nonetheless, he felt different somehow—less than reborn, but ascending to an unknown transformation. In his tossing and turning, he shrugged this off as the result of unfamiliarity. He was a pioneer in a wilderness of nameless trees and strange beasts.

Reality was still slightly off center, a dream state, that Kirkland believed might dissolve with the morning light.

★   ★   ★

APRIL 13, 1861

Firing resumed its awful, menacing growl before the sun was fully awake.

The concussions roused Kirkland from a pathetically shallow slumber, the shut-eye not nearly enough for his mind to climb from its deep-rooted murk. The clouds had retreated, and Kirkland wondered if those at Sumter were jealous of their departure.

Rubbing his eyes, he wandered again down to the beach for another day of expected fireworks. Smith was not far behind, having prepared two tins of coffee to take aim at their drowsiness.

"You look like you slept about as well as I did," said Smith, handing a cup to Kirkland.

"How can you sleep through a cannon fight?"

"I don't know. But they say that a seasoned soldier can sleep through anything."

Kirkland nodded. He had heard about Mexican War veterans who could sleep standing up while on the march and be lulled to sleep by the constant booming of guns. It seemed farfetched.

"That I cannot imagine," said Kirkland, stretching his arms.

"War can do peculiar things to a man."

"I guess maybe we'll find out."

"Maybe. But I'm willing to predict that this will be the only battle. We've made our point and now they'll probably leave us alone. Besides, who is Lincoln gonna get to fight his war, the immigrants? Or factory workers who've never looked upon a rifle? Why would they volunteer to take up arms against us?"

"Well, no conscripts are going to defeat a determined Southern army, that's for sure."

"Exactly my point. If Lincoln is smart, he'll leave us be and negotiate a truce."

Shielding his eyes from the brightness with a saluting hand, Kirkland obtained for the first time a clear view of Fort Sumter. Large chunks had been blown from the ramparts and its walls were heavily pockmarked.

Standing near the Iron Battery once again, Kirkland realized that the concussions no longer shivered him. It was if his body was now accepting and consuming the blasts, dispersing their power through his limbs and coiling his tendons. Yesterday's poison was becoming a tolerable meal.

As Kirkland congratulated himself on his newfound immunity and strength, he noticed smoke beginning to thicken above Sumter. It was slow and whimsical at first, but steadily increased as the minutes and then hours passed.

The beach where he stood began to fill with soldiers, who, with arms raised, barked a guttural ovation. The rabid infection spread to Kirkland and he screamed until his throat was sore. Sensing victory, the batteries again increased their hotshot, shells and mortars until the fort appeared as a lava-inducing inferno. With each passing hour, darkness loomed heavy over the fort, and even the bricks seemed aflame.

But the defenders would not yield even though nearly all of Sumter's guns had been driven to silence.

Approaching noon, a huge explosion rocked the fort, sending a shockwave that could be felt by those gathering on the beach.

Immediately, the firing against Sumter ceased and all watched in stunned silence. The atmosphere of victory was beginning to be tarnished. As minutes passed, Kirkland's stomach turned, feeling nothing but mercy for the men he believed were now being burned alive.

Eyes were turned to the fleet of three Federal ships standing idly by, and curses were thrown at them in liberal doses.

"Cowards."

"For God's sake, help them."

"Damn you yellow Yankees."

After a delayed silence, as if no man knew how to react, a single gun from Sumter invoked a desperate retort, sending the men into wild hysterics. It was a legitimate applause, their enemies' courageous perseverance having commanded unanimous respect.

Relieved, Kirkland joined the applause, and the battle continued.

"Those men deserve a better fate, a better fate," said Smith, shaking his head.

Kirkland's emotions were being deluged with anger.

"This is not war. It is a mockery. Where is the white flag?"

"Perhaps they would rather die."

Incredulous, Kirkland could not stand to look at the carnage any longer. Turning away, he left the beach. Smith didn't follow. Following the path to the dinner site of the previous day, he slumped to the sand and buried his face in his hands.

Meeting your enemy face to face is one thing, but this is something different altogether.

Confused at the dueling emotions in his head, Kirkland felt overwhelmed and physically exhausted, as if he had run for miles. He was sure that nearly all in the fort were dead. He was disgusted at himself for feeling so much pity and for being unable to share in the joy at victory's grasp. While railing against his mind's inherent nature, he noticed the cannons had once again stopped entirely.

Standing up, he could hear the sound of boisterous cheering from the beach and he sprinted there in curiosity. Rounding a dune, Kirkland saw the reason for the profound gaiety. Sumter's bold standard had been toppled and in its place was the coveted, colorless flag of truce. Victory, and mercy, was at hand.

Finding Smith, Kirkland shook his hand, and exhaled a dark cloud. Laughing with relief, the duo walked over to congratulate the men of the celebrating batteries, their ivory smiles contrasting loudly with their sooted faces. After the many handshakes, Kirkland and Smith returned to their dune dining hall.

Kirkland sat down, grabbed a handful of sand and watched the grains filter through his fingers.

"Tomorrow a new flag will rise above that battered fort, one with a beautiful Palmetto I would hope," said Smith, with obvious glee.

"There can't be much of a fort left."

"No. But we'll take it," said Smith with a laugh. "Back to its proper owner."

"The stories are true. War is a sight to behold. I only wish my friends back home were here to witness this. If this is the only battle, they missed quite a show."

"It's in Lincoln's hands now."

Anderson had surrendered Fort Sumter, and shockingly, no serious casualties had been reported on either side—until the next day. As one of the conditions of the surrender, Anderson had insisted on a 100-gun salute to the American flag. Halfway through, one of the guns exploded, killing one member of the gun crew and mortally wounding another.

Despite the nearly bloodless affair, on April 15th, Lincoln issued a call for 75,000 troops to suppress the rebellion. He was not going to back down. For the next week, the Camden Volunteers were drilled by cadets from The Citadel, waiting for further orders.

On April 17th, Virginia leaders voted to secede from the United States, pending a statewide referendum vote.

Kirkland, it seemed, would not be going home anytime soon.

Chapter 3

MAY 22, 1861
RICHMOND, VIRGINIA
6:45 PM

The man came straight at Kirkland. He was so old the wrinkles threatened to envelop his face. For some reason, the elder had picked him out of the crowd. With dual hardwood canes, he half dragged his failing legs until he was inches from Kirkland's face. But his voice, strong and true, belied his age.

"If I were twenty years younger, I'd be the first to the front," he offered. "God bless you young man. You will fight in my stead."

His eyes reflected a hard existence, yet maintained a purity and steadiness that affected Kirkland deeply, even more than his words. Momentarily caught speechless, Kirkland fell back on his newly-learned military bearing.

Head tall, he looked at the elder with directed poise.

"You can be assured I will conduct myself with honor. We will not let you down, sir."

Obviously pleased at Kirkland's response, the old gentlemen held out his hand. The grip was loose, though Kirkland could feel the man was attempting a more dignified clutch. But his strength failed him. When the elder had finished, he bowed and slowly disappeared into the horde from which he came.

This lean yet profound exchange had occurred at a memorable railway stop in Petersburg. At the time, Kirkland wished he had something more to give the man than a vanilla pledge, but he and his comrades had long run out of the Palmetto leaves, which they had twisted into cockades as tokens for their supporters at every depot on the route to Virginia. And he wasn't about to give up the South Carolina state seal buttons on his coat. One to a handsome young child in Goldsboro was all he was willing to part with.

Throughout the soldiers' journey north, the locals had rushed to see the saviors of the South, vigorously shaking their hands and offering nourishment and goodwill. Richmond was no different.

The women, with generous hearts and fascinated scrutiny, sought out the soldier camps to gift extravagant meals and hand out bouquets of fragrant flowers. Dressed in their best evening wear, they chatted with the soldiers, blushingly accepting all flatteries and attentions.

With equal gusto, the local men who were too feeble to pick up the rifle, did what they could for "the cause," arming the troops with words of gratitude and blessings for success.

Kirkland and the various companies of the newly formed 2nd South Carolina Infantry Regiment had begun arriving in Richmond during the last week of April, even though the results of the Virginia secession referendum had yet to be made public.

To his delight, Joe and Alex had arrived a week later with the Flat Rock Guards. Though he yearned to join up with his friends and neighbors, Kirkland held to his initial commitment. The joyous reunion of pals was amplified by the excitement around every corner. With their spirits carried on the shoulders of the Richmond people, it was only natural for the deedless warriors to puff out their chests and sprout bulging arms of valor. Even levelheaded Kirkland had caught his feet lifting from the ground. But before his feet touched the rooftops, there was Joe with his playful jabs, and Alex with his sobering wisdom, that anchored his legs back to ground level.

In and around the city, camps of instruction were being set up, and hundreds of troops were arriving daily from all over the South. Richmond was constantly doubling in size, with rows upon rows of white tents swallowing up every field and park.

Now almost 1,000 strong, the men of the 2nd South Carolina were placed west of the city in an elevated farm field, well supplied with water from a nearby reservoir. Here they drilled four times a day, the first beginning at 5:30 AM and ending with a dress parade in the evening, as the men began the transition from bumbling amateurs to professional killing machines. The rolls and flams of the drum were seemingly around the clock, and Kirkland often went to sleep with the cadences ringing in his ears.

The trio of Flat Rock friends found themselves during the brief times of leisure, especially on Sundays, when they traded their weapons for tourist goggles.

In their strolls, they watched cannons being forged at Tredegar Iron Works along the banks of the James River, and peered in awe at the Thomas Jefferson-designed state capital building, which towered over them like an ancient Greek temple. Perplexed, they gazed on the house of the pharaohs, an odd Egyptian revival building that was part of the Medical College of Richmond. But what was mundane for big city folk most interested Kirkland: the agricultural and hardware stores, where he window-shopped with an eye toward the future. And the extraordinary whiffs of fresh delicacies that massaged his nose whenever he passed a bakery or confectionary.

Ambling past the large cemetery directly in front of the camp, Kirkland looked at the scattered rows of weathered gravestones. He thought of the withered old gentleman at Petersburg who, in his frail condition, might soon find himself under a range of dates.

Strange place to put troops preparing for war.

Attracted by some of the intricately carved memorials, he wished that his mother had a more elaborate marker. Kirkland wandered the hillside graves often, casually filtering names and dates, and dreaming up their history, from child to moment of passing.

Was Richmond good to him or was he good to Richmond?

Of course, these questions were impossible to answer, and he was not naive enough to think the size of the marker had any relevance to either Socratic query. But this didn't halt his imagination and curious wonder. And while these blank-page graves would forever remain so, he somehow always ended up at one specific interment whose particulars were known. It was the Patriot James Monroe, the last US president who fought in the ranks during the War of Independence. This son of Virginia was severely wounded at the Battle of Trenton, a fact as much admired in the South as his political accomplishments. When Monroe's body was reinterred to Virginia in 1859 from his initial burying place in New York, the state government had spared no expense. Cast iron and skeletal-maze gothic, it loomed over the neighboring tombs like an ornate fortress. Depending on the weather, as Kirkland had discovered, the metal could sway wildly in personality.

In a James River-wafting haze, it was darkly mystical and foreboding. Bathed in sunlight, it took on the halo of a miniature cathedral.

"How goes it, chum?"

Kirkland turned to see Joe with his usual smile, Alex at his side.

"More than faire. How are your marching legs holding up?"

"Why, this ain't nothin'. Flat Rock boys can march all the live-long day."

"Sure, but you still don't know your left foot from your right," said Alex.

"You see, the college boy thinks he's a seasoned soldier now."

"I'm sure you're both the talk of the regiment," said Kirkland.

"Well, if not, I'm sure Joe can talk for the entire regiment," Alex quipped.

Joe laughed.

"I suppose you're right about that."

Kirkland returned his gaze to the cemetery, taking in the sobering graves.

"Something on your mind, soldier?" said Alex.

"It's nothing. Just thinking is all."

"A cemetery will do that to a man. But don't worry. 'Dust thou art, to dust returnest, was not spoken of the soul'."

"There he goes again," said Joe, throwing up his arms.

"I like that," said Kirkland, always more interested than Joe in Alex's book learning. "Never heard that one."

"It's Longfellow."

"Is he a tall man?" Joe joked, causing Alex to roll his eyes.

Kirkland tried to stifle a chuckle, but to no avail.

"This Long-Fellow… Is he a Yankee?" asked Kirkland.

"Yes, I believe he is."

"Them yanks can keep their words," said Joe. "We'll see how eloquent they are with a rifle in their face."

"The depth of your intellect is stunning," said Alex.

"Enough of this chatter," said Kirkland, stepping playfully between the two in a referee's stance. "Let's go help ourselves to some of them delicious victuals, graciously prepared by the finest of southern belles— while we still can. There are rumors that we're movin' out soon, possibly to Washington."

"Yes, we've heard them, too," Alex said.

"I hope so," said Joe. "These drills are getting right tiresome. If not for all of these fine ladies to look on, I'd be bored to death."

★   ★   ★

MAY 23
11 AM

"You must maintain proper balance, bend your knees and lunge with tenacity," said Drillmaster Claudius Francois Pardigon in a heavily congested, French accent. With hands locked behind him, dressed in civilian clothes, Pardigon roamed the dusty field, watching over his flock of bayonet practitioners. A veteran, having been wounded in the Crimean War, the Frenchman had been placed in charge of the final rudiments in the Richmond "school" of combat. Being a language teacher and newspaperman by trade did not disqualify him from being tapped for military guidance, as anyone with the slightest combat experience was welcomed due to the short supply of capable drill instructors.

A few squads of the 2nd South Carolina were in his charge on this day, including men from the Flat Rock Guards and Camden Volunteers. The sight was a little strange, since many of the men, like Kirkland, were equipped with a hunting gun that had no accompanying blade.

"Far too slow!" Pardigon screamed. "Your enemy will be able to deflect easily if you do not stab with fair-oss-etee."

One man in the Guards was having no issues with proper intensity, and even gave Kirkland the shivered willies. His stabs were violent and purposeful, yet filled with a combustible element that matched his dagger eyes. Well over six feet tall and cut of granite, it was if he descended from Nephilim giants. Even the cool, battle-tested Frenchman seemed alarmed by the man's murderous presence. While his commands remained of steady voice, Pardigon had trouble removing the brakes from his eyes. For several moments of trance, he ignored the rest of his pupils in need of instruction and focused entirely on the beastly man. Kirkland, however, was all too well-acquainted with this man of dark power. Hell, nearly all of Kershaw District had at least heard stories about Virgil Ratcliff.

The epitome of like-father, like-son, Virgil carried on the family paternal tradition of living at the bottom of a whiskey barrel, only coming up for air in brief attempts to share his insatiable anger with those unfortunate enough to stand in his path. Virgil was the only child of Frank Ratcliff, a legendary hell-raiser, who had squandered most of the family fortune on booze and gambling. His wife having fled years ago, Frank and his son eked out a living on a few acres of cotton. Forced to sell his slaves to pay off gambling debts, Frank resorted to hiring a couple of free blacks to work the farm. With more work than the hired hands could accomplish, Frank had pressed his youthful son into heavy manual labor, which was a source of extreme embarrassment to Virgil. At times, when inspired by liquid confidence, he refused to work and suffered savage beatings by his then much larger father. As a result, Virgil took out all his hateful vengeance on acquaintances and strangers alike, often prowling for a brawl into the wee hours of the night. As he grew and his body filled out, his lust for scrapping only intensified, as did his hated reputation.

Most folks in Kershaw District stayed well clear of Virgil, and many had more than a passing thought of putting a knife to his throat. Because of this, Kirkland couldn't fathom how Virgil had made it to his early twenties. Like the others, he tried to avoid Virgil at all costs, but one night they came face to face on Kirkland's return trip from an evening of courting Susan. In a moonless spring night, Kirkland was cautiously riding home in the twilight when an unseen object struck him on the side of the head, interrupting a revisit of the evening's romantic events, and knocking him from his horse. When he regained his senses, a liquored-up Ratcliff and his friend Wesley Hux were standing over him with sinister grins on their faces. Before the two assailants could say a word, Kirkland jumped to his feet and tackled Ratcliff, sending the two into a frantic wrestling match in the dirt. Although much smaller, Kirkland had Ratcliff pinned with his forearm across his neck until Hux joined the fray. Kirkland fought back with all he had, utilizing his sobriety and quicker reflexes to keep from being beaten into a pulp. As if leaping from the darkness itself, Joe appeared. By chance or divine intervention, Joe was traveling the same path from a similar engagement. With the help of Joe's impeccable timing, Kirkland and Joe quickly gained the upper hand, sending Ratcliff and Wesley retreating into the darkness. In the eight months since, Kirkland had dreaded and half-expected a similar encounter, but this rematch had not come to fruition.

In Richmond, Kirkland and Joe had simply ignored him, and Ratcliff, having joined the Flat Rock Guards, returned the favor. Kirkland had zero faith, however, that Ratcliff had dropped the matter entirely and figured it was only a matter of time before the bully returned for more.

"That's it! Magnifique!" said Pardigon, encouraging the brutality.

Joe was directly behind Ratcliff, and with Pardigon not paying attention, Joe moved a little closer, feigning to strike the monster in the ass with his bayonet. This caused an onslaught of giggles, and Joe quickly jumped back into position just as Pardigon wheeled, redfaced and screaming in his native tongue. Kirkland had no idea what the Frenchman was saying, but he assumed by its reckless speed and volume that they were colorful oaths.

While Kirkland was trying to contain a smile, he noticed Ratcliff glaring right at him, hard enough that he could feel its savage weight. Though he dropped his smile, Kirkland held his ground, and their eyes became locked in an uncomfortable stare down.

Still puffing, Pardigon resumed his normal position and Ratcliff clenched a fist in Kirkland's direction before harking back to run his blade through an invisible foe.

★　　★　　★

MAY 24
7:30 PM

With the evening dress parade finished, dinner eaten and the monotony of the usual sights contagious, they wandered farther than normal from their camp at such a late hour, east, toward the center of Richmond's commerce.

They headed down Main Street. In the distance, Kirkland spotted a familiar face.

"Come on, I want to introduce you to someone," said Kirkland, motioning for his friends to follow.

As they approached, the spectacled man, red in the face and sweating, noticed Kirkland and braked his blurred feet.

"Good evening, Kirkland," said the stocky man who looked miles from starving.

"Good evening, Smith."

They shook hands.

"Allow me to introduce the Flat Rock Guard's finest. Smith, this is Joe Duncan and Alex Morrison."

"Please, uh pleased to meet you both," said Smith, liberally shaking hands. "My name is Davis but everyone calls me Smith."

"Smith here is a blacksmith in Camden."

"Of course. Don't you have a shop on DeKalb Street?" asked Alex.

"Yes, that is my humble place of business."

"I've heard only good things about your work."

"Glad to hear it. I do what I can to satisfy the good folks of Camden and beyond."

Kirkland noticed a pamphlet tucked under his arm.

"Find something worth reading?"

Unfolding it, Smith read from the top.

"Sinner, you are soon to be damned. That's the title."

He chuckled. "Gets straight to the point, don't it? There's an old preacher down the road passing these out to the heathen soldiers."

Wiping his brow with his cuff, he tucked the propaganda into his belt.

"Warm today, warm today," said Smith, having to repeat himself after the first attempt was mumbled.

"Yes. Have you ventured far into the city?" asked Kirkland.

"Enough to take a gander. Figured this was my chance to see the world. Never thought I'd see Charleston, let alone…"

A scream cut him off, and they rushed in the female voice's direction. The desperate cry was emanating from inside a saloon's tobacco stained door, above which was a crooked, handpainted sign in block letters that read:

A St. Nicholas

Crashing inside, they saw a soldier holding a young woman, no doubt of ill repute, by the throat and pressing her down. Beside him were others of similar, grungy dress, lifting bottles of whiskey to inebriated lips, and ignoring the woman's pleas for help.

They were Louisianans, from a group of regiments that had already earned a reputation for fighting, overindulging in drink and for altogether lawlessness.

From his belt, Smith pulled out a bowie knife almost as long and wide as his arm and pointed it at the drunken soldier.

"Release her. Now," said Smith, his voice steady and a notch lower than in usual speech.

The Cajun soldier, gaunt yet sinister, looked at the knife and then at Smith. On the band of his hat was written, **Lincoln's Life or A Tiger's Death**. Flashing a smile of tobacco-stained teeth, he laughed in slow incantations. His friends stood up from their bar stools, equally as dismissive of the threat before them, but ready for action.

Kirkland counted them.

Ten against four. Not good odds.

Repeating his demand, Smith inched closer as the woman's teary eyes pleaded for help. The remaining patrons of the bar, and the bartender himself, sank to the ground, fearing the worst.

With neither side budging, Kirkland stepped in between the knife and the Louisianan, who tightened his grip around the woman's throat.

"Bartender," he said, "a round for the soldiers on me."

Placing his nose on the bar with wide orbs darting back and forth, the barkeep hesitated before fulfilling the request. Calmly, Kirkland walked over to the bar and bounced a quarter next to the shot glasses being nervously filled. Snatching a glass, he held it up, motioning for the Cajuns to follow. Squinting and looking Kirkland over, a man with a corporal's double chevrons, the highest rank in the room, finally stepped forward. Scooping up a glass, the man raised it to Kirkland's and threw the rye down his gullet. Kirkland followed, resisting the urge to cough as his throat burned.

58

Squinting again at Kirkland, the corporal spoke without eying the intended target.

"Let her go, Doucet."

Incredulous but following orders, Doucet released his grip on the woman's throat, pushing her toward Smith's knife.

"Enjoy fellas," said Kirkland. Tipping his hat, he backed up and gathered his friends through the door, making sure the prostitute was in tow.

Once outside, the woman, panting and trembling, broke down in tears, burying her head in Kirkland's shoulder.

"Thank you, thank you," she repeated over and over, between sobs.

"Go home, Miss," said Kirkland, gentle but firm.

Getting the message, the woman bolted into the night.

"I propose we leave with haste," said Alex.

"Agreed," said Kirkland, a little bewildered that his simple gesture had worked.

They stepped off with a brisk pace toward their camp, taking the next side street.

"That's a regiment of Ratcliffs," said Joe, shaking his head. "We should send them straight to Washington. They'll menace the Yankees to death in a week."

★   ★   ★

MAY 25

6 AM

"Kirkland, wake up."

Torn from the saddle of a dream, Kirkland regained his senses to see Smith standing over him, with drums calling in the background.

"Gather your things. We're movin' out. Oh, and by the way, I hear the Virginia referendum passed. They have joined us."

Kirkland jumped up and grabbed his brother's rifle. From his tent, he could see the frantic activity outside. He quickly dressed, gathered his

59

things, and headed out into the cool air. After helping Smith take down the tent, and before the cobwebs had faded from his brain, they were in line, marching toward the depot, where trains awaited the rising tide of charged-up South Carolinians.

His arms tingling with excitement, Kirkland helped Smith and his cumbersome baggage into an awaiting boxcar. He himself was carrying several extra shirts and drawers, along with numerous pairs of socks mailed by his sister, which weighted him down. As he was about to hop and roll in, he noticed Alex and Joe about to board another car down the line.

After exchanging knowing glances and adrenaline smiles, he took his place among the galvanized souls to whereabouts unknown.

Town residents rushed to the depot to see the troops off, handing their heroes packages of biscuits, cakes and whatever else they grabbed in haste on their way out the door. As the trains pulled away led by a heralding whistle, those in the crowd attempted to inspire with voluminous passion.

Every hat was aloft, every voice optimistic.

"Give them Yanks hell."

"Bravo palmetto troops."

"Show them boys what the South is made of."

"Godspeed gentlemen."

The Carolinians, every man standing and waving with pride, assured their well-wishers they would return victorious. Kirkland lingered at the entrance of the car and watched the throngs of supporters until their faces dwindled to silhouettes. Slowly, the trains ventured north, carried by the Virginia Central line and the hopes of a new nation.

Bent in a wide stance like an overloaded concierge, Smith was still trying to free himself from the arresting straps and ties that wound around him. Along with the monster bowie knife and gun were two pistols, a knapsack full of multiple layers of clothing, two haversacks bursting at the seams with food, his personal cooking equipment, including coffee pot, frying pan, canteen and tin cup, and two large poke sacks containing soap, shaving kit, sewing kit—dubbed a housewife—and other items of civilian luxury.

"Let me help with that," said Kirkland, amused, pulling off several blankets packed tightly around Smith's shoulder. "Expecting to be gone a few years? I thought *I* was overburdened."

Ripping his baggage away from Kirkland, he smiled.

"Essential items, every one. As we've now learned, the nights can be cold in Virginia. Patting the extra girth at his stomach, he continued. "And the food will need to be in abundance and cooked properly to keep my figure."

Kirkland laughed. "Remind me to stay close."

"Exactly. When all is said, uh, said and done, ya'll be knocking at my door, beggin.'"

"Fair enough."

Peeling off his own layers, Kirkland turned his thoughts to the obscured destination.

"Where do you think we're headed?"

"Too soon to tell. If I was a gamblin' man, which I ain't, I'd put my silver on Washington."

"That seems to be the consensus. I'm ready wherever these tracks put us out, to face the Yankees, I mean."

"I'd refrain from being too eager. The papers say quite a force is gathering in Washington. Cooler heads may yet prevail."

"Yes. A peaceful resolution would be the best of all courses."

"But you want to see the elephant, if for only a glimpse of the brute?"

"I must confess this is true," said Kirkland, nearing a whisper. "Drilling day after day, hour after hour, I need to know if I have the constitution for the real thing. Are my desires misguided?"

"Friend, curiosity is only natural after what we've endured and been prepared for. I, too, wonder at my fort, uh, fortitude when faced with a line of pointed muskets. I imagine we all do, whether we admit it or not. Do not be ashamed. It is a question that you cannot answer unless the situation is thrust upon you."

Kirkland knew Smith had spoken with uncanny wisdom. Aware that a magnetic craving had attached to his chest, pulling and hoping for his generation's Yorktown, he had allowed it to spread. The only tonic for his condition would be a great battle, a test of manhood. But for now, this knowing was still in the realm of the nervous exotic. And Kirkland, though not without fear, was ready to usher in the jungle.

★   ★   ★

ORANGE COURT HOUSE, VIRGINIA
1 PM

A shy, slender girl with her hair bound tightly with a pink ribbon, approached him cautiously.

Although her gait was timid, she floated between and under the gathered crowd, having precisely chosen the recipient of her mission. With her head bowed slightly, with eyes of pristine generosity, she handed him a package wrapped in white cloth. Glancing down at the package, Kirkland opened his mouth to speak, but the girl had already turned and fled before he could offer thanks.

"Thank you," he said, though only for his own gain.

"You have quite the way with women," said Joe, his arms folded, enjoying the awkward encounter.

"Ever present at moments of lethal embarrassment."

Kirkland opened the package, revealing delicious-looking ginger cakes.

"I don't see you attracting fine desserts."

"She's too young for you anyway."

"Thank you."

"All right men," said Captain Kennedy in his usual understated but forceful drawl. "Back on board. We're moving again in five minutes."

Though glad to stretch his legs on motionless ground, Kirkland made no complaint as he followed Smith back into the confines of the crowded boxcar.

"See ya'll at the next gala," said Joe, smiling as he jogged to his own traveling accommodations.

As the train pulled out of the station to continue its north-bound schedule, Kirkland lingered at the door for a spell, admiring the spring greenery passing by. In short order, however, the blurry images left him dizzy and he sat down next to a baby-faced man with freckles that seemed to be either coming or going.

"Beautiful country, isn't…"

Before the man could finish his words, a jolt sent him sprawling, his face crashing into Kirkland's shoulder. With the awful sounds of scraping metal and groaning wood pounding the air, both landed in a heap against the northern wall of the car, joined by several others who had slid into them as the train grinded to a violent halt.

Opening his eyes, Kirkland's first vision was a steady river of blood gushing from the freckled man's nose as he lay crumpled at his feet. Methodically twitching his limbs to see if everything was still in working order, Kirkland stumbled to his feet.

"You okay?" he asked the man, staring at the middle of his nose, which had shifted toward his left eye.

"I believe so."

"Here, take my handkerchief."

"Thanks."

Following others who were now rushing toward the car's lone opening, Kirkland watched the chaos of movement below. Already outside, Smith gave him a hand with his exit down the embankment.

"What the hell, uh, hell was that?" said Smith in bewilderment. "Did we run over something?"

They turned to the front and quickly gathered that this was more than a small accident. The car closest to them was overturned, and shaken men were climbing out of the skyward opening. Still somewhat dazed, Kirkland walked to the upended car. Seeing that there were already a dozen men helping to remove the passengers, he ran ahead to see what lay beyond.

His heart sank at what he saw.

The next car was hideously mangled and several men cried out in agony, lying a considerable number of feet from where they were ruthlessly launched. Feeling helpless, Kirkland saw movement out of the corner of his eye. A bloody hand appeared out of the thick foliage at the edge of the woods.

Walking over to it and fearing what he might find attached to it, Kirkland grabbed the hand and cautiously pulled out a groaning form.

Having assisted the heavily-bearded soldier almost to his feet, the man collapsed in pain, and Kirkland eased him to the open ground. Relieved to find the soldier in one piece, he knelt beside the man, unsure about what to do next.

It was then that he noticed why the soldier could not stand. His left foot twisted at a 90-degree angle from the rest of his leg, and Kirkland fought back the urge to recoil from the ugly wound.

"Please," the wounded man grimaced, "get me a surgeon."

"Right."

Kirkland bounced to his feet.

"This man needs a surgeon over here!"

His call heeded by a member of the medical staff, Kirkland moved on to find a group of men desperately working to free another from the wreckage.

The view sent him into a short prayer.

Before the accident, the unfortunate man had his legs dangling between the tender and the flat car, and the impact crushed his left leg below the knee. With their limited tools, the panicked soldiers were making no progress in freeing him. Though in obvious pain, Kirkland was stunned by the man's coolness and otherwordly patience. Someone had given the stocky man a cigar, and the exhaled smoke seemed to carry with it what must have been unbearable pain.

Joe and Alex.

The thought brought Kirkland to an about-face. Remembering that their car was several behind his, he felt reassured for their safety, but needles of doubt quickened his pace.

64

Running past his car, he found Joe and Alex on the same mission.

"Thank God you're okay," said Alex, grabbing Kirkland by the shoulder, who winced in pain.

"You sure you're all right?" said Joe.

"Yes, it's only a bruise. You?"

"We're tolerable. Where've you been? We were scouring for you."

"I went to see what we hit."

"I hear another train hit us head on," said Alex.

"It would appear likely. It's a terrible mess up ahead."

"Many wounded?"

Kirkland nodded.

"I also heard that it may have been intentional. The engineer of the southbound train can't be located."

"What?"

"Yes, our men are looking for him right now," said Joe, the veins on his forehead popping. "He best have jumped a ways back and found a good hole to crawl into. Otherwise, I'm afraid he's seen his last day."

"If it is true, then he is a coward."

Alex looked up at the sinister clouds gathering in eastern haste.

"I hope this is not a bad omen."

Chapter 4

As he had each day for the previous month, Kirkland looked himself over and took a few deep breaths to make sure the ravages of disease had continued to spare him.

This ritual complete, his next reaction was to feel for the weapon sleeping next to him, believing that today would be *the* day. And so it had gone since they'd arrived in northern Virginia at May's end, relief at his body's vigor upon awakening and frustrated at the moon's rise, shaking its head to announce the absence of the enemy.

Measles and mumps had been exposed to the rural Southerners for the first time and polluted drinking water infected the men with typhoid fever, dysentery and diarrhea. Dozens at a time were sick and nearly every morning, reveille announced the death of a comrade.

Despite the diseases running rampant through camp, the soldiers were occupied more by boundless estimation that a great battle was near. This was especially true for the troops of the 2nd South Carolina, who were farthest to the east and closer to Washington than any other. Now part of a newly formed brigade of North and South Carolina soldiers, a Virginia cavalry unit and two Virginia batteries, they were under the overall command of General Milledge Luke Bonham, with Colonel Joseph Brevard Kershaw leading the regiment.

The grandson of the "father of Camden," the thirty-nine-year old lawyer and politician was a Mexican War veteran, who looked the part of a born soldier. Tall and steel-backed, with a resonant voice that turned heads, Kershaw was a natural leader. And his men were grateful to have him.

The Camden Volunteers, posted as front-line pickets, were two miles from the quaint village of Fairfax Court House, on a hill overlooking three main roads that led to Washington and Alexandria, where any Federal movement could be seen.

Rumors had circulated for weeks that Yankees were about to advance. When orders came down on July 15 to send all extra baggage back to the main camp along a gentle waterway known as Bull Run, Kirkland was sure that the day of comeuppance was near. But he had felt that way ever since the regiment arrived in Fairfax in the middle of the night on June 21. Occasional meals of wine and Potomac herrings at the Powell Hotel were the zenith of the last several weeks, as the Federals had excluded themselves from sight.

After a light breakfast of blackberries and eggs, Kirkland wandered down the hill to relieve himself and capture a few moments of serenity. On an opposite knoll, two lambs were fighting over a twig, romping and wrestling it from each other like long-legged puppies. Nearby, their mother ignored the sport, head down and grazing; only occasionally nosing in their direction.

The simplicity was rinsing the nervous dirt between Kirkland's ears when the drums rolled.

Immediately, he took off at a run up the hill, the daily drilling having done wonders for his stamina and strength. Reaching the small plateau where he had slumbered under the stars, he dove for his brother's old musket. While some of the men had acquired a new gun in Richmond, Kirkland hadn't been among the fortunate as the number of troops far outnumbered the supply. For now, he would have to make do with the family's inadequate best.

Sprinting up the rising slope to the top, he skidded to a halt in front of Smith. But his friend's countenance startled and unnerved him. Like a statue frozen in a distant gape, his mouth was ajar and his eyes appeared ready to burst through his spectacles.

Turning to see what had gripped his friend to such consuming attention, Kirkland's heart tumbled forward and recoiled hard in his chest. There, coming down the road from Vienna from the northwest, was a storm of glistening flashes, ricocheting from thousands of bayonets pointed to the sky. Kirkland swallowed hard and his confidence took a nosedive into the dirt, until the call to form the company snapped him, as well as Smith, from their awed fixation. Gathering quickly in a jittery, disjointed marching formation, the "forward march" was given, and the company was recalled to Fairfax to link up with its regiment.

Captain Kennedy yelled, "Men, at the quickstep," for formal purposes only, as the men had already begun to scurry as fast as their legs could take them, knowing how badly they were outnumbered and with the enemy closing fast.

Tired, but with enough adrenaline to fill barrels, the men reached Fairfax, where the rest of the regiment was formed in battle lines and waiting for the pickets to join them. A short time later, a second company of pickets flew into camp just as the Federals fired off a few rounds of solid shot that harmlessly burrowed in front of them.

With the Yankees swarming in the distance, Kershaw ordered the men into marching formation, which was met with "you-gotta-be-kidding-me" stares. They had traveled dozens of miles, suffering months of impatient waiting, and at the first sign of the enemy, turn tail and retreat? Grumbling loudly and in mob numbers, the men followed orders. Knowing their disposition, and since the mutiny failed to surpass frustrated groans, Captain Kennedy allowed the protests without rebuke.

Kirkland, on the other hand, knew how ridiculous it would be to challenge a brigade, let alone the whole Federal army, and was not among the dissenters. Although he wanted a brawl as much as anyone, he was relieved, having seen the Yankee force up close.

Smith leaned in to Kirkland's ear.

"I'd stand here, uh, stand like the next, but I'm in no haste for suicide," he whispered.

Kirkland nodded in agreement yet said nothing. In truth, even against these odds, the withdrawal was painful. However, he imagined the back turning was only a temporary reprieve. As they marched west with feet kicking and whimpering against their direction, their necks twisted as if being constantly pulled by unseen reins. The men could barely walk four paces at a time without looking over their shoulders. When the bulk of the Carolinians saw for the first time just how many enemy pursuers were biting at their heels, it wasn't long before the gruff whining was muted.

With the Federals only 300 yards behind and closing, the regiment moved from a quick step to a jog, and finally into an all-out run. They arrived at Germantown just ahead of the enemy's flanking force, but still had seven miles to cover before getting to Centreville and a few miles more to their log-and-earth trenches at Mitchell's Ford on Bull Run.

But there was no time to rest.

Kirkland's eyes stung with sweat and as he ran, he struggled to find a dry piece of clothing on his arms, as he was constantly wiping his lathered forehead. Noticing the man on his left was no longer there, he looked back to see him struggling to keep up. His eyes were a vacant stare and his head was tilted upward, mouth open, his stubbly beard dripping with moisture. In the moment it took for Kirkland to gauge his place in the column and then turn back to the struggling soldier, the man had fallen out of step and lay face down in the dirt.

Smith, who was on Kirkland's right, saw Kirkland slow his propulsion. Seizing his arm, Smith shook his head.

"Ain't nothing you can do for him," said Smith, panting heavily. "Leave him be."

Acknowledging that Smith was probably right, but with a stricken conscience, he jumped back into line and they continued forward at the brisk pace. Many more fell by the wayside as a casualty of the July heat, and each time, Kirkland fought the urge to assist them. Each time a finger-wagging look from Smith kept his feet in motion. The weary troops finally reached Centerville ecstatic at the approaching friend of night, and even more so with the disappearance of the Yankees. For an anxious hour, they formed into line of battle. But the enemy failed to appear. Finally convinced the Yankees had halted for the night, Bonham gave the order to rest at ease.

Slumping to the ground, Kirkland put down his musket and raised his canteen by a quivering hand attached to a wobbly arm. While only a few drops fell to his dusty, parched tongue, it was heaven sent. Smith sat down next to Kirkland, yet failed to urge a trickle from his own empty vessel.

With sad, dejected eyes, Smith turned to his friend.

"Sorry, she's dry," said Kirkland.

"Not to worry. I'll manage."

"Are you sure?"

The pathetic face evaporated in Kirkland's scrutiny.

"Ah, compared to a few months ago, I'm fit as a fiddle." Smith patted his stomach, which had already lost much of its blubber since leaving Richmond.

"Almost skin, uh, almost skinny."

"Please, don't be offended but I had my doubts today. I was duly impressed with your fortitude."

Smith attempted to laugh, though it was minus its normal vigor.

"No offense taken. This old man is full of surprises. The sun ain't nothin' compared to the glowing heat in my shop. If you cut me open, you won't find blood, only fire. Only fire."

"Let's hope the day never comes where I see your insides."

"Indeed."

Kirkland sighed.

"What will happen to those men who couldn't keep up?"

"I don't rightly know. If they survive the night, they'll most likely be captured."

"I could have…

"Could have what? Dragged one of them here? No, you would have ended up just like them, dead or in the hands of the Yankees."

Smith lowered his tone.

"Believe me, my urge for helping them was as strong as yours. But you can't sacrifice yourself for a hope, uh, hopeless cause. For that end, nobody wins."

Kirkland drank the words, knowing their wisdom.

"Yes, I share in your sentiments. Yet it fails to relieve my suffering for them."

"Of course not. Words cannot cleanse the suffering we witnessed today. But hear this, friend. Our destiny was not fulfilled today. Only God knows when that will come to pass. Do not torture yourself. Your destiny will reveal itself in good time."

Smith's eyes clouded momentarily, and Kirkland worried that Smith was about to collapse.

"Hand me your canteen," said Kirkland, wincing as he stood up. "I'll hoof it to the nearest water source."

"I'd be obliged, obliged to you," Smith stammered.

"You rest now. I imagine our stay here will be brief."

As Smith stretched out in the cool grass, Kirkland wandered into the fading light in search of water and a tonic to creeping doubt that even Smith's wisdom could not wholly alleviate.

★   ★   ★

JULY 21, 1861
MITCHELL'S FORD ON BULL RUN
MANASSAS JUNCTION, VA
6:30 AM

The smothering shroud of anxiety combined with a lack of sleep was beginning to take its toll.

71

Kirkland, like the others, had shut his eyes for a few hours of fitful rest here and there, but the smallest sound across the river would send a jolt through his skull. A snapped twig or an owl's hoot would cause him to sit up in a hair-ascending tilt, with ears perked and eyes scanning the darkness.

On day four after the retreat from Fairfax Court House, Kirkland found his mind fluttering and his limbs apt to spasms and strange twitches, as if he had guzzled a stiff pot of coffee. Lying in the trenches he examined every nook of his rifle before checking and rechecking the ammunition supply in his cartridge box.

Bonham's brigade had been placed at the Confederate center and all expected an attack at this position. Yet at Mitchell's Ford, all had been quiet.

Because of Bull Run's steep banks, only a few fords were available for the crossing of large numbers of troops, and the Confederates were in force guarding these locations. Rising in all its brilliance as if unaware of the darkness gathering below, the sun habitually smiled at the pleasant Virginia countryside and tranquil waters of the Run. While the water moved along with a shallow grace, the banks were chest-deep with the nervous energy of men waiting for their first true glimpse of war. Always the last to know what the orders would be and what intelligence revealed about the enemy's movements, the common soldiers were at the end of their tethers, and ready to snap under the strain.

Sensing the unrest and atmosphere of severe tension, a regimental chaplain gathered the men for a morning prayer. Kirkland knelt in the cool grass with the others, and even the most chapel-delinquent realized the moment's gravity and joined with heads bowed.

With an expression of glorified anger on his vein-pulsing face, the preacher began in a booming, well-rehearsed voice.

"The enemy has defied the will of God by breaking the holy Sabbath with their profane mission of shedding our blood. May the enemy be thwarted in their Godless agenda. May you grant us victory against our oppressors."

Slowly, the preacher raised a blessing palm, and closed his eyes.

"Lord, be with these men, and give them courage and strength in the face of deadly fire. May they fight with your will in their hearts and righteous power in their guns. If they should fall today as a martyr to Southern independence, have mercy on them and accept them into your glorious kingdom. Amen."

When he was finished, an eerie silence pervaded the air as every man became lock-jawed with a sense of awe and purpose. The sole companion to this hush was a slight wind ruffling about their uniforms which failed to disrupt the collective meditation.

For the first time since he enlisted, Kirkland stared at his own vulnerability. Even the close call at Fairfax had not given him pause. Of course he wasn't blind to the danger, but never had death rested on his shoulder and whispered in his ear.

An uncomfortable heaviness took hold of his chest and admitted the truth: he was afraid.

"Hey Kirkland. After we chase these Yankees back to Washington, whatyasay we stick around and look for some local beauties?"

Thank God for Joe.

"Don't you have enough girlfriends?"

"On the contrary. Unlike you, I'm not married."

"Yes, well who in their right mind would marry you?"

"No one can turn down this fine biscuit of Southern charm."

Kirkland laughed, his confidence having returned.

"Well, I need to get back to my company, a *genuine* company," said Joe. "I'll see ya after we whip some Yankee be-hind."

Watching his friend walk away, Kirkland wasted no effort to contain a brimming smile. Someday, he thought, if the war drags on, he will transfer to the Flat Rock Guards. Having a calming influence like Joe going into battle would be the ultimate blessing. For now, though, he would have to rely on his own mettle.

Out of nowhere a cannon report was heard in the distance and a spinning ball dove into Bull Run with a mighty splash, sending the green troops running to take cover behind the breastworks.

Kirkland crouched in the trench but could not see any troops at his front. A second shot came and then a third, yet it was hardly a bombardment. Although a few scattered solid shot and shells were launched across Mitchell's Ford, they were sent from afar, and there was no hint of an immediate attack. As the morning wore on, the waiting became unbearable and seemed likely that the fire was nothing more than a ruse, and the real attack was to be made elsewhere.

Along with his comrades, Kirkland had nothing to battle but the stifling heat.

"Is the heat getting to me, or are the Yankees trying to deceive us?" said Kirkland to Smith, pointing his musket at the barren hills across Bull Run.

"I've been thinking the same," said Smith, adjusting his eyeglasses that were skiing down his sweat-lubricated nose. "It's a deception all right. We may be at the opposite end of the action."

The sounds to the northwest were subtle at first, building to a growling crescendo until there was no doubt blood had been shed somewhere up the muddy river. All heads turned to the direction of the strange, incongruous racket. At first no one spoke, or dared to move. It was if they were in a darkened theatre, an opera of peculiar vibrations, familiar yet somehow altered in its presentation.

Unseen, the performers left all to the untrained imagination. Listening intently, Kirkland adopted his Morris Island stance.

It was unnecessary. The field cannon were trumpets compared to Fort Sumter's tuba blasts. But as the battle sounds grew louder, he couldn't perceive whether the clouds of war were moving closer or just increasing in magnitude.

A feeling of powerlessness became overwhelming, not knowing what was happening beyond his sight. As the hours went by, his greatest fear was missing out on the action completely, which inflamed to a bothersome itch too deep within to scratch.

For a while he watched the hard-riding dispatchers reporting to Kershaw and Bonham, wishing he was party to their conversation. Neither officer could be read from afar, either, as each had on his poker face.

Aggravating the situation further was the mounting heat, as the shade trees along the banks had been cut to obtain a clear view of the approaches. For just a moment, Kirkland felt a steamrolling urge to bellyflop into the cool waters. The prospect was so gratifying that its absence was painful, and he quickly buried it in the trenches.

Refusing a tomb, however, was the dreaded unknown. He wanted to pick up his rifle and move somewhere, anywhere. Whether this was forward or backward, advancing or retreating, he didn't care. Of course, he preferred a glimpse of the Yankees with something other than his backside. Be that as it may, he needed some kind of direction and escape, and would take the first generous offer. Looking around him, he took heart that the rest of his company was just as miserable as he.

Some were staring blindly into the tree stumps, as if holding their gaze on a fixed point would settle their nerves. Others shifted uncontrollably in the trenches, hardly remaining in one stance for more than a few seconds. The worst were mumbling incoherently, trying to engage anyone in conversation, to speak of anything but the present situation.

Near the point of screaming for mercy, Kirkland and the others finally got their wish.

★   ★   ★

NOON

"Column of fours," Captain Kennedy barked, a faint smile on his lips. "We have our orders to advance on the enemy."

With a balloon-bursting cheer, the 2nd South Carolina leaped into marching formation in record time. No men in history were more impatient to be shot at. Along with the 8th South Carolina and a battery led by Captain Delaware Kemper, they soon headed northwest at the double quick.

As they advanced, the outward displays of alleviation soon dried up, replaced by features of nervous determination. Once again silent, the men tucked their emotional baggage close to their perspiring chests and shuffled toward their baptism of fire.

With his feet now moving, Kirkland was freed of the hatchet of inactivity pounding at his head, and for a moment, relaxed. While still blind to the dangers ahead, he found comfort in the realization that he would finally be able to use the mental and physical callouses born of grinding drill. After the men had gone two miles, they came into contact with the first of the walking wounded and terrified skulkers who were heading in the opposite direction. The latter was in numerous supply, as most did not display even the slightest of injuries.

Among them, a tall man with a splintered rifle and a faint limp cried out to all who would listen,

"The day is lost. We are whipped and broken."

Dozens more echoed his conclusions and their exaggerated whimpers of a slaughter drained the blood from Kirkland's face, leaving a pale wake.

Kershaw, sensing his soldiers were drinking in the gloom, rode over to counter the backpedaling propaganda.

"No!" the colonel boomed, startling Kirkland and his fellow troops with its snarling bite. "You are whipped and believe everyone else is. The day is far from over."

Inspired with renewed confidence and swagger, the men picked up the pace. Kicked up by the hordes of men, clouds of dust hung in the air and Kirkland found it very difficult to breathe. He reached for his canteen and brought it to his lips, but again, only a few drops remained. In the excitement, he had forgotten to replenish it with vital water.

After they had gone another mile, they reached General Joseph Johnston's field headquarters at Portici, a large frame house with monstrous double end chimneys. Halting briefly at the house while Kershaw received further orders, they were soon moving again, turning west on a forested road toward the Confederate left. The concussions of battle could be felt now, slamming into knees and searching out the weak.

Roughly fondled by waves of emotion like never before, a rolling succession of excitement and fear, exhilaration and apprehension tormented Kirkland's stomach. He thought of Susan, in her beautiful gown, but promptly eradicated the image from his purposeful mind. Breathing both erratically and heavily, he tried desperately to stay focused on the task manifesting before them. Realizing his hand was cramping from gripping the butt of his rifle too deliberately, he loosened his hold and gulped pints of air in an attempt to steady himself. Yet the air contained no buttress.

Nearing the Sudley Road, Kershaw halted the men and ordered them into lines of battle. Having been well drilled, the Carolinians quickly shifted into position. To the north, what appeared to be an enormous forest fire loomed overhead, swirling around a roaring, hellish ensemble of musketry and cannon. Second-growth pines blocked Kirkland's view of the raging struggle, and he had no idea which side was winning or what was poised to strike within or beyond the trees.

He had little time to let this latest round of the wobbles settle before Kershaw galloped ahead of the men. His charcoal horse was a little skittish, jerking his head and shuffling his feet, but his master soon had him under control and facing the troops.

"Fix bayonets!" the colonel tossed out with all his lung power.

With sweaty hands shaking with a glut of adrenaline, Kirkland went to remove the bayonet when he remembered he didn't have one. He glanced over at Smith, also minus a stabbing attachment, who shrugged before shouldering his gun.

"For-ward... March!"

No turning back now. We all must see this through. Breathe.

Looking to his sides, he was reassured to find the lines true and steady. The faces, however, were different shades, reflecting a wide variety of confidence and strain. Dealing with his own questioning feet, he did not judge or take time to ponder them. What he did center his attention on was the widespread determination to uphold the honor of South Carolina. It was not unflinching, as the eyes and posture told, but the men were not bowing to their fears.

Heading north towards the eye of the storm, the men entered the woods where the enemy's artillery soon found them. Branches and pine needles deluged the Carolinians as the Federals' long-range 20-pounders burst through, scouring the canopy. By reflex, Kirkland ducked as a large solid shot purred overhead and splintered a tree he had just brushed past. The crunching impact unleashed a shower of pine needles that covered his hat and decorated his shoulders. While the heavy ball struck well above him, the violent crack of wood jumped Kirkland's gait. His heart skipped a beat and raced ahead of him, and it was a full minute before he caught up with his chest.

Through waist-high brush Kirkland tramped, ignoring the urge to shuffle around them, only diverging from his path to get around a trembling pine. Unable to see the colors, he tried to keep pace with the man on either side and those in front, which proved difficult in the dense woods. As he stepped around one of these modest trees, a shot rang out, followed by a scattered volley.

Kirkland squinted but could only see bits of wildly colored uniforms filtering through the brush, as the Yankees were hiding behind the trees and crouched behind a rail fence. As the first line approached, the enemy arose with muskets leveled. In near perfect unison, they fired a volley at the Carolinians, but most of the shots were high. As they recoiled a few paces, Kirkland got his first good look at the enemy.

This was the 14th Brooklyn, decked out in French chasseur military uniforms, with pulsing red pantaloons and white gaiters. Covering their heads were kepis of alternating blue and red spirals, with a cloth havelock billowing down the backs of their necks. A navy blue shell jacket with a red false vest completed the striking garb.

Pointing to the New Yorkers with a finger of zeal, Kershaw yelled to his men: "There they are, boys! Down with them!"

The line in front of Kirkland's leaped the fence.

Within seconds, they were met with a blizzard of fire and Kirkland realized that the first Yankees must have been mere skirmishers who had retreated to a main line. The lead minié balls, invisible in their spinning, butchering flight, zipped through the gaps and tore into the flesh of the unfortunates.

Leaning his rifle against the fence, Kirkland attempted to jump over. As his feet touched the ground on the other side, a body slammed against him, throwing Kirkland back against the fence. Wincing in pain from another bruised shoulder, he looked down to see a stunned man clutching his right breast as blood poured out between his fingers. Terror amplified the blue hues in the wounded man's eyes and his jaw stuttered in a silent scream. A second man, recognizing the fallen, rushed to his side and fell to his knees in premature grief. Tearing off his hat, he jammed his palms into his cheeks, rocking back and forth over the death struggles of his brother.

Picking up his rifle, Kirkland noticed his company escaping him and he ran to catch up to the line, unwilling to interfere with the brothers' last moments together. Through the woods, the company officers screamed themselves into hoarse mutes in an attempt to keep the men in their lines, but to no avail. They had stopped to fire one semi-cohesive volley before order evaporated.

The trees and novelty of battle were making any coordinated attack futile, and the men began to fire at will even without orders. Here, Kirkland saw just how green the regiment was. Some fired so wildly that even the tree tops were safe. Others pulled the trigger with the muzzle empty of a round. One hysterical and impatient soldier fired with the ramrod still forced down the gun's barrel, the projectile making an odd whirring sound as it flailed through the air before wrapping itself around a small tree. Then there were those whose constitution failed them completely, the panicked men throwing away their weapons in a mad dash to the rear. In a more baffling demeanor, a few paused to collect blackberries, oblivious to the storm, munching carefree as if at a Sunday picnic.

Seeing Smith to his left, Kirkland moved abreast of him, content to go forward with a least one friend by his side. While he waited for a good target, a bullet rifled past his ear, so close he could feel its deadly wind as it passed. Although it spoke in an undecipherable language, it awoke something in Kirkland. Penetrating his skull, the shadow breath moved down his arms and into his chest, inflating his veins. In this moment, all fear melted away. He was at once a dagger of focused energy, a human arrow point.

Not wanting the shooter to gain a second bead on him, Kirkland stopped, raised his weapon, and calmly fired in the general direction the tickling miss came from. Continuing to hide behind trees and brush, the New Yorkers only showed themselves long enough to fire. With the smoke lounging between the trees, they were difficult targets. Kirkland maintained a close proximity to Smith, but the foliage and smoke soon separated the men into jumbled clumps.

Although they could hear the strong voice of Kershaw urging them on, at times the explosions of artillery and synchronized musket shots devoured his words. Seeing a handful of Carolinians who had crouched down together behind one of the larger pines, Kirkland grabbed Smith by the canteen strap and pulled heavily. Not arguing, Smith followed toward the confused and stalled allies. As they reached the wild-eyed band, Kirkland strolled past their shielding tree, the bullets thumping the gravel around him and creasing the air overheard.

Turning his back to the danger, Kirkland attempted to rally the wavering men, who were without an officer present.

"Form up and follow me!" he yelled, trying to make eye contact with each of them.

Smith stepped forward, and the men reluctantly followed. Together, they were a mere eight men, but they formed into an even line and advanced like reborn veterans. Kirkland, on the left flank and encouraging them, halted the squad at the next sign of opposition. The shots from the enemy were again high and harmless. In full view now, as the trees had thinned, Kirkland saw a handful of New Yorkers frantically reloading.

80

One bluecoat, a foot shorter than the rest, placed a cartridge into the barrel, but struggled to drive the shot home, and dropped the ramrod.

He was bending over to pick it up when Kirkland assumed the aggressor.

"On my command! Ready, aim, fire!"

In unison, the Carolinians pulled the trigger, and while the smoke wafted in front of his eyes, Kirkland discharged his own weapon blindly. The shots were wild, and Kirkland didn't notice a single man fall. The effect was enough, however, to send the enemy into hasty retreat.

With burning vision, and waiting for the men to reload, Kirkland directed his group to keep moving.

"On their heels! Shoulder to shoulder, march!"

Possessed by an insatiable urge to attack, he could barely recognize his own voice, it having taken a personality of its own. The noise of battle was met with indifference and time surged in mammoth leaps. Exploding shells no longer caused even a fleeting blink, and his customary reflexes were now stunted and pruned. The rivers of sweat at his brow and lower back dried up, replaced with a biting cold. His breathing slowed and eyes narrowed. It was as if a warrior spirit had attached to his heart.

Though he remained in control, he was somehow transformed, the holes of doubt plugged with feet-forward purpose. His usual pondering mind of normal consciousness was now a mere observer, in some sort of strange hibernation.

Still amongst the trees, Kirkland could not see the bulk of his regiment on either side, yet made the decision to keep moving. Spotting a remnant of the enemy 50 yards directly in front, he guided them forward, tossing aside branches as if they were an unqualified hindrance. They had gone only a few paces before the New Yorkers fired.

Hearing the man on his right scream, Kirkland looked down to see the fallen clutching a shattered ankle.

"Halt!" Kirkland yelled, trying to be heard over the shrieking wounded. "Form up!"

When the men were in place, he ordered a deadly reply.

"Ready! Aim! Fire!"

Without waiting to see the fallout of their volley, Kirkland pressed forward but noticed only Smith had advanced with him.

The remaining five were crouched around the man destined for amputation, arguing for the duty of a human crutch and passage to the rear.

"Leave him, the stretcher bearers will find him," said Kirkland, irritated. "We must keep moving."

His words fell on deaf ears and he was completely ignored, except for one man, who steadied his cap and abandoned the stragglers. This determined one had a crooked, freckled nose, caused by the unfortunate railroad accident on the way north. Kirkland had since learned his name or, rather, what his friends called him: Red McDowell. Approaching the two perseverant ones, Red simply nodded.

Knowing that three men advancing alone was foolish, absurd even, Kirkland took a long look at his surroundings. The peculiar absence of the 2nd South Carolina's flags was disturbing. Noticing a clearing up ahead, between patches of woods, he scanned the trees on the other side for any signs of movement. Seeing none, he proposed a plan to the duo.

"There looks to be an open field ahead. If we can get to it, hopefully there will be a better view of the grounds and we can find our boys. I don't see any sign of the Yankees but it could be a trap. Thoughts?"

"Even if we stay put, we could be captured, or worse," said Smith. "I say we give it a shot."

With eyebrows raised, Kirkland and Smith turned to their companion.

"Why not?"

"All right then," said Kirkland. "Let's move."

Traveling with caution, they advanced, eyes scanning with every planted foot. Somewhere ahead, the battle was ongoing and ferocious, and its ripples shook the trees like a mighty wind. But the enemy in the immediate vicinity had fled and they arrived at the clearing with no opposition.

Here, Kirkland saw his first Yankee up close, nearly tripping over the fallen in the tall weeds. The clean-shaven lad lay crumpled on his back, his head arched backward. While his eyes had relaxed from sentient fright, his mouth was clotted in a severed wail. A gaping, bloody hole in his neck made the cause of death obvious. The lifeless body didn't look more than sixteen, no older than Kirkland's brother Sam.

He was dismissing the wayward thought with a final glance when he detected movement from the corner of his eye. Wheeling in its direction, Kirkland raised his rifle at a man striding toward him.

Immediately the soldier stopped and threw up his hands.

"Friend!" he cried. "Friend!"

"What regiment you with?" said Kirkland, aiming his weapon at the man's chest.

"Sixth North Carolina. You?"

That was enough to ease suspicions, and Kirkland lowered his rifle.

"Second South Carolina."

Impatient, and wanting badly to find his regiment, he wasted no time with friendly chit chat.

"Everything's all jumbled up. You're welcome to take up with us if you like. That is, if you're not going to the rear."

"Oh, no," said the man, shaking his head emphatically. "Somehow I got separated from my command. I reckon I'll stick with you fellas, at least until I find my regiment."

"Are you loaded?"

"Armed and ready."

"Good. We've dawdled enough."

Boldly, Kirkland led the men across the small field. With every step, the land cradled more of the departed enemy, each with an exclusive pose of death. More curious than sick to his stomach, Kirkland was strangely detached. It was as if rough blankets had been thrown over the tender white candles of his mind, the flames snuffed and the wicks buried. The sight of runaway intestines and oozing brains only caused a muted reaction as if they were no more than spoiled sausages and spilled molasses. Through a window in the smoke on his left, he saw a blue flag with palmetto and crescent moon. The line of the 2nd South Carolina was not more than fifty yards away.

"There!"

Very much relieved, Kirkland took off at a sprint, sidestepping dead bodies, not bothering to check if the members of his little posse were at his heels. He caught up just as the regiment reached the edge of another woods. Here, the color sergeant planted the flag, signaling the troops to halt.

Finding himself next to Joe and Alex, Kirkland said nothing, acting as if his wandering adventures had not occurred.

"Where you been?" asked Joe. "Make a visit to the privy? You've been gone for a good while; must be plugged."

Before he could respond, Kirkland's companions fell in, and Joe looked over the Virginian with raised eyebrows.

"Who's that?"

"Woodsman."

There was but the slightest hint of a smile on Kirkland's grimy face, and Joe waited for more. But none followed.

"Woodsman, huh? Does he cure the piles?"

"No, but I imagine *that* will."

Kirkland nodded toward their destination.

"That'll do it."

Directly in front, Henry Hill was awash in blue smoke and fire-breathing flashes. A humble farmhouse perched in the center seemed to bewitch both armies, sucking in each side's limitless wrath. Even from a distance, Kirkland could see it had paid dearly for its magnetics, its sides and roof smashed by artillery.

Over this rise, a dark cloud hovered, mimicking the throes of night and creating an air of pure malevolence. The hill must have been taken and retaken numerous times, and at a fearful cost, each side plunging in only to be staggered by scorching flames. Tossed about in this inferno of rising ground were dozens of hapless men, Yankee and Confederate, mingled together in death. Their tributaries of spilled blood merged to form a web of ghastly rivulets that trickled down the hillside.

In force on the west and north sides of the incline, the enemy was now holding its ground against repeated attacks by Virginians to the east, under the command of a little known general by the name of Thomas Jackson.

Hearing through the onslaught of iron and lead both the huzzahs of the Yankees and the guttural shouts of Southerners, Kirkland had no idea which side was gaining more ground. Knowing he was with the wrong company, he signaled for Smith to follow him and they jogged over to the Camden Volunteers.

As they fell in with their proper company, three captured New Yorkers passed by, escorted by guards. Two of the prisoners leered at Kirkland, while the third had the hysterical, dilated look of a man being led to the gallows. On the brim of his kepi was written, "Richmond Or Hell."

Before Kirkland could digest the two-road slogan, Captain Kennedy pushed to the front of his men.

"We are the near the left flank and must prevent the enemy from getting around us. We will advance along the road... Ahhgh."

Clutching his side, Kennedy teetered backward and fell.

"Are you all right, Captain?" asked Kirkland, rushing to his aid.

Caressing his ribs where he was struck, Kennedy winced in pain. Repeating his question, Kirkland examined the captain for any sign of blood.

Still feeling his ribs, Kennedy pronounced himself okay.

"Spent ball," he said, as Kirkland helped him to his feet. "Only a bruise. It's nothing."

He attempted to continue his orders, but as he raised his voice, the pain sliced the end off his first word. Kershaw, however, his voice at full capacity, barked orders to advance upon the farmhouse in front. Fortunately for the Carolinians, by the time they arrived abreast of the little white home, the Yankees had abandoned the hill.

As the blue smoke dissipated, they came upon the remnants of an abandoned enemy battery. One of the gunners was slumped over the barrel of still-smoking gun, and as Kirkland marched by, the unmistakable aroma of burnt flesh inflamed his nostrils. The combined sight and smell of the roasting dead caused a few to gag and shield their heads. Despite being in close proximity, Kirkland's stomach did not quiver. And he breathed it in with the same numbed acceptance as the acrid gun smoke.

Now on the high ground, the Carolinians summoned the attention of several Yankee regiments and in an instant, the balls were whistling among them in alarming numbers. Men were being punched from the line, struck down and spun by nefarious bullets.

With no reinforcements beckoning, Kershaw had seen enough of the pointless sacrifice.

"Lay down!" he bellowed. "Lay down! We will wait here till our friends come up!"

In dropping to the ground, a cloud of dust assailed Kirkland's face, causing a forceful choke. He tried to spit out the dirt but little saliva remained. When he stoppered his mouth again, his defiled teeth crunched on the offending grit. Now reacquainted with an unbearable thirst, he tried to keep the engulfing urge for water at bay. But the work was not done.

Sprawled with his gun pointed at the Yankee lines, he was keenly aware that he had probably inflicted zero damage on the enemy, his primitive, unrifled weapon being of little use in anything but close quarters. As much as he cherished his brother's weapon, he knew he must find something more suitable at the earliest opportunity. Dreaming of a British Enfield or a Massachusetts-made Springfield, a growing crescendo to his left delayed his yearning.

The 8th South Carolina had come up, as well as General Kirby Smith's brigade, which had rushed forward from Manassas Junction, having arrived from the Shenandoah Valley by railroad. Even more help came from Colonel Jubal Early's brigade, further solidifying the Confederate line.

Bolstered by the reinforcements, Kershaw sprang to action.

"Rise, Carolinians! To your post!"

With a hungry cheer they leaped to their feet, and Kirkland could already feel the momentum shift. The fire directed at the 2nd South Carolina had slowed to a trickle, allowing for the men to align themselves with Smith's brigade which had arrived at the perfect moment.

Riding behind his regiment, the colonel pulled out his sword and pointed.

"At the double quick. Charge!"

Rushing forward, more mob than a straight line, before they were close enough to fire a shot, the enemy line wavered. At first it was gentle, a slow yielding, as the enemy started to back away.

The men around Kirkland erupted into a wild cheer. Kirkland attempted to join them, but his parched throat yielded only a slight shriek, which he quickly smothered in embarrassment.

At first the enemy backpedaled to a vibrant walk. Then it became a jog, with only the bravest pausing to unleash a parting shot. Before long, an altogether panic ensued, and whole regiments lost its nerve, the men sprinting away as if in a footrace.

It had become a rout.

As Kirkland watched, cavalry led by Colonel J.E.B. Stuart, swooped down with sabers drawn racing to cut off the fleeing Yankees from reaching the bridges over Bull Run. While the attackers failed to get there in time, this chaotic amoeba of pursuit caused many to throw away their weapons in an embarrassing, fend-for-yourself stampede. The 2nd South Carolina pursued as well, crossing the stone bridge on Warrenton Turnpike, and followed the enemy almost to Centreville before Kershaw called them back.

Addressing the ecstatic troops, the colonel smiled.

"You have won yourself glory today," he said. "You have made South Carolina proud. Today was a great victory, and although there will be empty seats around our fires, they did not die in vain. They went to God with honor and dignity. Much work is left to be done but today was a momentous day for Dixie!"

As Kershaw bowed from his horse in respect, the men flung their hats in joyous cheer, and toasted their leader with empty canteens.

Initially moved by the colonel's speech, Kirkland's euphoria quickly vanished as he scoured the elated, powder-blackened faces for his friends. He had lost all connection to them in the frantic chase and now fear was turning to panic. With his neck swiveled and eyes bulging, he desperately searched among the whooping throng. A great relief washed over him as he located Smith. Overwhelmed by fatigue in both mind and body, the two friends embraced in a wordless grip.

But what was the fate of Joe and Alex?

★　　　★　　　★

JULY 22
MITCHELL'S FORD

Kirkland awoke the next morning to paradiddles of rain against his uniform, with the concussions of battle still in his ears.

Having succumbed to a subterranean sleep brought on by extreme exhaustion, Kirkland wondered how long he had been lying unsheltered in the rain. His wool blanket, which normally kept him relatively warm in the rain, had no chance against this onslaught and Kirkland was soaked through. The ground around him had long since turned into a muddy pulp. Still too weary to rise, he remained on his back. Fearing that any movement would sink him into the mud's embrace, he remained still, the hat over his face his only comfort. When dawn finally appeared with a cloudy whimper, Kirkland found himself molded to the ground. With some difficulty, he tore himself from the mud's clutches.

Freezing, Kirkland made a beeline to the nearest fire, joining a handful of worn-out troops who were staring at the glowing embers. All seemed to be in some kind of morning stupor, almost catatonic as if drugged by the silence. Most in the camp were still sleeping, the officers allowing the troops an extended shuteye. Kirkland held his hands over the fire and rubbed them until full feeling returned. After eating a soggy biscuit from his haversack and sufficiently warmed, he decided to take a walk over the battlefield.

As he wandered, he let the events of yesterday roll through his mind. Thankfully, Smith, Joe and Alex had all escaped the battle without a scratch just as he did, and he had given each a bear hug when reacquainted the previous night. Knowing that his closest friends were still among the living, however, did not change the fact that many more were not so lucky. In the 2nd South Carolina, eight men were killed and 50 were wounded, many serious enough that they would probably not make it through the week.

It all seemed so surreal. Kirkland did his best to grasp its significance and weight. Though initially terrifying, once his feet had been dipped in battle's waters, the swift current had pulled him in before he knew what hit him. It was as if fear and the conscious mind had drifted away when the strain should have been the most severe. Time ceased to exist, distorted and sprinting. These sensory contradictions puzzled Kirkland, and every time he cast a questioning line into the deep, the hook came back empty. It was all too foreign and mysterious.

The more he walked, the more confused he became, trying to make sense out of the senseless. Realizing some kind of transformation had taken place while under combat's spell, he wondered if this was Nature's way of diluting the full effect. Even as all of his normal faculties of mind returned when the battle came to a close, the memories of the slain and bleeding remained in this cocoon of censored vision.

Do all men experience this?

Remembering the hordes of men who had flocked to the rear with minimal or counterfeit wounds, he dismissed this idea.

Maybe the experience is unique for each of us.

A stutter of movement to his left caught Kirkland's attention. He turned to see a large black horse appear out of the brush. It was limping badly and for good reason. The lower part of the animal's left front leg was missing, leaving a bloody stump that hovered off the ground and a large chunk of flesh had been torn from its left rib cage. It was an abominable sight.

Drenched and hideously wounded, it was a sad reality for such a beautiful mount. Sixteen hands high and solidly built, it was a draft horse of the highest quality.

Seeing Kirkland, the animal stopped and looked directly into his eyes, and Kirkland stood for several moments staring into its hypnotic brown orbs. Immediately he was struck by the horse's fearlessness and human-like comprehension, as he could sense it was resigned to its fate. The poise displayed by this suffering wretch shook him to the core.

Loading his weapon, being careful that the powder remained dry in the still-steady rain, Kirkland discreetly approached until he was parallel with the horse. Although it kept an eye on his movements, only its head shifted. Giving the horse a slight bow in admiration, Kirkland raised his rifle and aimed at the animal's head. Without hesitating, he fired, and the animal tumbled to the ground, dead.

Continuing on, the carnage grew worse.

On and around Henry Hill, the Confederates were busy burying both their own and the enemy's dead, but many still lay where they had exhaled their final breath. The numbers astonished Kirkland. In one area, smaller than a half acre, Kirkland counted 27 bodies of the Federal army. Inching closer, the putrefying corpses, robbed of their outer layers of clothing by scavengers, made him nauseous, the awful smell forcing a hand over his nose. The heat was causing rapid decomposition.

And these were bodies that were relatively intact.

One particularly gruesome body had been ripped in half, the poor man's serene face nearly kissing his detached feet.

He was probably dead before he hit the ground.

Other faces showed less tranquility. The next Yankee Kirkland happened upon had his jaw stretched in a diagonal, horrific howl as if the end arrived suddenly but with time to register the bullet's sting. Still others demonstrated the fragility of bones when met by iron shell and shot, with arms snapped like kindling and legs shattered as if made of porcelain. Although the rain had washed away the pools of blood, red patches remained. These were subdued yet calling for attention as if the soil was gorged and unable to swallow the multitude.

Everywhere, motley holes and furrowed grooves pockmarked the ground as if dug by rabid, overgrown gophers. Jagged pieces of artillery shells were scattered far and wide, washed ashore by the giant storm, along with various flotsam: splintered rifles, discarded haversacks and blankets, canteens and bayonets. Joining this madman's collage, spit out from the ravages of war, were herds of dead horses and mangled artillery wagons.

Having no interest in souvenirs but having spent the night without a waterproof cover, Kirkland seized a government-issued rubber blanket with no apparent owner and tossed it over his shoulder.

And he picked up a discarded Enfield, while hesitating, just for a moment, as he left his brother's gun behind. Kirkland recognized the gun, with the British "Tower" mark, as one that could have been issued to his own regiment. A fortunate few had drawn these weapons while in Richmond and Kirkland had envied these men. The person it had belonged to was a mystery, but Kirkland was glad to keep it in Carolina's company.

Near the ruins of the white farmhouse, he came to a corpse with an extraordinary uniform.

In the haze of battle, Kirkland remembered late in the fight running past injured men with the same regalia but didn't think much of them at the time. The man wore large, bulky trousers with blue and white stripes that extended from the hip to the knee, similar striped stockings, a bright red shirt and a red fez with dark blue tassels. Around the campfire the previous evening, Kirkland had heard men talking about the heroic charges of the Louisianans who wore this particular uniform, who fought hand-to-hand for possession of that tug o' war hill. "Tigers" they had called them, and by viewing the number of slain with the red shirts, these Louisianans deserved the nickname.

At Kirkland's feet, the tiger's eyes were open and dull, and he lay crumpled on his side with one knee raised to his chest.

"Them tigers sure put up a fight yesterday."

91

Kirkland looked up to see a soldier leaning against a shovel. Beneath a kepi, his soggy and dripping hair was matted against his face, almost completely roofing his eyes. Without even looking at Kirkland, he stroked his naked chin and peered down at the body for a closer look.

"No one can call this man a coward," he said, casually.

"Certainly not."

"Surely a lot of good men lost their lives on this damn hill. Even an old woman."

"What?"

"That's what I'm told. Her name was…" The soldier tickled his chin again. "Henry, I believe. Mrs. Henry. She was bedridden, and they couldn't move her in time when the Yankees showed up. I heard one of her feet was near blown off by a thrown shell. She didn't make it through the day, so I'm told."

Kirkland was stunned, as the thought had never occurred to him that someone might be imprisoned inside as the house was torn apart, piece by piece. Near the ruins, his attention was drawn to a small garden, around which was a hedge of althea. He had imagined this hedge and garden was an enduring labor of love for Mrs. Henry, with its palate of shimmering white and crimson blooms.

White and crimson.

"Excuse me, Sir, but it's time to get this man in the ground."

Kirkland nodded but was unable to speak. He had seen and heard enough, and turned with a thumping head, to walk back to camp.

Before taking three steps, he felt something squishy under his right shoe. Stepping backward, he looked down in horror to see a man's hand, palm up. Three fingers were missing, including the poor soldier's thumb, and whomever the hand belonged to was nowhere near it.

Whether it belonged to friend or foe, Kirkland would never know, and for the moment he didn't care. With his stomach petitioning for flight and the sound of a shovel greeting earth behind him, he walked briskly away from the carnage at Henry Hill.

Slumping as he trudged, Kirkland scolded himself for being squeamish and weak-willed. But below the surface, his anger was directed at allowing himself to be fooled into believing that war was glorious. It had become wholeheartedly apparent that war was brutal, hellish and a disgusting reminder of what humans are capable of when in opposition. Victory was sweet and cherished, but had arrived with a starless night.

More than ever, Kirkland wished to see Susan, to see beauty and light. He wondered what she was doing at that very moment, and was glad that her eyes were shielded from such a place of violent, contagious death.

Her eyes.

He missed those eyes, the sparking blue orbs and regretted being afraid of their spell.

How many glimpses did I shrink away from? My fervent prayer is that this battle will be the last, and I can return to them.

Lost in the medicating thought, the calling of his name broke through the beautiful picture, and for a split second Kirkland was annoyed to be called away from the opiate.

But then he saw Joe and Alex walking toward him and a smile cracked open the doom on his face. Joe was twirling a white parasol above his head.

"You make a fine lady," said Kirkland, shaking his head. "You trade in your rifle for a trinket?"

"Thank you, but I don't believe I'll be needin' my weapon today. My guess is the Yankees are still running, possibly diving into the Atlantic by now. We just walked half way to Centreville and found this in the hills. There were picnic baskets, even a pair of lady slippers."

"Strange."

"Yes. Apparently citizens, ladies, even Congressmen I hear, showed up in buggies yesterday to watch us rebels get a whippin'. They must have got caught up in the honorable retreat."

"Well, I assume they got their money's worth," said Alex.

"Indeed," said Joe. "I imagine the Yankees did as well, poor fools."

Kirkland nodded.

"Ah, yesterday, we couldn't find each other in a barn," Kirkland exclaimed. "Yet here we are."

"We're here when it matters least," Joe jested.

"I've just been roaming the battlefield. Terrible sight."

"Yes," said Alex, soberly. "Cicero once said, 'For among arms, the law falls mute.' I see his truth now."

"Cicero?" asked Kirkland.

"Roman philosopher, politician, and lawyer, among other things. We studied his writings extensively when I was but a college freshman."

"Enough with the sullen faces already," Joe beamed. "We gained a major victory and the Yanks are running back to Washington with their tails 'tween their legs. Cheer up, gentlemen. We'll probably be home in a month."

"I hope you're right," said Kirkland, his spirits rising, thinking of reunion. "I suppose you've anointed yourself a great hero of yesterday's battle."

"Of course I fought like the legends of old. You wouldn't expect anything less from me, now, would you?"

"Well, now that you mention it…"

"All right, all right, I will not boast." He giggled and then became serious. "But that Virginian you found in the woods had quite a story to tell about your exploits. He said you were quite fearless, possessed by the spirit of battle, even."

Studying his friend for confirmation, Joe tilted his head and waited. Laying eyes on the ground as if embarrassed, Kirkland said nothing.

"Lift your chin, boy," Joe thundered. "You did fine in your first battle. Better than most, Killer Kirkland."

With a mighty whack, Joe slapped his friend between the shoulder blades.

Flashing a look of severe revulsion, Kirkland growled: "Never call me that again."

Stepping backward, Joe held up his arms, in line with his scrunched up and puzzled face. But Kirkland turned away.

94

"I suppose I shouldn't ask him about the trophies he's carryin'," Joe whispered to Alex, who shook his head with admonishment.

For several tense, uncomfortable moments, no one spoke. Finally, Joe sliced through the invisible barrier, to the relief of all present.

"I meant no offense, old buddy. Come on, let's skedaddle. The air is getting ripe here."

★　　★　　★

JULY 23

2 AM

At first, the crawling sensation numbered only one.

He felt it under his arm, creeping for the pit. Holding still, with a mind magnified on the faint tickle, Kirkland waited. He had to be sure the invader was real, and not a rogue hair shifting in the humidity. Sitting up in the darkness, he came to a clear diagnosis: the vermin was true. Peeling off his undershirt, he blurred a hand from bicep to rib, sweeping his skin in the hopes of catapulting the insect into a place of no return.

Again, he waited, silent with blood pressure rising.

The armpit room was devoid of activity once again but the rest of the hotel suddenly awoke, with various floors opening a window of alarm.

Kirkland shuffled to his knees, panicking. His whole torso seemed alive and under attack. Although he knew what they were, the recognition was a failed comfort. The assailants had been making the rounds of unclean camps, hiding in the folds of clothing by day while howling for blood in the shadows of night.

While barely visible to the naked eye, the nighttime itch was a dead giveaway. Kirkland was not ready to be victimized and he jumped up from his disturbed sleep.

Not wanting to wake up his companions, however, he stifled his baptismal screams and maneuvered about on eggshells while fleeing the tent.

Now free of his snoring companions, Kirkland smacked his body with his hands in a frantic attempt to rid himself of his newfound sleeping partners—body lice.

Clawing at his chest and underarms, he leaped and thrust up his knees, running in place and twisting in repulsion.

When finally convinced that the pummeling body blows had killed his attackers, he dropped both hands to his knees, breathless.

Returning to his place of slumber, he laid back down and twitched his muscles, checking for the slightest movement and rolled from one side to the next until merciful sleep prevailed.

The next morning, after a night of little rest, Kirkland put forefinger and thumb to his eyes. A fog both in his head and on the landscape made focusing difficult. Slowly, the dimensions came together, and when they did, the realization and memory of the previous night returned. Sitting up again, Kirkland put both hands on his chest and ran counter circles, wondering if the vermin were still present for morning rolls.

Detecting no movement, he relaxed, but his mind was far from cleansed.

★   ★   ★

7:30 PM

Joe was galloping into one of his lengthy tales spun with a half-thespian, half-jester rhythm. A riveted audience of eight wide eyes followed his every movement and drank from every word.

Crossing his arms, with a knowing grin on his face, Kirkland waited, soaking up the anecdotes he had heard a thousand times. He had gone through a whole day of drill, begging for the hours to elapse so he could speak with his friend. Yet the more he wished, the slower the time passed. And now he would have to wait some more, until Joe finished his narrative. However, unlike drill, this he could easily stomach, despite its repetition.

"Kirkland," Joe interjected, acknowledging his buddy's presence, "you were there. Is this not a true, most unusual ordeal?"

Without waiting for a response, Joe continued.

"So you see, we were visiting my cousins in Lancaster and decided to detour on the way home to the battle site at Hanging Rock, where, as you probably know, Andrew Jackson, as a teenage patriot scout, was captured by the Redcoats. The moon was full, and we could easily see our way to the sacred ground. We tied our horses to a tree, and as we approached, a mist began to form as if emanating from the very rock itself. Within this rapidly forming cloud, not ten feet from where we were standing, a figure started to appear."

With a faraway look in his eyes, the teller slowly raised a hand, pausing for effect.

"He was wearing a blue coat with red facings, the uniform of the Continentals. In his hands was an old musket at the ready and he was staring off down the hill. Of course we were shocked at what we were seeing, and I'm not afraid to say I was trembling in my boots. The soldier became more solid with each passing second, until he looked as life-breathing as you or I."

As if aiding Joe's story, the sun broke from the heavy cloud cover, but Kirkland's attention was drawn downward again. Releasing his folded arms, his right hand settled between his nipples, detecting movement at the corners of his torso. In sly gestures, with thumb and forefinger, he attempted to annihilate the vampires feeding under his shirt. Crushing together his digits until they turned purple, he worked his way to every real or imagined disturbance, all the while keeping his eyes focused on Joe and his exaggerations.

Kirkland remembered the actual event a little differently. Although there *was* a mist around the legendary floating boulder that night, he saw no full body apparition. However, under a gluttonous moon, the swirling fog was definitely creepy enough to summon the willies.

To Kirkland's relief, Joe's tale reached its fevered conclusion.

"Slowly, the soldier's head turned and he looked right at us. Raising a bony finger, he pointed down the hill as if he was telling us to get ready for the British to attack. Then just has quickly as he arrived, his form dissolved back into the mist, which was then swallowed by the rock. We had seen enough! I practically leaped onto my horse with a single bound to get the hell outta there. When we returned to my cousin's house a month later, I told him about our experience. To my surprise he didn't laugh and accuse us of partaking in too much whiskey. In fact, he said the phantom soldier appears frequently on the anniversary of the battle, which unbeknownst to us, was the very night we happened to visit the Hanging Rock."

"No!" said a bewildered spectator.

"It's true!" said Joe. "Ask any oldtimer around them parts. They'll tell you straight. Well, gentlemen, I bid thee goodnight," said Joe, bowing, walking straight for Kirkland.

"More, more!" called several in the audience.

"I need to save a few yarns for another occasion," said Joe, waiving off an encore, to the groans of his devotees.

Ignoring their pleas, Joe stabbed at Kirkland without mercy.

"I see you have finally allowed the graybacks quarters."

Kirkland's eyes fell to the ground and he shifted his feet.

How?

Joe smiled, enjoying the uncomfortable reaction.

"It's no cause for alarm. They are more numerous than the Yankees, and with a more considerable bite."

Almost incredulous, Kirkland raised his head.

"I'm surprised it took this long," said Joe. "Are the Camden elite a tad more impervious? We've been infested for some time now."

Taking a deep breath, Kirkland shook his melon and relaxed, finally able to smile.

"I was afraid I was alone in the filth."

"No," Joe giggled. "Not in the slightest. I don't care how many times you swim the Run or pick through your clothes, the little devils are here to stay. I've boiled my clothes several times, but I'm afraid it's only a temporary solution."

"I thought the mosquitoes and black flies were enough to annoy a man."

"They ain't paradise, either. But at least a swat brings their end."

Kirkland nodded.

"I was determined to play ignorance to your plight," said Joe, needing to get one gentle jab in, "but you looked ready to burst."

Kirkland gritted his teeth in a mock smile.

"I just may have. But now that I know that you have been more fouled than me for some time, I feel all warm inside."

"Ha! You elitist sow. Jealousy is a nasty curse."

"My fingernails are black with envy. Care to relieve them of Virginia dirt?"

"Not likely. Embrace the filth, my friend. You'll be better off."

★   ★   ★

SEPTEMBER 18, 1861
TWO MILES SOUTH OF FALLS CHURCH, VA
3 PM

"They just might finish that behemoth by the twentieth century," said Alex.

"What?"

Alex pointed beyond the Potomac River, just below the horizon.

"That's the Capitol building. They've been working on that structure for almost seventy years, ever since George Washington himself laid the cornerstone."

Although miles away, Kirkland was able to clearly note the skeleton of planks rising from the center of the unfinished dome.

"We're so close."

"Don't let that deceive you. The Yankees are well entrenched before us."

Alex was right, as usual. Shortly after the battle of Manassas, the enemy had begun fortifying the ground in front of Washington and the Yankee picket line was only 300 yards due east. For weeks, the Carolinians had taken turns at the front to maintain a constant watch, waiting for a vengeful strike. However, neither side budged nor even flinched. Stuck in a daily rut of staring each other down over fields of no-man's-land, troops on both sides appeared to be getting antsy. With each day of inaction, they grew bolder, daring the marksmen to pull the trigger. Although there were a few close calls, no one had been seriously wounded in these taunting challenges.

Kirkland busied himself more with swatting at the mosquitoes than presenting his head as a target. These tiny bloodsuckers were much more irritating and vile, and closer. After many failed attempts to eradicate them, he grudgingly accepted that the graybacks were here to stay. But he wasn't about to share his crimson with the mosquitoes too. Feeling another pinch, Kirkland slapped at his forefinger, splattering blood across his knuckle.

"Shouldn't have gotten greedy," said Kirkland out loud, which brought quizzical looks from his neighbors. In show-and-tell, he raised the back of his hand.

"Greed *and* gluttony," Alex agreed. "Let's hope his brothers fall short of adopting wrath."

Kirkland giggled.

"Ah, hell," said Joe, "this is getting awful tiresome."

"The killing of innocent mosquitoes?" mocked Alex.

"Nooooo, you damned fool. This sittin' 'round doin' nothin'. How about sloth? We're here, the Yankees are there. What is the complication? This war ain't gonna end with a blinking contest."

"What do you propose we do?" said Alex. "Maybe the three of us can just casually stroll into Washington and ask Lincoln for his unconditional surrender."

"Now you're talkin'. You ain't as dumb as you look."

Alex turned to Kirkland.

"We purposely seek out his company?"

"I'm afraid so."

Joe took the jab and pounced.

"I'm telling ya'll. Give me some chicken guts on these sleeves and we'll be marching down the streets of Washington by tomorrow evening."

He winked and smiled in a fashion for which Kirkland and Alex had no defense. Before Joe's brow creased, his friends had surrendered to laughter.

Next to them, however, Jesse Locke had a different kind of entertainment in mind. Raised along Granny's Quarter Creek not far from the Kirkland plantation, Richard knew the family well. Though they were not as prosperous as the Kirklands, the Lockes were known to be hardworking folk, but unwise in business dealings. Yet they were resourceful and didn't want for much, and when they threw a party, people flocked from miles around. For not only was their whiskey a notch above and in plentiful stock, the Lockes didn't mind sharing.

"I'm gonna get a closer look," said Jesse, with a waggish, confident smile indicative of his eighteen years.

"That's not a wise idea, Jesse," said Alex. "They have sharpshooters."

"Let's see how good they are, then."

Before they could object, the man took off in a sprint toward the Yankee lines, followed by another diseased by boredom. As they watched, the men crossed a grassy field of fifty yards, bullets rummaging the dirt around them, and safely reached a dilapidated barn. Slamming their backs against the barn's front doors, they caught their breaths. Raising his gun in the air, Locke threw a victorious whoop toward his spectators, who were equally divided between the gleeful and the horrified. Peeking around the corner at his foe, Locke's fever was unsatisfied, and he left his refuge in search of a warmer climate.

Four steps in, Locke suddenly lingered in midstride, as if frozen by a blast of icicle wind. With one foot in the air, he teetered for a moment before shuddering backward in a slow-motion heap. Once Locke hit the turf, his slouch hat spun on its edge, curling towards its master before collapsing at his outstretched hand. Locke himself wasn't moving. Only the hairs on his head stirred, rolling with the wind like a field of wheat as if the earth had already claimed him.

Recovering from the initial shock, Locke's trailer dove to his side and proceeded to drag the corpse behind the barn. For whatever reason, whether they admired the man's bravery or if they were stupefied by the direct hit, the enemy held their fire for the duration of the soldier's recovery.

Slumping within the breastworks, Kirkland removed his headgear and turned his back on the scene. Along the picket line, a grim silence howled. If they grieved, they did so in silence.

The hideous wail from the man cradling his friend's body spoke for them all.

Chapter 5

Cradling firewood up to his chin, Kirkland set off for camp, with the pleasant burn already in his nostrils. He had always enjoyed the smell of a good campfire, and despite its repetition, daily use had failed to dull the cathartic essence. With quality wood harder to come by, as the area close to the camps near Bull Run had been picked clean, he had wandered more than a mile to the fields of the epic battle.

As he walked over his own baptismal grounds, Kirkland relived a few trivial yet branding memories: bursting, widening eyes stinging with sweat, the pain in his hands as he choked the polish from his rifle, the rabbit who sprinted in a frantic circle between the enemy lines, desperately looking for a hole to crawl into. That last vision came days after the battle. When it actually happened, he'd hardly noticed the frightened creature, if he had even saw it at all.

Out of all the rolling boulders witnessed that day, it was these pebbles that tumbled through Kirkland's head as he retraced his virginal steps. And he was grateful for them, as many a time during the last few months he had awoken in the moonlight, with a heaviness pressing down on his chest.

Now even further from the enemy since they had arrived back at familiar territory along the banks of Bull Run a week previous, there was plenty of time for wayward thoughts. As summer came and went, both sides continued to balk at assuming the aggressor and appeared to be leery of igniting another major battle. Other than a sharp skirmish on September twenty-fifth with minimal casualties, the waiting game dragged on.

The day before, Kirkland received a letter from Susan, along with eight pairs of knitted socks. Though impressed by the quality, he only kept two and shared the rest with soldier friends who were footwear challenged. The letter itself was barren of major news from home, but he cared not. Susan was still writing him and he took pride in her reporting that none of the womenfolk were marrying any man who refused to enlist for the Southern cause.

Kirkland longed for her. The pain was made worse by a rumor that the Federals were planning to land on the coast of South Carolina. Through a second, much more pleasant grapevine, the soldiers heard that they would be sent home to defend against the invasion of their state. Yet this gossip turned out to be another falsehood. They weren't going anywhere.

As Kirkland left the shelter of the pines, he noticed a man in the distance on his knees, bent over and digging with a shovel. With his back to the observer, the man rose and turned, brushing the dirt off an object, which he soon held up in admiration as if it were buried treasure. Kirkland closed in but kept his distance, curious. When within twenty yards, he felt a twinge of pained recognition.

Ratcliff.

The twinge eloped to abhorrence when Kirkland realized the idol of Ratcliff's worship: a human skull.

Sensing an intruder, Ratcliff wheeled, but kept the morbid prize aloft.

"Ah, Kirkland," said Ratcliff, in a mocking tone, ignoring the wooden bounty Kirkland carried. "Bloodthirsty on this afternoon, are you?"

He slowly licked the skull's forehead and curled his tongue, with eyes closed as if relishing sweet potato pie. When his eyes snapped open in a fiendish stare, he took on the appearance of a vertical corpse, waiting. As Kirkland stood dumbfounded, Ratcliff tossed his head back and laughed gruffly.

104

"There ain't much Yankee meat left, but if you's hungry, I reckon you'll find a few scraps on the bastards buried deeper."

He laughed again, as Hux materialized in his shadow, clawing the air with a skeleton hand.

"Come on, Wes, we found *our* mantelpiece. Happy hunting, Kirkland."

Tossing the head back and forth between his hands, Ratcliff started to walk away but stopped abruptly.

"Oh, and one more thing. If you find a real fresh one, be a gentleman and cut me a sirloin. I'll pay top dollar."

Licking his lips, Ratcliff smiled coldly. As he ambled by, he sampled Kirkland's ruffled mane for several moments before turning away. Hux was in tow, pointing a bony finger at the outraged bystander as he passed. Kirkland opened his mouth in rebuke, but thought better of it.

And old dog is an old dog.

Desecrating a grave, whether friend or foe, was inconceivable to him, a place where only the most wicked of barbarians would tread. Hopping mad, but feeling the weight of the firewood, he continued on, looking down at the disturbed grave. Like a soiled butterfly, a rib cage was all that lay exposed. As Kirkland pulled himself away, he admonished himself for examining too close.

And then he walked briskly back to camp, attempting to reclaim the campfire in his nostrils.

★   ★   ★

DECEMBER 25, 1861

"Welcome, Mr. Kirkland. May I take your coat?"

"Thank you, Mr. Duncan," said Kirkland, amused. For Northern Virginia in December, it was rather balmy but far from tropical.

"We have quite the Christmas dinner awaiting. Please sit."

Joe motioned his friend to a log chair, grooved and cut for the special occasion.

"Do not lean too far to either side, as yours truly is not the most able chairmaker. Not like your brother, Dan. It is slightly uneven, I'm afraid."

Kirkland put his hands on the folksy chair and pretended to analyze every feature.

"I'd expect nothing more."

Joe smiled, ready to ambush.

"If our humble abode does not suit your aristocratic tastes, I hear they're eating squirrels down by the river."

"If I have offended your gentleman spirit, I apologize." He paused for effect. "Though squirrels do sound delicious."

Leaping at his friend, Joe grasped him by both arms, before smothering him with a bear hug and giggle.

"I'm glad you left that inferior company to join the Flat Rock Guards on this day of celebration."

"Hey, we were there at Fort Sumter. Where were you?"

"I believe I was wooing one of the South's finest on that particular day."

"Now *that* I believe."

Alex sauntered over with outstretched hand.

"Good evening, Richard," said Alex, with true gentlemanly flair, as if trying to upstage Joe's attempt.

Taking Alex's hand only briefly, Kirkland threw it to the side and wrapped arms around his buddy. He then greeted the others, one by one, who were sitting at the crude holiday table made of boards between barrels. Uncharacteristically, they were not playing cards.

"Red, Jim, Taylor, Merry Christmas."

"Merry Christmas to you," said Taylor, rising to check the food cooking in a small cast iron pot suspended over the fire on a tripod.

A clerk in pre-war life, his attention to detail had suited him well as a cook, and his talents with food had far surpassed the others. As a result, he had been nominated for cooking an appropriate meal with the limited ingredients on hand.

"Wait. Before you sit down, I've got something for the occasion," said Alex, in a rare outburst of excitement.

Disappearing into the mess' tent for a few moments, he produced a small piece of tupelo with three crude holes notched in its face. With care usually given to an heirloom centerpiece, he placed it on the table. And then with his right hand, which had been concealed behind his back, he held up three long, green candles. Anchoring them into place, Alex folded his arms and beamed.

It did not have the desired effect.

Red and Jim McDowell, the quiet brothers who had already seemed to be devoid of Christmas cheer, stared at the fire with blank expressions. Kirkland removed his hat and dropped his eyes to the trampled turf. Fidgety and uncomfortable, Joe shuffled his feet. With his back to the fire, Taylor peeked over his shoulder, realizing the sudden quiet. His eyes met the table's fresh decoration and plunged downward.

For a moment, time wavered and rippled. The giddy faces in mouth-watering anticipation appeared to Kirkland in an all-too-real vision. There was father, at his customary position at the table's head, stoic yet content, watching over his family with silent pride. His brothers and sisters were all there, buoyant and glowing with holiday spirit as the farm's most prized animals were toted in for the rare indulgent feast.

The years were interwoven and fleeting, until Kirkland settled upon one of his oldest memories. There he was, kicking Sam's shins and tickling his ribs underneath what had been their mother's favorite tablecloth. Sam, tiny and demonstrative, was blubbering wildly after learning from a cruel brother that his favorite pet chicken had been dispatched for the lavish meal.

The scene adjourned for a sing-along astride a roaring, waltzing fire. They read from the Bible about the Magi and a Bethlehem birth. And to cap the utopian evening, there were stories of Christmas past about Mother and her guiding hands, always ensuring each child went to bed with stomachs full and hearts of lasting warmth. She was their most welcome present, unwrapped and grasped by the tiny curling hands. As she tucked them into bed, squirming at night's end, a kiss to the forehead was their lullaby, rendering limbs paralyzed with contentment.

Awakening as if from a dream, Kirkland realized Alex was staring at him, wise to his sudden travels. Looking at the other faces, he knew they were similarly distant and had yet to return.

Joe, however, was the next to recover from nostalgic ghosts, and he did not wait for the others to rouse.

"Alex, I believe you've been holding out on us. What else do have in that bag of yours?"

"Well, even *I* did not foresee that we would be away from home this late in the year. But I knew the possibility was there. Unfortunately, this simple offering is all I can bestow for this occasion."

Joe reached into his pocket and pulled out a tin match safe. Striking a Lucifer, he lit the candles one by one, hoping the wind would remain kind and dormant. At least for the moment, it cooperated.

"In our predicament, I'd say this is mighty fine."

He giggled, returning to form.

"Well, Mr. Kirkland, I doubt your mess has furnishings of such luxury. We have another surprise in store for you. Taylor, how is that fine pot of meat coming along?"

The fresh odor was suddenly profound.

"I believe our humble feast is ready," Taylor announced.

"Well, then allow me to set the table," said Joe, placing tin plates and forks in front of each voracious man as Taylor approached with a bowl of steaming stew.

Placing the morsels on each plate, Taylor shook his head.

"We placed quite a few traps on the outskirts of camp, but only got two scrawny ones."

Kirkland looked at Joe for explanation.

"Rabbit, but we were able to purchase a fine turkey as well," said Joe, smiling.

"And potatoes!" said Taylor, with mock zeal.

In addition, they supplemented their meager table with items sent from home: jars of pickles, apple butter, buckwheat bread and chestnuts.

"A feast for kings," said Kirkland, without contempt. "It smells delightful."

As the fowl and cottontail chunks and potato bites slid onto their plates, he took the high road, grateful that he was spending Christmas with the next best thing to family or a certain love interest. As Joe and Taylor took their seats, he stood up.

"Allow me to give the blessing."

"Please do," said Alex.

Clearing his throat, Kirkland purged his mind of all negativity even though one foot was planted far away at home.

"Dear heavenly father, we thank thee for this meal and fellowship of friends. Please bless it to our body's use and let us remember that even through these difficult times of war, we must always remain cloaked in your image and conduct ourselves with humble honor. Jesus, we remember you on your glorious birthday, and the sacrifice you made for mankind. May we strive to follow your example, and ask that you help us to ignore the trappings of evil. Please watch over our loved ones at home in our absence. In your blessed name, Amen."

"Amen," each man repeated, and the forks were unleashed, digging in.

For several minutes no one spoke, as all mouths were occupied by chewing and reloading.

Between forkfuls, Alex finally articulated a note above the grunt or the slurp.

"My compliments to the chef," he forwarded.

"Indeed," said Kirkland. "This is the best meal I've had since I began playing soldier."

"Thank you," said Taylor, "throwing together a stew is not exactly a culinary feat."

"Maybe not," said Joe, "but I've ruined much easier fare."

"He ain't lying," said Alex. "Black and crispy is an understatement. Which is why we always pass him over when it's his turn to fill our rumbling stomachs."

"Hey," said Joe, elbowing Alex in the shoulder. "I can peel a potato, and some might say even drop it into the pot when I'm done."

Chomping his food with exaggerated smacks, Joe giggled.

"Forgive me," said Alex, shaking his head. "I was under the impression that you were completely useless."

"Ooh. Professor, if your academics fail you, I'll have a job waiting for you in my kitchen."

"Then you will remain eternally waiting. And you will starve."

Joe shoved another large forkful into his mouth, the juices dribbling down his chin.

"Mmm. Not today."

"No, my friend," said Kirkland, smiling as he rose, "not on this night. I will return with more for your belly."

Walking over to the fire, Kirkland scooped up another bowlful for the table. As he did, he looked down the lane at other messes in similar holiday cheer. While the scenes warmed him, he couldn't help but notice that the numbers had fallen off substantially from what they were even a month ago.

Diseases like typhoid fever and pneumonia were still rampant, and every week a few more unfortunates passed their final breath. In addition, the fight at Manassas had convinced a multitude that joining an artillery or cavalry unit was a safer way to get through the war in one piece. As a result, more than a hundred had already transferred out of the regiment.

Also in December, the Confederate Congress decided it was time to start bribing the soldiers to reenlist for two more years, by offering bounties and furloughs to those who would sign.

The pull was constant in several directions, and Kirkland had attempted to remain neutral, waiting to see how things would shake out. But he had resisted turning his back on the regiment. No, he couldn't do that. While some clung to high hopes of a peaceful resolution with the Union,

Kirkland knew better. Although the two sides continued to be idle, there would be more bloodshed, and plenty of it. He could feel it like a punch to the gut.

"Kirkland, you gonna make it back by the year of our Lord, eighteen hundred and sixty-two?"

Kirkland sighed.

Why can't I be more like Joe?

"Sorry, boys," said Kirkland, passing the second helping around.

"Come down out of that old hat of yours. What's on your mind, private?" said Joe.

"It's nothing."

"Kirkland, look who you're talking to. You can tell me."

Of course, all were staring at Kirkland know, shrinking his confidence.

Tread lightly.

"Joe, have you made up your mind to reenlist?"

"Ah, the most pressing question. I thought that was it. On one hand I don't take kindly to these politicians and generals forcing our hand. And who knows? We could sign on for two more years, get our bounty and furlough, and before we have to come back, the war could end, with a little extra money in our pockets. But would that tarnish the reason why we enlisted in the first place, to defend our state, our kinfolk and, especially, ALL the fine ladies in Dixie?"

Kirkland smiled.

"Well, of course, you wouldn't want to ruin your reputation with the ladies."

"No sir. I, for one, plan on sticking around. I'm not going to sign them papers just yet, though. Nothing's going to happen until spring anyhow. I reckon I can wait. I'm having fun in heaps presently."

"Alex, what do you think?"

"As much as I yearn to continue my studies, I agree with Joe that both armies will remain idle through the winter. The possibility that this could be a lengthy war grows with each day, and if this fact holds true, it will be inconceivable to return to my prior commitments. The South will need every man and my loyalty must stay true to its cause."

Kirkland nodded, gargling his response before allowing its outward passage.

"The last time we were in this predicament, I failed to listen to you. I had my course and I took it, jug-full stubborn as you know. The longer I'm away from Carolina, the weaker I feel in her absence. Yet we can't abandon her now. No. She needs us here."

It was getting dark. Tilting his head back, Kirkland sniffed the stars and gazed into their innumerable glitter. Joe and Alex did the same, and as they were enjoying the night sky, Jim opened his voice in song.

"Oh, come, all ye faithful, joyful and triumphant…"

While not destined for the stage, Jim's voice was both mournful and cathartic, homesick mixed with a determined pride. As he sang, all politics and hovering burdens were at once set aside, luring his tablemates into a cleansing. The wind picked up slightly, enough to blow out the holiday candles, yet no one seemed to mind.

Unable to resist its pull, Kirkland joined in the festive vocals, while keeping his eyes skyward. And then it was Joe, followed by Alex, and the second McDowell brother until all were under the song's spell.

But it didn't stop there.

From campfire to campfire, the song bowled, arousing more voices to lift upward, demanding an audience of the heavens. Before long, the entire regiment was caroling, trancelike but impassioned. The men sang as if the words would reflect off the stars and beam down on their loved ones back home.

"Oh sing, choirs of angels, sing in exultation…"

Chapter 6

A mild winter had been chased away by bone-chilling cold. The brigade, which now consisted of the 2nd, 3rd, 7th, and 8th South Carolina regiments, was finally allowed to begin constructing winter quarters in early January.

This delay, unjustifiable to the men as the enemy had made no aggressive movements, was made worse by having to trudge two miles through the snow, over half-frozen streams and hills, just to arrive at the work site. While Kirkland had been lucky, more than a few on this hazardous journey had made an errant step on the ice, finding themselves waist-deep in frigid water.

Despite the elements, Kirkland and Smith, along with two other messmates they'd become friendly with, had worked quickly to build a crude, but cozy hut, into which they moved on February fourth. The structure had split pine log walls chinked with Virginia mud that was as tough as hickory when dry. Made from a canvas tent and weighted down with straw, the roof was stable, but prone to leaking, and a fieldstone fireplace on the north side brought much needed warmth. The chimney was topped with a cut molasses barrel, lined with mud to prevent it from catching fire.

With brass hinges and an iron gate latch obtained in a gift pack from home, a southside door helped stunt the winter drafts, but when it was closed the lack of windows caused an extreme darkness that even an enthusiastic fire could not fully diminish. While just large enough for Kirkland to stand erect in the middle, the shanty demanded twists and wiggles when fully occupied.

Inside, bunk beds were constructed on each side, which doubled as seats in the cramped space. On the bottom bunk, all one had to do was swing his legs over the side to be seated at the table, which was made from laying two ammunition box covers, nailed together, over two old whiskey kegs salvaged from a local farmer. On this rough surface, the men dined, and slammed down many a losing hand in the ambition to break the drab tones of a motionless army, where weapons in hibernation slept on the walls.

Besides Kirkland and his spectacled friend, two others shared duties and long nights in their humble abode. The tall, mountain-reaching one was Banbury Jones, shortened to Bury, as if he were either adamant about taking a shovel to the enemy or in a hurry to dig his own grave. Kirkland wasn't sure which was more legitimate. At Manassas, the six-foot three-inch Jones had to be dragged back into the lines after an assault stalled, all the while cursing at the Yankees. He'd been wounded twice, a flesh wound in each leg, balking at medical attention or even slowing his advance to even the score. After the battle, the officers attempted to promote him, but he refused, preferring the life of a private. Away from the flying bullets, Kirkland had found Bury to be a gentle giant, unassuming and polite. As such, he had no trouble making friends after returning from a three-month hospital stay, and was much respected within the ranks.

Twelve inches shorter, but just as fierce as Bury, was George Washington Fain. At Manassas he had risked his life to wrestle the relative stranger, Bury, back from certain death in an almost comical scene that the

114

men who witnessed it enjoyed retelling. Fain had curled his entire body around one leg of the rabid giant, pulling with all his might. He at least had stopped the enraged Bury in his tracks, allowing for others to help drag the wounded man, kicking and screaming, to safety.

Later, after the intoxication of battle had escaped from his pores, Bury had come to respect the diminutive fireball. They became instant friends, though complete opposites in campfire disposition. Fain was by any measure a loudmouth, always trying to prove his height was no disadvantage. The slightest affront would set him off, and he was often restrained by his friends to prevent a visit to the guardhouse or worse. This was done almost exclusively to those he wasn't properly acquainted with, as a way, Kirkland suspected, of judging character. In these cases, no semblance of a provocation was needed, as Fain would conjure one.

Once properly challenged, if they met Fain's unintelligible criteria, they were safe from future calls to fisticuffs, if not from his pranks. Like many, Kirkland had received Fain's unnerving initiation. While strolling through the camp in Richmond, not watching where he was going, Kirkland bumped into Fain.

★   ★   ★

"Excuse me," Kirkland said, continuing on.

"You can take your excuses and shove 'em where the sun don't shine."

Kirkland turned in surprise to see the bulldog-like Fain, clenching his fists.

"I apologize," said Kirkland, walking away from the confrontation.

"Your mother not teach you proper manners?"

Kirkland stopped and wheeled.

"Or maybe you don't know who your mother is?"

With lava surging through his brain, Kirkland launched himself at Fain, tackling him to the ground. As they wrestled in the dirt, they were quickly separated by their fellow Carolinians. While knocking the dirt from his trousers and glaring at his opponent, a peculiar thing happened. Fain flashed a sincere smile and bowed, holding out his hand.

"Forgive me," he said, with playful innocence in his eyes. "I like to know who I'm gonna play soldier with, when it matters."

After taking a few seconds to recover, Kirkland skeptically approached the outstretched hand. Peering into Fain's eyes, he scrutinized them for any hint of deception. Seeing none, Kirkland shook his hand.

The judgment complete, Fain nodded approvingly and sauntered away, whistling "Yankee Doodle Dandy."

What a peculiar man.

★   ★   ★

After that introduction, Kirkland found Fain no less outlandish, but once his trust was gained, he was a loyal and generous friend.

And he was, after all, daily entertainment for those not subject to his wrath or odd humor. For when Fain ran out of soldiers to challenge, his pranks became the irritation of the day. His most notorious juvenile caper caused a near panic.

No doubt with his usual intimidation, Fain had convinced a drummer boy to loan him his percussion. With this instrument, in the middle of the night, Fain stood in front of his hut and sounded the long roll. Kirkland, Bury and Smith had rushed out into the snow, half naked and bewildered, to encounter their friend in stitches. As the entire regiment joined them in the freezing moonlight, Fain's laughter shrunk to a nervous giggle. Needless to say, the officers were not amused, and Fain spent the rest of the night freezing in the guardhouse without a fire.

Except for the coldest of nights, winter camp had been very comfortable, with poker and pranks keeping Kirkland and his messmates entertained. Drill had been suspended for the winter, and only a dreaded stay, freezing at the picket post remained for military duty.

Thankfully, the days away from the warm huts were infrequent, and Kirkland had plenty of daylight available for long-winded letters to Susan and ramblings of a somewhat shorter variety to his family. Thoughts of home and its sacred faces often drifted through his mind, settling in for long periods of affliction.

116

Kirkland tried to dwell within positive reveries, and keep the portly, burdensome stones from filling his shoes. But days upon days of inactivity left too many opportunities for walking down the hillside of clinging memories. Some days of course, were worse than others, when the longing for Flat Rock approached intestinal sickness.

When these pains attacked twofold, in his gut and his mind, he kept to himself and wandered a mile away or more to gather firewood. He would remain there for hours at a time, chopping much more than he could carry, giving the extra fuel to other soldiers who had journeyed to the closest patch of woods near the camp. Many a soldier went back to his cabin carrying a full load of firewood without ever having to raise an axe above his shoulders.

As a result, Kirkland's supposed generosity had won him widespread gratitude. He was glad to have helped out, even if the root of the perceived altruism was more about busying a troubled mind for a few hours.

Most of the winter, though, he kept an even keel, waiting for spring to melt the boredom away.

★　　★　　★

On one particular night, winter seemed to wrap a blanket of ice around their dwelling, inhaling all warmth that even a large fire couldn't replace.

Having maneuvered from his seat several times to hover in front of the flames in an attempt to sustain feeling in his extremities, Kirkland finally gave up and decided to wander over to the huts of Company G. Leaving Smith and his messmates trying to stop shivering enough to keep a poker game alive, he resigned himself to the stranglehold of the Virginia winter outside.

As expected, the village dubbed Camp Greenville, in honor of the South Carolina city, was deserted. Taking a quick look around, Kirkland chuckled nervously as the frigid wind slapped him in the face and burned his nostrils.

I must be out of my mind.

Smothering his face in a blanket with only his eyes uncovered, he walked briskly to the western side of camp and into the unforgiving wind. After what seemed like an eternity of porcupine breaths, he came to a familiar residence. Above the door was a charcoal inscription with the words "Plato's Cave."

Kirkland and his messmates could never agree on a proper name for their domicile, nor did they care much for a moniker, so they left their hut nameless. He was amused, however, at the creativity of others with names like "King Haigler's Inn," "Carolina Resort," or "Yankee Killers."

A knock at the crude wooden door was quickly answered by Joe's worried eyes.

"Kirkland! What on Earth are you doing out in the cold? Get in here."

Closing the door behind him, Kirkland noticed a similar atmosphere to the one he had just departed.

The McDowell brothers and Taylor were huddled close to the fireplace, throwing down cards on a box marked "hardtack," the table on "loan" from the enemy.

Alex was also in front of the fire but with a book in hand, ignoring the others.

"Alex, put that waste of paper down," said Joe. "We have a caller."

The poker players nodded at Kirkland, which was returned. Alex finished the paragraph he was reading and put the book down.

"Hello, woodchopper extraordinaire," Alex uttered, in his usual sophistication.

At the comment, Kirkland blushed. Apparently his deeds had become more well-known than he had imagined or intended.

"You're making quite a name for yourself."

"Naw, I was just bored," said Kirkland sheepishly.

"Well, what brings you to 'Plato's Cave' on such a dreary night?"

Joe rolled his eyes. "I had nothing to do with that name, I assure you."

"What does it mean?" said Kirkland, knowing that with Alex, it must have a deep significance.

118

All he had was time and a lengthy discourse by "the professor" was just what he needed.

"Here we go," said Joe, rejoining the card game. "Let me know when you want to discuss something interesting."

"Like your favorite color of lady's undergarment?" Alex shot back.

"Not a bad idea. That's the best topic of conversation you've come up with in a week." He smiled, sat down and said, "Deal me in."

Kirkland hunkered down next to the fire across from Alex. Although indeed curious, he was craving anything to keep his mind from diverting to Susan and away from the tired, trivial subjects of debate that he'd heard a thousand times this winter.

Clasping his hands together, Alex stared at the ground for a moment, thinking of where to begin and how to explain it in a way his friend could understand. Although he did not doubt Kirkland's intelligence and had spoken of Plato with him before, it was never in this kind of depth.

"Yes, the Allegory of the Cave. Okay," Alex began, animating his hands. "Plato, as you know, was an ancient Greek philosopher and one of the most brilliant men to have ever lived, in my humble opinion."

"Yes, I've heard you quote him before. He was a student of Socrates, right?"

"Very good. Yes, he wrote a series of dialogues that cover many topics including the nature of knowledge and the nature of the soul. He was also a soldier noted for his bravery. But that's not important in this discussion."

Clearing his throat, Alex accelerated into the parable.

"Imagine a group of people who for their entire lives have remained imprisoned in a cave and tightly chained facing an ordinary rock wall. Behind these prisoners, at the opposite end of the cave room, is a raging fire. In front of this fire is a passageway where other people travel to and fro, carrying various goods and making assorted noises as they move. You with me so far?"

"Seems simple enough."

"Good. As these people and objects pass in front of the fire, all the prisoners see are wild, distorted shadows on the walls. These shadows,

119

with their accompanying sounds, are all they perceive of the outside world. They attach names to these images and believe these dark projections represent truth, as this is all they know. For these prisoners, their reality is one of ignorance. It's the old adage, 'seeing is believing,' so to speak. But what they perceive are only fragments of truth."

Kirkland nodded, but was a little unsure of where this ancient philosophy fit into the present situation.

Alex continued: "I believe humanity is the prisoners, still shackled in that cave, unaware of the truths and light that remain a short distance away, yet completely beyond its grasp. How else can you explain war, not to mention war between brothers? It's a plague on both our houses. We will forever remain in ignorance until we break these chains and escape the shadows. Occasionally someone catches a glimpse, with toes inching past the threshold. But they eventually retreat to the safe haven of their known experience. It will take immense courage for all of us to venture into the light, but I don't believe we're ready. No, war and suffering are here to stay. We are many miles from the cave's mouth. We are taught from birth what to believe, who our enemies are, how to act. But is this truth? That is a question we all must ask ourselves."

Kirkland let the philosophical notions swirl around in his head, beginning to understand its inherent wisdom.

"If that is what you believe, then why did you choose to go to war?"

In extended silence, Alex shook his head as if more than a little exasperated trying to come up with a meritorious answer. In the end, he just threw up his hands.

"If you swim against the current too long, you'll either drown or find yourself alone. At least in the cave, I have my pals."

"You would stay in this cave for Joe?" Kirkland quipped.

"You're an astute observer, Kirkland. What was I thinking?"

"Well at least in this cave I've got a pair of kings," said Joe, gleefully throwing down a winning hand as his poker mates groaned in disgust.

"Too bad we haven't gotten our fighting wages. I woulda cleaned you guys out."

"See what I mean, Kirkland? Dark, dark cave."

"If that Abigail Lynum is a mere shadow, then ignorance is bliss. She was the most beautiful girl I ever saw, from up in Lancaster…"

Kirkland allowed Joe to regale his gambling pals with one of his belle sightings, wanting more answers from Alex.

"How does a man escape from this false cavern?"

"You must not allow the darkness to swallow the light within. You must embrace the slivers of intrinsic truth, no matter the sacrifice, amidst the most extreme opposition. Only then will you be truly free."

★   ★   ★

MARCH 1, 1862

"Kirkland, snap out it," said Fain, with his usual amplified abruptness. "I asked you a question."

Kirkland looked up at his accuser, having slipped away from the conversation in an unintended flutter. Susan's face evaporated.

"Forgive me. What do you wish to know?"

"We've spilled the beans on our respective affairs concerning the fairer creatures. We all know the object of your desires. It's your turn to ante up."

As Kirkland hesitated, Smith attempted to lessen the demand.

"Forgive my uh, uh, vulgar friend here," said Smith, stumbling over his words. "What we are looking for is a good story, don't we agree, Bury, Fain?"

"Vulgar?" Fain's complexion was turning blood red.

"Hold your dirty drawers," said Bury, interjecting peace. "The notion my friends are offering, some with more subtlety than others, is that we have all shared something of personal note. We are not asking for chivalry to die with your words, but the winter is long and we are running out of fresh narratives."

This was no revelation to Kirkland, who was cognizant of the fact that he had been less than forthright with personal anecdotes around the winter fire. Though he had warmed to his messmates, even the most mundane experiences with Susan had been kept in his breast pocket and unshared. The trio had been badgering Kirkland since the day before when he had received a package and letter from Susan. It contained a homespun cotton shirt and a handkerchief, along with pound cakes and brandied peaches. He had passed out the well-traveled victuals generously before taking the letter and disappearing in a quest for solitude's lair. Although he immensely enjoyed receiving a letter from his dearest, her sudden presence could bring on a lasting melancholy. At its worst, this shroud could envelope Kirkland for days, during which he spoke little and kept to himself, creating a distance between him and his messmates.

"Uhh.." Kirkland weighed the decision in his mind, before casting out the fear of being teased.

"All right then, you need not press me further," said Kirkland, with a twinkle in his eye that made his messmates immediately intrigued.

"It was very early on a Saturday morning, a drowsy sun resting among the trees, yawning before the rise…"

A half mile from the Godfrey property, Kirkland's nerves were falling behind his horse. He pulled on the reins to allow for them to catch up.

Excitement had turned to fear, coupled with a healthy dose of doubt.

What are you going to say to her? You've got nothing to say.

Kirkland remained motionless in the saddle for several minutes, his amiable horse not arguing, dropping his head to munch on the trailgrass.

She's much too handsome and sophisticated for me.

Growing up motherless, he'd often wondered if it had left him a little rough around the edges. After all, his father had often shown contempt for the overly refined.

"What do I have to offer this fair maiden? Have I completely lost all sense? Why am I talking to a horse?"

Dismounting, Kirkland patted Brimstone on the shoulder.

"No offense, old boy."

Pacing back and forth, he attempted to rehearse a greeting. But the more he strained for honed perfection, the more insecure he became. This was, after all, an important occasion. He would be calling on Susan at her home for the first time. Although they had met at social gatherings where she seemed to display an interest, their shared words were polite and trivial at best. He had played the role of gentleman with difficulty, for he was irrevocably smitten.

And it had taken several, painful exchanges before Kirkland found the nerve to ask Susan if he could court her.

He would never forget her response.

She giggled, arose from her chair and began to walk away. Kirkland was crushed, but as she passed him standing there defeated, she turned her head and provocatively smiled before answering, "I thought you'd never ask."

Complicated. Independent. Free. Dangerous.

Susan was unlike any woman he'd ever met or even heard of. And Kirkland knew he was making inroads to her heart. This didn't prevent him, however, from getting the jitters before each encounter, at least for the first month. And certainly, this first visit to the Godfreys was an occasion high on the butterfly scale.

Kirkland was about to give up on memorizing a poetic impression when his foot landed in a hole, throwing him off balance and pitching him sideways off the trail. He landed on his back in a patch of brush. When the shock subsided, he felt even more foolish.

I deserved that.

And then he laughed out loud at himself, staring at the pines until his confidence mimicked the tallest, or at least the middling ones. Regaining the saddle and pulling the horse's head away from his nibbling, Kirkland guided the animal to a slow trot.

No rush.

Kirkland stood at the menacing steps and took a deep breath, hoping the extra oxygen would swiftly bring life to his cemented knees.

What happened to that confidence, gathered among the trees? Remember, she agreed to the courting offer. But what if that opinion has changed? Aw, hell.

Surrendering himself to fate, Kirkland's right foot broke free from its imagined vines and he started a rhythmic ascent. Visualizing the sturdy pines, he walked to the door. Pausing only to clear his throat, he knocked three times, careful not to sound too eager. He could hear footsteps opposite the door, which soon was ajar.

A servant with a white apron and poised stance greeted him.

"Good morning Sir. How may I be of assistance?"

Kirkland removed his hat.

"Yes, is the man of the house present?"

"Of course. May I ask who is calling?"

"Richard Kirkland."

"Just a moment, please."

The middle-aged, graceful woman disappeared around a corner.

A slight itch appeared on Kirkland's hand, barely noticeable, a transient thought on a preoccupied mind. Within moments, the servant returned.

"Mr. Godfrey will see you now. Follow me, please."

Here we go. I didn't even prepare myself for her father!

She led him to the parlor where her father, seeing Kirkland, stood up immediately.

"Mr. Kirkland, do come in."

"Thank you, Sir."

"Can I get you some coffee?"

"No, thank you."

"Are you sure? It's the finest bean money can buy—from Costa Rica."

"I'm fine, Sir. Thank you."

Mr. Godfrey smiled. He was a dignified fellow, fine in manners and well-respected in the community. One of the wealthiest planters in Flat Rock, he was known to be an honest and astute businessman, equally versed in the country handshake and the lawyer's contract. His silver, impeccably groomed beard and layered hair added to his polished

124

mystique. Of course this perceived aura of flawlessness only made Kirkland more uncomfortable.

"Very well. Please, have a seat."

"Thank you."

Kirkland sat down stiffly on a well-worn couch, trying to pass for a gentleman. Sitting down across from his guest, Mr. Godfrey began with polite conversation.

"So, tell me. How is your father?"

"Very well, Sir. Busy as always but the crops look bountiful this year."

"That's good to hear. He is a fine planter who knows how to get the best out of the land."

"I'm sure he would return your compliments."

This seemed to please Mr. Godfrey.

"Unfortunately, I have not had the pleasure to see him recently. Please give him my highest regards."

"Of course."

Kirkland started to fidget but caught himself. There was an awkward pause, which he discerned was Mr. Godfrey's way of testing him. Doing his best to remain composed, he kept his gaze steady.

"So, what brings you out to Scarlet Hill?"

The abruptness and shift in conversation caught Kirkland off guard.

"I, uh, came, uh, to…"

Mr. Godfrey chuckled.

"Of course, I know why you are here."

He clapped his hands and a second, younger servant arrived.

"Brenda, Susan has a visitor. Please announce our guest. Mr. Kirkland wishes to see her."

The servant bowed and ascended the adjoining stairs.

"While we wait, I was hoping to get your opinion on something."

Another test?

Perspiring greatly now, Kirkland hoped it was not too noticeable.

Whether this shedding was noticed or not, Mr. Godfrey did his best to put the visitor at ease.

"I don't mean to be so forward, but in these turbulent times, a man should not be short on dialogue and decision. Despite what some may say, I do not consider myself an expert in political affairs. But war is on the horizon, and may be a foregone conclusion. Many are hasty to jump from that cliff and are easily swept away by the rhetoric and grandstanders. Now, I've always been loyal to the Union while also being an ardent supporter of South Carolina. And of course, all the while I'm looking out for my business interests. These lines have become blurred, and eventually, I'm afraid, sitting on the fence will not be an option. Please, as a young man, of a different generation and from a family I respect, I would appreciate your perspective. If I may be so bold."

Stunned, Kirkland was unsure how to respond. Here was a man whom many in the community sought for his wisdom in all matters of politics and economics, being absolutely open and asking a question of a novice in worldly affairs. Sure, their families had known each other for years. But this was not a time for honesty. Failing to show 100 percent support for the "Southern Cause" could tar and feather your reputation in a hurry.

And he wants my opinion?

This time, Kirkland's facial expression was a dead giveaway.

"I know my hesitance is unpopular," said Godfrey. "But please understand, war is not as glamorous as some may think. Of course, if South Carolina decides to secede, I will follow. Even if it means blood up to our ears."

His eyes were pained, as if he knew what was coming, and he appeared to look beyond the walls, momentarily forgetting Kirkland was there. But the gentleman's politeness soon returned as did his demand for Kirkland's response.

"Forgive me for my long-windedness. Please, I welcome your opinion."

Kirkland was about to stutter a response when Godfrey's daughter was announced.

"Sir, Miss Susan."

Immediately, the men stood up.

Saved.

"Father, have you let our guest get a word in?"

He seemed only slightly embarrassed.

"I must confess I dominated the conversation, as usual."

To keep his composure, Kirkland looked past Susan's face and away from her eyes.

"Your father was very generous with his opinions. I only hope that one day I will be so wise."

Instantly regretting his response, Kirkland hoped he did not sound patronizing or weak-willed.

"Susan, I will not hold him any longer. The room is yours."

"Actually, I would like to take advantage of the pleasant evening. Would you object to us taking tea on the porch?"

"A splendid idea."

He clapped his hands.

"Brenda, put on some tea."

"Thank you, Sir," said Kirkland, stiff but respectful.

He turned to follow Susan but stopped short, feeling her father's words demanded a response, equal to the man's honesty. He faced his possible future father-in-law with all the courage he could muster.

"Thank you for deeming me worthy of your sentiments. I believe your caution is admirable. I, too, have my reservations about rushing to judgment. Reason must persevere. However, if South Carolina calls for its liberty, I will be the first to enlist in her defense."

Mr. Godfrey said nothing but bowed slightly, and Kirkland could not ascertain whether the gentleman was in approval of his words or if he had been too forward. His gut told him the former as he followed Susan out the front door, unsure if he was escaping one delicate cage for one of the same discomfort.

She smelled like orange blossoms, and the aroma caused an involuntary shudder.

"I must apologize for my father," said Susan. "He is consumed by worry for his family and business."

"There's no need," said Kirkland, grateful that she spoke first. "Your father is wise in his views. If more were as conciliatory and openminded, this world would be much the brighter. He says he does not have the aptitude for politics, but I beg to differ."

"Yes, he is almost too modest. He is well connected and versed, and many want him to campaign for this office or that."

"I'm not surprised."

"But he likes you. That is obvious."

"I'm not so sure."

"Please. He would not have allowed me to breach the front door with you if he didn't approve."

Naturally, Kirkland was pleased to hear of it, but he was more curious if his daughter shared her father's high opinion. He put his hands behind his back, scratching them slightly, as the door opened.

"Miss, Sir, your tea," said the servant. "Thank you, Brenda, you may set it down here."

As the servant disappeared inside, Susan motioned to a small table. She poured a glass and handed it to Kirkland.

"All this talk of war. It never ends."

Kirkland nodded, again grateful for Susan's forwardness, but eyed her carefully to see if it was small talk or genuine loathing for the topic. Or was this also a test? He could not read her just yet.

"You must not blame your father for his unease. Much is at stake. He is only looking out for your family and to the future."

"Of course, I am well aware. And I am grateful. He is a good man. I just worry the topic will consume him."

"Fear not, Susan. We are all swept up in this climate of unknown. Your father is sensible to consider all the possibilities."

"Yes, my father is wise. But I'm afraid my mother passed down her tendency for persistent worry over him."

Kirkland laughed.

"My father tells me my mother was of the same constitution."

128

"She must have been a tremendous lady. My father spoke highly of her."

Sipping his tea, Kirkland held the liquid in his mouth, before swallowing hard. He was taken aback that Susan's words summoned such powerful emotions. Afraid it was noticeable, he turned from Susan and placed a hand on the porch railing. Resisting the urge to gulp the drink down, he took another modest sip and pretended to take in the plantation surroundings.

"From the little memories I have of her, she certainly was."

Susan, sensing his discomfort and embarrassed, changed the subject again.

"You said that if war came to South Carolina, you would enlist?"

Kirkland, ready for her question, couldn't resist.

"I thought you were tired of this discussion of war."

Susan looked away nervously, and Kirkland kicked himself inside. But it was too late to recant.

Stumbling to come up with something before Susan responded, Kirkland went blank, and this time gulped a mouthful.

"My apologies," said Susan, pulling on her left ear. "It is not my place to speak so carelessly."

Placing his nearly empty glass on the tray, Kirkland looked at Susan with gentle eyes and attempted to speak.

But his brain and his tongue had lost their connection.

"No, uh, forgive me, I, um…"

Susan appeared ready to bolt, and Kirkland knew it. In an attempt to gather his faculties, he focused on a daguerreotype of his mother that, for as long as he could remember, held the place of honor on the fireplace mantle of the Kirkland home. His father had always refused to let anyone touch it. Every Sunday morning he would stand before it in contemplation for several minutes, before wiping whatever dust had accumulated from the previous week.

"Your question was legitimate, and proper," said Kirkland, recovering. "I did not mean to throw it to the wind with disregard."

He was about to say more when an intense itch in his hands finally caught his attention. Looking down at his hand, the recognition hit him like a fallen brick on his toes.

Susan smiled, pleased with his response.

"My brave soldier. If off to war, will you write?"

Noticing a leaf stuck to Kirkland's shirt, Susan boldly reached for it and plucked the greenery from its captor.

Kirkland's eyes widened, realizing what kind of irritation he had just passed on to the object of his adoration. He panicked, his hands now burning uncontrollably.

"Of... of course I will write," Kirkland stammered, his horror growing as Susan passed the leaf between her hands.

"I, I've stayed past my welcome. I have things to attend to. Important things. I must take my leave. Please thank your father for me... for his hospitality."

Kirkland bowed, placed his hat on his head and abruptly hustled down the stairs. Without turning to face her, he called out,

"Good day, Susan," leaving her confused, holding the poison ivy that would soon cause an inflamed rash on her palms.

★　　★　　★

The audience was in an uproar, pleased with Kirkland's generous offering.

They laughed until their ribs hurt, while the storyteller's giggle was less than convincing. Although it was a story that eventually Kirkland and Susan could tell their potential grandkids about, it still made him cringe as if it happened yesterday.

While Susan and her father would make light of the incident at their next meeting, Susan's mother, away shopping that day in Camden, would not let the matter of Kirkland's negligence go so easily. It would take months for her to warm to her daughter's man of affection.

Fain, always ready to spin a yarn for drooling ears, was nearly foaming at the mouth to relate to Kirkland's tale. The laughs were still kicking before he attempted to one-up Kirkland's story.

"Oh, oh, I have a similar story, without the girl, though."

"That's shocking," said Smith, teasing. "All right then, don't hold back. Kirkland sure didn't."

"A good story to be sure, but not in the same caliber of my next chapter."

Standing up, Fain transformed his hands to storytelling mode, gesturing wildly.

"Several years ago, I went hunting for deer with a friend on his family's extensive, wild property. We left the dogs and jacklights at home for more of a challenge. All day we waited by a clearing, on a trail that led to a creek where the deer would come down from the hills for a drink. We saw a few, but they were either does or young and unworthy, and we waited for something larger.

"But the large bucks were nowhere to be seen. It started to get dark, and not wanting to come home empty-handed, we decided to camp out for the night and try again the next morning. As I was about to close my eyes for the night, my bowels started acting up something fierce. So I got up to relieve them, wandering far enough away from camp as to not disturb our hunting sights. It was a cloudy, moonless night and you couldn't see the hand in front of your face. Well, I did my business as best I could and scrounged for a few leaves to wipe my behind."

Fain giggled, anticipating the climax of his story.

"The next morning, I woke up to an intense itch that would not go away. I tried to ignore it as we set our ambush, waiting for a great beast to walk to the slaughter. Before long, a huge buck with an enormous rack wandered down the trail, snorting. With everything in my power, I tried to ignore the urge to scratch my bottom, which was now burning something severe. As the deer approached within my sights, I couldn't ignore the urge any longer. I dropped my gun as softly as I could and reached around with both hands to ease the suffering. But the buck was wise to my movement

131

and took off in fright, my friend firing but missing. By this time, I was rolling in the dirt, pulling down my pants to get at the deer's best friend."

Smith fell backward off his chair as he strained to hold in his convulsions. Bury and Kirkland couldn't contain themselves either.

Fain was clearly enjoying the response, but he wasn't done. Taking breaths between his falsetto spasms, he continued.

"My buddy was beside himself, cussing me out and screaming. And here I am, with my ass hangin' out, rubbing it to near bleeding, wallowing in the dirt."

"You are victorious," said Kirkland, howling with the others.

Fain clapped his hands, celebrating his supremacy. But unlike the others, Kirkland noticed that there was something about this memory that detracted from his pure joy. It was very unlike Fain to display any form of weakness, and as Kirkland eyed him curiously, the fireball was struggling to hold it together. As the laughter died down, to the surprise of Kirkland, Fain volunteered the information.

"My friend's name was Hugh Tiffany. He joined up with the 8th Infantry, Darlington Rifles. He was killed on that damn Henry Hill."

The room went silent, and Fain clenched his jaw, staring at his feet.

"I searched for him but couldn't find his body. No doubt he lies buried for eternity in some unmarked grave in the Virginia countryside."

The sober stares into the fire went into full effect. No one spoke or uttered a sound.

As if blown to his feet, Fain moved with such force that Kirkland flinched.

"I will redeem him in Yankee blood tenfold before this thing is over."

Pulling off his brogans, he climbed to his top bunk.

"Well, I bid ya'll goodnight. Good story, Kirkland."

Chapter 7

MARCH 9, 1862
NEAR MANASSAS JUNCTION, VA
7 PM

Standing in the doorway, Kirkland lingered for one final vista of reflection. The comfortable bunk, the blackened fireplace of warmth and sizzling aromas, the simple table of a thousand games, epic recitals and down-home conversations. Certainly, it was no Valley Forge and he could still hear the laughter as he closed the door.

"Come, come on Kirkland," said Smith. "Time to play soldier again."

Nodding with mixed emotions, Kirkland followed, slinging his rifle over his shoulder.

"I was getting mighty bored anyhow."

Smith giggled. "You and me both."

"Any notion of where we're headed?"

"Richmond or Hell?" He smiled broadly, adjusting his eyewear.

"That sounds plausible," said Kirkland, giving his friend a slight shove. But it was enough for the top-heavy Smith to nearly fall over.

Just as he had left Richmond the spring before, Smith was overburdened, with a knapsack and haversack bulging, a heavy overcoat courtesy of the Yankees, and enough blankets for a Minnesota winter, all tied haphazardly around him.

"Easy," said Smith, bending his knees to regain his balance.

"You sure you can carry all that? We could be in for a long march tonight."

"I sent all excess baggage to the junction like we all did. What's left are pure necessities."

By Smith's jerking adjustments, Kirkland thought otherwise, but refrained from additional probing. To shed weight, he decided to leave behind his knapsack and overcoat. Saving the few items that he deemed necessary (including the shirt Susan had made) in tightly rolled wool and gum blankets, he doubled over the roll, binding the ends together with string. Adding a second string in the middle to keep the form intact, he then tossed the hoop over his left shoulder, where it curled around his right hip in a position where he could fire his gun without removing it. Just in case.

"All right then, let's get a movin'," said Kirkland.

"To, uh, the south. Somewheresville!"

As if escaping from prison, Fain and Bury had already rushed ahead and the duo jogged to catch up. Once they had gained the long, uninterrupted lines of enthused men, willingly closing the chapter on winter drags, they marched slowly toward the supply depot at Manassas Junction. The men knew what was coming and were licking their chops.

The previous evening, the soldiers had been told that all excess baggage at the depot would be destroyed when they left the area. However, the men were welcome to stuff their pockets and bags of whatever they wished, and the stores were rich of everything in a soldier's imagination—mountains of food, clothing, shoes, and the most sought-after item: whiskey.

When the depot came into sight, a mad rush ensued, as the men converged on the goodies with child-like hoarding.

"Take what you will boys, but take heed that you must carry your spoils for untold miles," said a chuckling Kennedy, recently promoted colonel of the regiment.

It was almost too much for the shut in, neglected soldier to absorb. While they certainly had not been suffering for supplies during most of their stay in Manassas, free loot was another realm. It was Christmas in March, with temptation calling from every shelf.

Scanning the tonnage, Kirkland crammed a dozen potatoes, a poke sack full of salt and an extra pair of cotton socks in his haversack. Next, he filled his pockets with a new toothbrush, comb, and match safe. Eying a pile of shoes, he picked a few pairs up and measured them against his feet until he found the right size. But it would be an awkward carry, no matter where he put them. And he certainly did not want to begin a march with stiff shoes containing rusty feet. After agonizing over the decision, he left the extra pair behind.

Kirkland had the first pick on most items as the majority of men were crowding around the whiskey, knocking open barrels, and filling their canteens and tin cups. The smaller jugs and bottles were quickly snatched up and carried away, but Bury was unsatisfied with the puny treasures.

As Kirkland watched in awe, Bury picked up a 10-gallon keg and dropped it on his shoulder with a red-faced grunt. Spinning an effortless 360 degrees as if to accent the inferior nature of its weight, Bury teased Fain, who was carrying a mere cup filled to the brim. Of course, this only encouraged an outpouring of sailor oaths and a demonstrative chug. When it was over, Fain was back in a whiskey line, pushing for a second drink.

Perched on his horse, Kershaw waited patiently for the men to get their chance at the wells. He had recently been commissioned brigadier general, replacing Bonham, who had resigned in a dispute with President Jefferson Davis. Although the men hated to lose Bonham, it was quickly forgotten when they learned who would be his replacement. They had seen the stalwart presence, the way he led in battle, and had full confidence in his abilities.

When satisfied all had an opportunity or three at the trough, Kershaw cut them off.

"Column of fours," said the general.

Facing a legion of groans and no stranger to imbibing, the general dismounted and strolled to a whiskey barrel, where he filled his canteen. Raising it high, he toasted the men.

"Carolinians, I salute you. Drink now and be merry, but be ready to whip our enemy, wherever they may appear."

He took a long swallow, amid boisterous cheers and gave the command to move out.

★　　★　　★

MIDNIGHT

Warmed by whiskey and blinded by the usual silent treatment about the destination, the men marched southwest following their commanders to whereabouts unknown. While it was clear that the enemy had its sights on the Confederate capital of Richmond, the possible routes and strategies to reach the city were numerous. Would it be by land or by sea? The lanterns had yet to be hung.

As the troops sipped their fire and became increasingly drunk, the marching columns rapidly deteriorated. While some preferred to stumble forward on the measured steps of the railroad tracks, others drifted to the parallel road.

Sober but under the influence of winter rot, Kirkland had chosen the latter, and was already feeling the strain on his soft legs and laden back. In the darkness, he could see the outline of Bury, who was beginning to hunch slightly under the weight of the barrel. Next to him was Fain, who was acquainting himself with the entire road, incapable of walking a straight line.

Behind them, a faint glow arose as if a premature sunrise aspired to light their way. Turning, Kirkland noticed the light growing in its severity and instantly knew its cause.

Manassas Junction was burning.

"I was under the impression that it wouldn't be torched until tomorrow evening," said Smith, gaining Kirkland's side.

"That's what they told us. The townsfolk were supposed to have the opportunity to take what they found useful before it went up in flames."

"Well, I don't think they'll find much of use now."

"Careless drunkard, no doubt."

"Hey," Fain snarled.

"Relax, Fain, I wasn't speaking about you."

"You…"

An explosion drowned out the rebuttal, followed by several more in rapid succession. Before long, the fires had reached the artillery rounds and rifle cartridges, blasting holes through the drowsy night, as if the hostilities of Manassas were being reenacted.

Even though the men had advanced several miles from the depot, the ground seemed to tremble and shake. The fireworks were enough to halt the entire brigade in its staggering tracks and the men watched the dancing illuminations in silence. A wave of prickly sadness caught Kirkland off guard.

The junction was, after all, a symbol of warrior birth and it had become home. Though it represented a confusing and painful chapter, its pages were not without brotherhood and joy. As he watched the flames destroy this adopted roost, a thousand moments replayed in his head and he wondered what the next few months would bring.

"That's it boys," said Bury, dropping the keg to ground, and nearly somersaulting in the process. "I'm not carryin' this another step."

"I got it," said Fain.

Attempting to lift the keg without the strength of his legs, the whiskey defied him, flinging the dynamo into a hissy of slurred epithets. He tried again using better form, but as he got the keg to his shoulder, he teetered backward and fell to the ground.

"God damn it, son of a bitch," Fain growled, hulking over the object of his wrath.

Breathing in shallow bursts, he grunted and lifted the keg again, bending his legs in support. With both arms trembling, he held on as the whiskey balanced precariously on one shoulder. But when he took a step and straightened his legs, he teetered sideways, keg and man crashing to the road in a heap.

Bury walked over to help him up, but Fain angrily shoved his hand away. Brushing himself off, the defeated stood up and repeatedly slammed the butt of this rifle into the keg until a leak was sprung. Replenishing his canteen and taking a long swig from his newly filled cup, he beckoned for others to follow.

"Come and get it, you assholes."

★   ★   ★

MARCH 11
NEAR RAPPAHANNOCK STATION, VA
5 PM

Clinging to the rubber blanket with a numbed hand under his chin, Kirkland shivered as he walked.

His other mitt, gripping his rifle, was even more frigid, and he alternated hands frequently in a desperate attempt to keep both from sleeping. The day before it began to rain, the clouds rejoicing in their incontinence, for they had been dumping torrents nearly unabated for 24 hours.

Even with the water proof cover, the steady downpour had threatened to penetrate Kirkland's bones. He was miserable, having spent the previous night spooning with Smith in a failed attempt to stay warm without a tent. Dawn brought no relief, as the onslaught from the heavens continued. The men had taken to the railway exclusively, which saved them from a road of sloshy pulp, but the added weight from swamped blankets and overcoats had incited a mass ditching of personal gear. All but the most essential were discarded and Kirkland had parted ways with nearly every item gained from the depot's trove. Forced to throw away the potatoes, save a couple, and the bag of salt, his one comfort was knowing he'd made the right decision about the extra pair of shoes.

Becoming almost unbearable, the wet clothes and haversack straps were chaffing his skin into red, yelping cinders. Never in his life had he craved a fire more, and this blazing vision consumed his thoughts. Despite the weather, they had traversed a remarkable twenty-two miles in less than two days.

"Smith, tell me a story," said Kirkland, barely above a whisper as if his tongue was also waterlogged.

"Well, uh, well, let me see. Hmm."

He looked up to ensnare a tale and instantly regretted it, as his spectacles were overrun with droplets.

"Ah, hell," said Smith, attempting to wipe them clean, but only smearing them in the process.

"Story. Hmm. Okay. One night as I added a log to the fire…"

"Please don't mention fire."

"Can't get it off your mind either, huh?"

"I would trade my rifle for it."

"As would I. Maybe the wagon trains with our tents will catch up with us tonight."

"I won't hold my breath. Not in this weather and with these roads."

"The rain has got to, got to slow one of these hours. It might even cease altogether by next Tuesday."

"Alex told me once that there are places in the world, such as in South America, where the sky opens nearly every day. They call them rainforests."

"An appropriate title. Remind me to stay away from South America. They must have a long growing season, however."

"Good for the crops, terrible for the soldier. Tell me, why are we doing this again?"

"To save the South, and your sweetheart."

Tripped up by a crosstie, Kirkland nearly fell on his dripping nose.

"Apparently I've forgotten both 'the cause' and how to walk."

"Your head is just a little soggy," Smith giggled. It'll uh, it'll come back around."

"If Richmond is our destination, I aim to board at a fancy hotel, like the Spotswood."

"I reckon I'll settle for anything with a roof over my head."

"The Yanks are no doubt salivating about marching into her. And I'm sure wherever they appear, we'll find ourselves blocking the road."

"I just hope we can corner them somewhere right quick and put an end to this war."

"You are optimistic, my friend. But for now, I pray for the clouds to part and for the radiant sun to break through."

Removing the rubber blanket from his head, Kirkland shook off the accumulation.

"May the sun emerge before I drown."

Noticing Smith tossing aside another blanket, he couldn't resist.

"Say, it would appear your necessities are rapidly shrinking."

Grinning, his chum removed his knapsack, and with an exaggerated stance, heaved the dead weight into the trees.

He sighed: "Moment of weakness, I'm afraid. I will come back for that."

"With or without a bloodhound?"

"Have you seen my nose? I have no use for a hunting dog. I can pick up my own scent for miles. Besides, my property may just float alongside us to Richmond."

Sharing a chuckle, the men relished any distraction from the monsoon.

"If only my Enfield would drift along as well," said Kirkland, "washing ashore in a flood to the Spotswood's doors. I must carve my initials into it, so it will fall into the proper hands."

"May I hold court in your suite, orate, uh, orating to the masses from your balcony?"

"Indeed. As long as you preach about the virtues of traveling light."

"Ouch. Are you still in possession of your lover's nobly made blouse?"

Confirming with a playful smirk, Kirkland retaliated.

"Are blacksmiths even allowed to marry?"

★   ★   ★

APRIL 21, 1862
NEAR YORKTOWN, VA

He tore into the envelope, and seized from it a paper heart.

All along its border was pink lace, carefully stitched and surrounding an elegant penmanship that Kirkland had come to cherish at every observance.

The words were simple, yet delivered an immortal kiss.

To my beloved soldier
On Saint Valentine's Day

Kirkland read the words twice.

beloved

Attached to the valentine was a lock of auburn hair, and with thumb and forefinger, he caressed the strands from top to ending curl. He then brought it to his nose. It smelled like orange blossoms, which rolled his eyes back. She had worn this perfume before, on the day of their last face-to-face at the Godfrey home.

When his eyes ceased revolving, he closed them and winced, pulling the card to his chest. In an instant she was standing before him with that lambent but mischievous smile.

Oh, my Susan.

Cradling the valentine as if it were her essence, Kirkland greeted her, holding tightly. After a lengthy journey home, he finally, painfully, opened his eyes. Once more reaching into the envelope, he plucked an accompanying letter, folded with feminine care. Carefully, he opened the letter, knowing the distant conversation would arrive with unintended teeth.

Taking a deep breath, he dove in.

My beloved Richard,

I take this moment to send a Southern patriot my heart. For when you left many months ago, you took a sizable portion of it with you. Ever since, I've longed for its return. But this is a selfish desire, a weakness that I'm well acquainted with. God and state have flung you into the wilds of Virginia and I do not desire to keep you from your noble work.

When I gaze at the dipping sky, I often see you there, just above the horizon, smiling down at me. This brings me comfort and the strength to endure the distance between us. I know that someday you will come back to me. Yet I also know, that there is much work to be done before our future together will commence.

Do not concern yourself with matters at home. While luxuries are strained, we want for nothing. As terrible as the present may be to you, always remember that I'm by your side. No miles or barricades can separate us. This simple valentine cannot begin to convey the pride I have in your sacrifice.

Do not doubt for a moment that we will reunite again, for I await your return with every breath, trusting in God for your deliverance. Until that glorious day, I will surround myself with hope and your gentle presence. Keep me close and I will guide you home.

Forever,

Susan

Waiting several minutes for the words to fly around his head and settle, Kirkland gradually placed the letter back in its envelope. He gazed at the rain-threatening heavens, waiting for an image to manifest. But Susan was not there.

Time had dimmed her image and Kirkland now wished she had posed for a tintype. For as much as their last meeting together was unforgettable, the acute edges and succulent details were beginning to lose their color and definition. Momentary panic aside, where a whiffed urge to sprint due south uncorked his resolve, the letter only served to bathe him with added determination.

Having finally made the decision in early April to reenlist for the war, he would fight for Susan, her name branded on his trigger arm as much, or more than, Flat Rock, or Camden or Carolina. She was the propelling force, the fuel that would sustain him for however long the war continued.

And then there were his soldier pals, to whom he was fiercely loyal. He could not, and would not, abandon them.

In the end, the decision to remain in the army was an easy one, and even assisted in saving him from the embarrassment of April 16, when he learned the choice had been made for him anyway. On this day, General John B. Magruder, commanding the forces at Yorktown, ordered all of those who did not want to reenlist to leave. Later that day, the men who left were recalled after Magruder learned of the Conscription Act being passed in Richmond, requiring all white males between the ages of 18 and 35, with a few exceptions, to enter the service.

Of course, the men had returned to ribbing questions: "What's the news from home? How was your visit? Did you eat and run?"

Meanwhile, Union General George B. McClellan had amassed 120,000 men and over 70 huge siege guns on the peninsula south of Yorktown. To reinforce Magruder, Kershaw's brigade had sailed down the James River and up the York to the swampy lowlands.

Although Union forces greatly outnumbered the Confederates, the overly cautious McClellan had ordered his army to entrench.

By making an embellished racket and marching his men around in circles, Magruder had fooled the Union general into thinking he opposed a much larger force. But such deception would not save them forever.

★ ★ ★

MAY 2, 1862

For weeks the road had lived on a diet of steady rain, and now wanted a more substantial meal.

Having indulged in Confederate feet, it had become greedy, with knees next on the menu. Kirkland worked to free one leg, but sank deeper with the next step.

"Give me a hand, I think I'm stuck."

Leveraging his friend under his arm, Joe pulled, and the road suckled in earnest, holding on to its victim. He yanked again, this time with more strength, but the leg wouldn't budge.

"Third time's the charm?" said Kirkland.

Grunting, Joe heaved with full force, and with slurping protest, the mud mouth finally released the extremity.

"This is fun, ain't it?" said Joe.

Kirkland looked at him as if he had gone insane. Realizing Joe wasn't joking, he concluded that his friend was indeed a practicing lunatic. The dots had been connecting for years.

"Joe," said Kirkland, unable to resist a bewildered smile, "I've always known you were not all there, but you are really not all there."

"No," said Joe, giggling. "That's probably a correct assumption."

Kershaw's brigade had been roused in the middle of night to advance to the furthest picket line, to cover a secretive retreat. Still vastly outnumbered, the Confederate braintrust had decided, after weeks of anticlimactic staredowns, to move closer to Richmond and draw the Yankees away from their supply base at Fort Monroe.

Before moving north, one final ruse was in the works. To reach the pickets, however, the brigade would have to traverse a dangerous landscape. While the moon was an outlying beacon, the pervasive darkness made it impossible to judge the ground in front.

Breathing heavily, Kirkland strained to keep his balance, trudging through the muck.

It only got worse.

When the road ended, a swamp commenced, and he found himself in waist-deep water, holding a rifle above his head. With every step, the mud gliding past his shins beneath the murky water felt like a horde of snakes in a circling orgy.

Remembering his father's lesson of the cottonmouth, he shuddered. This was not how he had imagined the serpent would take form. Kirkland followed hard the silhouette of Joe in front, to distract from thoughts of what could be swimming below. At last the water grew shallow, and Kirkland gained a foothold on dry land. He could have kissed it but in his puckering, he noticed the enemy's fires in the distance, on the opposite side of the Warwick River.

"Halt."

Colonel Kennedy walked down the tired and water-logged column, speaking with the company commanders.

"Tell your men to gather all the wood they can find," Kirkland overheard him say. "Here, we will build as many small fires as we can to deceive the enemy into thinking we have the advantage in numbers."

Following orders, Kirkland made trip after trip into the canopy by the swamp, breaking off dead branches and dragging fallen timber to a pile near the edge of the river. All along the bank, shallow pits were dug and filled with mounds of twisted limbs, splintered logs and pieces from a rail fence. Because the wood was damp, or worse, it took a while to get going, but before long the fires were crackling and dancing skyward.

"There are a lot of fires over yonder," said Kirkland, tossing a clump of bark onto a growing flame, while at the same time beholding the other side of the river. "What is weighing down McClellan's head?"

"I don't pretend to know," said Alex, throwing a fence post into the pit. "But I also don't intend to argue with him. Let's hope he stays the fool."

Kirkland scratched at his itchy face and neck. He hadn't shaved since the regiment left Manassas Junction, and the unaccustomed skin was getting irritated by the growing fur. This was only mildly annoying compared to his shoes and trousers, which had rarely been dry during the previous month, and he was near shivering.

Inching closer to the fire, it wasn't long before the mud on his pants began to smoke.

"Tell me, why did I reenlist again?" said Kirkland, only half-joking.

"I believe it must have been your desire to become a fish," said Alex.

Kirkland laughed.

"That must be it. I may sprout fins yet. In fact, I have forgotten what the sun looks like."

"It's round and commonly yellow," said Joe, stacking another log on the fire.

"Ahh, thank you, Joe," said Kirkland. "Where have you been hiding it?"

"I'm saving it for a rainy day."

"That makes a lot of sense," said Alex, unimpressed.

"Well, professor, I won't be loaning it to you anytime soon."

Hearing a groan from the next fire pit, they looked to see officers moving down the line giving instructions quietly, man to man, so as not to alert the enemy. By the reaction, Kirkland could see that the news wasn't good.

As the officers approached, Kirkland's fireside mates saluted them.

"Column of fours. We're moving out," said a captain by the name of Haile, barely above a whisper. "Sorry boys, but we must return the same way we came."

The officers moved on and even Joe lost his agreeable attitude.

"Good. I was almost getting warm."

Chapter 8

FRIDAY, JUNE 27, 1862
SOUTH OF THE CHICKAHOMINY RIVER
EAST OF RICHMOND, VA

T he sun had peeked around the dripping trees, stretching in a lazy
yawn, before shoving aside the rain clouds.

With it, the enemy had come out to play, advancing on Richmond.
Although outnumbered nearly two to one, the Confederates had slammed
into the enemy in several bloody battles, forcing the Union army into
retreat.

After General Joseph Johnston was seriously wounded defending the
city at the Battle of Seven Pines on May 31, Robert E. Lee took control of
the Army of Northern Virginia the next day. Twenty-five thousand men,
including Kershaw's brigade, under General Magruder, were sent south of
the Chickahominy River to block the eastern approach to Richmond.

On June 18th, the Carolinians were ordered to push forward and scout
the Federal position. After light skirmishing and coming within two
hundred yards of the Yankees' main line, Kennedy recalled his men,
having accomplished their goal. Being in such close proximity to the
enemy, Kirkland and his fellow troops were anxiously awaiting—and
expecting—another major engagement.

But more than a week went by with no further action. On the 25th, orders came down from Kershaw that the men should prepare rations and be prepared to move at a moment's notice.

Two days later, they were still waiting.

Impatience was setting in, brought on by several mornings of waking with the dark cloud of battle hovering above their faces, close enough to tickle their ears. Its breath mocked them, and was a constant vortex of energy, unpredictable in its madness. While they stood idle, awaiting their turn, the ominous sounds of raging combat were ever nigh.

Although the 2nd South Carolina was involved in a sharp skirmish just outside of Williamsburg during the retreat from the peninsula, it had been almost a year since the soldiers had experienced a major engagement and the men were more than ready for another crack at the enemy.

★   ★   ★

With his back to a small cottonwood tree, Kirkland stared at a copy of the *Richmond Examiner*. His eyes fell on a critical review of Lee's appointment to command the Southern forces: "A general who had never fought a battle and whose extreme tenderness of blood inclined him to depend exclusively on the resources of strategy."

I hope they're wrong.

"Richard."

Looking up from the newspaper, he was pleased to see William Truesdel approaching him and rose to greet his old Flat Rock friend.

"Hello, William. How are you?"

"Fine. Fine. And you?"

"Splendid. Just reading up on our new commanding general. Doesn't exactly inspire confidence."

"Well, what do the newspapers know? I say, give the man a chance before condemning him as a failure."

Kirkland nodded.

"Anyhow, Richard, I just spoke with a dispatch rider. It appears your brothers are camped not far from here."

149

Kirkland's eyes perked up, the reading glaze singed away. He had heard by way of a recent letter from his father that Dan and Billy had joined the Kirkwood Rangers, a local cavalry outfit.

"Where?"

"Just over them hills," said William, pointing north. "I say we pay 'em a visit."

Receiving permission, William and Kirkland headed toward the camp of his brothers, the latter carrying a box of desserts that had been sent to him from his sister-in-law, Rosa. Having not seen his brothers, or any family, in more than a year, Kirkland was set in a youthful hurry, barely able to restrain his feet from catapulting out of his brogans.

Though his legs had also caught the fever and beckoned for a run, Kirkland's immediate company called for a more relaxed pace. He doubted William would be pleased at a sprint and so he held at bay the springs in his mind and body.

After walking for 30 minutes and twice asking for directions, they found the camp of the Rangers, tucked away from the main road along a grassy brook. Again asking more specifically for his brothers' whereabouts, they were pointed toward the eastern side of the camp. Kirkland's step quickened this time, the brakes on his calves no longer holding. Devouring the ground in his path, he left William in his wake.

William said nothing, but smiled, jogging to catch up to his friend. At last, Kirkland spotted Billy brushing the mane of his horse, his black derby hat a sure giveaway.

Coming up behind him, the younger brother disguised his voice.

"Kirkland," he said, in his deepest voice, "you call that a well-groomed horse?"

Billy turned slowly, expecting a lecture from one of his superior officers. His stolid face morphed instantly into a knowing grin when he saw his playful accuser.

With a boyish shout, he grabbed Kirkland by the shoulders and tossed him to the ground, the brothers wrestling in the dirt as they had done a

150

thousand times along a similar creek back home. Gaining vertical and wiping the dirt from their trousers, the grapplers embraced.

"Brother," said Billy, "it sure is good to see you."

"Fate can't keep us apart. Not for too long, anyways."

Billy finally acknowledged the second guest, who was waiting patiently for the brothers to reacquaint.

"William. How are ya, neighbor?"

"Very well, thank you. How are the horsemen?"

"Can't complain. Haven't seen any action yet, though."

"I'm sure your time will come. Where's the other distinguished gentleman of the Kirkland clan?" asked William.

"Yes," Kirkland added, "where's that proud papa?"

"Oh, so you've heard. He's fixing up some grub. You both must join us for supper, if you can call the meager portions that."

"Of course, we're used to that. We did bring along Rosa's molasses cakes, however."

"That Rosa is a fine woman, for a Truesdel," said Billy, giving William a jab in the stomach.

"She certainly did lower her standards by marrying a Kirkland," William replied.

"Now that's a fact. Follow me, boys."

The three men found Dan in front of a small fire throwing some Irish potatoes, wild onions and slab bacon into a spider skillet, recently confiscated from an abandoned Yankee camp. Glancing upward, Dan did a double take, shaking his head as he rose.

"Hey, little brother. I kinda figured we'd run into you 'round here somewhere. I don't care how many thousands of fighting men we have here, I just knew. Billy, was I not confident in this fact?"

"He was."

"I was."

"Well, then, what else can you forecast for us?" said Kirkland. "Do you see a bloodless victory on our behalf?"

"Bloodless? Shoot. I ain't a fool. Victory, however…"

151

He passed a hand in an all-seeing rainbow in front of Kirkland's face before continuing.

"Now that's a more reasonable prognostication. But if I could predict the weather, I'd be a rich man."

Kirkland chuckled.

"If your condition advances to include the weather," said Kirkland, "please share the information with your brothers. I could use that lucrative enlightenment when I have land of my own."

"Don't hold your breath. But if that brilliance strikes me in a lightning storm, I'll let you know."

"Speaking of a lightning storm," said Kirkland, "I hear you've received a new gift, born but a few days ago."

"Yes, Rich. My wife and I have been blessed with a girl," said Dan, beaming. "We named her Ella. I hear she's a spitting image of her mama."

"Congratulations."

"Yes, congratulations," added William.

"Thank you. I do wish I could have been there. But…"

"You woulda been pacing the porch, sweating like a hog in a slaughter pen," said William, laughing. "Of course you wanted to be there, but distance may have saved you a pair of shoes."

All shared a liberal giggle at his expense, and Dan's sheepish bow proved the vision may not have been off the mark.

"This war can't last much longer," said Kirkland, collaring the back of his brother's neck. "You'll be home before you know it."

Although each gave an affirmative nod, their faces told otherwise. There was little light in that tunnel and Kirkland knew it.

"Please sit down," said Dan, motioning to his guests. "I'll have dinner ready in a jiffy."

★   ★   ★

As the food was served, Kirkland quickly downed it in half-choking gulps, more eager for conversation than to fill his stomach.

"How long have you been in these parts?" he asked.

152

"Bout a week in this general area," said Dan. "They've kept us moving. You just missed Sam. He followed us here but was sent home on account of him being too young."

Kirkland tossed his head back and winced. The missed opportunity struck him hard.

"It's just as well," he volunteered, though the words had wings dragging on the ground. "Father needs him."

"Yes. He ain't getting younger."

"How is father, at least before you left? Of course I've received letters, but as you know he's not one for offering complaint."

"Certainly not, but he's in good health," said Dan. "I think the extra responsibility has brought a spring back in his step. The crops look good. He keeps to himself mostly."

"I sure would like to see him if I can get a furlough," said Kirkland, staring off into the scaly bark of a sycamore tree.

"Yes, he would like that very much, I'm sure. Mayberry takes good care of him. Tom, too."

"How is that boy?"

"Growing into a man. He's really shot up in the last year."

Kirkland tried to imagine what Tom might look like taller, more mature.

"Have you seen Susan?" he asked quietly, almost under his breath, expecting a good-natured teasing from his brothers.

But none followed.

"Before we left, I ran into her in Camden," said Dan.

A canyon of a silence followed.

"And?" said Kirkland, impatiently.

Dan looked at Billy and smiled.

"She looked as handsome as always."

"Yes."

It was all he could say, and he caught himself daydreaming of a future encounter, a joyous reunion.

No, I must not waste this time with my brothers.

William took out the cakes his sister Rosa had made and handed them out.

"You know, in Camden, they even took down the church bells for casting cannon," said Billy. "Can you believe that?"

"God have mercy," said William. "That's one way of bringing Him down on our side. Will we stop at nothing to win this war?"

"Everyone must make sacrifices to defeat these invaders," said Kirkland, forceful but without malice. "We have no choice now. The enemy is here and we must cast them out."

"If we use our resources like Jeb Stuart has, I say our chances for success are fine and dandy," said Dan. "Have you heard about Stuart's ride around the enemy?

"Yes, it's remarkable," Kirkland said.

"Unbelievable is more like it. He rode a clear circle around the enemy and lost but a single man. It's been the talk of camp. He must have gained some invaluable information. Yes, I suspect we'll use that knowledge and attack soon, before the Yanks make their next move."

"We've been expecting a brawl for some time now," said Kirkland. "We were involved at Yorktown and Williamsburg, but nothing too heavy. At Yorktown we built huge fires and marched back and forth to deceive the enemy into thinking we actually outnumbered them."

His audience erupted into laughter.

"At Williamsburg," he continued, "we were the rearguard and the blue bellies hit us hard. But we were protected well by earthworks and casualties were few. They retreated when darkness came. Since May we've been marching and drilling, marching and drilling till blisters took hold. I can't take much more of this waiting."

Sighing, Dan cleared his throat.

"Don't be in too big a hurry to go and get yourself killed," he said. "I get antsy at times to get in the thick of it as well, but you've never been a sheep, so don't follow them to the slaughter."

Looking up at his brother, Kirkland saw the worry in his eyes.

154

"Don't worry, Dan. I'll be all right. I've got a good set of men about me."

"That's right," said William. "There's not a better regiment in the whole Confederate Army than the 2nd South Carolina."

"Well, save a few kills for the Kirkwood Rangers," said Dan, winking.

"It's gonna be dark soon," said William, standing up. "We best be gettin' back."

Kirkland had lost all track of time and gazed up at the retiring, velvet-tinged sky. Though his feet were whimpering and sullen, he knew William was right.

"Thank you for supper," he said to Dan, reaching out his hand.

His brother took it and gripped it heavily.

"You take care of yourself, Richard."

"Don't try to be a hero," said Billy, also shaking hands and giving a brotherly shove. "We'll see you soon. Before you know it, we'll be sitting around a well-lit fire with pa, telling war stories."

Taking William's hand, Billy smiled.

"Give my best to the Truesdels and give our regards to the other Flat Rock boys. Tell them the Rangers are a-comin'!"

Chapter 9

The camp was surprisingly vacant, the orphaned flames rising and twisting into heavy black spirals.

Expecting to find the enemy in force, all that was discovered were supplies left behind in haste. Much of it lay in haphazard piles burning on either side of the railroad, but in their hurry, the Yankees surrendered large quantities of food, clothing and personal items.

At dawn, General Kershaw had sent four companies of the 2nd South Carolina, including Kirkland's, to ascertain if the enemy was camped at Fair Oaks Station. But they had moved on—by the spirit of the fires, very recently.

Many of the Carolinians filled their haversacks with Federal rations, much of it hardtack in heavy waxpaper wrapping, and bagged extra items of clothing or replaced their shoes. Kirkland, however, again chose to go light, expecting a long day of marching ahead.

Tearing off the cover of a hardtack package, he smashed the granite-like cracker with the butt of his rifle and placed a chunk in his mouth, allowing his saliva to moisten it before chewing. He stood on the railroad tracks, keeping a safe distance from the fires in case the Yankees had hidden ordnance among the burning piles.

Staring down the perfectly straight lines heading somewhere to the east, Kirkland wondered just how far the tracks drifted.

Where will this iron road take us today?

At about 8 AM, the rest of the brigade joined those in front and the march continued. Following the roads in a generally eastwardly direction, the men moved quietly in columns of fours.

On several occasions, when there was a sniff of the enemy, they spread out into lines of battle. But each time was a false alarm, the men exhaling before weaving back into marching alignment. Kirkland and the 2nd South Carolina found themselves abreast of the railroad once again, being the left flank of the advancing brigade.

When the tracks came into sight, he was intrigued by an enormous siege cannon mounted on a platform car that, with the help of a pushing locomotive, was keeping steady pace with the regiment. It was a Brooke naval rifle, a 32-pounder, nicknamed the "Land Merrimack."

He grabbed Smith's shoulder without looking at him, but it didn't matter, as the whole regiment was walking with their heads cocked to the left and staring at this novelty of war. And then there was a violent red flash, a massive thunderclap and a torrent of black smoke as the giant recoiled violently, shelling the distant woods in front of them. After the initial surprise, Kirkland chuckled to himself, glad that the big gun was on their side.

Smith read his mind.

"I wish this, this uh, gun would follow us always."

"It wouldn't hurt."

"Reminds me of the siege guns on Morris Island, yet mobile."

"Yes, and my nerves are now better prepared."

Smith laughed.

"I'd have, uh, I'd have to agree with you there. We have come a long ways my friend. Both in distance and grit."

"I wish I could see what they're firing at."

It was getting late in the day, but still very little was seen of the enemy. Occasionally, shells were lobbed at them from Federal redoubts but the batteries seemed to retreat after every shot. Dodging these was easy enough and no one was hurt. Entering a small valley, the advance halted, the men resting in battle formation. In front was a thickly forested area that extended for at least a hundred yards.

Kirkland lay down in the declivity, watching for any stirring over the hill. Clutching his rifle with gouging thumbs, his body was rigid with a mind far from composed. While the weather was Virginia-summer warm, the sweat at his brow was induced by the unseen. The enemy was close. He could feel it.

Anticipation had burned the last remnants of saliva from his mouth and he nervously gulped at his canteen. Staring at the ominous woods, he could detect no movement other than a flickering leaf here and there, wiggled by a blind bullet.

Wait. I think I see something.

Before he could get his bearings on what it was, a form came leaping threw the underbrush, nearly falling on top of him. On the man's heels, miniés came whizzing by like overgrown mosquitos, and Kirkland recognized the fleeing man as one of their own skirmishers. He was followed by the rest of the frontliners who quickly dove to the safety of the natural trench.

Without delay, the familiar voice of his brigade commander soared, with a hurtling gusto that would have cauterized the yellow from the most trembled of hearts.

"Charge!"

Liberated from their chains, the men of Kirkland's regiment, with the 3rd South Carolina on their right, plunged into the woods ahead, screaming.

Attempting a lion's roar, he coughed after a minimal bay, his parched throat corking a suitable showing. This underwhelming squawk was contrary to his peers, who fairly shook the trees as they passed. Although the force of this utterance sent a shudder of calm through Kirkland's body, it failed to penetrate his core.

Almost immediately, the enemy's batteries lobbed shells overhead, but the tree cover was so thick, it absorbed most of their fury. Occasionally, a rifle flash could be seen ahead, yet they were lonely and the triggermen were still far off and invisible.

To his left rear, the massive discharge of the railroad cannon could still be heard. Its beefy song brought comfort to Kirkland's nervous psyche. Like the rest of his company, he ran straight through the underbrush, not bothering to side-wind around obstacles unless a sturdy tree blocked his path. As a result, at times it was an off-balance rush, but his attention was mostly drawn to hacking at branches looming and biting at his head.

As he passed a scraggly oak, a bullet cracked against its base and Kirkland knew the gap was closing. The flashes were in bunches now and the flames brighter. Still, he could not see a single soul who opposed them.

"Companyyyy… Halt! Close ranks!"

Behind the men, Colonel Kennedy was pacing, ready to retaliate.

"Men, we will fire a volley and then reload quickly. We must keep moving. When you see a flash, aim under its glow."

As the difficult terrain had impeded all attempts to keep everyone together, men were still trying to find their way into their spots and Kennedy was getting impatient.

"Come on, come on. Get into line!"

To Kirkland's right, a man jumped into formation and he did a double take, as the soldier was from a different company, the Lancaster Invincibles.

Noticing Kirkland's stare, the man just shrugged his shoulders. Kirkland knew him only as Hilton, a sergeant who had a reputation of unworldly tenacity when the long roll sounded.

"Attention company! Ready! Aim!"

Kirkland pointed his weapon at the invisible enemy, straining to see any movement.

"Fire!"

Pulling the trigger, Kirkland absorbed the kick into his shoulder. It felt good and the puff of flame at the barrel's mouth was strangely euphoric.

"Reload!"

Kirkland shoved another round down the barrel as the suffocating smoke hung under the green canopy, shuttering the light. As the last ramrods were slotted, Kennedy ripped out his sword.

"Carolina, CHARGE!"

Kirkland took one step forward but Hilton had already taken two. As Kirkland lurched forward to keep pace, Hilton doubled over, clutching his stomach. He let out an angry, almost sinister groan as he hit the ground. Continuing on, his pulse elevated, Kirkland found the dense underbrush of briars and timber extremely difficult to traverse. Trying his best to keep pace with the man on either side, he eventually gave up, and concentrated on keeping a rhythm to his march. It seemed the enemy was falling back, as the flashes in front were getting no closer. At times, he perceived the outline of a man among the sparks, but he wasn't sure. To these ghostly images, he raised his rifle and fired, unaware if his shots were eating meat.

While reloading, a bullet nearly creased his left temple. In reaction Kirkland ducked and somersaulted, crashing through a sapling, its branches smacking him hard across his face. Despite the close call, Kirkland resumed loading, placing a percussion cap on the gun's nipple. The rotten smoke began to settle between his ears, and he shook his head to regain equilibrium. By this time, the lines of battle had become unrecognizable.

Kirkland looked for an intimate face between hurling bullets at the flashing darkness and straining onward. In a small clearing ahead of him, just big enough to let a small portion of the smoke escape and allow light to rush in, Kirkland saw William Truesdel raise his gun to shoot. He started to make his way toward his friend.

Too late.

To his horror, a bullet ripped out the back of William's neck as his body kicked horizontal, lingering in the air as if thwarting gravity before tumbling to the earth.

Stunned and locked in place, Kirkland choked on the vision before running to the spot where his friend had fallen. Dropping down to one knee next to him, he fired his rifle at the nearest spark of flame. Then, grabbing William by an arm, he quickly dragged him behind the largest tree he could find.

Finally safe for the moment, Kirkland peered down at the lifeless eyes and knew his friend was gone. The bullet had left a trail through his front teeth and throat, killing him instantly. Cradling William's head in his arms and lap, he shuttered his friend's cooling brows and said a short, naked prayer. The words were barely audible, even to Kirkland, drowning in the enveloping tempest.

"Dear heavenly Father, please greet this brave friend of mine in heaven. Amen."

He kissed William on the forehead and tenderly rested the limp body on the ground. Gritting his teeth, Kirkland picked up his rifle and began reloading.

Peeking around the tree of death, he could make out the enemy now, at least a few of them, anyway, visible through the foliage. His eyes widened as he noticed two rifles leveled in his direction. Wheeling again behind the tree, Kirkland pulled together his limbs to shrink, just as a shot splintered the wood near his head.

Taking a deep breath, Kirkland tiptoed the fingers of his left hand around the Enfield's barrel. When they were in place, he gripped the weapon hard and thrust his head back against the tree.

The impact was more violent than he intended, though its cracking resonance somehow snuffed the burning in his nostrils. His fear evaporated, replaced by a simmering calm. Without peeking, Kirkland flung himself around his temporary shield, and reset his wings on a course with the enemy.

This time, there was no stumbling, no wayward movement. It was as if his feet hovered a few inches from the ground as he bowled through the suddenly capitulating thicket.

Kirkland could see the enemy was in full retreat now, and this only emboldened his legs. Glancing side to side, he looked for his company commanders, yet even the regiment's flag had been swallowed by the canopy of smoke. Men struggled in clumps but it was obvious that the lines were still jumbled.

Squinting, Kirkland could detect more and more light ahead as if daylight was thrashing to push out the premature night. As he shortened his stride to make out the changing landscape, a figure brushed past him, and Kirkland could almost feel the man's rage as he passed.

He was astonished as recognition took hold.

Hilton?!

Retracing his steps in his mind, he wondered if the remembrance of Hilton's gutshot was true. Picking up the pace to catch up with him, Kirkland surmised that it must have been a spent ball. It had to be!

As Kirkland reached the supposed soldier of charm, however, he could see that a large quantity of blood had pooled at Hilton's lower back. It was all he could do to even keep up with the wounded man, but eventually Kirkland gained Hilton's side. With a mouth as wide as a river, Kirkland cocked his head to the side, and slung his eyeballs at the miracle man's face.

Hilton's countenance was one of unworldly determination, flushed with creeping death, yet molded into an ancient, thrusting spear. His eyes were unmerciful and hostile and he did not seem concerned in the least with his fate.

The man was gone, and only a vengeful purpose remained.

Both strengthened by the sight and utterly disturbed, Kirkland at once made up his mind that he'd march with this man over glowing coals if necessary. When they finally reached the woods' end, side by side, Kirkland was nearly breathless. Yet Hilton appeared unwinded and strong. Though his face was becoming pale, his eyes and jaw retained their fierceness and hellfire scowl.

They kept moving and as they ran past the final tree cover, the Yankees were less than 150 feet away, running for their lives across an open field.

An officer stepped in front of them, his sword unsheathed and parallel to the ground. Kirkland was relieved as he was of the belief that Hilton would have kept charging until he had plunged a bayonet into a Yankee's spine and died trying, with him in tow.

The officer was swearing wild oaths, more at the situation, Kirkland surmised, than at the men who were stumbling into the clearing.

"God damn it, where is my company? Hold here, we must wait until we have a line. Any damn line. I don't care what company you're from. Wait here. We've got 'em running. We must not delay for long."

He sidestepped along the treeline, gathering up whatever troops he could find. Toward the railroad tracks, other officers were doing the same, trying to form some semblance of order. Through all of the ruckus, the railroad battery could be heard still, exploding its intimidating loads at the enemy. Men arrived almost one at a time as if walking through a thin, canvased doorway, and found whatever empty place was vacant in the waiting array.

When the lines were in order, Colonel Kennedy stepped to the front and growled for an advance.

"Charge!"

They were halfway across the field when Hilton was stuck again, blasted from his feet as if he had hustled into a wall. He was far ahead of the nearest man when hit, this time in the shoulder. Rolling to his side, he attempted to get up. Both sides of his flannel shirt were now dilating with violet, plunging toward his waist. He made it to one knee before fainting.

Having gained on the warrior with the rest of the Carolinians, Kirkland rushed to his side. Although Hilton had regained consciousness, he was mumbling incoherently.

"Can you walk?"

Thrusting his jaw with an emphatic "Yes," he attempted to stand once more, and Kirkland set down his gun to help. Twisting both hands in the cotton folds of his chest to avoid Hilton's injuries, he was about to lift when a captain screamed at them.

"Go to the rear, Hilton!"

Then he pointed at Kirkland.

"You! Keep moving."

Kirkland immediately obeyed, leaving the direly wounded man panting on his back.

When he retrieved his weapon, he noticed that both palms were covered in blood. The color was brilliant, almost glowing. Fascinated in a detached examination, he dropped his hands to his trousers, but instead of wiping the gore away, he fused it with his gun. And then he fell in again with the assault line.

The enemy had retreated to a small hill and was reforming. As Kirkland raised his gun to shoot, a shadow distracted him as he was about to pull the trigger. Somehow, Hilton was back, moving step for step with his brothers. The vision sent a fury of adrenaline bouncing through Kirkland's heart, causing his fingers to tingle.

But as he looked closer, the confidence faded to alarm.

The luster was gone from Hilton's eyes, and his mouth was agape and falling. The steadiness in his gallop was gone, and Kirkland feared he would drop from loss of blood at any moment. While Kirkland kept his eyes forward, his peripheral vision and attention was on the miracle man.

He barely noticed when a volley from the enemy exploded in his front.

To his left, the nearest man was knocked backward as if crushed by an invisible two-by-four. On the opposite side, however, Hilton stood tall as a bullet ripped through his chest.

As Kirkland watched in astonished recognition, the man's eyes glazed over and slowly, he dropped to his knees. He coughed just one time, reanimating his broken body long enough to vomit blood before collapsing into the grass.

Chapter 10

With a single, dreaded purpose Kirkland walked down a crowded and tantalizing Main Street. Unlike in past visits, his normal head swivel stalled and was rusted. This time, the oyster dealers held no fascination and the confectioners failed to inspire a sweet tooth drool. The laughter-tossing saloons likewise were ignored, as were the peddlers selling their wares. He even denied the hardware and agricultural stores a casual glance.

On this day, Kirkland's gaze fixed on no certain point—just somewhere down the street. His neck might have enjoyed the morning off, if it weren't holding up his welling head.

Though the enormous Federal army had come within six miles of the city limits, passersby he encountered floated past as if oblivious to the situation. Two portly, middle-aged women laughed as they ambled by. If they noticed his bloodstained clothes, they didn't show it. Kirkland was by no means offended, however, for he gave them little thought either.

Like oiled images on a passing train, memories of William Truesdel from his youth sped before his mind's eye. They came at once, fierce and unrelenting, and he was passive at the controls. While most of the remembrances were of pleasant and cherished times, he could not feel their warmth. As in dreams, they were devoid of color and cohesion, tumbling through a limitless void.

Eventually, Kirkland gathered enough strength to slow the blurred images until one unforgettable set of events was framed.

It was 1850 or thereabouts, on a particular balmy December day, perfect for an afternoon of outdoor games. Kirkland and his brother Billy had conjured up a round of hide-and-seek with the neighbor Truesdel, always an eager participant. It was Kirkland's turn as ambushing predator, creeping around the outbuildings and crevices of the Kirkland farm. He'd always relished the vanishing art more than the sleuth, and was usually more daring than William in his hiding, since Kirkland's father cared little if he returned with clothes doused with moisture and grime. At least the elder Kirkland didn't raise a fuss like William's mother did.

However, on this day, Kirkland found his brother in the corn crib with relative ease but William proved a more formidable challenge.

The outhouse? Vacant. In the barn among the cottonseed? Nope. How about the slaughter pen? Not there, either.

Kirkland went from building to building and leaped behind the shadow trees, but William was nowhere to be found. As the minutes crept by, slow as molasses, he was ready to call out and summon William from whatever rock haven he had crawled under.

As the words curled on his tongue, a high-pitched shriek came from the smokehouse.

Running to the building, he arrived in time to see William burst through the door, hands clawing at his throat. He ran in circles, hopping and lunging in a panic, all the while making an otherworldly choking sound that reminded Richard of the time his brother Jesse mistakenly inhaled at his first encounter with a cigar. Eyes bulging and searching for relief, William finally straightened his crazy-eight highway and made a dash for the creek. Falling to his knees at the water's edge, William dunked his head hysterically, exchanging one pain for another, as the frigid

166

waters needled into his skull. He recoiled violently and landed on the seat of his pants, stunned and breathless. By now, the Kirkland brothers were beside themselves, colliding in fits of heaving laughter. They knew just what had happened. William had shut himself in where hams and pork shoulders were being smoked with red pepper on the coals. In his quest for concealment, he had lingered too long among the spicy fumes.

★　　　★　　　★

While this was a pleasant memory, Kirkland quickly slammed the door, unwilling to traverse too far down memory lane.

The grief was slowly building inside, made worse by the task awaiting him. Intentionally, he avoided looking at the storefront windows and their reflections of him, not wanting to see his friend's crimson insides splattered on his coat. He was exhausted, having tossed and turned the previous night after burying William where he fell, but knew this task had to be done and had volunteered to do it. Despite the best opportunity in months at scoring a decent meal, he ignored his howling abdomen. This was a mission bred by a desire to seek fulfillment with the greatest of haste before the inevitable slap of mourning could find his cheek.

A sign on a building loomed ahead, in large black, stenciled letters:

THE SOUTHERN TELEGRAPH COMPANY

Approaching the door with heavy feet and a swollen heart, Kirkland took a deep breath and walked in.

An old man with brilliant white hair and shaggy side burns greeted him.

"Hello, young man. May I help you?"

"Sir, I need to send a message to Camden, South Carolina."

"Yes, of course. Here is the necessary form. Just write the name of the recipient and the message. It costs a dollar and nine cents for ten words. However, you probably want the message sent back repeating your words to ensure accuracy. This will cost half of the original message…"

The clerk looked closer at Kirkland's clothing. Noticing the bloodstains, he quickly changed course.

"I'm sorry. You need not worry about the extra charge. I assume you have an important message. My apologies, Sir. I would let all you brave defenders send messages for nothing if it was up to me. Take your time filling out the form."

Kirkland dabbed the pen into ink and took another deep breath.

Under the words, "By Telegraph from Richmond," Kirkland wrote:

To John Kirkland of Flat Rock

Father I am well

His hand began shaking and he made a ballasted fist, before continuing with the roll of the Flat Rock community dead.

William Truesdel killed. D Stover, J Sheorn, Baskin Jr also dead. L Robertson, R Love, seriously wounded. Please inform families.
RR Kirkland

Kirkland put the pen down and his legs momentarily buckled.

He handed the message to the clerk, who immediately read the message. Looking up from the paper, the clerk nodded at his customer, with eyes of pure empathy.

"No charge."

With a dry swallow, Kirkland nodded back and walked out. Normally, he would have protested vigorously at this special treatment. But a profound desire to bolt constrained his manners.

Leaving the building, he ran several blocks to the former St. Charles Hotel, where he'd left his horse, briefly on loan from his brother Dan. Now known simply as General Hospital No. 8, the cobblestone streets in front had been covered in sawdust to deaden the noise of passing vehicles.

Kirkland had wanted an unhurried walk before delivering the somber message. In his clouded vision, he hadn't noticed the hotel's transformation. Next to a sign advertising a billiards saloon underneath the building, a plain-clothed soldier leaned on a wooden crutch puffing a cigar. His left leg was missing below the knee and its hollow trouser, partly tied up, dangled awkwardly above the ground.

As Kirkland was about to jump on the horse, he noticed the amputee craning his head east as a wagon came barreling down the street in a reckless hurry.

It was filled to the brim with dead soldiers, obviously piled higher than the wagon's normal capacity. Behind the driver and his rider, were several shovels at the ready, muddied and bent from overuse.

While passing Kirkland, a body shifted and rolled off the back end of the wagon, slamming into the ground as if impatient to find rest beneath it. The rider, who'd been keeping an eye on the rotting cargo, shook the thin, black driver's shoulder, and the two dashing horses were immediately reined in. The smell was overwhelming, and a young woman on the opposite side of the street pinched her nose while hustling her two children away.

Vaulting off in disgust, the rider, whose sun-cooked face was nearly as dark as the driver's, spat a long stream of tobacco juice into the dust as he turned to retrieve the fallen body.

"God damn it," he cursed. "Come on, Levi. We ain't got all day."

The driver followed the bossman's wishes and they walked unceremoniously to the lost cargo.

"Shit," said the rider. "How many times we gonna have to do this today? They ain't payin' us enough for this. Damn it all."

Both he and his partner looked as if they'd dropped down and rolled in the mud. Each walked with a stiffness gained from hard physical labor.

It was likely the duo had been putting soldiers in the ground for several days, Kirkland surmised. Though William Truesdel had lost his promising young life to nothing more than a stalemate at the battle of Savage's

169

Station, Richmond had been successfully defended in several battles around the city and the enemy had been shoved backward.

Safe for the moment, the citizens of Richmond were now faced with overflowing hospitals and overwhelmed graveyards.

"Get his legs, hurry up," said the rider, who was about to grab the soldier by the wrists but realized he only had one.

Compensating, he picked the man up by the shoulders. As they lifted him, the soldier's head dropped and hung limp, and a crumpled kepi fell to the street.

Kirkland, his foot still in the stirrup, released himself from the horse, and stood there, watching. He wanted to flee, but his eyes refused to blink.

The two men struggled awkwardly toward their wagon. When they reached it, they heaved the soldier onto the body pile as if it were no more than a fire-destined log. Launching another bloodlike spatter into the matted cobblestone, the gopher-cheeked rider shoved at the body, compacting the hoard of flesh.

"Hurry up, damn it, I wanna be home for supper," he said, sneering at his expressionless companion, and climbed aboard the wagon.

Jumping on, the driver scooped up the reins and flicked his wrists. The horses obeyed and the wagon was gone, leaving Kirkland staring at the kepi, forsaken in the middle of the ungrateful street.

He imagined the hat's unlucky owner being tossed into an unmarked grave, perhaps in view of President Monroe's climbing labyrinth of iron in Hollywood Cemetery. In this bitter injustice, he would be lost to his family forever, the truth of his final resting place a locked door for which there was no key.

Throwing down the half-spent cigar in forceful descent, the amputee snatched the other crutch leaning against the hospital's wall and muscled for the door.

Having seen enough, Kirkland quickly gathered his horse and headed east toward Williamsburg Turnpike, to the source of the alarming inventory of death.

★   ★   ★

JULY 3

1 AM

The looks on their faces told it all. No one was spared. Walking by with their heads stiffened and pale in the bright moonlight, their minds were far from their feet. They seemed to be suffering from a peculiar stupor. An uneducated observer might diagnose exhaustion mixed with callousness, but Kirkland knew better. Lack of sleep contributed to their appearance, for sure, yet this did not explain the hollowed out sockets, as if the skin had been peeled back to make way for the skull's impatient emergence. All appeared to have aged before their time. Kirkland hoped, prayed even, that this was a trick of the light. But he wasn't convinced and wondered if his own mirror would reflect the same.

After all, none of them had ever seen such butchery of men. Blood stained their vision and the smell of it remained in their nostrils. By the vacant stares, Kirkland knew he had missed a deadly encounter with the enemy. Having returned his brother's horse, he had spent half the night searching aimlessly for his regiment, and came upon them entirely by accident.

When, in near desperation, he finally encountered the marching column, no one spoke. They just drifted slowly by, barely acknowledging Kirkland. None of this surprised or bothered him. In fact, at this moment, he preferred it. For his spirit was winded and his tongue was broken. He did not want to speak of where he had been or learn what the men had trudged over while he was absent.

More than ever, he wanted to be home in Flat Rock, far away from the deafening presence of war. This was no longer the chance of a lifetime to breathe history. It was no longer an adventure.

The skin of youthful naïveté had been painfully shed, stripped and wrenched away before a new layer could be formed beneath.

Tender and depleted of armor, Kirkland had crawled into a numbing stupor. He'd inhaled reality and was choking on it. He hoped the Federal

171

flood would recede to Washington never to return, and that a medicating sun would rise in the morning, drying the infested swamp of a ludicrous war. But he knew that Susan and a life together would have to wait for the dueling beasts of war to gorge themselves and become dormant.

Not bothering to look for his company, Kirkland took his place among the weary masses and assumed the melancholy march.

In the aftermath of the battle of Malvern Hill, the regiments of Kershaw's brigades were separated. They had marched for miles back and forth in the unforgiving darkness, the commanders searching for the missing units until all were together again.

As soon as the order to halt was given, the men dropped to ground where they stood. Kirkland, his mind and body failing, collapsed in mid-flight hibernation, snoring in a blackened hole.

The next morning, he awoke to roll call not knowing where he was or how long he had been slumbering. As he staggered into line, he regretted being summoned to a most painful routine. It was a bitter and jarring awakening. Many names, too many, were followed by a daggered silence. Each familiar surname called by the first sergeant brought remembrances of words exchanged and times shared, which at the time of occurrence seemed trivial. Yet a brotherly face, now muted for eternity, brought these simple conversations into a different library altogether.

Kirkland knew them all. How much or how little didn't matter. Too many of the boys had not escaped the clutch of the reaper—the brigade had suffered 300 casualties at Savage's Station and Malvern Hill. While the fortunate ones may yet recover and were in some Richmond hospital or local home, all who were absent seemed lost forever.

And in that moment of questioning, Kirkland made a decision. He would transfer to the Flat Rock Guards. His sanity demanded it. Several of his beloved friends were already lying in shallow graves and he'd missed the opportunity to serve at their shoulders. To live or to die, he wanted fate to carry him to whatever end, touching elbows with his country brethren. He would settle for no other alternative.

"Jonathan Davis."

The name snapped Kirkland out of his resolute mindset. His face grew tense and he held an anguished breath.

When Smith answered the call, he exhaled in deep relief.

Smith, thank God you're Okay.

Although many in his current company had earned Kirkland's admiration and respect, Smith had become a close friend and confidante. In the early weeks of the war, it was Smith who had singed away the rough edges of loneliness and isolation.

He hoped his friend would understand his decision.

As roll call finally, mercifully, ended, Kirkland stood in place while his fellow soldiers dispersed into the morning light. Holding on to several names, he whispered them in reverence and said prayers for both the dead and wounded. While far from adequate, this, along with dreamless sleep comforted him a bit, gave him a cursory level of internal peace. In this shallow rebirth, he allowed each name to bounce around his skull before releasing it to the wind.

The ceremony complete, he bee-lined to Smith and found him in his customary position.

★   ★   ★

Detaching the handle of his self-made frying pan from the barrel of his musket, Smith placed it on the small fire he had prepared and added some bacon grease squeezed from a heavily saturated poke sack.

Reaching into his haversack, he pulled out a small bag of cornmeal. Searching again, he failed to produce what he was looking for. Opening the bag wider, he gave the empty bottom a once-over before realizing this was to be expected.

Looking up, he spotted his messmate, who was waiting patiently for the common, futile hunt to end.

"Hey, Kirkland, can it be that you're one of the wise who didn't eat the three days rations in one gorging?"

"I believe I have some left," said Kirkland, a small, knowing grin on his face.

Like many prior to marching orders, Smith was always gulping days of rations in one sitting. In the past, Kirkland had figured the blacksmith had more mass to feed, so he gladly shared whatever meager portions he had saved. That belly from '61 was now long gone, but his appetite to regain it had not receded. And as Kirkland had learned on Morris Island, Smith's culinary talents could make a dull meal taste a few notches sweeter.

Over the previous few days, however, his friend had been allotted precious little time to wander from the march to forage for enticing victuals. Reaching into his haversack, Kirkland pulled out roughly a third of his three quarters of a pound of salt pork ration, which for once had been distributed to the troops in the full amount. It was bluish, with a few hairs and a patch of skin attached, and smelled terrible, but it was protein.

Handing Smith the meat, he sat down by the fire to watch the chef work his magic. Knowing that with the transfer of companies, he might be forced to cook more, he followed his friend's preparations more intently than normal.

All around, soldiers were busy preparing breakfast. Kirkland tried in vain not to notice that many of the messes were depleted of drooling men.

Smith first soaked the pork in a tin cup filled with water. Eying the liquid carefully after a short period of time, and apparently satisfied that at least some of the salt content had been released, he added the meat to the frying pan. The sizzle alone made Kirkland's stomach twist in hunger and he placed a hand over it to hide its beckoning call.

It was a fruitless gesture.

"Don't worry," Smith said with a giggle. "I'll have this cush up in a jiffy."

Dumping out the salt water, Smith handed him the tin cup.

"Why don't you, uh, fetch me some more water from the stream."

"Of course."

Sore from both riding and marching long miles, he stretched his back and kicked out his legs as he ambled to the water source. It was a comfortable walk. The July heat had yet to rear its smothering presence. An absence of wind, though insignificant in the morn, could prove a detriment as the sun climbed. Kirkland sent a wordless plea for its later company.

More pressing on his mind, however, was a proper way to divulge his intentions to Smith that he was going to leave him.

Am I being silly?

After all, it was not as if he was moving to New York or grasping for the Yankee flag. He was not even leaving the regiment. Smith would only be a campfire or two away on most nights. While the words and their gravity swirled around in his mind, he caught himself gesturing with his hands as if he were conversing silently with a ghost. Shaking his head and acknowledging how foolish he must look to a spectator, he noticed a hulking man shuffling toward him along the path.

Ratcliff. Great. The perfect observer.

Shifting to a more confident gait, Kirkland continued, wondering what kind of rebuke or searing taunt would arise from the beast's lips. As Ratcliff approached, he tensed and waited for the bully to roar.

"Good morning," said Kirkland, casually, minus any threads of history.

But Ratcliff passed without even a glance in Kirkland's direction.

Perhaps I have become the ghost.

While strange, especially for Ratcliff, and entirely rude, the silent treatment beat the alternative and Kirkland arrived at the stream without lingering malice.

Crouching down to dip his canteen into the shallow water, he made sure to navigate the container into a scum-free pool. Images of William and a familiar creek surfaced again, and he did his best to wipe the dried blood from his uniform.

But he was unwilling at this moment to traverse down memory lane, and quickly tossed aside all that brought thorns to his gut. Searching his mind for an obstacle, Kirkland realized an unread letter remained in his pocket. He had picked it up on the battlefield, and it was forgotten until now. Pulling the envelope out, he sat down. On the upper left of the envelope was a star and shield, with the words "The Union For Ever" written within the star. It was addressed to:

Mrs. Bjorn Andersen
Dodge Co.
Wasioja, Minnesota

He unfolded the letter and began to read.

Dear sister,

I received your letter on the 28th instant, and I'm glad to hear that you are well. Please have faith that mother will recover from the fever. From what I've witnessed, God has taken his share and filled his quota for scores. I was bothered by the flux for a spell but feeling a heap better now. The health of my company is not very good and we've had some long marches in the heat that will try a man's soul. I'm glad that Sven is doing well in school. I always knew he would turn out to be the brightest of us all. Tell him I am proud of his efforts but that he needs to stay the course and not get lazy.

Please let me know how the crops are doing. When I rushed off to war, I was of the belief that farming was a noble but boresome life and that playing soldier would be exciting. I was grossly mistaken. There is nothing glorious about being a soldier. However, I swore to do my duty and I will do so till death if necessary. I do not know how long this war will last but I suspect it will go on a good while longer. My only desire is a quick end to this war. If we can push through to Richmond, the Rebs will have no choice but to wave the white flag. Then I can return home and live the good life, beneath the pines.

I must keep this short as we're about to move again. Please write soon as each letter is devoured by a homesick soldier.

Nothing else is new at present. Give my kindest regards to ma and pa and hug my sisters for me.

Your brother until death,

Jacob Erikson

Carefully shoving the letter back into its carriage, Kirkland stroked the ends of his mustache with his thumb and forefinger, and watched a large crow across the stream hop from limb to limb as if searching for the perfect roost.

"Kirkland. How are you, friend?"

Wheeling, Kirkland found a man he knew only as Riddle staring down at him with a tail-wagging grin on his face.

"Pardon my interrupting your private affairs, but I have something to show you, since we are now crossing paths on this fine Virginia day."

A little befuddled by Riddle's transformation, as he had seen him the previous night under the same peculiar funk that had overtaken much of the regiment, Kirkland was more than curious about his remedy.

"Here, take a gander," said Riddle, handing Kirkland a small book. It was a Bible. Upon opening the volume, he discovered a minié ball buried in its pages. Shuffling through it, he was astonished at just how narrowly Riddle had eluded severe injury or worse. The bullet had stopped but a few pages from the conclusion of Revelations.

"Luck was on your side," said Kirkland, handing the Bible back to its owner.

"Luck, hell. It was Jesus who stopped that bullet."

Squinting, Kirkland scratched his head and met Riddle's grinning eyes. This was no small enigma as Riddle was not known to be a pious man. In fact, you could say that he was much closer to digging for the devil. With his penchant for boozing, gambling away his wages and visiting ladies of ill repute at every opportunity, he was a soldier of very questionable morality. Whatever the reason for Riddle's miraculous slip from death, Kirkland humored him and his divine intervention.

"Forgive me. God must have a special plan for you."

This seemed to please Riddle, who folded his arms and tilted his head, all the while maintaining a toothy exuberance.

"Of course, as I'm sure yer aware, I've never had ears for preaching. But these Bibles do have power."

He pointed to the wounded copy.

"This proves my sins have been forgiven. Hallelujah! From this point forward, I will spread the word that the Good Book can be your shield. I even secured a second Bible from a poker game this very morn and I will carry them at each breast when the long roll sounds."

Kirkland opened his mouth but hesitated.

"Well, Kirkland, good day to you," said Riddle, jogging off toward camp, before Kirkland could utter a response.

★   ★   ★

He shoved a fork into the thick gravy and ate in silence. Nothing but the direct and honest approach would suffice.

"Something on your mind, Kirkland?" asked Smith.

Before answering, Kirkland took another bite, swallowed slowly, and looked Smith directly in the eyes.

"Yes, well... I've decided to transfer to the Flat Rock Guards."

Clenching his teeth, and desperately holding his gaze from falling wayward, he waited for a response.

"Of course you are. It's about time."

"What? You don't mind."

"Hell, no. I'm surprised you didn't do it earlier."

"You are? I..."

Smith laughed heartily.

"Don't worry about me. I'll be fine. You belong with your kinsmen. If I get lonely, I know where to find you."

Kirkland was embarrassed. Always amazed at Smith's never relenting nucleus of cheerfulness with a cup filled to the brim, he should have known that he needed Smith much more than Smith needed him.

178

"You've been a good friend," said Kirkland, unsure how to express the magnitude of his feelings. "When all this is over, I look forward to paying you a visit at your shop in Camden."

"You'll see me a good deal before that. The regiment isn't as, uh, big, big as it used to be."

He paused briefly.

"Did you, did you hear we lost Tom Brownfield?"

"No," said Kirkland soberly.

"I'm not sure if he is with the beyond yet, but I saw him get cut down. And it looked mortal."

"Let's hope you're wrong."

Smith nodded, but his face was not one of conviction.

"It was both an ugly and inspiring sight. He was hit by a ball in the head, but he refused to leave the field, and he stayed with us until the order to retreat was given."

Thomas Sumter Brownfield was considered the regiment's amulet, a larger than life offspring from a legendary family, although this was a most unfair burden to carry. However, when your grandfather is arguably the most revered hero in South Carolina, it's a legacy that can't be ignored. Thomas Sumter, nicknamed "the Carolina Gamecock" for his guerrilla-style tenacity in fighting the British, no matter how outnumbered he was, was the last surviving general of the Revolution before he passed in 1832.

"What exactly happened on, uh, I hear it was called Malvern Hill?"

"The enemy held the high ground, with considerable artillery and help from gunboats on the James. By God's fortune, we were not at the front for that was certain death. But we kept charging that hill, that damn hill, until better heads prevailed. So many good boys were lost."

An awkward silence followed, and Kirkland was overwhelmed with regret for not being there, at his post.

"Enough of this sentimental speak. Eat up, skinny boy. You're going to need it."

★   ★   ★

JULY 9, 1862

Kirkland took one gander at the lazy, enticing water and leaped in.

Immediately, the cool water of the Chickahominy swallowed him, leaving him feeling better than he had in weeks. Resurfacing with a galvanized spirit, the water carried away days of lingering stress and piles of mental rubble. He put his fingers through his still matted hair and dunked multiple times in slow vanishings.

"Come on in Joe, Alex."

Needing no further invitation, Joe made a running jump from the banks into the healing liquid.

Alex, however, tiptoed his way in. Others were whooshing by him and eagerly joining the growing number of bathers. They treaded water against the gentle current, watching Alex impatiently.

"Get your intellectual ass in here," said Joe.

Thus motivated, "the professor" finally dove in.

For the next half hour, they breathed in the peaceful calm of the Virginia river. Silently, Kirkland tossed his head back, leaving his ears exposed above the water to catch the songbirds uttering their joyful ballads. Treading, he took in somersaults of passing clouds as golden rays dashed through their gaps.

These balms of pleasant warmth were glazed across the soldiers' faces, giving birth to the hypnotic textures of serenity that only a summer swim can produce.

"Kirkland."

Hearing his name thrown with formal edges was a rude punch against his revival. A man with a face of over-exuberant importance was standing on the shore, staring down at him.

"Yes, corporal."

"Captain Cunningham wants to see you. Now."

★　　　★　　　★

He saluted his captain, a little uneasy, not having the faintest idea what Cunningham had requested him for.

"You wanted to see me, Sir?"

"Yes, Kirkland. Let's take a walk."

"Certainly, Sir."

Putting his hands behind his back, the captain led the way. A graduate of South Carolina College, the twenty-seven-year old Joseph P. Cunningham came from one of the wealthiest families in the state. Of course, this mattered little in war, but he had proved to be a capable officer who was liked by his men.

"I'm sorry to take you away from your swimming hole."

Kirkland was taken aback by the apology, which served to bate him with increased curiosity.

"That's quite all right, Sir."

Noticing that the captain was sizing him up, he tried to walk as erect and soldierly as possible.

"I'll get straight to the point. I know you are new to the company, but most of the men are well acquainted with you."

"Yes, I grew up with many of them. Very good men."

"It appears that they hold you in high regard as well."

"That may be true, Sir, but I'm of no better quality than the lot."

Avoiding a launch to conclusions, Kirkland tried to feel where the captain was going with his veiled manners. But he was coming up empty.

"I've also spoken with your field officers in the Camden Volunteers. They say you are a model soldier. Brave in battle, and principled."

Moderately embarrassed yet suppressing a rumble of pride, he attempted to display an oaken core.

"The fact is, Kirkland, the men look up to you. Because of this, I'm promoting you to first sergeant."

The captain stopped abruptly and scouted Kirkland to gauge his response. Bewildered and speechless, his balance struck down, Kirkland wore a countenance of shock.

"Thank you, Sir, but I'm… I'm not sure I'm deserving."

"Listen," said Cunningham, firm but not overbearing. "We've lost several capable officers of late. The need for quality replacements is of the highest importance. You are now a veteran soldier and I assume you're well-versed in Hardee's tactics?"

"Yes, Sir."

"Good. Columbia will soon be sending us several new recruits. I will need your help to get them up to snuff. Can I count on you?"

He held out his hand, which Kirkland took.

"Yes, Sir. Whatever I can do to help, Sir."

"Excellent. I will get you the insignias appropriate with your rank when they become available."

They saluted each other, and Cunningham left him standing there, hesitant and overwhelmed.

Sergeant Kirkland.

1st Sergeant Kirkland.

He was flabbergasted at the promotion and harbored no beliefs that he had performed any better than the average soldier. If this was the pervading impression, he felt it was an illusion. He had learned that bravery was a bullshit word. At times, he had been as terrified as the next man.

Once a person passed through the hellish anticipation of battle, however, instincts took over and fear was relegated to trouser pockets until the next prelude to a fight. Of course, not all men reacted to being shot at the same way and he had seen a wide spectrum of reactions. But in his experience, soldiers with elongated panics were in a thimbleful minority.

Would the men accept such a leap-frog advancement?

It was not a position for the weak-willed. The first sergeant was in charge of roll call and keeping the company roster. Like a foreman, he must assign camp duties and supervise the non-commissioned officers, and has the authority to confine men to the guardhouse and arrest those who fail to do their duty.

I don't even have a corporal's experience!

182

With a meditative gait, Kirkland strolled through camp in an effort to clear his throbbing head, taking care to inhabit the periphery. He was in no mood to join in any reveries or soldier play but resigned himself to being an acute observer. Many were playing cards, their laughter bouncing off one another in contagious ivories of joy. Others seemed unaware of the swirling din of camp life among them as they sat beneath a writing tree, pencil in hand, scribbling furiously about their latest adventures and no doubt inquiring about loved ones at home.

Kirkland walked for several hours, greeting men when they acknowledged him, but he politely declined all requests to include him in their casual affairs. When the initial invitations sprouted to playful demands, he excused himself to the river and waited for the sun to relinquish the day. The water was still flowing and the moon made a triumphant return. Concentrating on these simple facts, he relaxed. The world had stayed true to its rotations, despite the upheaval. A giggle arose from a vision down the pike, nasty but delightful. He now had the power to order his friends around.

Private Duncan. Private Morrison. Go dig a latrine.

Chapter 11

A covered ambulance rumbled by, its damaged inhabitants groaning in horrid unison with each axle squeak. From the cracks in the undercarriage, a staccato of ruby drizzle fell in jagged rows as if sown by a mad gardener.

This furrow of blood preceded the walking wounded, and like a ghoulish parade-head, escorted the soldiers away from another deadly encounter with the enemy. Heads bandaged, arms in slings, or troubled with makeshift crutches, the men hobbled along at the best of their limited ability.

Despite their obvious pained expressions and grimaced footwork, Kirkland noticed a quiet dignity in their struggles. They did not appear as defeated men, with hollowed eyes and drooping, bruised shoulders. Though unmistakably trialed and exhausted, their faces carried an aura of bullish pride.

Many of the South Carolinians asked for news from the front, for positive information that Kirkland was confident he already knew. Somewhere in front of them, the Confederates had won a major victory, and Kirkland was sure of it.

It took little prodding for the walking masses to share the glorious exploits of the Battle of Second Manassas.

"We whipped 'em," said a tattered and ransacked fighter, walking with a limp as sizable as his graying beard. "That bastard Pope got what was comin' to him. The Yanks is on the run."

The news brought cheers up and down the marching lines. All of them were well aware of Union Major General John Pope's boasting in the papers. Although he had achieved some success fighting on the Western front, he had taken command of the newly formed Army of Virginia with bombastic and conceited pronouncements, confident that he could march to Richmond with ease.

"What unit you with?" came a shout from somewhere behind Kirkland.

"4th Alabama," said the injured man, proudly.

"Take care of yourself, friend."

With renewed vigor, the men of Kershaw's Brigade marched ever closer to the battle's aftermath.

Having marched 120 miles in six days, with very little rest, Kirkland and his brothers in arms had received trickles of reports from the odd passersby.

However, these supposed first-hand accounts were contradictory and unreliable. As a result, the Carolinians were unsure of which extreme to pocket. While still unconfirmed, it was swiftly becoming evident that Robert E Lee and Stonewall Jackson had embarrassed another Yankee commander. This made two battles of Manassas and two landslide Confederate victories. Although certainly not dejected that he missed the second installment, Kirkland would have relished witnessing the Yankees in another panicked retreat.

As he neared the battlefield, however, he wished the 2nd South Carolina had circumvented the area altogether. The awful smell struck the marching troops like an invisible hammer, well before the culprits were in long-range view. It was as if the lid to a box of rotten beef had been thrust open directly beneath their noses.

Kirkland's gut reaction was to turn and head in the other direction, not wanting to see the inevitable horrors that waited ahead. Rounding a corner, onto a portion of a collision field, the scene was even worse than expected.

Rapidly deteriorating corpses lay where they had fallen, unburied and blackened by the merciless sun. Stripped of their layers of clothing, the enemy's dead resembled bloated, featureless masses of burn victims. To Kirkland, they didn't even appear to be human, only globs of gelatinous flesh. Where the soldiers had fallen on steep inclines, the heads had separated from their decomposing bodies and rolled away. Others had been savagely run over by teamsters' wagons like roadkill, with no one bothering to remove the dead from the road.

The wind picked up, showering the wide-eyed troops with the revolting odors, leaving nearly every man horribly nauseated. Without orders, the Carolinians summoned the double quick, pinching their noses and bolting from the place of lingering death. They kept on running until the air was at least tolerable once again, where their stomachs could relax into their empty but amicable state.

Joe looked at Kirkland and couldn't help let a giggle escape, as his friend's nose was a vivid cherry from his attempt to strangle the abusive fumes.

Kirkland, however, was far removed from a joking manner and barely even noticed Joe staring at him. Taking the hint, Joe remained quiet. Eyeing Alex, Joe could sense his intellect busy at work. His forehead was creased in disgust and his jaw was set with perplexes.

"Snap out of it you two," Joe erupted. Slightly embarrassed, he lowered his voice a notch. "Lee has shown us the way to victory. We must follow."

"Yes," Alex and Kirkland answered in succession, each with passive tones.

But they were staring firm at Ratcliff and Hux, who were laughing heartily. Ratliff closed his eyes and sniffed a long trail from his chest to the sky. He then exhaled in hedonistic thrill as if the choicest ham had been brought before his palate.

186

★   ★   ★

SEPTEMBER 6, 1862

WHITE'S FORD ON THE POTOMAC RIVER

Kirkland stood on the Virginia shore, on the precipice of invading the North. Pausing momentarily to take in the grand sight of hundreds trudging through the water of the famed Potomac, sounds of reverberating joy came up from the water. Slowly at first it came, building as if from a wind-spun fire, tree to tree. In a moment, fifty thousand diaphragms were tapped to their essence, and from this source of collective power, the words of "Maryland, My Maryland," began to thunder from inspired tongues.

The bands kicked in with accompaniment, and before long, the entire Confederate army was proclaiming in melody that the South was here. For beyond the words exuding from pitch perfect to the barking flat, was an optimism that only Marse Robert Lee and a string of victories could provide. Leaving the supply lines of Virginia was not a popular decision. Mixed feelings and even words of opposition were prevalent. This included shouting whispers that many would halt defiantly on the Dominion's shore and refuse to cross into enemy territory.

Kirkland, too, was vacillating in his support of the brash move to take the fight northward. This would be invasion, after all, one of the major reasons for so much animosity toward the Yankee government when they had the gall to try to reinforce Charleston or move on Richmond. Always one to loathe hypocrisy, he struggled internally with the contradiction.

However, when the threshold was breached, and it became apparent that nearly all of the men would cast their lot with Lee, Kirkland found himself swept away. The song became more than just a marching chant. It was a fever that spread from tongue to tongue, a molding of purpose and an affirmation that they were of one mind. It was ammunition of the veins, stored in the heart for later use when the next great battle pounded at their chests. Now, more than ever, the path narrowed to a conclusion of resounding victory and the birth of a new nation—or sudden death.

The men knew they were making history, and were poised to shake the gigantic shoreline trees with bold declarations of a new revolution. Kirkland could feel this determination cradle him, and he felt its pride. Singing became not just the right thing to do but a calling.

Avenge the patriotic gore
That flecked the streets of Baltimore,
And be the battle queen of yore,

Maryland! My Maryland!

Kirkland hoped their voices would carry all the way to Washington, penetrate the White House walls, and induce a peaceful solution. Somehow, he hoped, the invasion would scare the Federals into thinking twice about continuing the war. He knew better, however. More blood, much more blood, would have to be spilled before peace would reign.

As he stripped and entered the water, Kirkland became sorry he had removed his shoes, as the sharp rocks tore into his feet with every step. He was glad to reach the sand bar island in the middle, where he promptly put his shoes back on for the second immersion before reaching the Maryland shore. With renewed comfort, and his rich, if flawed, baritone voice still carrying strong above the shallow waters, Kirkland reached the other side. He would follow Lee, trusting in his wisdom, with his beloved friends in arms even if the Potomac was his River Styx.

★   ★   ★

SEPTEMBER 7
NEAR FREDERICK, MD

As Kirkland walked, the discomfort, at first, was gradual. His stomach awoke with a low rumble, and began to twist and constrict.

It arose like a salty tide into his chest, until everything below his neck seemed to tremble. The sudden onslaught knocked his step out of rhythm

188

and he clenched his lower cheeks in fearful anticipation. Perspiring as if his entire body was aflame, Kirkland alternated between shuffled steps with bent knees and a falsified, back-arching canter. He closed his eyes and prayed that the feeling would just go away, and that his bowels would smother the impatient gallopers.

Now beginning to feel self-conscious, his pained attempts at normalcy only made him look more ridiculous. Alex shot him a concerned eye, while Joe seemed to be enjoying his friend's distress. Joe said nothing, but his lips tremored, waiting.

Kirkland's walk became even more awkward. His arms struck out in pained angles and he nearly lost the grip of his rifle. A high-pitched squeak, audible but elfin, escaped from his behind, and his eyes tripled in size, fearing the infant's mother. In near panic, Kirkland leaped from the line and sprinted, one hand flailing wildly and the other on his backside as if it had the power to halt the coming storm.

Running behind a stand of Loblolly pines, he looked for the closest downed log. Zigzagging left and then right, his body contorting and jerking, he finally spotted prostrate timber. Launching himself toward the woodland privy like a cougar with his tail on fire, he skidded to a stop. Hopping from foot to foot, he ripped his lower clothing to his knees and crouched.

As his bowels emptied, Kirkland felt a most profound relief. Panting like a wild dog, he closed his eyes and waited for the prisonbreak to complete. The accompanying stench made him wince and hold his breath, and he wondered what mouthful had made a mockery of his insides.

Probably the green corn.

Whatever the culprit, it mattered little now, as he had little to say about what went in one end and out the other. Rations had been tight to the extreme, and living off the land was an unfortunate necessity.

As Kirkland caught his breath and felt the plug in his ass had reasserted itself, he gradually stood up.

The beast has passed. All right then.

He took one step, slowly, and then another, without any dire stomach cramps, then proceeded to catch up to his place in the march. As he found it after a short jog, he maneuvered into line with as much silent grace as possible.

Joe waited for fifty yards or so, before pouncing into a racket of laughter and finger pointing.

"I didn't know you could run so fast," he finally stuttered, between fits. "Of course, the runs can press a man."

Even Alex couldn't contain himself, and he burst through his normal steadiness, giggling like Kirkland had never heard him before. Kirkland said nothing, and just shook his head, this time his top cheeks in crimson distress. But after seeing his two buddies in unrepentant stitches, the absurdity of it all swallowed his mortification.

And he laughed carefree for all of a minute, before a gas fire was stoked below once again. This time the utterance from below was no pixie horn, and a tuba-fart escaped before Kirkland could soften the blast. It was thunderous enough for the whole company to hear, and rousing cheers carried down the line before impacting into fits of crowded laughter.

Kirkland didn't waste another step before beelining ninety degrees into the wooded privy once again.

"Oops. Another round of the two-step," Joe offered, between spasms of laughter, watching Kirkland leap like a deer into the foliage.

"Some fallen tree is about to have a very bad day."

★   ★   ★

SEPTEMBER 11, 1862
BURKITTSVILLE, MD

The town's Main Street seemed to rise in ascent from the center of an enormous cornfield, all the while being dwarfed by the hills behind. Kirkland half expected to see stalks pushing through the roof tops and church steeples.

In the first visible window, an old woman thrust open the shutters and glared at the passing soldiers. A long, crooked nose thrust itself from a mass of swarming wrinkles. Her eyes were but creases waiting for God's closure, yet she held her frosty-white head in defiance, looking down over that beast of a nose. She said nothing, content to be seen and not heard. Others though, younger and bolder, took her stance and unleashed its restraints, with no mercy.

They were all young women, four in all, unrestrained by marriage or fathers off in the fields, and they came out of their humble abodes to glare at the Carolinians.

"Traitors, God will have judgment upon you."

"Turn around and go back where you came from."

"Death awaits you over the pass, you creatures of filth."

Kirkland was both taken aback and curious, in both extremes. Joe, however, while taking the medicine without retort, could not help but let a giggle escape his quivering lips. While he tried hard to stifle it, the women were too close not to hear, and it only served to stoke the vilifying breaths.

Two of the most vocal walked right up to where Joe was fighting his face, and strutted parallel to him, seething and volatile.

By now, however, the men were used to such opposition. At first it had surprised them, as it was thought that Marylanders were sympathetic to the Southern cause, and even Lee hoped to recruit large numbers as they passed through the border state. In this pursuit they had been vastly disappointed. While there were a token few willing to donate much needed food and supplies, they had been outnumbered by indifference and outright loathing. The supporters would venture from their front doors, while those true to the Union would keep their shutters latched and curtains drawn. At least until now. This was the first outright tongue-lashing at the hands of a Marylander.

And Joe couldn't help but find humor among the hornets. He even latched a hand to his face to try to hide his snorting, but it was no use. The women were ready to pounce on any utterance.

191

Walking alongside the column, their eyebrows flexed downward and their lips streaked of menace.

The apparent leader of the feminine mob, with curly red locks, and pretty in a simple way, Kirkland thought, grew closer in her wild paces. She was wearing a lubricated apron as if she had been disturbed from churning butter.

Throwing up her hands as if ready to strangle one of the passing soldiers, she unleashed a verbal tirade that chafed Kirkland's ears.

"You are devils, I say, Satan's messengers. You will find no quarter here except in the cold cemetery. And we will mourn your passing by dancing on your graves. Be gone and leave here, filth."

Kirkland looked at Joe, who initially looked surprised. But then his face contorted, cheeks bubbling, holding his breath in mock silence as if ready to burst.

He waited, and waited, and Kirkland knew how painful it was for Joe to keep his tongue behind bars. To his credit, however, Joe waited until they reached the edge of town before he spoke again.

Blowing out his held air as if near suffocation, Joe took a few exaggerated breaths and grinned.

"For a Yankee, she was cut from a handsome cloth," he finally allowed. "If we had more time here, I believe I could convert her to our cause."

"If you were Shakespeare himself," Alex huffed, "you would fail to breach that woman's outer shell."

"You have no faith," said Joe, faking incredulous. "I believe she winked at me, at the conclusion of her oaths."

"No, you were mistaken for an invitation to the town's noose. Don't let the brigade keep you, if you would like to stay awhile."

"Naw," drawled Joe. "I've never been too fond of redheads."

As they moved on to the center of the rancorous town, they passed two fine churches, side by side. The first, taller house of worship was a Lutheran structure, with rosy bricks and an octagonal belfry. It had an oven-fresh appearance as if the cornerstone had been laid the day before.

192

Gleaming with a whitewashed façad, Ionic, fluted entrance pillars and pointed Gothic windows, the German Reformed church was much older, though no less appealing.

Both were welcome visuals, devoid of fertile scowls and threats, and as the men reached the end of the buildings, they were pleased to have the town behind them.

Just as the slope to South Mountain began to punch at their calves and they were fated to leave the valley behind, a simple farmhouse materialized on their left. It appeared ancient and in need of young hands. Snarls of paint curled and withered from its façade, tired of its grip and standing sentinel to seasons of contrasting abuse. The foundation dipped slightly to the east, as if slowly submerging. Despite the antiquated exterior, however, the embroidered, color-beamed curtains, parted at the four-frontal windows, spoke of a grandmother's light.

Flower pots, dashed with Blue Flag Iris, hung between two worn rocking chairs on the weathered porch. The grounds around the house also held roses, whose impeccable forms were no doubt a combination of princely sire and generations of nurturing. The corn behind was tall and strong, planted by a master, with decades of trial and mastery.

As Kirkland passed the house, enamored with its charm, an elderly man stepped from behind a dense crab apple tree. He seemed as old as the house, with silver locks struggling for freedom beneath a top hat and farmer's dirt accumulated proudly on his high-waisted pantaloons and suspenders.

Moving slowly, the elder squinted at the parade. His head moved from left to right and then his chin dropped at the passing feet kicking up the dust. Before long, he appeared to be slowly falling, teetering painfully, dropping to the seat of his pants.

Grimacing, the old man reached the ground, pulling his knees to his chest in obvious pain. He labored for a few moments in his hard-fought destination, resting, and then proceeded to untie and remove his shoes. Continuing with his downward gaze, the man searched until he found his match. Pointing a boney finger at the object of his hunt, he called to a soldier with naked feet.

The chosen one was only a few paces in front of Kirkland, and he heard the conversation in its entirety.

"Young man, take these shoes. You will need them in the pass ahead."

The soldier stood over him, unsure, and looked around him for either rebuke or encouragement from his fellow soldiers. Finding none for each verdict, he still hesitated.

"Sir, I cannot accept your offer."

"Nonsense," said the old man, dismissing his objections with stout arms that were twice or even triple as youthful as the rest of him. "My son is a cordwainer. I can get a new pair lickety split."

Still hesitant, but eyeing the shoes as if they were gold, the Carolinian acquiesced. Dropping next to the old man, he pulled on the well-cared for brogans, and slipped them on.

"Thank you, Sir. Please accept this…"

"No," the man waved, obviously offended at the suggestion of pay. "Take these and do your duty."

The soldier had no choice but to tip his hat and move on, but he lingered for a moment in silent admiration.

★　　★　　★

SEPTEMBER 12, 1862
SOUTH MOUNTAIN, MARYLAND

Breathing heavily, Kirkland paused and looked up to see a Peregrine falcon riding the mountain winds. No bigger than a crow, but with a wingspan of several feet, the graceful creature circled overhead, seemingly oblivious to the intrusion of the climbing army.

Suddenly, the falcon lurched downward at an incredible speed, disappearing behind the stunted, witnessing trees.

Kirkland pondered what prey had twitched and called down the hunter. He also wondered if the falcon was successful in its dinner flight and more, anything to keep his mind off bodily aches and the climb ahead. The alleviation was short-lived and brought forth a divergent pain. Rabbit meat never manifested a more enticing fancy. Even a morsel of squirrel would be a meal catered by a haloed chef. In the last three days, Kirkland had eaten little more than a few apples and a handful of turnips foraged along the march. At least his diarrhea was left behind in the valley below.

Since dawn, the brigade had been scaling Elk Ridge in an attempt to dislodge the enemy perched on Maryland Heights, which overlooked the key Union garrison and town at Harpers Ferry.

They, along with Barksdale's Brigade of Mississippians, were but one wing of General Lee's plan to surround the town and force its surrender. While Kirkland's entourage had the shortest route to travel, it was also the most difficult terrain and vital for securing Lee's objective.

Up the unforgiving slope of South Mountain, the Carolinians and Mississippians struggled to maintain their footing. The path was so treacherous that all horses had to be left behind. They would have no supplies, and even worse, no artillery to support them.

At times, the trail disappeared completely into a maze of boulders and dense foliage that had forced their will in little colonies between the rocks.

"I didn't recall signing up for mountain climbing," said Joe with a laugh, maneuvering over a large outcropping of stone.

"I don't suppose you ever thought on being in Maryland, either," Alex retorted.

"No, I suppose you're right."

Kirkland grabbed a thin root protruding from the rocks and attempted to pull himself up. Nearly over the obstacle, the root snapped and he landed with a skidding thud.

"Rich, you okay?" Joe cried, scrambling over to his wincing friend.

His friends helped him to his feet.

Kirkland's pant leg was split open at the knee, revealing a smarting but slight wound.

He examined his leg, probing another opening in his quickly deteriorating marching wear.

"It's just a scratch. Nothin' to make a fuss about."

"This trail might kill us before the Yankees have a chance," said Joe, shaking his head.

"Let's hope neither gets its fill."

"I aim to be in Harpers Ferry by morning. There, I will help myself to their stores and prevalent grub."

"While I enjoy your optimism, please refrain from any mention of food. I beg you."

"I can rightly imagine all of the wondrous victuals they must have at their disposal. And I aim to dispose of it, right down my gullet."

"Joe…"

"Tender hams and chicken thighs, fresh bread with apple butter…"

"You are incorrigible," said Alex. "Do you wake up in the morning with the intent of unleashing misery?"

"Someone has to keep ya'll motivated."

"Us or the enemy?" said Kirkland.

"Oh, my friends, save your wrath for the blue bellies up yonder."

"That's SEARGANT Kirkland, to you," said Kirkland, nudging Joe forward with the butt of his rifle. He pointed to the three chevrons pointed down with a parallel diamond, indicative of his new rank, recently added to this sleeves.

"See," said Joe, turning to Alex playfully, "I told you the promotion would bring on airs."

"Someone has to watch your back sides, as painful as that vision is."

Joe looked down over his shoulder, knowing full well that the stitching on the seat of his pants had seen better days.

"Just more room for the wind to flow."

The three shared a good laugh, though it was filtered through hollow insides. To the ignorant observer, it would have appeared less than genuine.

"You are, by far, the most vulgar man in the Confederacy," said Alex.

"Did you hear an oath pass from my lips?"

"No, but I swear I heard it from below."

196

Joe looked over his shoulder again.

"Naw, you need food to make it speak."

And at this punctuation, they laughed, momentarily weightless and free from all Earthly burdens.

"Just wait until we get to Harpers Ferry," Joe continued. "Then I'll have lots of ammunition. You, however…"

He pointed at Kirkland.

"You might want to give me your portion. Last time I checked, the local food went through you like the Potomac."

"How could I forget?" said Kirkland, sheepishly.

A distinctive report ended their pleasantries, at once a familiar and back-straightening sound. The pickets had encountered the enemy, and the command to form battle lines quickly followed.

The men obeyed, although the rock pile they had entered made the maneuver almost comical. They teetered on the reef of rubble, stumbling and tripping over the loose, uneven stones.

Uncharacteristically, the 2nd South Carolina was in the rear of the brigade and the men did what they could to follow the leaders.

Although Kirkland tried to keep the line intact, so many had either disintegrating remnants of shoes, or worse—nothing at all. The soldiers in front had no choice other than to carefully navigate the jagged trail, eyes down and rummaging for their next safe foothold. Kirkland himself was enduring the needles, his brogans resembling a foot sandwich. The tops and bottoms were intact, but the middles had torn away gradually from the long weeks of daily tramping. To keep from going completely barefoot, he had wound together what was left with strips of cloth, but this was only a temporary solution. He knew his toes would be naked before long.

Finally there was some relief as a lane no bigger than a cattle trail was reached, but this eventually appeared to dead-end in emphatic greenery. It was as if the road was absorbed by a secretive, Quaker mountain, unwilling to let a bloodthirsty army pass.

The Carolinians soon picked up the trail of the advanced regiments, throwing aside the outstretched, pleading limbs of the brush. It soon became obvious, however, that the enemy pickets had been driven off, and the moon had aligned with the mountain, at least delaying the fight for another day. As darkness made any more progress impossible, the men were halted for the night.

Reaching into his haversack, Kirkland knew he would find nothing resembling scraps. He did it anyway in the delusion that God Himself had taken pity on him and placed a small nibble of food where previously none had existed. It was no use. Tired and thirsty, Kirkland lay down on the mattress of stone, curling and contorting his body in a failed attempt to rest entirely on the softer earth.

Knee aching and stomach empty, he licked his chapped and weathered lips, and blinked hard. Trying desperately to refrain from allowing hunger visuals to gain momentum in his head, it was no use. An apple dipped in mud sounded good at this point. He even craved the green corn that had purged his being so violently that he swore it would be the last ear he would bite down on for the remainder of his life.

One sip of water. Just one sip of water.

Having made it to the crest, the Southerners rejoiced in the fading sunlight and the end of an exhausting climb. The Yankees could wait.

Most were fast asleep, even on their bed of rocks, but not Kirkland.

There were times when he could instantly fall asleep, brought on by exhaustion or a mind dry of worry. Regrettably, this night wasn't alleviated by either category and he cursed the men who could fall into slumber effortlessly. And then he called back the jealous rant. Looking up at the stars, humbling in their brilliance, Kirkland exhaled deeply.

"Can't sleep, either?"

He looked over at Alex, who was also gazing skyward.

Kirkland shook his head, saying nothing.

For several moments, they stared silently into infinity's garden.

On top of a mountain, Kirkland was acutely aware that on this very night he was nearer the great constellations than he had ever been, and most likely the closest he would ever be. In this recognition, he cradled a dream that gravity was no longer binding, that for one night, he could rise up and greet the twinkling mysteries. Holding this fleeting warmth to his breast, he closed his eyes and floated higher. But Kirkland's wings slowly evaporated, and he drifted back to the mountain, still enraptured by the stars' embrace, yet knowing more would have to be endured before he took his place among them.

"When I was very young, I would sit with my father on the porch and we would look up at the stars," said Kirkland, in a soft tone, so as not to disturb others sleeping around him. "My father would tell me that my mother was up there, one of those stars, shining her everlasting love down on us. One night I asked him which one was my mother, and my father told me, 'I don't pretend to know. I like to think she's one of the brightest ones.'"

Kirkland pointed to the brightest one in the sky, circling it with his forefinger.

"I wonder if she is looking down at us right now. Do you think she can see us?"

"I imagine she can. And that she's very proud of her brave sergeant son."

Kirkland turned to look at Alex, who nodded assuredly and turned over on his side.

Looking up once more at the motherly star, Kirkland closed his eyes and soon entered a deep slumber, dreaming of home.

She walked away, glancing back, intimating for him to follow. How pristine she looked, her eyes were dazzling, beckoning. The curves of her torso were illuminated by a rush of morning beam. Her hair bounced on her shoulders, again and again, exposing the white velvet of her neck as if guided by a teasing wind. He tried to follow, but it was as if his legs were swamped and weighted. The distance between them never changed, only mocking his struggles.

"Susan, wait!"

Hearing laughter, Kirkland hesitated, trying to hold on to the image of his faraway love.

"Susan, wait," the falsettoed ridicule from behind him melted the cobwebs. Turning about, Kirkland eyed Ratcliff, who instantly burst into an exaggerated fit of laughter, making sure all within earshot could hear him. Next to him, Hux followed his buddy's cue. More angry than embarrassed, Kirkland glared at his badgers, but held his tongue.

"Dreaming of that sweet Godfrey piece of ass?"

Kirkland jumped to his feet and started to lunge, but Alex cut him off, hooking Kirkland around the waist.

"Just ignore the bastard," Alex said quietly. "He's not worth getting your dander up."

Ratcliff gave both a sinister grin, eyed the gathering witnesses and walked away with another exaggerated laugh. Nervously, Hux shuffled his feet before gaining composure to follow his idol.

Just entering wakefulness was Joe, in time to observe the instigator strutting away with his one-man flock and Alex relaxing his grip on Kirkland.

"What I miss?"

★   ★   ★

Soon the offensive march resumed and the encounter with Ratcliff was dropped quickly at the wayside.

While the 2nd was still in the brigade's rear, this fact failed to suppress Kirkland's anxiety about the upcoming assault. As before prior brawls, the adrenaline tingled his hair at the roots and jolted his heart into gallops. Just how many Federals awaited them at Maryland Heights was unknown. Even if the troops were few, if they were well entrenched, a dangerous surge of will would be petitioned and every man would be called to the gauntlet.

Kirkland could hear the scattered shots of the pickets in the distance, and soon the familiar bass-jawed warble of Federal cannon announced their greeting.

Rounding a bend, he could finally see portions of the enemy's defensive works in the distance, between the smoke-foliaged trees. The faraway vision sucked out an already laden breath and inflated his eyes, as it appeared that the enemy front line was manned by a row of massive cannon. Immediately, he feared for the safety of men assuming the ramming head, but he saw no movement or powder-smoke bellowing from the large guns.

He kept his feet moving, stepping over fallen logs and around the shivering trees. Glancing to the corners, he was surprised to see the battle formations intact and steady, in spite of the impeding terrain. The landscape had improved little from the day before, the only disparity was that the slope had steadied, and the vertical climb was mostly behind them. As Kirkland drew closer to the Yankee entrenchments, he realized that he had mistaken downed timber for cannon. The enemy had fallen back to an abatis of logs stacked tightly together with their ends raised and sharpened to impalements.

Though it was a minor relief to Kirkland, the immobile lances were a formidable hazard to traverse.

While the firing intensified, the canopy of smoke descended ever lower, obscuring his view. But where his eyes failed him, the fiendish growl of the rebel yell curled his searching ears, and painted a desperate scene. Through pockets between the cloud layers, the 7th South Carolina could be seen moving toward the abatis and he clutched his rifle hard with silent encouragement.

What Kirkland didn't know was that Barksdale's Brigade was simultaneously advancing along the eastern shelf of Maryland Heights, while the 8th South Carolina was taking to the western route, determined to turn the Yankee flank and rear.

While the 7th regiment was momentarily checked, the men stubbornly pressed on and Kirkland could now see their flag climbing over and through the enemy's defenses. Men were falling in alarming numbers, and Kirkland saw one of them fall backward, his stomach crashing down on one of the wooden beams. There the unfortunate rested, his arms dangling on one side and his legs, the other.

With Barksdale's men and Kershaw's 8th closing in, however, the enemy fell back, realizing they were flanked. As they fled down the mountain in a panic and out of Kirkland's view, the sun cut through with penetrating beams, spotlighting the growling victors. Rifles shook skyward and heads pulled back, invoking the conquered mountain and claiming it as their own.

Congratulatory handshakes followed, but Kirkland moved with purpose toward the sword trees. When he arrived at the fallen who he had seen through the smoke, he eased the young soldier down from his awkward position of arrested flight. He was young, barely able to grow a stubble beard in a month's passing. The wound of death was not the first noticed. It was his shoeless feet, savaged by the mountain climb. The blood had pooled there, between his toes and cascaded to his heels. Taking the man's arms, he crossed them upon a crimson breast, and said a prayer for deliverance to a better locale. If he had met the dead one, Kirkland couldn't recall, and he hoped this omission in his head was a true fact. That he hadn't forgotten.

Either way, the young man was another lost martyr to Carolina dreams, and Kirkland regretted the unknowing, the name lost on the mountainside.

But this was no time for burdened sorrow, and he, in truth, felt both relieved to be alive and elated in the short work. After all, while the casualties in the leading regiments were harsh, it took less than thirty minutes to crush the enemy and send them running toward the safety of the garrison at Harpers Ferry. The Yankees would have no choice but to surrender now, and good old Jackson and Lee had done it again, embarrassing their foe into submission.

★   ★   ★

SEPTEMBER 15

"That's quite a view," said Kirkland, standing inches from the cliff's edge, yet bearing it no mind.

"Quite a view indeed," said Joe, at an unusual loss for color. Even he was stunned, unwilling to cheapen the moment.

"If I were an artist, or even a poet, I might linger here for days," said Alex, taking his place alongside the two bewitched gazers. "Forget the strategic military importance. We ought to reclaim this land on beauty alone. If I fell from this perch, I might not hit the ground."

Below, the Shenandoah and Potomac merged in shimmering delight, their waters drifting among glazed boulders and the pillars of a sacked railroad bridge. Rising from their banks in jade-crowned artistry, the Blue Ridge in mid-day's glow challenged the stars for polished majesty. Kirkland's geography was learned enough to know the granite range extended all the way to Carolina, kissing the northwestern edge. And while he had ventured nowhere near that part of his home state, his toes at this moment were somehow connected. With eyes closed, he could feel Carolina's heartbeat, stern and independent, yet welcoming and familiar.

The wind picked up, not in powerful intimidations, but in slow, purposeful gusts as if the mountain was communicating an ancient language, long forgotten by mankind. Kirkland didn't pretend to understand its message, though he perceived a gentle scolding, for disturbing a sacred realm of natural wisdom.

"I'm sure both of you are aware that George Washington, as president, chose Harpers Ferry down there for a national armory," said Alex.

"Absolutely. Who wouldn't know that?" said Joe, rolling his eyes. "Thank you for that history lesson."

"That's not all," said Alex, ignoring Joe and speaking directly to Kirkland. "Lewis and Clark stopped here for weapons and supplies before embarking on their great Western adventure. And, of course, there's John Brown."

"Really? Lewis and Clark?" said Kirkland, surprised.

"Yes. They spent a month here while their rifles, knives, tomahawks, and a collapsible iron boat frame were conceived."

203

"Them weapons were put to good use. What were them monstrous bears they discovered?" asked Joe.

"Grizzly bears," said Alex.

"Right. My father used to scare us with tales about them," said Kirkland. "With my father, there was never a shortage of Lewis and Clark stories around the fire. But it was grizzly bear tales that scared us the most. Is it true that they grow to ten foot and a thousand pounds?"

"That may be of slight exaggeration, though not too far off, from what I've read," replied Alex.

"Sounds like Ratcliff, without the bite," said Joe. "Now that would be an entertaining quarrel."

"Please. A grizzly would tear Ratcliff apart," said Alex.

"Exactly."

Joe grinned widely.

"Come on, my friends," he continued, motioning toward a winding trail down the mountain. "Let's return to the Virginia side and see what the Yanks have cooked up for us."

★   ★   ★

As they entered Harpers Ferry, more than 12,000 Yankees were being escorted from the garrison.

While defeated, their bristling eyes and vengeful tongues showed a healthy aspiration for Confederate demise. Few dropped their chins in shame, and many had harsh words for the outpost's conquerors. Kirkland had never been eye to eye with so many boiling over with overtures of loathing.

"Enjoy it now," said one particularly tall and cocky Federal. "We'll be back to whip you as soon as we're exchanged."

Kirkland said nothing, but Joe couldn't resist.

"Didn't I just see you running down the mountain? I swear it was you."

The soldier stopped and his neighbors, for the first time, looked uneasy and pale. The prisoners' guard moved in quickly.

204

"You men keep moving now or you'll face the butt of my rifle," said a burly lieutenant, raising his weapon in a show of force.

But the prisoner wasn't done, and unleashed a few parting stabs directed at Joe.

"We'll see you in Richmond—when it's burning."

He spit at Joe's feet before turning away in a huff.

"You are a true gentleman," said Joe. "But I'm afraid you are grossly mistaken." He raised his voice. "Richmond don't take kindly to strangers. You should know that by now. Right, boys?"

A cheer went up through the victorious ranks, and both sides moved on without further incident. With expectant spoils on their minds the Carolinians entered the city.

"Look," said Alex, pointing to the right. "That must be John Brown's Fort."

Kirkland wasn't impressed. For a building of such far-reaching infamy, which had captured the attention of a splitting nation when the bold move was made in 1859, it appeared lonely, a runt of scarred brick. There wasn't a man on either side that didn't know the story and its implications. When the fiery abolitionist laid siege to the arsenal, along with twenty-one followers, they took residence in a building at the armory's gate after taking a few dozen citizens hostage. Intending to raise an army of slaves, Brown had no qualms about committing murder to achieve his goals, having done so in the past. None other than Robert E. Lee was sent to retake control of the armory and town, and J.E.B. Stuart had attempted to negotiate Brown's surrender. Brown would not back down, and when it was over, the mayor of Harper's Ferry was dead, along with seventeen others. News of the violence spread quickly, causing fear throughout the south of more uprisings. While Brown was eventually convicted of treason and hanged, he became a martyr to the abolitionists.

"At the gallows wouldn't be a terrible way to meet your end," said Joe, matter-of-factly. "Of course, that notion assumes an instant snap of the neck and you didn't strangle to death for twenty minutes."

"I'd much rather go quietly into the night, like my grandfather did," said Alex. "He said goodbye to his family as if he was leaving for nothing more than a moonlight stroll, laid down on his bed and breathed his last." He sighed. "Peaceful, and on his own terms."

"Boresome, but I like it," said Joe. "What about you, Rich?"

"Me?" said Kirkland. "The circumstances of my end do not concern me. I just know I ain't ready yet."

"You will not find a rebuttal for that argument, at least not from me," said Alex.

"Me neither," said Joe. "Brown sure met his match in old Marse Lee, though. I'm sure glad he was loyal to Old Virginia."

Kirkland shook his head.

"He was only doing his duty. Just as he is prevailing now, but under a different flag. You are right, though. If he had chosen his former allegiance…"

Joe whistled, in high-to-low crescendo, imitating a falling shell.

"I prefer not to think on it," said Joe, not allowing the missile to explode. Kirkland was on the same wavelength, knowing that Lee had been offered the keys to the entire Federal army, yet had turned down the honor of leading it. Virginia, his home and heart, was too dear to take a pugilistic stance against the soil of his nurturing.

A halt was given, and the Carolinians sat down, not realizing the true scope of their weakness and exhaustion until at ground level. It was a delirium Kirkland had felt before, but the mountain had taxed his legs beyond normal marching wear. Combined with a body screaming for the slightest morsel, the light began to waver.

Just as he was dreaming of the Yankee warehouses, sure to be stocked full of mouth-watering provisions, Kirkland felt a black shade enveloping the whiteness of his eyes, speeding downward, and he collapsed backward in a heavy swoon.

★ ★ ★

Lucidity ricocheted and bounced around inside his head, its wheels struggling to find their track.

Kirkland blinked several times, the darkness only serving to delay coherency. Just as his eyes finally centered on a quarter moon, two heads created an eclipse. Joe and Alex were staring down at him with both worry and amusement.

"You okay, Kirkland?" asked Alex.

Still unsure of his place in reality, Kirkland looked at his crowded surroundings and hesitated. Harper's Ferry was a mass of wagons and men, coming and going, further swirling his foggy mind. While Kirkland had no inkling of the repose's duration or how he had fallen into its capture, it didn't take long to perceive that it was a cavernous sleep, born of necessity.

Rubbing his eyes, he yawned them open several times, but his lids fought to clamp down again.

"How long have I been out?"

"Oh, about eight hours or so," Joe offered.

"Is that all?"

"You passed out and we couldn't wake you," said Alex. "We gave up after a while. Figured you weren't missing anything and could use the shut-eye."

"Really? Eight hours, you say?"

"We poured a little water down your throat and before long you were snoring like a barn dog," said Joe, grinning.

Kirkland wasn't sure if it was the act or the retelling that his friend enjoyed more.

Sitting up, he groaned, his tight legs giving pained resistance.

"Help me up, my knights in shining armor," said Kirkland, smirking playfully. His good humor was cut short as he reached his feet. Adding up the miles of the previous days, his knees locked up and demanded toll.

"The suspension's gone on these things," said Kirkland, wincing. He massaged his legs and stretched them until they were in working order. "Rip Van Winkle comes to mind."

207

Alex laughed.

"Rip who?" said Joe with searching eyes.

"You know, the man who fell asleep for twenty years and awoke with a rusty musket and long beard?" said Alex, astonished.

"Never heard of him. He from Dixie?"

"It's a sto-ry," said Kirkland, amused. "Takes place in New York, I believe."

"Who cares about a Yankee in a coma?"

Alex threw up his arms and grunted, turning his back on the literary ignorance.

Kirkland smiled, never tiring of the incredible opposites. Putting his arms around Joe and then Alex, he grinned and pulled his friends together in a mock butting of heads.

"The academic and the heathen—to each his own."

"I prefer knight, thank you very much," said Joe.

"Well, Sir Joseph, have we helped ourselves to the Yankee stores yet?"

"No," Joe grumbled. "It appears that Stonewall's men hoarded it for themselves. And our commissary wagons have not yet arrived."

Kirkland groaned and clutched his midsection.

"I believe my stomach has folded, in the act of eating itself."

Joe laughed.

"Yes, well…"

He was intruded upon by orders bouncing among the stars, stiff and unmerciful.

"Fall in men. We must leave in haste."

Chapter 12

SEPTEMBER 16, 1862

SOMEWHERE BETWEEN HALLTOWN AND SHEPHERDSTOWN, VA

4 PM

Eight hours of comatose slumber was not nearly enough. Without rations, Kirkland quickly returned to a state of crippling exhaustion. The brigade had marched through the night since leaving Harpers Ferry, turning north at a blink of a village called Halltown. Walking under the phalanx of bashful stars had been tolerable enough. Since dawn, the dusty turnpike had been less kind, and the array of hills became cruel under the oppressive sun.

With every hour and temperature spike, the climbing of the smallest knolls became tortuous exertions of will. Brief stops for water were the only comfort, and in this hiatus, Kirkland would dunk his soiled head in a cool stream and drink liberally until he choked, before refilling his empty canteen.

These brief respites were hardly a complete rejuvenation, but to Kirkland, the limbo between sleep and alertness was a cherished gift. On the march, his mind would glaze over for hours at a time, his body locked into a ghostly cadence, steady and resilient, yet piloted by an absentee landlord. During these times, his soul would drift, taking sanctuary in the pine-root chambers of his red clay heart. Here it suckled, gaining strength from memories and distant faces, before recoiling to its usual position.

Despite its triumphant return, it was not a joyous reunion. For during these times, the fog would lift with a strangling gasp, and the pain would start at his feet, scaling upward with wondrous speed, biting at his elbows and clawing against his skull. His temples would crease and flicker, the sensation turning inward until his eyes bulged and flamed, turning browns to scorching blue. The pain was excruciating, yet in these moments Kirkland knew that somewhere, deep within, the embers of endurance had been stoked and reborn. At least for a little while… enough for the next hill.

Alert again, he scratched the jutting stubble on his cheeks. His itching face was only slightly more comfortable than his blistered feet and receding stomach. Looking down at his hideous shoes, he was not optimistic that the frayed strings would hold them together much longer.

As he pushed on, many fell by the wayside. Some of these men slowed to a leaden creep, taking themselves out of line while continuing forward in plodding steps, unwilling to yield to their bodies' limits. Others simply gave out in a dramatic heap, teetering sideways as their legs cramped and abandoned their hosts. These "played out" men hit the ground, panting and delirious, completely incapable of moving any further.

Kirkland could summon no pity for them, as the energy he had left was concentrated on keeping his own two feet in labored motion.

Another hour passed and he fell into the narcotized state once again. In this haze, he barely noticed Joe fall out of line and disappear into a stand of trees. While Kirkland had turned his head in sluggish recognition, it slowly withered back to the frontal position, his eyes trained on the dusty brim of the slouch before him.

Before the column had trudged a quarter mile, Joe appeared alongside with an apple under his chin, hugging several more against his chest. For a brief moment, the walking dead sprang to life, clamoring for Joe's foraging delights, however meager. He passed out all he had, allowing the

210

last to fall from his chin into his hand. Reaching over to Kirkland, he nodded.

"Take it," he demanded.

"I will not take the last. Save it for yourself."

"You need not worry," Joe giggled, pulling an apple from his pants pocket.

It was all the convincing Kirkland needed, and in one motion, he snatched the apple from Joe's hand and shoved it into his foaming mouth.

His first bite was so large, he nearly gagged, and so he resurrected a state of beguiling calm. But what he really wanted at this moment was to become an eager snake, to stretch his jaws abruptly around the quivering fruit, swallowing it whole. For this was harvest season, and the apple was painfully ripe, a hallowed sphere of glowing red, overflowing with juiciness. This fact, coupled with his starvation levels, negated any attempt to enjoy the small meal. This was devoid of slow savoring, and with each bite, he grew more rabid. The inner snake had won out and he didn't stop at the core or the stem. It was all inhaled in rapid fashion and when this was complete, Kirkland searched his whiskers for any wayward juices, sucking on his fingers until all sticky remnants had been devoured and accounted for.

Tonguing his dusty molars in an attempt for one last taste, he craved more. While he was indeed grateful, the after-effect was immediate and callous. His stomach now aroused, it screamed, demanding more. And not as a nesting baby bird, either, but like a full-grown raptor.

Having grown accustomed to its tantrums, Kirkland shrugged it off as best he could, confident that the token meal had saved his weakening legs, and more importantly, a doubting mind. He was now sure he could finish the journey to wherever Lee, Division Commander Lafayette McLaws or Kershaw needed him. Presently, he tried to force "are we there yet?" from his mind and hoped the destination wasn't too far beyond the next summit.

He would be disappointed.

The sun grew bored with its torments and began to fade. But they kept moving. Unfortunately for the soldiers, even darkness failed to put a stop to the forced march. They had now been on the move for eight hours, with little rest and no end in sight. As usual, the officers of the brigade were tight-lipped about the destination, despite an onslaught of pleas from their exhausted men.

Around midnight, twelve hours after the march began, the order to halt was finally given and the entire column slumped to the ground.

Kirkland's legs were so drummed and mechanical, he had to rein them in, knocking his thighs with fists to cease their runaway movement. But his upper half was almost as wandering, and he closed his eyes to regain balance.

"Kirkland."

"What is it Joe?" said Kirkland, barely above a whisper.

"Where do you think we're headed?"

"I don't pretend to know. Probably joining up with Lee somewhere yonder."

"Maryland," said Alex, interjecting. "If we keep heading north, we'll cross into Maryland again. We can't be too far from its borders. Of course, we'll have to cross the Potomac again."

"This time I will keep my shoes on, at least if these old things survive the currents," said Kirkland, not forgetting the cuts he received on the last go round.

Joe giggled. "Mine ain't much better."

"Lee must be in trouble, or we wouldn't be in such a damn hurry," said Alex. "The Federals must be close."

"If that's true, maybe I can requisition some new brogans," said Joe.

"You may want to make sure the Yankee is with the Beyond first, or he will rightly quarrel with you," said Kirkland.

"I'll wait patiently. Until he breathes his last."

"I may join him with the Beyond if I don't get some food in my belly."

"Your prayers may be answered," said Alex, standing up. "I believe the wagon train has finally caught up with us."

The threesome, in addition to everyone in the regiment not snoring, turned to view the commissary wagons coming up in the rear. A collective drool spread across the regiment, yet the men were too fatigued for a rousing cheer. Kirkland licked his lips, and the mere expectation of food punched at his midsection. He wanted to run to the wagons and tear into the first box or barrel he encountered. The contents were irrelevant. Anything to stifle the knives and knots fighting for superiority in his belly would be gluttonous paradise.

"Fall in, men."

Kirkland turned, incredulous, hoping—praying, that he had misunderstood.

If three words could inspire mutiny, this was it. No one moved.

"Fall in men, column of fours. Move."

Accustomed to following orders explicitly, the men did as they were told. But the grumbling reached a thunder of near insubordination. Kirkland met eyes with Joe and didn't like what he saw. All remnants of good humor had evaporated from his crestfallen face, which surely resembled his own.

Am I too selfish, Lord, to request sustenance?

★   ★   ★

SEPTEMBER 17, 1862
OUTSKIRTS OF SHARPSBURG, MD
8:30 AM

With a fine, serrated hand, the courier saluted the general. Dismissed with orders, the dust-encrusted rider threw himself upon his glistening horse and spurred, and the stallion launched itself toward the thunder smoke ripening east on the horizon.

Sitting Indian-style with his hands on his ankles, Kirkland watched the bolting horse and rider disappear into and beyond the fated village of Sharpsburg, Maryland.

Despite the alarming crescendo of cannon and musket fire in close proximity, the vast majority of the 2nd South Carolina was snoring. The brigade had crossed the Potomac into Maryland at dawn and soon found themselves before General Lee's headquarters, where the men were allowed a brief rest. Kirkland, however, forced himself to stay awake, believing that an hour or two of slumber would only encourage cobwebs difficult to shake. By the immense cacophony roaring in the distance, he knew the morning's work would be deadly, perhaps the worst yet seen even with his veteran eyes. He needed his full capacity of mind, or at least mostly so, hoping adrenaline would fill the void.

It was a difficult bearing, ignoring the pillow's enticements, even if that pillow meant blades of grass. The men of the brigade had, after all, marched through the night on empty stomachs, and most hadn't eaten anything resembling a meal for several days.

Kirkland, however, was no longer bothered much by the hunger pains, as his stomach had for most stretches become numb, having grown tired of its own clamoring and knocking at a heedless door.

As his eyes became heavy and his brain threatened to shut off, Kirkland stood up and arched his back.

"Just in time Kirkland."

Kirkland turned to see Colonel Kennedy standing alone, tapping his fingers on the hilt of his sword.

"Sir?"

The colonel smiled, but behind it, Kirkland could feel a heavy gravity.

"Sergeant, I could use your help rousing the men. We will be moving in a few minutes."

"Certainly, Sir."

He cleared his throat, and threw his head back, as if loading a tired lung. Whatever the source of conjuring, Kennedy found it.

"Fall in, men! Awake!"

Kirkland hesitated and found himself staring, but a get-on-with-it blink from the colonel put motion to his step.

"Fall in! Rouse yourselves."

Men rolled with groans, jerked unhappily from oceanic sleep and more than a few oaths escaped from its waters.

214

Kirkland moved among them, shouting with all the volume he could gather until he was before the prostrate Alex and Joe. Alex had moved, squinting at the painful sunlight but Joe remained in a fit of sawing logs.

Although he wished for a bucket of ice water, Kirkland did the next best thing. Licking his forefingers sloppy, he bent over and needled them into Joe's ears. Kirkland's mischievous grin vanished, though, as his buddy failed to stir. Rubbing his eyes, Alex was stupefied as well.

"I thought you had him there."

Recovering from his blundered prank, Kirkland flashed a deviant smile and moved on, curling his dirty toes into a less-than-subtle jab into Joe's midsection. This did the trick and Joe lurched forward to a sitting position with a beastly snort.

"Good to see you're still with the living."

"I'm not so sure about that," said Joe, between incomprehensible mutterings.

"Well, unless I'm speaking to a banshee, we're moving out."

"All right, all right."

As the men stumbled deliriously into line, Kershaw appeared on his neighing horse. He trotted his mount in front of his brigade, beholding the men with a countenance of severe expectation and trust.

Kirkland followed his gaze and was taken aback at what he saw, even slightly embarrassed. They did not have the look that would strike fear in an opponent, unless that foe happened to be head mistress at an etiquette school. Nearly every man resembled a whiskered youth on extended recess, who had trudged through miles of blackberry brambles and jumped in mud puddles. Pants were ripping at the knees and splitting at the seams, in a few cases a trip or over-extension away from a complete disrobing. Elbows and armpits had similar designs on tasting the clean air.

However, bare skin, unless recently exposed, was no longer pale, but cooked to a rusty brown. Or was it dirt? Kirkland wasn't sure anymore, as the last bathing was a distant memory, and he knew of not a single man who burdened himself with an extra change of clothes. Examining himself, Kirkland discovered new wardrobe malfunctions—tears at his left thigh and both shoulders. Maybe the rough exterior made them look physically tough, but he dismissed this notion as ridiculous.

Let the enemy be betrayed by their perceptions.

Spotting Smith, Kirkland gave his friend a flexing nod, which was returned with the same intensity.

When the men were in position, the general gave them another long gander before addressing the ragged brigade.

"I know you're tired. You have suffered greatly to get here. And in doing so you have proved your worth, that you are the best of Carolina. I know you will continue to honor Her by standing tall on this day. Today you will show what Carolinians are truly made of. Men, show the enemy the cold steel and face them with the courage I know each of you possesses."

Pulling out his sword, slowly and deliberately, Kershaw raised it above his head.

"Forward…"

His voice was humble yet savage, instilling a confidence for all to follow.

"March!"

As he moved, Kirkland gazed up at the blackening sky, closed his eyes, and said a prayer for the safety of his friends.

While heartfelt, it was a simple prayer, without extravagant pleas or excess language. From past experience, he knew war spared neither the pious Christian nor the rampant sinner, and he did not pretend to understand His plan. All that Kirkland knew for sure was that if it was his time, it was his time, and he surrendered himself to this design. But this fact didn't deter him from sending upward what little energy he still possessed, in the hope of mercy for his friends.

After all, it couldn't hurt.

His subtle petition complete, Kirkland lowered his chin and attempted to allow the war mask to overtake him. But it failed to cover. He would have to wait for the lead tailor and iron seamstress to greet him.

As the long column marched through the mostly deserted town, a wagon carrying a frightened family came rushing past. The driver, no doubt the husband and father, who had changed his mind about a basement holdout, was flicking the reins in wild convulsions. The horse was just as scared, as if unaccustomed to such bold commands or hurried movements.

Tears deluging down her cheek, the mother was doing her best to hold on to both wagon and screaming child. Crouching in the rear, a boy of about seven was restraining a large dog, barking wildly in confusion and fear, and attempting to jump from the fleeing vehicle. The child was bouncing around the wagon dangerously, yet his bearhug and perseverance was true, and Kirkland was sure if either went over, it would be a pair.

And Kirkland said a prayer for that Marylander child and mutt, as well.

Moving on through Sharpsburg, thankfully, no more civilians appeared in distress, most having long vacated the range of danger.

At the eastern edge of town, they veered northward into a grass field bordering the Hagerstown Turnpike. It was like stepping off a blind cliff into a forest fire. Fortunately for the Carolinians, this leap was in sound only. While errant shells passed over occasionally, the raging battle was a still a ways off in the distance.

But Kirkland already could smell its coiling breath, and see that they were entering a treacherous landscape beyond what his battle-tested eyes could fathom. As they drew closer with each step, the racket from cannon and musket appeared to rip the clouds from the sky, roll them into iron and drive the metal in waves against his head. In response, Kirkland reached up and patted the top of his slouch hat, half-wondering if the concussions would split it down the middle.

Once again, the lands of cultivation and nourishment were being torn apart, overrun by carnivores with a thirst for scarlet. In contradiction, the bulging red veins in Kirkland's tired eyes shrank to white, as adrenaline hammered them into his skull. His legs sprouted a strong, cadent rhythm and his arms no longer tired of the heavy Enfield across his shoulder. While nervous, he knew this would pass at the first volley and he didn't

217

concern himself with shudders of fear. If this were to be his last day on Earth, he would meet it with honor.

The brigades of Thomas Cobb's Georgians and Barksdale's Mississippians took the lead through fields that had been recently harvested, the first of naked, raven dirt and the next of corn stubble.

Directed to angle northwest, they disappeared into the irregular files of a large cornfield. The enormous stalks were taller than even the loftiest of men, blocking the view in front, but not the sounds.

While the leaves swirled gently in the wind, tranquil and harmonious, they seemed to magnify the wrathful clamor and hideous growls from sights unseen. Blind to their origins and proximity, they became all the more ominous, and Kirkland found the lack of vision almost unbearable. As he marched through the green spires, even the corn itself turned against him, the fine-edged leaves sawing and scraping against his neck and face. He wanted nothing more than to escape the tormenting maze, hoping that each passing stalk would be the last.

By the time they entered an open field, from the neck skyward was one big itch, and Kirkland clawed at the loudest before a falling screech drove away all bodily irritations.

Before he could move, the shell slammed into the ground not ten feet in front of him, furrowing the ground as if pulled by a mule with its tail on fire. As its path grew closer, the men in front jumped out of the way, and the hot metal stopped at Kirkland's naked toes. He held his breath and froze. For what seemed like minutes, the shell grinned and hissed, but failed to explode.

Stepping carefully around it, Kirkland exhaled his stomach as Kershaw rode up to halt the men.

"At the double quick by the right flank!" he shouted, repeating the order several times in an exasperated attempt to be heard over the beastly roar. He pointed northeast across the field. "Enter the point of those woods and drive the enemy!"

As Kershaw rode off, Kennedy stepped in.

"Right, face!"

It was an order for the 2nd South Carolina only, as Cobb's Brigade had gone astray along the Hagerstown Pike forming a gap in the attack formation. Well-drilled, the regiment moved effortlessly into position.

As Kirkland jogged forward, he peered into the woods but saw nothing. No flags, no movement, no enemy. Nevertheless, the West Woods shunned all warmth of feeling.

Resembling a haunted forest of whispered rhyme, with massive centenarian oaks, it was just the sort to harbor all kinds of mythical creatures and dark forces bent on gobbling up men who dared to enter. Or worse—hidden Yankees with loaded rifles. A split rail fence cut off access to the woods and Kirkland wondered what the cross beams were holding inside.

As they reached this obstacle, Kennedy screamed for the men to climb over.

"Quickly, form up on the other side!"

He had scarcely spoken when the enemy suddenly revealed itself among the trees. Leading by example, Kennedy had one leg over the fence when the Yankees fired their first volley. As he hurried to gain entry to the other side, a bullet tore through his ankle. Tumbling to the ground, he landed on his back, writhing in pain next to several others who were similarly welcomed across the threshold by lead.

Momentarily stunned by its leader's wounding, the regiment paused. But Major Franklin Gaillard was ready. The former newspaper editor and fire-eater, widely read for his secessionist views, had his chance to prove that he could back up his rebellious words.

Leaping over the fence, the major stood with his back to the enemy, raising his sword with calm assurance.

"Come on boys, there they are! Form up!"

At least those were the words Kirkland perceived, for the garish clamor relegated the commands to mere lip reading.

The men in front quickly rallied. As Kirkland reached the fence, he could see that the Yankees, the 125th Pennsylvania, were not more than sixty yards away, leveling their rifles for another volley.

Leaning his rifle on the opposite side, he hurdled the rail as a bullet struck inches from his hand. He could feel the impact ripple through his forearm as he vaulted to the ground. In discharge of his sergeant duties, he helped to close the ranks with a mellow push to those slightly behind or peripherally challenged.

As he knew it would, the fear had evaporated, riding on the coattails of the powder smoke. Time began to skip by in blurred chapters, and the frayed nerves of the cornfield were now sanded down to an acute awareness. The liberal pints of adrenaline were both euphoric and mesmerizing, inducing a machine-like response to the senses.

There was no soul in this realm, for its tuning fork had been silenced and buried deeply. As much as Kirkland tried to hold on to its vibrations, he knew that gripping it too tightly could destroy his mind or leave him exposed. Sometimes yielding to reflex and the will to survive held its purpose. For if Kirkland was to survive the war, in body as well as psyche, he wanted all of him to return to Susan. And so he allowed, and fought for, a small window of light to shine between his eyes and remain connected to his toes. But now, despite Kirkland's objections, this light was rapidly fading to a dark gray, and growing swiftly to murkier pigments.

Before the enemy could reload, the 2nd South Carolina was in line, with one eye draped and the other centering on a mortal puncture.

"Ready! Aim! Fire!"

Kirkland's gaze was on the enemy's center as much as his own, and when the Carolinians erupted in one large burst with a few tardy followers, the flag company, as usual, was a favorite target.

Before the volley's smoke drifted among his eyes, he watched the blue-clad color bearer slump heavily as if his spirit had been harshly yanked from its shell. Flag and carrier crumpled forward as if dying together, the stripes wrapping lovingly around its defender, as if desiring to rest with him in a Maryland tomb. Together they rolled once, and the soldier found his end, bearded face to the sky with the rest of him in a red blanket that now held less than equal measures of white.

The interment wasn't to last, however, as a small boy, no more than sixteen, struggled to free the regiment's standard from the corpse. He tugged and pulled for several moments, his baby face thrown back with exertion. Finally it yielded, and the boy unfurled and raised the flag high as the troops around him cheered its rebirth.

The Carolinians released another volley and met the enemy's huzzahs with their own version. As they advanced, the rebel yell sprung forth with a power and zeal far beyond what the exhausted tongues should have been capable of producing.

The Pennsylvanians held their ground but advanced no further, and to their left and rear, a New York regiment, the 34th, entered the storm but also was checked.

As the 2nd South Carolina halted to fire, a soldier in Kirkland's front was examining his weapon, it having jammed.

"Here, take mine," Kirkland shouted. Dropping his rifle, the man grabbed the offering and wheeled around to fire. Before he could pull the trigger, he was hit in the bowels. As he fell, the rifle bounced high in the air, landing at Kirkland's feet. While the wounded man demonstrated in agony, Kirkland snatched up the weapon and picked out a bluecoat for reprisal. Locating a target, he fired and could see that his aim was true, as the intended victim reached for his chest, keeling over.

Near the man Kirkland had just put a bullet through, the boy color bearer slumped to the ground. As he fell, the youth held the stars and stripes aloft with one defiant arm. And he kept it there, while his face burrowed into the leaves. The lone appendage shook as if the last ounce of vigor was draining into it, consumed by the weeping flag. Just as the boy's strength was depleted, and as the standard began to tilt, a compatriot pried it from his fingers and raised it again. This new bearer was no mere boy, but a strapping man, and his eyes flashed anger as he waved it in the Carolinians' faces. Right to left and right again, the tarnished flag was swung, before the flash disappeared from the third bearer's eyes, and he toppled into the row of brave corpses.

221

On both sides, bodies were falling among the giant elder oaks in terrifying numbers, soaking their roots with lavish offerings of blood.

The Pennsylvanians began to give, slowly at first, but then reinforcements under Jubal Early and Tige Anderson charged into the woods on Kershaw's left. The Carolinians shook their rifles and then the trees with their hollers, joining in the charge.

This time, the Pennsylvanians broke and stampeded, the New Yorkers following their lead. Smelling victory, the Confederates increased their speed and vocal hysterics.

Unlike at Savage's Station, these woods held little undergrowth and the 2nd South Carolina moved through with relative ease and order. The largest obstacle was stepping around the scores of writhing wounded and silent dead, which were so numerous that if they had been replaced by rocks, a man could hop from one to the other through the entire expanse of trees without touching the ground.

As Kirkland maneuvered between two prostrate victims, a third took hold of his shin as he passed. Looking down, a young man with a carefully groomed, anchor-shaped goatee and a face pale with fright, called out for mercy.

"Please, I need a surgeon," he pleaded, almost tearfully. The man pointed to a shredded arm, dangling uselessly at his side.

Kirkland patted the man on his good shoulder, but said nothing, knowing it could be hours before medical help would reach him. And if he survived to make it to the surgeon's table, the arm would be sawed to a stump, unceremoniously tossed onto a pile of rotting limbs. As gently as possible Kirkland moved on, pulling his leg away from the Yankee's grip.

Before long, the regiment had reached the edge of the forest. Directly in front was a small, whitewashed church, which Kirkland mistook for a schoolhouse as there was no steeple or ornamentation of any kind. The ordinary brick structure was pockmarked with bullet holes and sliced with shell trails. Whatever its purpose, it had been ravaged without mercy.

Halted behind it, having received further orders, Major Gaillard moved along the regiment, shouting orders to the officers. Reaching Company G, he spoke to Captain Cunningham as Kirkland strained to hear over the barbaric din.

"We will pass the school and when formed on the other side, will assault a battery posted in a field across the pike," exclaimed Gaillard, pointing. "The regiment will split as we go around. Understood? Good."

Cunningham turned to face his company as a shell screamed overhead, nearly kissing the roof before disappearing into the trees.

"We will move around the school to the right. Move quickly and into line once we're on the other side."

They were off before Kirkland caught his breath. He was sucking air, his frail limbs needing extra oxygen in his condition, as the adrenaline was now sputtering in his veins. Lack of food had severely lessened the dosage, and he wondered if his heart would splinter his rib cage. While his mind still cradled a dull flatness, his muscles began to jerk slightly in uncontrolled spasms. To his credit, he ignored the bodily hiccups and held fast to his rifle with each runaway jolt. But the short rest, in fact, was damaging to limbs kept in propulsion by rote.

As Kirkland went between the church and a cord of firewood, he tripped over a small limestone ledge, stepping over it with all the grace of a newborn fawn. He caught himself, however, without the use of skidding hands. The maneuver became more like a haphazard sprint, and as he rounded the place of worship, the discordant ruins of the morning's struggle frowned in rued glory.

To his left in the distance, an overmatched cornfield seemed to have risen up against trespassers. It was hacked and cut, as if a dull sword had sliced through, leveling at various installments.

The last remnants of Yankee soldiers who had streamed out of the West Woods were still close and running before friendly batteries. At the guns, the artillerymen were waving their arms in wide arcs in desperate attempts to get them to move from the path of fire.

Fifty yards ahead, Kirkland's attention was drawn to one of these infantrymen, bent over at the waist, too exhausted to continue retreating. A ball struck the ground next to him, throwing up a smattering of dirt, and restored his motivation. The blue-clad man started off in a panicked run, but only made it a few steps before being laid out by two bullets in his back. Head flung astern and arms limp, the man's rifle hit the ground and somersaulted sideways, as its former master crumpled to the ground in an uncoordinated heap. All around him, men were falling in similar fashion, the brave ones backpedaling, dragging their rifles on the ground as they reloaded. Most, however, had witnessed their fighting spirit evaporate like a Georgia mud puddle in July and were running for their lives.

As their pursuers reached the edge of the woods, hollering like Creek Indians, the artillerymen could wait no longer. The guns flashed and recoiled, one after the other, chopping down both friend and foe in their indiscriminate highway of iron.

Turning away and to his duty, Kirkland helped to guide the Carolinians in front to a walking, symmetrical blade. But it was a long open field between this knife and the Yankee guns.

When they were in position, Gaillard paced in front, reflecting calm, but saying nothing. His steps were measured and long, and although he refrained from looking into the faces of his men, Kirkland detected no hesitance between the ears.

With a sudden, unflinching rigidity, the major turned and pointed to a battery in rapid preparedness two hundred yards away across the wide, barren field. Behind it, a farmhouse had been reduced to a delinquent bonfire. Black hordes of smoke rose above it like an obsidian dagger, and for a moment Kirkland couldn't decipher which end held the point. Whether it was rising to strike the heavens or being thrust downward to send the Maryland farm to oblivion, he wasn't sure.

Twisting his head around, Gaillard's eyes flashed louder than his command as he gestured a steady hand toward the battery.

"Silence those guns! Readeeeeyyyyyy… March!"

Fortuitously, the massive fences that had lined both sides of the Hagerstown Pike had been to a great extent hacked down and splintered—one less obstacle to deter their advance.

Thus they crossed the road with little difficulty, and the men could see no infantry supporting the battery. However, the six 10-pounder Parrott guns had wheeled into position and were ready to feed the 2nd South Carolina all of their attentions.

This would be a charge of will, musket against the cannon's mouth.

Kirkland breathed in short spurts, as perspiration collected at his forehead and dripped from his cheeks. His nostrils seemed plugged from the inhalation of smoke, lessening his perceptions of smell and taste. Likewise, his ears had withered from the relentless pounding, and were no longer capable of full operation. Sight was now the dominating force, and he didn't admire the vista before him.

They entered a swale, reducing their vision of the enemy guns, with only the sponge conspicuous, standing tall at the ready.

Once over the gentle rise, Kirkland knew that for many, this would be the last few footprints at the edge of destiny's night. The fear was there, certainly, but it was muted and stagnant, and Kirkland's internal alarm was strangely monotone in its warning. Time was restless and narrowing, threatening to fling itself from the grandfather clock.

Moments after the spiraled mouths appeared in full array, they vomited and disappeared within the vapor of their own entrails.

The first round tore off the arm of a soldier near Kirkland's front, and passed Kirkland's left ear, the diabolical hum of its rotation felt more than heard.

He flinched a trifle, but it was more a subtle nod than insistent duck, and his feet never stopped moving. Without looking down, he passed the despondent man, yelping at the severed arm swimming in a crater of his own blood.

The double canister had struck the Carolinians before the explosion registered between their ears, each shot heaving tin cartridges that incinerated upon discharge. These containers carried seventy-five iron balls, each weighing twelve pounds, and were devastating to infantry. The artillerymen had aimed at the ground immediately in front of the charging rebels, to create a more controlled shotgun pattern that would bounce and rise, tearing through the lines of men as they marched.

A dozen or so around Kirkland had been either killed instantly or horribly mangled, and he quickly pounced to fill in the gaps. A few of the new recruits had stepped backward and hesitated, but the sergeant was behind them in short order.

"Keep moving!" he shouted, applying as much pressure as needed with a rifle crossed at their backs. "Close up ranks. Close up!"

Stepping around the fallen, they converged until all were shoulder to shoulder once again. Kirkland could plainly make out the enemy furiously sponging and reloading, and he had advanced no more than a few yards before the Parrotts spoke again. The iron balls tumbled through flesh, knocking men off their feet and misting the air with the scent of blood.

Having seen enough, Cunningham halted the men for a volley, which was accomplished in searing haste, the guns eager for torrential revenge. Although a few of the cannoneers withered under the flame, it was not enough, the rise in the ground causing many to fire high. Directly in front, a man stumbled and fell, and as Kirkland was helping him to his feet, he also tripped badly, the woodchuck burrow claiming its second victim.

The man he had rescued to vertical was Fain, who grinned knowingly, though Kirkland didn't return the cheer. For he had twisted his ankle badly and the next step forward nearly doubled him over as the pain rolled up nearly to his thigh. It was then that he noticed that his toes were finally free, having generously left behind the leather sandwich for a groundhog meal. Stopping briefly, Kirkland ripped off his other crumbling shoe to maintain a walking equilibrium. Regardless, it was all he could do to refrain from limping badly, as the call to "fire at will" was passed down the rapidly shrinking force.

With the shooting mechanism now up to the discretion of the individual, who would pause differently from his neighbor to fire, Kirkland struggled to keep the lines in his care orderly. Especially on a bum ankle.

Though he could perceive an increased anxiety among the artillery foes, they bravely held on and kept the fire uncomfortably hot.

Just as it appeared they were about to break, help arrived at the crucial moment. Coming up on the battery's right were fresh infantry, and before Kirkland could wrap his head around the threat, the Yankees cursed them with lead.

As Kirkland was checking the battle line on his right, a man in front teetered backward and wheeled against him. He seemed momentarily stunned, but remained on his feet. Putting a fearful hand delicately to his face, the soldier patted the area around his mouth. The right side of his mustache had been shaved by a bullet. The blood began to appear in tiny pinpricks on the familiar face, whom he recognized as Heywood, a recruit who had joined up in the months after Savage's Station.

Bright but with a cocky vinegar seemingly all young fireballs carried on their sleeves at their enlistment, Kirkland had helped to drill him and turn him into a capable soldier. Yet there was something odd about the tall redhead, just a feeling really, that behind the bravado were holes in his character that might leak his steadiness at the most inopportune of times. Kirkland had shrugged it off since no evidence of any major faults had aroused suspicion, but here his inner voice proved regrettably accurate. Staring at the blood stamped on his fingers, Heywood moved his hand back and forth from the still-whiskered upper lip to the side of sudden baldness.

As the soldier was only slightly wounded, Kirkland grabbed him by the arm and attempted to carry him forward but Heywood threw him off with a look of drunken confusion. His eyes glazed over for several moments in a strange stupor, his legs anchored in place.

When the haze ended, Heywood's whole countenance changed. Lifting his head back, his mouth opened in maniacal laughter. Reanimated, Heywood stumbled about, hopping in wild circles, out of his mind in macabre giggles. As his turbulent movements brought him facing Kirkland once again, he suddenly jerked violently and his face grew ashen. Struck by a minié in the back of the head, blood poured from his nose, joining the shallow basin at his lip and ran down, flooding over his chin. Dropping to his knees, Heywood pitched forward, already in merciful death.

"Fall back! Retreat to the road. Fall back!"

Gaillard was gesturing wildly and Cunningham followed suit.

The regiment had been butchered enough.

As Kirkland backpedaled, his shoulder was rammed with enough force to spin him, and his already hobbled ankle balked at the dance. Landing on his back with a cushionless thud, he peered up at the forlorn sky, unsure if the heavens were calling or if the realm of terra firma would persist.

★   ★   ★

SEPTEMBER 18, 1862

Kirkland trudged barefoot and limping through the premature autumn canvas of oak, cut down by hordes of exuberant miniés darting and crashing through the wood. Rubbing his aching shoulder, he was grateful for the gold and violet bruise under his shirt. For upon inspection, the bullet had not pierced his skin, and as ugly a mark as the impact had left, it was greatly superior to the alternative. And while his ankle was swollen and sore, it was a minor injury.

Many others were not so lucky. In the charge across the Hagerstown Pike, the 2nd South Carolina had suffered horribly, and half of its men were on the casualty list. Although the West Woods were still in Confederate possession, little more was gained, and the most violent day in American history ended in a stalemate.

Where the fighting was thickest, Kirkland could not walk ten feet without passing a Federal in perpetual sleep, hugging the ground cold or staring upward with wick-blown eyes. Their faces demonstrated the grittiness of the blue-tinged foe. Black smudges trailed from mouth to mid-cheek, the result of biting off numerous paper cartridges as they loaded time and again.

Having spent the night in the woods, the dead seemed to outnumber the living, where campfires mourned the legion of empty places among them.

Joe and Alex had come through unscathed. This deliverance, along with a long overdue meal of beef and bread ravenously devoured, had prompted a lengthy, indebted prayer.

When he awoke on this morn, Kirkland's first act was dropping to his knees, repeating this litany of thanks. His next thought was for the men of the regiment who had been killed the day before and who inevitably lay unburied and uncared for on the lethal Maryland plain.

As a result, he had asked for and received permission to go to the picket lines, to seek out the regiment's dead if the enemy would allow it. Arriving at what Kirkland now knew was a Dunker church, a German Brethren sect of peace-loving farmers, so named for their penchant for baptismal submersion, he sighed. The church's condition was appalling.

While he had noticed the raggedness and damage when he passed the building the day before, his preoccupied mind had not given it much thought. And he'd believed it was a school. Walking gingerly to a window, he peered through the broken glass. A large bible sat undisturbed on a long table at the opposite end, open and unruffled. Rows of wooden benches encircled a warming stove, and faced the plain minister's counter. Without so much as a cross to proclaim the Baptist's faith, the walls were equally barren.

Simple, country folk. Not unlike my own.

Pleased that at least the inside of the church had survived relatively intact, Kirkland was about to move on when he noticed four Yankees passing by, carrying one of their own on a stretcher. A lifeless arm dangled from its side, nearly scraping the ground.

Curious, Kirkland went up to a man in butternut puffing on a wooden pipe, the bowl whittled to resemble a stovepipe hat.

"Is there a truce?"

"On a soldier's honor, I suppose," said the man, between exhales. "The generals, of course, would not agree to it in principle, but the pickets on both sides are silent for now."

"Then we may retrieve our dead unopposed?"

"It appears so, though I wouldn't wander too far."

Kirkland nodded, and began to follow the same path he took into battle the previous day. Rounding the skeletal church, he was stunned and the bruises at his shoulder sank to his heart.

A dictionary carried no words for the voluminous carnage.

It was as if an epidemic straight from the book of Revelations had descended upon the countryside, rolling over the gentle hills and farmlands, striking down all with as much warning as a lightning strike. Yet these prostrate victims were not grazing cattle, but men, and the plague that swept through was of nothing more than iron and lead. If this was prophesied, it was cruel in its finality.

Crossing the pike, Kirkland passed more burial parties, some carrying the departed on stretchers, others gripping chilled wrists and eroded feet. The pallbearers, though unceremonious, were reverent and silent in their harvest, moving with precision and haste.

Since no one had any notion how long the unspoken truce would last, it was paramount that they retrieve all of their dead as quickly as possible to ensure some semblance of an honored burial. Even if most would find their place of rest with a crude headboard or nothing at all, hundreds of miles from a family plot, it was the best that circumstances allowed.

Although Kirkland, of course, had pondered this anonymous epitaph before, whenever the enemy was close in metallic salutation, he was beginning to question the gloomy nature of it. After all, dying with face to foe would be considered an honorable last act for his bones, no matter the soil of their rest.

Would it truly matter where I succumbed to dust?

Stubbing his naked toe, he hopped in pain, searching for the aggressor. The culprit was a large shell fragment, half buried in the grass, perhaps upset at not inflicting the ambition of its birth. As he bent over in a rocking wince, a foot shone like a white light at his periphery. Upon it was a shoe in immaculate condition, without so much as a scratch upon its leather.

Kirkland stood over the man, obviously dead by the ugly wound at his throat. His foot was extended and raised at an angle as if offering, tempting even, a passerby with its bequeathing nature.

Looking around, both to his immediate vicinity and within to his soul, Kirkland attempted to stroke his chin. But even elevating his hand the short distance returned the pain in his shoulder. Grimacing, he switched to his good arm.

For several moments, the arguments in his chin were stroked. He paced around the man, and sat down, hand still on his chin but facing inward, in Rodin-like fashion.

Finally, he raised his road-weary foot to the dead man's and it was almost too good to be true, a perfect match. But still he hesitated.

While he had raided discarded items on the battlefield before, he had never scavenged from the dead. At least not knowingly, and certainly not from a corpse. But he was in Maryland and barefoot, with the potential for many miles on unprotected toes. Sighing deeply, he looked around to make sure no one was watching. Satisfied that his morbid deed would go unnoticed, he proceeded to untie one shoe and then the other. He cringed at the stiffness of the corpse, but he gathered his nerves enough to pull, squinting almost to the point of blindness. When the shoes were free he opened his eyes. The army-issue socks were almost new as well, nary a hole and dry.

Glancing around again, Kirkland shook his head, but the forecast was too vivid to ignore. He envisioned miles of additional tramping on shoes that had yet to conform to his feet, stiff and blistering.

Since he had gone this far, he took a further leap, pulling off the socks in one cringing motion. Practical won out over skittishness, defeating shame. Sitting down beside his benefactor, he thanked his host out loud, hoping the voiced words would appease the ghosts. And then he put on the socks and shoes as his own— though painfully at his wounded leg— before giving one final nod in candid thanks.

Moving on, Kirkland came to an artillery limber, still entangled with a butchered auburn horse. One of the wheels was missing several spokes, and the ammunition chest was pockmarked by bullets, its cover twisted back by a shell.

On the other side, a gun crewman was torn nearly in half, his intestines spilling over barricading fingers, iced in death. Wincing at the gore, Kirkland turned away, determined to get close to the high water mark of his regiment's charge, where he knew many of Carolina's best had fallen.

But his hands were starting to tremble and red spots formed before his eyes, growing and threatening to flood his vision. The roar of hellish conflict and the pleading cries of the wounded returned, haunting him. It was as if Kirkland's entire body had absorbed what his eyes and ears couldn't. These sensory memories threatened to implode his weakened constitution.

Dropping his eyes to a surrogate ground, the grass did little to ease his climbing panic. A smudged and erratic road of blood led one way or the other, as some unfortunate had dragged his ransacked body away from his hunter. Whether donated by friend or foe, he was not about to follow it to conclusion. By the liberal amount of crimson, he knew that the effort to escape must have been futile and abbreviated.

Gravity pressed down on Kirkland's shoulders like hands of granite. As he reached the first large grouping of recognized corpses, he felt he could go no further.

When his knees were about to buckle, a man who surely must have risen from the dead approached him. His homespun shirt of blue flannel was stained red in a large oval on his chest, and the blank expression on his face was lifeless and chilling. Walking as if blind, he moved toward Kirkland in slow, uneven steps. When it appeared that a collision was near, Kirkland got out of his way. As the quasi-phantom passed, he wheezed in shrill gaspings, which caused the hair on the back of Kirkland's neck to bolt sideways.

Initially paralyzed by the vision, he attempted to speak but his tongue was cowering in a fetal position.

"Sh-should I call a surgeon?" Kirkland finally stammered. "I can guide you to a hospital."

But the wounded man just ignored him, and continued on toward the Dunker Church. Shaken, Kirkland watched him drift away in measured toe drags, arms wilted and uncooperative.

Turning his back on the daymare, Kirkland closed his eyes for a moment and clenched his fists. It was too much to breathe in, veteran or not. Sending these images aloft, he opened his eyes again. The farmhouse in the distance was still smoldering, yet the columns of smoke had lessened to the appearance of fragmented puffs. They were no longer obese in their darkness, nor did they hold to an unbroken chain between heaven and earth.

Around the farm, Yankee burial parties were busy at their retrievals.

As he was watching their movements, two Negroes close by dropped a stretcher before their next customer. The man was a captain, whose rank entitled him to better treatment, even in death. Perhaps he would be carried home, or buried in a local cemetery.

Both Negroes were cooks in his regiment. While one man was steady in his macabre work, the other looked beaten down with fatigue, his face perspiring with dread. Kirkland knew him as Spice, valued by his mess and beyond, as a chef with powers of flavoring alchemy, who could produce delectable meals beyond what supply should have allowed. Known as a gifted forager, he always came back with the right additions to turn drab rations into a little extra. Even Smith had sought his culinary wisdom, but he wasn't in this former Mississippian's league.

Kirkland could plainly see that Spice was not nearly as adept in this new role. Nervously walking around the corpse, he reached down to grasp a foot but jerked his arm back in reluctance. His companion gave him an irritated look, already having the dead man's hands in a hoisting stance.

Walking over, Kirkland intervened.

"I'll stand in for this one," he said.

Spice was mortified.

"No Massa, you done 'nough already. You's should be restin' after dis fight."

"It's quite all right," Kirkland assured him. "You wait here for a spell."

Spice paced nervously, obviously in disagreement but hesitating to speak. But he found the nerve.

"Massa, please don't leaves me here with de dead. I beg you."

Taken aback, Kirkland attempted to gauge his response, but the cook quickly averted his eyes.

Seeing his distress was all too real, Kirkland relented.

"Carry on," he said.

This time, Spice had no trouble lifting the corpse, and as they loaded it onto the stretcher, Kirkland waited in discomfort for the duo to leave him. When the cooks were a considerable distance away, he allowed his knees to accomplish what they had long desired. Falling to the ground among the Carolina dead, he surrendered to his grief, which magnified when he noticed a bespectacled man among the bodies laid out in rows, awaiting burial.

It was Smith.

The previous evening, after holding roll call with the Flat Rock Guards and eating dinner, Kirkland had immediately gone to sleep.

Although his intention was to seek out his friends in the Camden Volunteers to make sure they had escaped the day's butchery, his body had given out. In the morning, he questioned several members of Company E about Smith, but none were sure about his fate. So Kirkland held out hope, unwilling to accept that his friend was gone.

But here he was.

His pant leg soaked with blood, with a bullet hole in his thigh, it was likely that an artery had been severed. Smith had probably bled to death in minutes, at least not suffering long. For that, Kirkland was grateful.

Removing a handkerchief from his pocket, he wiped the powder grime from Smith's face.

"Thanks for everything, good chum."

Gathering himself, Kirkland rose, allowing the tears to remain at his cheeks, unswept and wholly unpolluted. And then he surveyed the row of Carolinians on the field of Antietam once more, saying the full names of those he knew out loud. He ended with Smith—Jonathan Davis.

As a survivor, he would carry these names with him, until the time would come to join that fraternity in rest. Whether this reunion would come to pass in days, months or white-haired with grandchildren pulling at his trousers, that day would beckon. Some day.

But he had made it this far and had no intention of gliding silently into the night.

Thy will be done.

Noticing a gleeful whistling, Kirkland looked up to see Riddle gliding by, almost skipping. He patted the bulges in his chest pockets where the Bibles were cooped. With a wink, he rhythmically strutted away.

Chapter 13

A modest fire thrust vibrating shadows on the nervous remnants of an oak tree grove.

It was a pleasant fall evening, the warmth of the fire holding the lightly chilled air at bay. Like most days over the past month, the brigade passed the time drilling and taking turns on the picket line with little or no action to speak of. Many of the slightly wounded had returned to their regiments, and new recruits and conscripts were arriving steadily. The roads were thick with those returning from furloughs and recuperation from injuries, as well as with those headed home to heal bodies broken from the Maryland campaign. And there were a lot of broken bodies. The number of casualties for the one-day fight at Sharpsburg was staggering: 25,000 for both sides. Losing nearly a hundred, including 19 killed and many more seriously wounded, the 2nd South Carolina had limped back across the Potomac having fought for nothing more than a draw.

The wounded included the McDowell brothers, who each lost a leg to amputation—Red, his left, and Jim, the right. But at least they had gone home.

Lee's first invasion of the north had failed. But McClellan, fatally cautious, did not pursue with any significant numbers of Federal troops and gave Lee a chance to regroup.

While camp duties were tedious and unexciting, few were complaining. Except about the politics of Lincoln.

"That scoundrel and his villainous administration keep proving how much they loathe the Southern states," said a man in Kirkland's company whom everyone called "Nail," as he was known to be tough brawler in his younger days. Much of the trouble in his youth could be attributed to his penchant for whiskey. While sober—he'd been on the wagon for several years—Nail was a good-natured fellow who loved a good laugh. Now in his mid-thirties, he didn't go looking for a fight unless it was with the Yankees.

Where many men had transferred to artillery units to increase their chances of survival, Nail did the opposite. He had enlisted in the Palmetto Light Artillery, which had been sent west to Mississippi, but found long-distance warfare boring, craving a more personal view of the enemy. Besides, the "real" action, according to the newspapers, was in Virginia. Despite joining the 2nd South Carolina only two weeks prior, he had no problem making quick friends.

Rough around the edges and a bit uncouth, he fit right in with the veteran unit, where the traits of a gentleman were apt to erode without the presence of wives and sweethearts.

Even Fain had welcomed him with open arms, but not before instigating a fight that led to a bloody draw. Kirkland was forced to throw both in the guardhouse for a few days, where they found in each other a kindred spirit and became fast friends. Though of Flat Rock, Nail was of a different generation, and Kirkland knew him only by reputation and insignificant encounters.

"I would love to be in a room with Lincoln right now," Nail held forth, forming his hands into fists. "That emancipation proclamation will only encourage the darkies to rise up against our women and old men, when we can't protect them."

237

Lincoln, five days after Sharpsburg, had released the preliminary version of the document to free the forced labor of the Southern states, and it had become the talk of camp for much of the last month.

"Yes, it was his intention to cripple the South, but it only frees them in areas where the Federals have no control, so I don't see how it will do much of anything," said Alex, who, of course, had studied the document at length after seeing it in a Virginia newspaper.

"Exactly," said Joe. "He can't get his pathetic generals to do it in battle, so he had to resort to other measures. Right now, it's just a piece of paper."

"I only see one immediate impact," said Alex. "England will certainly not enter the war with us now, not in a war against slavery. It will be up to us and us alone, to ensure the Confederacy's survival."

"We're doing just fine without 'em," said Joe. "We don't need any foreign influence. We've got Lee."

"Amen to that," said Nail.

A commotion could be heard at a nearby campfire, and all in the group turned to its general direction. It didn't take long to figure out who was causing it.

Two men were standing on opposite sides of the fire, and Ratcliff was making his opinion of the other known.

"You goddamn conscripts are not welcome at my fire," he bellowed. "Where you been, huh? Cowering among the women and the children, that's where! We don't need you yaller dogs. Get the hell away from my fire."

Kirkland got up and walked over to the new draftee, for whom over the last two days, he'd given pointers and guidance during drills. The greenhorn's name was Davy Clyburn and many in camp had mocked him because he was a draftee and not a volunteer. Small in stature and weight, he was understandably perplexed at his new surroundings but Kirkland thought he had learned quickly. However, knowing that battle was a much different animal than drilling, Kirkland had long given up on predicting how a soldier would respond when "seeing the elephant." He had seen strong men reduced to trembling cowards at the sight of a fight. In contrast, Kirkland had also seen those depicted as frail and unsteady, transform into dashing lionhearts under the thickest hail of shot and shell.

Davy stood his ground in front of Ratcliff, but his eyes betrayed his stance. He looked unsure of what to do or say, and Kirkland stepped in.

"Private, come with me," said Kirkland firmly.

Relief washed across Davy's face and he quickly obeyed. Kirkland turned to walk away, with Davy in tow.

"I'm not finished with him," Ratcliff screamed.

"Yes, you are," said Kirkland, turning his head to look directly into Ratcliff's steaming eyes.

They kept walking.

"You going to let him talk to you like that?" said Hux.

"Shut your trap!" yelled Ratcliff, kicking the log out from under Hux, sending him doubling over backward.

"Sit down, private," said Kirkland, handing Davy a thick piece from the fire supply.

"Thank you, Sir."

"Would you like some coffee? It's not the real thing but it's the best we got."

"I'm obliged."

Kirkland poured him a cup of acorn mixture.

"I suppose proper introductions are in order. This is Nail, Joe and Alex."

Davy shook their hands.

"Don't worry about him," said Kirkland, motioning behind him. "He's woken up on the wrong side of the bed every day of his life."

"That's a fact," said Joe laughing. "He's always been the ornery thorn in everyone's side."

"You knew him before the war?" said Davy.

"Unfortunately," said Joe. "We all did. The three of us grew up together and Nail, here, he's also from Flat Rock. Where you from, private?"

"Round Columbia way."

"Ah, Alex went to school there at South Carolina College."

"Really? I would like to have gone there myself, but I'm not much of a book learner. Nor could we afford it. We have but a small farm. I wanted to enlist, to fight straight away, but with my brothers off fighting, someone had to stay behind to take care of the crops, my father being in poor health."

"Well, you're here now," said Joe, raising his glass.

"How old are you, young man?" said Nail, looking the new recruit over.

"Just turned nineteen."

"I would've guessed not a day over seventeen, no offense."

"None taken. I was kinda the runt of the litter. But I can hold my own."

"We shall see. If you can fight like that waterbug Fain, you'll do all right. Size has nothing to do with it."

"Fain?"

"Oh, you haven't received the honor yet?"

The dancing shadows on Davy's face amplified his confused expression, and Nail cackled against his ignorance. But he didn't elaborate, and Davy looked around for an explanation that didn't follow.

Taking a puff from his whittled pipe, Nail ignored him as an awkward silence rung in their ears.

Kirkland was about to divulge to Davy to expect an initiation, but sensing he had enough for one night, decided against it.

"Nail, I hear you've got a start on a big family. How old are your young'uns now?"

Nail put a forefinger to temple and thought for a moment.

"My oldest, Robert, is ten. He's a strong little buck. Then there's Melinda, she's eight, and a spittin' image of her mamma. George is five and full of vinegar like his dad. Nora is a sweet child. She's three."

Nail grew more serious, and took a few drags from his pipe.

"I sure miss them little ones. And my wife. I haven't seen the lot in over a year."

For a moment, the fire consumed the intoxicating joy and torched the serene. Thoughts of home could be either debilitating or redeeming, or both, in a strange colliding.

Kirkland, fearing a lapse into gloom, changed the subject.

"Remember old man Tidwell, who lived in that shack on the outskirts of Kirkwood?"

"Sure. They called him Colonel Tidwell. His porch was bigger than his house," said Nail. "He was a salty fellow. Used to scare the bejesus out of people, pointing his old musket at all who happened by."

Kirkland nodded.

"I was very young when he passed, but my grandfather told me he was a great war hero, one of the last survivors of the Revolution, who fought with Daniel Morgan at Cowpens.

"Yes," Nail replied. "My grandfather felt sorry for him and would bring him food, as did many others. He was greatly admired, which probably kept him out of the asylum. I heard he slept with that rifle, dreaming of battle every night, and woke up shooting holes in the ceiling."

"Really?" said Joe. "I hadn't heard the particulars. But I do know that he died penniless and alone, a sad end for a noble patriot."

Kirkland now wished he'd steered the conversation in a different manner, especially since he'd woken up several times over the last month in a cold sweat, the tenor of battle piercing his ears. The post-war life of Tidwell seemed like a fate worse than death. Would his constitution hold up? Kirkland wasn't sure.

And it scared the bejesus out of him.

Chapter 14

DECEMBER 9, 1862
SOUTHWESTERN OUTSKIRTS OF FREDERICKSBURG, VA
6 PM

Kirkland pulled at his rectangular, red-brass belt buckle, tagged "CSA" in proud lettering, his new pants of minor unfitting, a size too large. He wasn't complaining, however, for the new uniform was devoid of large tears or seams that threatened to expose skin to the increasingly dreary elements. After months of tramping around with clothing that dishrags would take offense to, new duds had finally arrived. Just in time for winter.

Joe was in opposite adjustment, his sleeves cosying beyond his wrists and bullying his knuckles. While he had rolled up these defiant aggressors on several occasions since the morn, the poor material of the cloth had thwarted attempts to abide in folds. And as this day was no different than most others for the last month, the men taxed by manual labor, the subtle efforts to curb the wardrobe deficiencies were futile, at best.

Throwing back his sleeves for the umpteenth time, Joe gritted his teeth but his tongue had other ideas.

"Rich, can you fetch me an axe?"

Kirkland was in slight bewilderment, waiting for a joke's climax.

"I have a strong urge to make more than subtle adjustments to my uniform," said Joe.

"You might regret that," said Kirkland, "on account of this weather we're having. At least the new armor is free of vermin and undesirable chambers."

"I may be completely peculiar, off my rocker, even, for I almost miss the crawling bastards."

"Yes, you are crazy as a loon," said Kirkland, unable to resist. "That's a fact. But I'm confident that you'll have a reunion with your little buddies in the near future."

As if of joined intelligence, they moved abreast in the same motion, studying the other's rapid browning. Both of their brogans were nearly devoured by the mud, and the disease had spread upward past their ankles in swarming patches.

"Well, cleanliness ain't a virtue in this army," said Joe, giggling.

"No, it is an impossibility," said Alex, who'd been listening silently in the background. "Ever in the caves."

"For once, Morrison, I agree with you."

Fain moved closer, intrigued by Alex's response.

"What's this about a cave? Is it near? Large enough to sleep in?"

"Don't bother about that," said Joe. "Alex is speaking in his usual metaphor nonsense."

Alex beamed a knowing wink at Kirkland, unwavered by Joe's lashing

"Ah, hell," Fain snorted. "Nonsense, all right."

He wandered off muttering to himself.

★   ★   ★

On All Hallows Eve, Kershaw's brigade began the long journey south. Lee had organized the army into two corps, under the commands of Stonewall Jackson and James Longstreet. McLaws was now part of the latter, and he ordered Kershaw to maneuver through the Blue Ridge at Chester Gap, towards Culpeper. The men, as usual, were not told of their destination.

It was a pitiful, four-day march covering seventy miles: wading twice through opposite, frigid forks of the Shenandoah and several more biting streams, and over steep mountain passes. Still without replenished or adequate clothing, the brisk winds and stinging rain taunted them. Once the men reached the supply base at Culpeper, the Palmetto troops were finally refitted, and they camped for several days among the mostly tree-barren, farming community.

Kershaw's brigade arrived at the outskirts of Fredericksburg on November 22, and immediately got to work, slaying the trees in front, opening a window in which to view a possible attack. Once this was done, the men began to fortify the hills.

Kirkland's regiment was camped next to a sunken lane, cut by years of heavy wagon travel, called the Telegraph Road, that curved west and then north around two large hills—together called Marye's Heights—before continuing northward to another series of hills and ridges. Ordered to entrench along the road west of town, they dug in, sharing what few shovels they had, the others doing their best with dinner plates and bayonets.

On the opposite side of Fredericksburg, beyond the Rappahannock, the enemy was posted on a bluff known as Stafford Heights, waiting for pontoon boats to arrive so they could cross the river. The Confederates had burned the bridges leading into the historic town, and while the Yankee army greatly outnumbered its foe, they were helpless until materials were obtained. The river was too deep to ford and the new commander of the Army of the Potomac, the furry-cheeked General Ambrose Burnside, waited impatiently as Lee raced against time to secure the high ground.

Much was at stake, for Fredericksburg was at the halfway point between Washington, DC and of Richmond. If unchecked, the Union troops would be salivating for the Confederate capital. And worse, they would have a sustained confidence in finally besting that wizard known as General Lee.

★   ★   ★

8:30 PM

A familiar, brass crossfire ascended from the river below, instantly recognizable and warm.

The bands were at it again.

With lips pursed on fire-warmed instruments, and mallets clubbing the frost on a bass drum head, the strut of "Dixie" blared.

By the strained vigor, Kirkland deduced that the band was on a competitive mission this night.

They were pushing the meter to new gallops, as if fueled by a religious awakening.

Though the Carolinians were quite a stretch from the river, the song carried on the frozen air, and reached their ears as if belted from a nearby fire.

"I sense a battle afoot," said Alex, his hands reaching for warmth over glowing coals.

"They're raising a ruckus tonight for sure," Kirkland agreed.

It was not uncommon for the bands on either side of the Rappahannock to stage an evening concert, battling it out for supremacy as they alternated songs.

"Give me turkey, give me mutton, plums or pie, or even squi-rrel," Joe sang, in lyrical parody, "look away, look away, look away, Dixie hams."

Kirkland, and even Alex, giggled at the new version.

"You have a one-track mind," said Kirkland, shaking his head.

"It's not that I don't appreciate that melody," said Joe. "However, due to the alarming number of times it has been thrown at my head, a fresh rendition can do no harm."

"Indeed. And you have more versions than anyone I know."

"I accept that honor freely."

"I'm sure you do."

The song ended, and the Yankee band wasted no time in patriotic rebuttal, launching into "John Brown's Body."

"Ah, too predictable," noted Alex. "We've heard enough marches to last a lifetime. And the same ones at that."

"I cannot disagree," said Kirkland. "But I must say, the quality is above the normal racket we're normally exposed to from regimental bands, even if the song selection is in great need of additions."

Alex nodded. "Remarkably better than the normal fare, this is true."

"But it's the same tramping songs, over and again," lamented Joe. "Can someone please write a new standard?"

The enemy band finished with a rousing crescendo. And the Southerners were waiting, not even allowing a few seconds to pass before "The Bonnie Blue Flag" shattered the silence.

A thunder from adjacent fires arose in choral tag-alongs and cheers, and Kirkland's fire-ring pals were swept away in the moment.

While the songs were of a repetitive nature, they were lively, boisterous, full of pomp and nose-thumbing glee, if only partially authentic in their arrogance.

They were propelled to sing.

First gallant South Carolina nobly made the stand
Then came Alabama and took her by the hand
Next, quickly Mississippi, Georgia, and Florida
All raised on high the Bonnie Blue Flag that bears a single star.

When the chorus hit again, the hills seemed to shake with bass and tenor, drowning out the trombones and cornets, and charging ahead of the band. When the brass was heard again, it was measures behind, bringing laughter at the soldier's inability to maintain a vocal cadence.

Naturally, when the song ended to rousing ovations, the Yankee band responded with "The Star Spangled Banner."

Of course, the Southerners, despite knowing every word, booed and heckled the War of 1812-inspired anthem.

In response, the Yankee singers increased their volume, making every effort to outdo their enemies.

And the rockets' red glare, the bombs bursting in air,
Gave proof through the night that our flag was still there;
O! say does that star-spangled banner yet wave,
O'er the land of the free and the home of the brave?

The power of their voices was unnerving, the sheer numbers in their haunting choir unfathomable. While distant, and across the river, it was a pure rumble, as if the entire continent was here to oppose them.

As the last notes of brass and percussion faded, and the voices died out, an uncomfortable, almost unbearable silence followed.

Unconsciously, Kirkland's ears perked and his head tilted. He was about to stand when a lone voice broke the silence, as if it came from the river itself.

It was a single bugler, from the opposite shore, with an encore that stripped away the antagonism in a few gusts.

It was "Home, Sweet Home," the song generals on both sides feared, worried that its gentle longing would incite desertion. But to the common soldier, it was pure gold, a window to a better place the writer so poetically desired.

But what these generals failed to grasp was that the song only repaired breakages in patriotism, calling for those to remain steadfast in defending those they left behind: girlfriends or wives, children and siblings, mothers and fathers, and extended family.

What should have been of greater concern to the chieftains was the song's ability to stack arms, to unite all in earshot to crave a sudden cessation to war.

When these notes penetrated their weary bones, the enemy became invisible, the river between them disappeared. All were in the same longing, wanting a swift end to the misery and bloodshed, hoping to return in one piece to those they loved. But when the last strains faded into the

247

night, the soldier stood a little taller and walked with more purpose. He was reenergized for the trials to come, to defend home, sweet home.

And at this performance, the effect was no different.

Kirkland, originally caught off guard, became aware of the sniffling masses. All were moved, even Joe and Fain, to the threshold of tears, or beyond. And many wept freely, a rare moment of shared grief, without fear of ridicule. For a few moments, the Rappahannock had been siphoned, and all differences, all politics put aside. Memories of family, of home, were the only principles. It was all that mattered. This was what the men on either side were truly fighting for, whether stamped on their forehead or lodged deeply within. Home, sweet home was their rock, their patriotism.

When the bugler's last vibrato faded into the hills, Kirkland wiped his eyes and found his mates doing the same.

It was a profound silence and no one spoke. Although the hush may have been for mere seconds, it was a painful dragging. And then, slow at first, a low rumble began to rise from both sides of the Rappahannock. It quickly gained steam and climbed above the river valley, bowling over all in its wave. The cheers were of unanimous approval, minus possibly a few generals, recognizing truth beyond what words could accomplish.

The applause went on for several minutes, as if neither side wanted to back down first, until eventually, it died out from campfire to campfire. Later, when tattoo was drummed, signaling for the troops to bed down, Kirkland drifted from the fire in a strange stupor. It was as if Flat Rock had appeared in a swift brilliance before his eyes, and was then yanked away just as quickly in a cruel gesture. But a homesick gut wasn't what was bothering him.

At first light, the fellowship of the bugle would be cast in the river and the enemies would be poised to kill each other once again.

Chapter 15

Kirkland doubled forward and awoke with a robust, startled inhale, the cold air stinging his lungs. Before he could take in what was happening, a second cannon roared to life, echoing alarm through the hills and valleys surrounding Fredericksburg. As if in rebuke, the bell from Saint George's Episcopal tolled in haunting frowns.

The familiar long roll sounded and within seconds hundreds of men sprang to life.

A much less fearful rumble could be heard next to Kirkland, and he was astonished at its source. There was Joe, snoring, completely oblivious to the action swirling around him. Kirkland grabbed his hat and struck Joe across his chest, startling him in mid-snort. Rubbing his eyes, Joe looked around at the men running in every direction.

"Aw, hell, sometimes the dreams are better than the drums," said Joe with a giggle, pulling off an overcoat and two blankets, which he had shared with Kirkland during the night.

"Did you kiss her?" asked Kirkland, an amused grin on his face. "Come on, the company is forming. The pontoon bridges must have arrived."

"Why can't the Yankees wait until after breakfast, like proper gentlemen?"

"Sure, run down to the banks and yell that we ain't had our coffee yet. I'm sure they'll oblige you."

"I've heard worse ideas from you, Kirkland," said Joe, stretching before reaching for his gun. "But with these here frozen legs, I ain't runnin' nowhere."

With Kershaw barking orders astride his horse on the right of the Telegraph Road and the troops in line, the men stepped off into the darkness.

Heading east toward the city, the soldiers were halted before their legs had a chance to warm, and with the sun still lurking in the shadows.

Unable to see what was happening, the troops could only listen intently as the scatter of musket fire cracked from the Rappahannock below. Although it was common for the 2nd South Carolina to be on the move at night, actual fighting while in the grip of darkness was a different story.

This possibility of blind combat, with dawn still curled in bed, was enough to make even these veterans uneasy.

"Talk to me, Joe," said Kirkland, surprised that he said it out loud.

"Don't worry," Joe replied. "Even if they make it across, we won't see them for a good while, well after dawn. I hear Barksdale's men are holding the town. Those are good men down there. They'll delay the Yanks for a good while."

Joe was right, Kirkland conceded, for the Maryland campaign had proved the Mississippians' worth.

"Yes, they're good men," said Kirkland. "But they won't be able to hold off the entire Federal army for long."

"No, but I'm sure Old Lee will come up with something. It'd be a shame to give up Fredericksburg, though."

"Indeed," said Alex, who, along with Nail and Davy, had been listening silently to both the growing clatter below and Joe's prognostications. "They've already trampled over George Washington's boyhood home."

"And don't forget them poor, little cherry trees," said Joe. "If young George didn't annihilate the orchard with his axe, its children are now firewood. He may have shifted in his grave to our side."

"You know, Rich, George learned the surveying trade as a young man, just like you did," said Alex, ignoring Joe's remark.

"Yes, but I was nothing more than a chain carrier. Don't expect me to run for president."

"Why not?" asked Joe, butting in. "The similarities are striking. He was a surveyor. You're a surveyor. He was a soldier. You're a soldier. You should stand on the river bluff and announce you're the second coming of GW. They'd be sure to pack up and leave then."

"Is this revenge for my morning coffee remark?" asked Kirkland.

"Absolutely not," said Joe. "I'm just pointing out that you're in exclusive company."

"Sure you are," said Kirkland.

Inwardly, however, he was glad for the light-hearted chatter. It was obvious another deadly battle was near and everyone felt it, whether voiced with honesty or downplayed with a buffered cockiness. The atmosphere was saturated with gloom. When the rooster light poked through, it failed to brighten the shadows, as if its rays were accompanied by heavy hands slanted toward the low notes of a pipe organ.

Even the trees appeared to sway with nervous trepidation. The enemy was here, poised to strike. While in a strange meditation as he dug in the hill with his bayonet, Kirkland became absorbed in his father's story of the cottonmouth. The voice was crystal, as if the old patriarch was at his ear. If they were to be cornered or outnumbered, he hoped the regiment would take his father's advice and become the snake, refusing to back down, waiting for a moment to strike.

It was then that Kirkland and his pals noticed the last remnants of citizens fleeing to the countryside. Although most had in preceding days left their endangered city, a few remained, and now thought better of it.

Children, hastily dressed in jackets over nightwear, were running alongside their frightened mothers, who were holding their delicate hands and urging them on. They carried small bundles of food and extra layers of clothing for the cold nights ahead. Men corroded with age, followed closely behind, summoning the legs of their youth while reassuring their families in flight.

The more fortunate ones rode in swift-moving wagons, maneuvering haphazardly around those on foot, carrying unsecured baggage, which threatened to bounce free between each rut.

Watching with a helpless gash in his chest, Kirkland said a prayer for the innocent victims, caught between two ravenous beasts that spared no one in pursuit of territory and death. When in heat, these gluttons for destruction had no conscience, no hesitation in their tramples of civilian property and daily living. Blind, unconditional victory was all that mattered in times of war, and this had been a hard lesson for Kirkland to accept.

He knew that when these citizens of Fredericksburg returned, they would find their homes and gardens, businesses and stores in cratered trauma or worse—completely destroyed. It would take much brawn to rebuild their lives and fortunes, to regain their place in civilization.

"You know," said Alex, "I don't believe an American city has been sacked since the British burned Washington in 1814."

"That…"

Before Kirkland could reply in full, the earth seemed to rupture. One hundred and forty cannon, including huge siege weapons, opened from Stafford Heights, sending a shock wave in all directions.

Hoping to dislodge and break the Mississippians, who were frustrating Federal efforts to cross the Rappahannock and enter the city, the Yankees held nothing back in their impatient wrath.

The sheer power of the guns was startling to Kirkland and the South Carolinians. It was the loudest and most ferocious roar the southern farm boy had ever heard. Even Alex stared with mouth agape at the destruction occurring in the distance.

Davy stood petrified.

"Davy," Kirkland called out. But even though he was only a few feet away, the bombardment stifled his shout.

Realizing the futility of speaking, he stepped in front of Davy, blocking his intimidating view.

Davy's eyes shed a couple of sizes as they met Kirkland's calming browns. Patting Davy gently on the shoulder, he simply nodded an air of composure and willed it to take hold.

The gesture seemed to work—for now, but Kirkland made a promise to himself not to let Davy out of his sight for the remainder of the engagement.

The bombardment lasted for several hours, and it became obvious that Barksdale's boys were putting up a good fight in delaying the Federals' efforts to cross the river.

Inevitably, however, crowns of thickening smoke began to rise above the city. The cannon fire slackened, and musket fire could be heard within the city's ruins.

Fredericksburg was falling.

★   ★   ★

DECEMBER 12, 1862

Unable to sleep, Kirkland followed a small grassy path along Hazel Run, hearkening to its temperate passage. His footfalls were meditational and quiet, he having no ambition to distract from the serene current of the water.

Nearby, with its massive wheel huddled against the building and sleeping, an old two-story gristmill looked recently abandoned.

A sliver of orange pierced the darkness, but it was mostly dark, sans the numerous, ghostly glows flickering from campfires within the city.

Chilled from the frigid night, Kirkland had decided a short walk would encourage the blood to melt and be reborn in his extremities. It was uncannily peaceful at this time in the morn and he'd resolved long ago to make a habit of it whenever slumber failed to take. As he usually did on these pre-dawn jaunts, he meditated on Flat Rock and home, father and family, and most of all, Susan.

While embracing these memories and traveling ambitions, he realized he wasn't alone. Just ahead on the trail, a spectral figure crouched in the shadows.

Curious though with timid step, Kirkland inched closer.

The figure was staring off into the birthing light, pencil in hand. The man alternated between scribbling furiously into what appeared to be a journal and returning his eyes to the dawn's greeting.

Bolder now, Kirkland approached.

"Good morning," Kirkland announced.

Startled, the man jumped and scampered in the opposite direction.

"Wait, I didn't mean to disturb…"

But the man was already gone.

Although something about him was familiar, Kirkland had little time to ponder the mysterious stranger, as a group of riders trotted into view.

As they neared, the leader slowed his iron gray horse to a walk and the entourage followed.

The sun had now begun staggering to full bloom and Kirkland had no problem identifying this stranger: it was the old general himself, Robert E. Lee astride his favorite mount, Traveller. Among his escorts was General Longstreet, wrapped in a blanket like a shawl, and General Stuart, dressed impeccably with a yellow sash and ostrich plume flaring from his curled, slouch hat.

Unbeknownst to Kirkland, Lee had set up his headquarters directly behind Kershaw's brigade on Telegraph Hill.

Lee raised his palm and halted his muscular, coal-maned horse. Retrieving his field glasses, Lee observed the city before him and surrounding areas, carefully scanning the ground from left to right and back again. He appeared irritated at the fog that concealed much of the river bottoms, but said nothing.

Neither Lee nor the other riders noticed Kirkland standing off the road, or if they did, they didn't pay any attention to him, and Kirkland had no intention of disturbing them.

I wouldn't want his responsibility.

While Kirkland had seen the general on two other occasions, at Sharpsburg and when he reviewed the troops a short time later at Brucetown, he was never this close to the legend. Lee had grown his beard longer than Kirkland remembered, giving him a dignified appearance beyond his simple dress. While his understated attire was by no means on a level with his rank, Lee carried himself like a gentleman in charge, graceful, and with a nobility that could not be explained alone by his Virginia stock. Age and the dominance of white consuming his face had failed to dull the razor aura emanating from his face.

But this was no time for elevated awe.

Kirkland was just hoping Lee was formulating a good plan. And he hoped that Traveller would hold up under the battle strain better than he did at Second Manassas, where spooked, he knocked a walking Lee onto a tree stump. Attempting to brace his fall, Lee suffered two broken hands.

After a few minutes, Lee signaled for the riders to move on to their next scouting position and off they went, heading south.

Kirkland watched until they were out of view.

God be with you general.

"Hey Rich, where you been?" said Joe, curiously. Kirkland had made his way back to the trenches, where most hovered over remedial fires.

"I was meeting with General Lee."

"Of course you were," Joe chuckled. "Well, does he have some grand strategy to demolish the entire Yankee army in our front?"

"He didn't say."

"That's expected, being the highly unimaginative man that he is. Let's hope he has another card up his sleeve."

"We're on good ground here. If the rest of our army has a position like this, we'll be fine indeed."

"I wish I was privy to that kind of information. There's talk that we're stretched for miles to the south, where Stonewall has command."

"If this is true, then we're in good hands. You know he won't back down."

"You have to admire his aggressiveness."

"Back down?" said Fain, incredulous, moving closer to bludgeon his two cents. "Have you ever heard of Stonewall in a defensive posture? No, sir. He will attack them, and drive them to hell."

The little juggernaut became irritated by his own words.

"Let 'em come," Fain ejected. "I desire the front when they move. They will pay for destroying this great city, and I want to be there at the cold greeting."

No reply was uttered, as if all were fearful to instigate a battle of words with Fain, which could lead to worse. They had learned better, and Fain seemed disappointed in their silence – angry even.

"Well? Am I alone in my desire for a reckoning?"

Kirkland, though sure he would regret it, finally spoke.

"No, Fain, you are not alone." He walked over to Fain, uncomfortably close, and met him inches to eye.

"While I do not share your enthusiasm for a reckoning, I stand beside you as a Southerner, wanting to end this war in a great victory. And if we can accomplish this pursuit today, then I also desire to be at the forefront, rifle in hand, and will gladly give my life to the cause."

Fain, taken aback, but not by miles, returned Kirkland's hard look. He searched for truth in Kirkland's eyes for several moments. After a few blinks, Fain grinned, and began to laugh in deep, almost sinister measures.

"Kirkland, you are a continuous surprise. At one time, I thought you were borderline soft."

He slapped Kirkland firmly on the shoulder.

"Bury! You got any whiskey?"

Fain walked toward his friend, and Joe tilted his head at his leave.

"That man scares me," said Joe. "But I must say, we need more like him."

Alex, having witnessed the exchange, shook his head, as if in battled agreement.

"He has found his calling. In a time of peace, I'm afraid that man would find the end of a noose for lack of purpose, but here…"

He hesitated, as if afraid to announce a hard-swallowed truth.

"Here," Alex continued, "he has a destiny, a reason for being. It's as if he was born to be a soldier, born for this war."

"I can't disagree with you, professor," said Kirkland. "But please keep your head down, for I have no confidence that your destiny calls for your presence here. I trust that God has plans for your intellect."

"You may perceive too much," said Alex. "But don't forget, I left academics to serve our beloved state, and like you, I will offer up my spirit if necessary."

Kirkland felt more than a little embarrassed.

"Of course, I know your mettle," said Kirkland. "You have no need to prove your loyalty to Richmond or South Carolina."

A shriek from Joe spared Kirkland from further elaboration.

"Food!" he exclaimed.

The commissary agents were passing around half a hoe cake and a piece of skinny beef per man. It was hardly a king's ration, and the same meal as the night before, but the hardened soldiers had experienced much less. Kirkland and his mess had relied on boxes of dried fruits, chestnuts, sausages and pickled vegetables sent from their generous homes but this supply had run out.

Removing his bayonet from its scabbard, Joe attached it to his rifle and impaled his meager breakfast. Thrusting the meat over the fire, he shuffled left and blinked away the smoke attacking his eyes.

"Kirkland, I reckon I don't have to eat you today after all."

★　　★　　★

In the early afternoon, as if someone had pulled the drapes from a window, the fog suddenly lifted.

Kirkland's heart tripped as the scene before him was revealed.

Thousands of bayonets flashed and blazed, invoking the sun, their extreme numbers reflecting with intimidation.

While the entire city of Fredericksburg was now in the Yankee's possession, the enemy was still crossing the Rappahannock with vigor. The pontoon bridges were full of massed troops walking out of cadence to keep the bridges from swaying. Lengthy supply trains and ordnance wagons followed in a seemingly endless progression. Cavalrymen, with their stout horses and glittering sabers, trotted across handsomely.

In response, shells were lobbed at the crossers but they were only pebbles thrown into a vicious wind.

"It's too bad we had to give up Fredericksburg," said Kirkland, beginning to sweat, though only partially due to the rapid temperature spike. "I feel for those people. But I think Lee made the right decision. It will be difficult for them to dislodge us up here. Dare I say, I hope we are attacked rather than the other way around."

"Yes," said Joe, giggling, yet with a slightly nervous bite. "That's a heap of troops down there. I've never seen so many blue devils."

"They're sure taking their sweet time to get motivated. If I were them, I wouldn't give Lee this much time to prepare."

Having overheard the conversation, Riddle gave a high-pitched cackle and moved in.

"I'm with Kirkland, here. God is on our side. They can throw at us all the troops they want. We'll hold."

Patting the Bibles in his chest pockets with a double thump, he laughed again.

"Praise Jesus, them bluebellies are fixin' to die."

★　　　★　　　★

DECEMBER 13, 1862

Kirkland squinted and tried to peer through the spectral mist. Although the abducted city lay several hundred yards in front, the sounds of industrious movement were carried on wings of foreboding moisture.

The night previous was one of merciless cold, and sleep was in short turns. Kirkland awoke so frequently he questioned whether he slept at all.

With morning, however, the temperature rose quickly, and his fingers and toes reassembled to make his body whole again. While he craved fetal, the lack of substantial rest did little to curl the sharp edges of death's imminent touch. The foul breath of battle was on Kirkland's cheek and stung his nostrils, filling his lungs with dread. Colliding images of Sharpsburg swept inward from his ears, tightening around his normal base of composure. Removing himself from the breastworks, Kirkland began to pace.

"Not to worry, Sergeant."

Colonel Kennedy dismounted from his bay.

"Good morning, Colonel," said Kirkland, trying to act poised.

"This is better ground than at Sharpsburg," he said, as if reading Kirkland's thoughts.

"Yes, but fighting near a church somehow felt more empowering, even if I didn't know it at the time."

Kennedy gave a hint of a smile.

"A shame what happened to that place of worship. It's peculiar to say, but I hope the fight comes today, and it will be over by tomorrow's Sabbath."

Kirkland presented the colonel an inquisitive look.

"These days, time seems to run together and the names fall away," Kennedy continued. "Sunday, unfortunately in times of war, is but another ending in d-a-y. I don't mean to be blasphemous. I do miss the days when I took my dear Elizabeth to Bethesda Church in Camden. As they say, a good sermon wears away the rust of the week. Someday, God willing near, this war will be over and the Sabbath will be returned to its rightful place. But for now, we must do our duty."

"Yes, Sir."

He wanted to say more, as in "be careful," since the colonel seemed to be a lightning rod for Federal bullets, but he decided against it.

Instead, Kirkland saluted the young commander and Kennedy returned it.

Boom!

The Washington Artillery, an elite unit of Louisianans entrenched just north of Kershaw's brigade on the high ground called Marye's Heights, had inhaled its metallic reapers and spit. In position behind and to the side of the Heights, Kirkland's view was obscured, and he couldn't see what had tempted the battery to rouse.

Just as the Washington Artillery came alive, the enemy's guns answered its challenge.

"Kirkland, get down!"

Regaining his surroundings, he saw the whole of his fellow Carolinians hugging the ground, along with Alex's pleading eyes. Kennedy had moved away to gain a better view, leaving Kirkland alone in his fixed wonderment. Quickly discerning the recklessness of his vertical, he joined his comrades in the dirt.

The enemy's shells, with their trumpeted screams, were meant to fall elsewhere, on Marye's Heights and in front, but errant missiles fell among the Carolinians.

"Steady, boys. We'll be in it soon enough."

General Kershaw was walking behind the recumbent men, his voice confident and reassuring.

But Kirkland wasn't his double in spirit. Unable to witness what was happening on the other side of the Heights, or on Stonewall Jackson's front to the south, his nerves took temporary flight. In an attempt to nullify this dread, he reminded himself that Lee and Jackson were in charge. Furthermore, he had confidence in his Carolina brigade, and his veteran regiment, surely at least the equal to any the Yankee's could throw at them.

Taking a few deep breaths, Kirkland looked at Joe, who returned his sheepish gaze with one of ridiculous play. Taking up his gun, Joe raised it above his head like a spear, in a mock hunter's stance. He went through the motion of throwing his weapon like an indigenous warrior, before returning it to his side. Smiling, Joe nodded at Kirkland, who could only respond by shaking his head in bewildered glee. And in thanks, again, with simple gestures, for removing much of the anxiety from his head.

Black mud kicked high in his wake as the lone rider hustled his horse toward them on the Telegraph Road. The horse slid to a halt in front of Kershaw and the messenger quickly dismounted. Saluting the general, the rider handed him a note and Kirkland knew the wait was over.

Immediately Kershaw, calm yet forceful, relayed orders to his staff and the brigade officers. Kirkland strained to hear the one-way conversation, but could only make out a few disjointed words. When he was done, Kershaw mounted his horse and pulled the immaculate sword from its scabbard.

Raising it high he trotted along his lines of men, who had already jumped up in anticipation.

"This is it boys," he shouted. "Do Carolina proud."

Then it was Colonel Kennedy's turn.

"Hurry, column of fours! Company commanders, get your men ready."

The men didn't need to be told twice.

Within minutes, after a brief check of ammunition, the marching formation was in order.

"Here we go, Rich, here we go, professor," said Joe, his face twisting into a mischievous grin. "Time to save the day and steal the glory. Bluebellies be-ware."

Alex feigned indignation at the "professor" comment.

Looking at Kirkland, he said, "Time for Joe Blowhard to seize the day with his mouth."

Kirkland started to smile, but one glance at Davy Clyburn stumbled the loose moment. The battle virgin's face was of pure terror, white with apprehension. Having almost forgotten his inward pledge to monitor the uninitiated one, Kirkland felt careless for leaving Davy alone with his expectations. Gently grabbing his shoulder, Kirkland looked into his foreboding eyes and tried to send a message of assurance and calm.

"Don't worry, Davy. These are veterans around you. Just stay close to me and you'll see it through. When you fire your weapon, aim low. Just remember, I'll be right behind you."

The pep talk seemed to soothe Davy some, but his nod in return was with less than complete conviction.

"Steady men. At the quick-step. March."

With Kennedy's fiery command, they were off.

Kirkland took one step and nearly fell out of his shoe. The frost had melted with the afternoon boil, turning the road to a muddy bog.

"Hey Rich, you might need that shoe later. Better hold on to it."

Pulling his shoe free, Kirkland continued, glaring playfully at Joe's humor. He wasn't the only one struggling to jog through the mud. The whole regiment was fighting the mire's grip. As they stumbled down Telegraph Road, the enemy's artillery noticed their movements, and shells began to find their range. With every blast and ricochet, Kirkland watched Davy duck and jerk, much more so than the enhanced reflexes of the veterans, when one got unnervingly close. He wanted to call out to him, but refrained from doing so in front of the other men.

As the Carolinians continued several hundred yards down the road, the missiles became more abundant, their screams more deafening. Blessed with good fortune, few located their mark and the men reached the bottom of the hill relatively unscathed.

Crossing the bridge over Hazel Run, they filed past the mill buildings and a sandstone quarry onto a freshly hacked road through the backside woods of Willis Hill. The 8th South Carolina followed up the steep and narrow trail leading to Marye's Heights. Now briefly removed from the sights of the Federal artillery, the Carolinians climbed northward, escorted by the rumblings of the growing tempest.

Exiting the ravine near a large, brick-walled cemetery with marble gateposts, they were given a most unwelcome greeting by enemy shells. The sky was filled with them, as if a flock of ravens were exploding, one bird after another.

Out in the open, there was no place to hide, as behind the rectangular walls of the family cemetery were artillery horses attached to limbers and caissons, along with crews of stretcher bearers waiting for a lull.

Directly in front of this habitat of disturbed rest were gunpits housing a 3-inch ordnance rifle and a 10-pounder Parrott of the Washington Artillery, attracting the enemy's sting. Also prominent was the Willis residence, an odd mixture of two chimneys at its gabled ends stabilizing wandering walls of avid expansion. Kneeling close were two other brick outbuildings, whose masonry were being severely tested.

"Form into line of battle, form into line of battle!" Colonel Kennedy screamed, trying to be heard over the incessant explosions.

"Lay down men, get down!" Kennedy repeated after the men were in battle formation.

Kirkland hit the ground, keeping his eyes on Davy in front.

Within seconds, a shell burst to the left of him. The concussion knocked Kirkland sideways and he rolled to a stop against Alex, who cushioned the blow.

"Are you all right?" Alex pleaded.

"I think so."

He was pawing his various body parts for damage when he heard Davy in animalistic wails. An arm had dropped from the sky, splattering mud on his face, and derailed him into hysterics.

Hopping to his feet in panicked recoil, Davy began to flee to the rear. Before he could take three steps, Kirkland tackled him to the ground. Kicking and howling, Davy tried to wriggle free, but Kirkland held firm.

"You're okay. You're okay, Davy," he caressed with a mother's tongue. Then he played the reputation card. "Don't let them see you run. You'll never hear the end of it. Do you want to return home a coward? Listen to me. Gather your faculties. I know you have strength in you. Take hold of it and breathe it. It will get you through."

Davy stopped fighting him and went limp.

"Stay next to me. When we move, stay close."

Out of breath from the struggle, Kirkland brought his chin up and pointed.

"Look, look at Kershaw," he said, taking his own advice, stunned by the vision.

There, the general casually rode to the front of the hill surveying the battlefield in front as bullets struck the ground all around him. He maneuvered his horse slightly but paid little attention to the grave danger of his position.

Then a strange thing occurred—the bullets stopped flying.

Incredibly, Kershaw's total fearlessness had struck a chord with the enemy and in admiration, the riflemen sought out a more deserving target, leaving the general alone.

Staring in disbelief and awe, Kirkland watched as Kershaw finished his survey with impunity. Realizing the enemy's show of respect, the general removed his headgear, and bowed gracefully.

"You see that?" said Kirkland with renewed confidence. "Who wouldn't follow that man through the Valley of Death?!"

Though unanswered, Kirkland could sense Davy's yellow spots evaporating.

Kershaw rode to the front of his now rabid, emboldened men.

"Get up, men," he said, with an inspiring growl. "Our brothers below need us."

With a rousing cheer, the Carolinians rose up and took their places. At "forward!" they launched on the plateau, between the cemetery and the Willis buildings. Against the wall of one of the smaller structures rested an elderly cast iron stove, which sang in triumphant pings as if lured into a game of target practice.

Through the smoke, Kirkland saw little of their opposition, but caught a glimpse of the bold, emerald flag of the Irish Brigade. Glowing in otherworldly brilliance, the flag rippled in gouging waves, as if sailing through a nor'easter. While beautiful in display, as if highlighted by a Judas orb, it was an undesirable spotlight. A perfect target.

As the 2nd South Carolina began to descend Marye's Heights, bedeviled kisses fanned Kirkland's cheeks on each side, the bullets skirting his whiskers. The terraced hill was muddy and perilously steep, and the trek downward was anything but coordinated or graceful. It wasn't long before Kirkland lost his footing and rolled several feet before regaining his balance.

Likewise, Joe slid and stumbled, teetering on one leg for several paces. He started laughing uncontrollably, which became contagious, spreading to a dozen men around him.

With deadly missiles buzzing among them, they giggled like children on a Saturday frolic. Despite the utter ridiculousness, Kirkland caught this wave of purity, and merrily in the face of death, he laughed down the hill.

Skidding to the edge of the drop-off to the road, he collected himself and was about to jump when something gently rolled into his legs. A peach-fuzzed mug stared upward in bronze tranquility.

"Come on, Davy, let's get out of this storm," he said, not looking down.

There was no response.

Grasping Davy's arm, he pulled, but the body was limp. Leaping into the road, Kirkland reached back and jerked Davy over the edge.

"Davy?"

From a small hole in Davy's coat, directly over his heart, a trickle of blood oozed, barely noticeable.

As the recognition swept over him, Kirkland heard a rowdy whisper and ducked from a sharp pain at the top of his right ear. Instinctively he put his hand to the source of the pain and framed it before his eyes. His fingers were laced with blood.

"That's not even a two-hour furlough," said Joe, examining the minor wound.

Ignoring both Joe and his own blood, Kirkland looked down at Davy.

"There's nothing you can do for him," said Joe, yelling over the suffocating noise. "Get to the wall!"

Kirkland started to obey, when Major Gaillard caught his eye, nearing the bottom of the Heights. His face was covered in blood, but he seemed unaffected, nonchalant even. Noticing Kirkland's concern, he held up his hand as if to say he was okay. It was a premature response, for moments later, he grimaced and fell backward, his foot mashed by a ball. Despite the wound, Gaillard crawled the last few paces to the safety of the road. Not far behind Gaillard, Kershaw was descending the hill with the 8th regiment when a shell exploded above, the shrapnel decapitating his horse. Somersaulting over his mount, Kershaw landed awkwardly and rolled twice. Briefly stunned, the general looked back at his mangled steed in bitter remorse and less so, as if in minor annoyance, at his lacerated arm. Despite the close call, Kershaw dusted himself off and rose, walking the final lengths down the hill with parading stride, exuding both calm and a hint of livid bristle.

Turning around, Kirkland spotted Captain Cunningham directing his company to double up behind the 24th Georgia, which was to the right of a humble, roadside residence known as the Stevens house.

Along with the 27th North Carolina, Kennedy's troops backed four regiments of Georgians, and the files behind the wall were now four deep. The 8th moved farther down the road and into place as the right flank.

"The Guards are over there," Kirkland yelled, grabbing Joe by the arm. Together they ran toward Cunningham.

"Captain, what are your orders?" said Kirkland.

"Sergeant, take your position behind the men here and keep an eye on the ammunition. If it starts to get low, I want to know about it. Stay low. We have a good defensive position here but they are coming hard. Any questions?"

"No, Sir."

"Good, now move."

Kirkland squinted, trying to see through the scowling heavens, where day had become night. The afternoon sun wilted in flight, as if driven hard by an indignant moon. It was a maddening, constantly wavering switch with blinking windows of transient view.

Mingled with the Georgians, Kirkland sought one out for a sketch of the heretofore battle.

"I can't see a thing through this smoke, friend," he said, still squinting. "What has gone on here?"

"It was a sight to see," said the Georgian, who Kirkland guessed must have been a stocky, well-proportioned young lad before the war by his square dimensions, but now ravaged of girth by hard campaigns.

"They came at us bravely, but our artillery tore 'em up before they were even in musket range. We took care of the rest, and I don't blame 'em for falling back. We have good protection here at this wall. It's like pickin' off buzzards. I reckon though, that they will keep comin' and the day ain't won yet."

He was obviously a veteran, having seen the way battle can turn in an instant from a conquering rout to a backpedaling retreat, and how ground can be won and lost in multitudes before the declaring ink dries.

"Yes," said Kirkland, knowing how outnumbered they were. "We may be in for quite a scrap today, before all is done."

The Georgian only nodded, peering over the wall with a hard rifle grip.

"General Cobb has been wounded. A shell went right through the roof of that house and struck him. But we have our good Colonel Robert McMillan yet."

"Well," said Kirkland, "the 2nd South Carolina will greet them with you."

"You have arrived with Providence. I do believe they're coming again."

But they were a long and treacherous distance away. Between the edge of city and Marye's Heights was a half mile of mostly open ground, with several obstacles sure to slow any advance. First, the enemy would have to get over a millrace five feet deep and fifteen feet wide. The Confederates had removed the floorboards from the three existing bridges, leaving only the dangling stringers. It was now a moat of freezing water, and Southern artillery had already perfected the range.

Those who made it safely across would then have to traverse 600 yards with little cover, and over fences bordering a ten-acre fairgrounds. Though a few random houses and their dependencies interrupted the open plain on their right, it was small consolation. And the ground was incredibly flat, with only a gentle swale in the center of the fairgrounds offering any notion of hiding.

The Sons of Erin, having lain down at the swale to catch their breaths, rose in unison, and they began to pick their way through the crowd of prostrate men. They were now 150 yards off, but their progress was slowed by the remnants of previous assaults. Although the lines were uneven, with artillery shells exploding all around them, on the Irish Brigade came in bold strokes, its emerald standard with a golden harp ever defiant in glowing ripples through the smoke.

Cunningham paced behind the men, repeating the same message so all would hear.

"The Georgians will fire by company, then you'll take their places at the wall. Load! Load!"

As the Carolinians rammed cartridges down their barrels, the Georgians leveled their rifles and the air above the wall burst in shuddered flame.

"Guards, move!" Cunningham screamed. "Guards, move!"

The Georgians, staying low, maneuvered behind them while the Palmetto troops took their places.

Crouching, Kirkland followed, watching for tardy or choked ears. He was pleased to see all had their wits as they moved in perfect harmony.

When they arrived at the wall, Cunningham wasted no time calling forth a volley.

"Move behind and reload! Move behind and reload!"

This went on for several minutes, the Georgians and Carolinians taking turns throwing lead into the Irish in a constant, withering blaze.

Even with limited visibility, the effect of their fire was plainly seen. Despite the enemy's remarkable determination, their lines began to splinter and waver. Regiments were attacking one at a time, and faced the devastating wrath of the wall's defenders alone and unsupported.

It was becoming a massacre.

But onward the Irish lunged, as if their children were being held captive behind it.

Kirkland watched the display of courage with unfettered admiration. This was beyond what even heroic men should be called to do.

The Irish were now swarming around both sides of a two-story, Greek Revival house owned by the Stratton family, and among the half dozen buildings of the accompanying wheelwright complex. To Kirkland, they appeared like spectral silhouettes, visible then obscured, then reappearing a few steps closer among the small orchard of peach trees west of the home.

At Kirkland's right, however, the Irish regiments were in great peril. In the preceding days, Cobb's Georgians had torn down the planking of the closest fairground fence, and stacked the boards into a maze of timber. The few that ventured beyond these obstructions were quickly shot down, and the attack collapsed, the survivors retreating to the swale for cover.

In and around the Stratton house and orchard, the other wing of the Irish Brigade had also stalled, the men butchered in alarming numbers.

A shorty, scrawny Georgia man removed his coat as if the red-checkered shirt underneath had burst into flames. He could contain his enthusiasm no longer, vaulting onto the wall. His eyes were wild and his mouth stretched to its limits. Raising his rifle with one hand and swinging his jacket with the other, the Georgian tipped his head back and let out a cry that was half wolf howl and half cougar growl.

As if all were one creature with a thousand tongues, the Southerners raised their hats and cheered with unfiltered delight. The ensemble of confident airs centered and rose before the winds shifted toward the prostrate foe.

Even those not known as uncouth mocked the Yankees with vehement oaths.

Kirkland attempted a cavernous shout, but his parched throat failed him. Of course, Joe had just walked up to hear his pathetically mild utterings.

"You sound like a wounded cat," said Joe, proud at his good fortune. He handed Kirkland his canteen in jest, which Kirkland swatted away.

"Ever there to find me in my glory."

"Someone's got to do it," said Joe with an exaggerated show of ivory.

"Hey, what's that?" Kirkland pointed to the enemy.

Joe wheeled around.

With Joe not looking, Kirkland snuck a sip from his own canteen. But he made sure the water dripped from his chin, when his friend turned back.

"Can't believe I fell for that."

"You are, gullible by nature."

"I'll remember you said that."

For a brief fifteen minutes, the storm took a breath, and the fire from each rival slackened. In the fairgrounds, also known as Mercer Square, Kirkland watched several Yankees drag and prop corpses into a grisly wall. Even in death, these unfortunates would continue the fight.

As Kirkland feared, this lull was only temporary, and at the city limits, another brigade was readying to take the heights.

★   ★   ★

"Here's what we're going to do," said Captain Cunningham, making the rounds with new orders passed down from Colonels McMillan and Kennedy. "Instead of alternating companies at every volley, those in the rear ranks will load weapons and pass them forward. Those in front will exchange their empty barrel for a loaded one."

He looked each individual square in the eye, imposing his will and making sure all understood.

"We will fire at will, but only when they are within easy range and when given the command."

A cheer from the fairgrounds alerted the men of another charge.

"Here they come again boys," yelled Cunningham. "Remember to hold your fire until instructed."

The Washington Artillery on Marye's Heights sprang to action. Now well-versed in pinpointing the range at each Federal step, the rounds exploded among the newest challenge, and the Yankees disappeared within the smoke.

Reaching into his cartridge box, Kirkland plucked a round and loaded as quickly as he could, waiting to pass it forward when the enemy appeared within the slaughter pen.

Those in the fairgrounds were amped by the reinforcements, and fired at the wall with renewed vigor.

Forced to kneel, the soldiers waited again in blindness behind the wall for the command to rise against their attackers.

The Federal artillery also seemed to rejuvenate, launching shells in vengeance at its nemesis upon the hills.

Doing his duty, Kirkland looked left and then right at the defenses behind the wall, witnessing no shirking, nor paleness of heart. While grossly outnumbered in manpower, the wall was an equalizer at the least, an impenetrable rampart at best.

Or so he hoped.

Now over the millrace, the Yankee brigade came on, ignoring the decimation from shell and shot, closing the gaps as their brethren fell. Cunningham and McMillan were pacing behind the lines, but Kennedy was motionless, his arms folded in deep concentration. A shell fragment burrowed the earth near Kennedy's feet, yet he reacted with mild annoyance, kicking away the dirt thrown upon his shoe.

His back to the wall, Kirkland massaged his loaded rifle, searching for any sign from his commanders that the time for eruption was near.

A glance at the stoic Camdenite was what the doctor prescribed, and he relaxed a few notches.

The minutes passed, and still there was no command to fire.

In his mind's eye, however, Kirkland perceived the enemy was, by leaps and bounds, closing in. Unable to see their progress, they were galloping like horses, frothing in mad retribution. He wanted to peek above the wall, but decided against it, trusting the leadership's judgment.

Sucking in air, Kirkland shut one eye and then the other, beckoning for the rancid smoke to disperse. Yet the wind had stalled, offering no relief to the sulfur bubble encircling the men at the wall. By ghostly image, Kirkland was sent home, recalling his father's lesson about the cottonmouth.

Without warning, McMillan halted his footfalls and stood next to Kennedy. Nodding to each other, they separated and called down the thunder.

Cunningham screamed, with a power Kirkland's ears had yet to behold.

"Fire! Fire! Fire!"

Above the stone wall, agnostic flashes mingled and danced, steered by forefinger strings. With barrels leveled and sure, they released a shuddering pyre of death.

Passing his rifle to the front, Kirkland stood up enough to see the Yankee lines waver. Approaching the crowd of men dug in at the swale, the Federals were falling in bundles, slaughtered by metal merchants large and small.

"Keep the fire hot," yelled Cunningham, again pacing behind his company. "Give it to 'em hot!"

As he passed a newly charged musket to the front, Kirkland's eyes narrowed to the sight of a single man carrying the stars and stripes. He was too far away to see the expression on the soldier's face, but his legs told of resolute motion. For a split second, Kirkland pictured his great-grandfather, running with a similar flag against overwhelming odds in the battle of Camden.

As he looked on, the flagstaff was reduced to splinters, and the proud colors of his granddaddy came crashing down, swimming in the mud. Its guardian slowly slumped to his knees, still clutching a jagged piece of the standard, and pitched forward on top of the flag.

The Yankees, realizing the madness in further steps, joined their flag in the dirt. They could advance no further. While the bravest had ventured to within 50 yards of the wall, they had paid the ultimate price for their daring.

Another brigade had failed with horrible casualties.

Gazing upward, Kirkland knew that the light, although stunted, was still far from relinquishing to night. Two questions, balanced in weight, rapped against Kirkland's skull. His heart, impressed by the enemy's fortitude and sacrifice, desired the butchery's end. Yet with each charge, the enemy had gotten closer to the wall, and he knew the victor was far from decided.

Will night ever arrive, to put an end to this bloodletting?

Could superior numbers eventually overpower our defenses, stout as they are?

Kirkland prayed for haste of the first petition and infinity's hold for the second.

★   ★   ★

At his side, Alex was having trouble ramming a cartridge down a barrel fouled from heavy use.

"Here, let me help you," Kirkland yelled above the storm.

Placing the rifle between his feet, he held it firm. Just as Alex was about to shove the round in, the ramrod jerked out of his hands. For a long moment, they looked at each other in surprise and then down at the twisted piece of metal. Instinctively, they dropped lower and shared a nervous giggle, now well aware that they had been standing a little too tall.

"Take this," said Kirkland, handing him his gun. "I know this one is clean."

A roar from the fairgrounds chilled their discussion. The prostrate Federals were waiving their hats in a robust cheer as a new brigade stepped from the city limits.

"They just won't give up, will they?" said Joe.

273

"How many hornets you have left?" said Kirkland, checking his cartridge box.

"About 15."

"We're going to need more ammunition."

Kirkland went around to several other men in his company inquiring about the number of remaining rounds.

He then sought out Cunningham.

"Captain, we are down to 10 or 15 rounds per man."

"Damn it," exclaimed Cunningham. That will not do."

After giving an order to a courier, he turned back to Kirkland.

"We must conserve our ammunition. Tell the men to hold their fire until the enemy is close enough to fire accurately."

"Yes, Sir."

Moving with heightened purpose, Kirkland went from man to man in his company.

"Hold your fire until your aim will be true," he yelled. "We have sent for more ammunition, but until then you must make every round count."

Joe removed his hat, and bellowed with exuberance at something occurring on Marye's Heights. Turning to understand the nature of his glee, Kirkland saw the 25th North Carolina Regiment swarming around both sides of a large mansion known as Brompton. The reinforcements boosted morale and those in the sunken road welcomed its arrival with stirring notes.

But as the Tar Heels rounded the Marye house, exposed in the open, the buoyancy at the wall was stifled as the tired defenders witnessed their aid being mowed down by the dozens.

Kirkland felt a mighty urge to reach up and pull them in one gargantuan swoop to the road. Instead, he found himself waving loudly in circular beckons. While an absurd gesture, it was one of desperation and helplessness, and when the survivors finally dashed from the heights to the relative safety behind the wall, Kirkland smacked his hands together in relief. Winded from the visual, his straining lungs were ramming against their cage.

274

With the Tar Heels solidifying the left, it proved to be a fortuitous buildup, as the Yankees were testing this flank more than ever before.

While the attackers had stalled again among the Stratton buildings and orchard, it became obvious that a fierce battle was occurring sight unseen at both edges of the line.

Continuing to load and pass readied muskets to the wall, Kirkland couldn't help wondering what was occurring beyond his limited range. To this point the Confederates were holding firm, the wall of stone and men impenetrable. Few Yankees had even reached within a Scottish hammer throw, let alone broken through the defenses.

But ammunition was now at critical levels, in grave danger of running out. During this lull in the fighting, Kirkland again polled the men of his regiment for the number of remaining rounds, fearing their answer. Reaching into his own cartridge box, he pulled out the last two rounds, staring them down in the palm of his hand.

"Joe, we're in trouble."

Chapter 16

2 PM

Immediately, Kirkland turned to seek out Cunningham, but the captain was already heading his way.

"Kirkland, how many rounds do the men have left?" said Cunningham, with a poised stance but nervous tone.

"Sir, we're running extremely low, two to five rounds per man."

The captain twitched violently and sucked in the bad news, holding it within his chest. His eyebrows pressed together, magnetized by a current of desperate searching. In a shuffling trepidation, his pupils danced between the corners, staring at nothing and everything.

Finally allowing a liberated breath, though it rushed from his nostrils more like a fiery snort than a calm heave, Cunningham bowed. He was composed, but at the very limit of possession.

"What is the status of receiving more ammunition?" said Kirkland, attempting to be mild in color.

"It's coming, but we were forced to move it far in the rear as the Yankee guns were getting too close."

"My orders, Sir?"

"Gather what you can from the wounded. I've sent word of our dire need. As you can plainly see, they are coming again. I don't want to see a shot wasted. Conserve to the last."

"Yes, Sir."

With graveness of step, Cunningham departed, sending his message of willful restraint to each company officer. Kirkland, reborn with purpose, followed his command.

The first man he encountered was Nail.

"I know you're low on ammunition," said Kirkland. "We've got more coming but take Alex and get all of the cartridges you can find from the dead and wounded. Whatever you find, split it up and pass it out to the ranks behind. We will load the guns that we have. But do *not* pass them forward to the wall until Captain Cunningham gives the word. Now go."

Kirkland turned to Alex, who had already overheard the order.

"Alex, make sure whatever rounds we have left are distributed evenly."

He thought about saying more but muted himself. There was little else to recommend.

"We'll make what we have left count," said Alex. "I will keep you informed."

"I know you will. Be careful and keep your head down."

With his scavengers off, Kirkland looked downward and picked up the nearest stray rifle. The barrel was empty and it felt cool to the touch. He hoped it wasn't among those rendered useless from heavy burden. Upon cursory examination, the weapon appeared in working order, still efficient for serving Death.

As Kirkland continued to move about relaying orders, Riddle, careless in exposing his upper body above the wall, had his slouch knocked off by a bullet. Grinning, he patted his chest, and then was bludgeoned by a minié to the forehead. Blood and brains showered the men behind him, and doused the road with gore.

Sharpshooters had taken refuge in the upper story of the Stratton house and were picking off the overly curious and reckless. Ducking lower, Kirkland yelled for the men to take cover. Before his eyes fell below the wall, however, a shell crashed into the building's attic, obliterating the floor. The sharpshooters were no more. Offering up a fist to the amazing marksmanship of the Washington Artillery and its allies, Kirkland shook his head in awe.

Without its fearful precision on this day…

He chose not to finish the image or give credence to the alternate reality.

While his first encounter with Louisianans at a Richmond saloon had planted a bitter seed, it had grown ripe with age and with an acquired taste. Though some of the bayou men, especially in the infantry, had deserved their reputation as brawlers and thugs, in battle they were tigers who more than proved their worth in every battle.

"Here they come again boys!" Kennedy growled behind his men. But before he could give further commands, he was knocked off his feet.

Kirkland ran to his side in horror.

Wincing, Kennedy reached for the spent bullet that had bruised his chest, but failed to penetrate the skin. As he rose, he looked at Kirkland and spoke casually.

"Souvenir."

Incredulous, Kirkland feared he was worse than letting on.

"You sure you're okay, Colonel?"

"A mere annoyance," he said, rising to his feet and peering over the wall. "Don't bother about me. We have visitors."

Wheeling about, Kirkland caught sight of the 11th New Hampshire Regiment entering the field. The men wore dark uniforms, which contrasted loudly against the faded, battle-spent attire of the other regiments from previous assaults. Kirkland mused if this was a new regiment or one that had been refitted. Either way, they were coming straight at them, in good order.

As usual, the smoke obscured the full scene in front, but Kirkland knew that this regiment was not alone and that more brigades were being thrown at them in rapid succession. This new threat scrambled into the fairgounds through torn holes in the fences and over surviving barricades. All along the wall, the officers were screaming, trying to be heard above the ferocious roar.

"At the ready! Hold your fire! Hold your fire!"

Kirkland, still holding the discarded rifle, loaded it without trouble.

As the regiment from the Granite State formed up in Mercer Square, the order to fire was snarled, and volleys ignited the wall into blazed lightning. Again, the smoke was blinding, denying the hunters a glimmer of their prey. Kirkland dug a small hole, just large enough to hold the butt of a rifle, where he could ram home a new bullet on his knees without the gun slipping.

He loaded one weapon, and then another, and then another, without pause. He had no idea what was happening on the fields in front, or the effect of the loaded guns he passed to the wall. All Kirkland knew was that they were putting up one hell of a fight, and the artillery on Marye's Heights was matching their intensity.

An inhuman, guttural roar to Kirkland's front and left broke his concentration. He turned, wondering what odd echo could smash through the aural chaos.

Ratcliff had yanked a rifle from an outstretched hand and leveled it toward the rushing foe. It balked from his agenda and he lifted the fouled weapon above his head. With a condemning growl, he flexed his biceps until they shook before slamming the rifle against the wall with such force that it splintered. Bloodshot and bulging with hatred, Ratcliff's eyes were more than predatory. They had lost all light and reason. It was as if cold, demonic membranes had eclipsed them, leaving two orbs of destructive yearning.

Lunging for another weapon, Ratcliff wheeled. His long, dirty locks followed, whipping across his face. In one motion, he pointed the rifle toward the beckoning haze, and fired blindly into the mist of the phantom regiments. Various cords of disheveled hair stuck to Ratcliff's grimy face, and fell individually, as if alive and slithering.

And in this whirlwind, Kirkland felt connected with Ratcliff's madness, as if they had become of one mind. Kirkland's stomach quivered as if burdened by boulders. He looked away and grimaced, clutching his midsection. Shadows invaded the last den of serenity between his ears.

Stomping his foot against his loading base, Kirkland attempted to run the cobwebs, and banish the darkness. Dropping an empty rifle, he latched his eyes, clenched his jaw and curled his toes. The candlelight within was flickering in a mighty wind, desperate in survival.

After several deep breaths, he opened his eyes to see Joe staring at him with alarm.

"Are you hit?"

Kirkland unclenched one fist enough to wave him off but said nothing.

Joe was unconvinced.

"Are you okay, buddy? You look like you've seen a ghost."

Kirkland just nodded. He tried to mold the words to allay Joe's fears, but gibberish prevailed. With the thunderous battle raging around them, it was almost impossible to speak in sentences anyway. To prove to Joe that he was "back in the saddle," Kirkland took one more cavernous breath, and picked up the rifle at his feet. It was a mirage, but the last thing Kirkland wanted was to show weakness in front of those in his command. And he hoped that his fellow soldiers had not witnessed the brief transition from oak to kindling.

Unsure of what had just transpired, Kirkland returned to his work and hoped the dizziness was fleeting. While bothersome in the extreme, it was not cowardice. Yellow lines had never bleached his spine. Of course, he was acquainted with fear. Any man who denied its presence in mortal combat was a liar. But fear and cowardice were two entirely different manifestations of war.

And Kirkland had always done his duty. His feet would go where his mind screamed against. He had earned the respect of his peers and of his superior officers. There was not a man in the 2nd South Carolina, other than Ratcliff and his worshipper, Hux, who didn't regard him in the highest esteem. However, for the first time, Kirkland had felt totally disconnected from himself.

A mind aligned with Ratcliff?

It was a fear worse than death. The narcotic rage had buried its talons in Kirkland's skull, begging him for acceptance, and he found it hard to push away.

Passing a loaded musket to the front, Kirkland grabbed another, and noticed Joe glancing backward at him before drawing a bead on another unfortunate Yankee. Rifle empty, Joe crouched down and crabbed over to his friend.

"Kirkland, me boy," said Joe, in a mock Scottish accent, "can A giv ye a haund?"

"What?" said Kirkland, the talons already releasing their grip.

"Ma Scots is poor." Joe slapped Kirkland on the back, sending a wave of sentient verse up and out through Kirkland's ears, then gathering momentum while heading south, exiting again between his toes.

Laughing, Joe smacked Kirkland again, this time on the behind. It stung, but brought relief.

"Joe, you heathen. Do that again and there'll be hell to pay."

"Oh, of course, chicken legs is gonna give me a beatin'."

"In due time, my friend. In due time. We're a little busy at the moment."

"Och aye."

But in truth, another wave of the enemy had been obliterated. Those with legs still in vitality retreated to cover while others fell to the ground to continue the fight. Another lull reigned, and General Kershaw took advantage by sending down the 15th South Carolina from the heights to reinforce the wall. The artillery fired intermittently, and scattered musket shots kept knuckles tense and eyes wary.

Kirkland hesitated, but looked into his cartridge box, afraid of what he might find. His fears were confirmed. Although he had replenished his ammunition from the dead and wounded, he was again down to two rounds.

Joe looked over Kirkland's shoulder.

"Two balls, huh?" he said, reaching for his groin. "Me too. Still there. For a moment I thought they had burrowed toward my stomach."

But Joe wasn't laughing at his own joke.

"How many do you have?" said Kirkland, trying not to sound disturbed. "Miniés that is."

"I'm empty."

Sitting down, Kirkland removed his hat, exposing a white forehead, a striking disparity to his powder-blackened face. He ran a fingered plow through his sweaty, matted hair.

The gloom was too much for Joe.

"We have plenty of sandstone here," he offered. "We could just throw rocks at 'em."

Kirkland looked up with eyes of disbelief. They locked on Joe's with a countenance devoid of humor or tolerance for the jester. This was a wordless argument Kirkland had never won before, and the underdog wouldn't start a victory streak here. Joe's innocent smirk and half-wink could never be painted black. The face was impervious to cold rain. Though he tried to hold it, it wasn't long before Kirkland was laughing to the point of breathless tears.

When he regained his composure, he glanced around for an additional pint of affirming light.

"Our wounded and dead are few," said Kirkland, more a voiced thought than commentary.

"Don't worry," said Joe, reading his mind. "I'm sure we will be resupplied soon."

"I…"

As if at the same instant, both men noticed a vacancy of sound on Marye's Heights. The Washington Artillery, so effective at keeping the Yankees at bay, had become eerily silent, like a preacher who had lost his place in a grand sermon. A thousand heads turned and looked up the hill, waiting for the orators to extend their God-fearing message.

The uncomfortable silence rose to disbelief as they watched the artillerymen, out of ammunition, hitch up their steeds and drive their guns to the rear.

★   ★   ★

5 PM

No one said a word, as if all tongues had become paralyzed by the untimely exit of a guardian spirit.

Peeking over the wall, Kirkland could see the Federals organizing for another attack.

A light breeze blowing from the west had pushed much of the smoke and opened an aperture of foreboding.

Thousands of Lincoln's warriors stepped off, their bayonets pointing to the heavens as if channeling the wrath of God. Line after line of blue appeared, marching as if on parade. Out of musket range and with very little artillery to harass them, they looked cool and confident. Worse—they looked pissed off. Although their faces were illegible, their steady gait spoke of revenge.

Kirkland was smack dab in the center of the enemy's concentration and he knew it.

Joe saw it all too vividly as well, and while he tried to adhere to his nonchalant stance, the new threat betrayed him. He stood with mouth agape until he became cognizant of Kirkland's stare.

"Well, buddy, thrust your Palmetto in your heart," said Joe, calm but serious. "We're gonna need it."

Without answering, Kirkland threw himself into action.

Grabbing a cartridge, he was about to ram it home when a commotion from behind stopped him.

New batteries were tearing up the road behind Willis Hill. Led by horses with desperate hooves, their riders bounced to their haphazard rhythms, digging in with their velocity spurs. Shells burst over them and tunneled the ground beneath, missing by hairs.

Trailing behind on a caisson, a man held on with white-knuckle grips while his red kepi threatened to elevate from its perch. Releasing his hold from the iron handle with one mitt, the artilleryman pulled the brim to his nose and was nearly ejected from its precarious seat. With legs in midair, dangling from the side of the wagon, he was saved by the driver's fortuitous turn. Oblivious to the trials of the rider behind him, the horseman had maneuvered in such a way for the rider to regain his foothold. While this gunner retained his seat, with every bump, the old hat lunged closer to its ambition.

The enormous, spinning wheels of the carriage also seemed to renounce gravity, lifting from the ground at the strike of a mud tumor. In time, the rider lost his daring, and held on with both hands. Feeling its opportunity, the headgear, calling the wind, could be restrained no more. It dove upward briskly and then flipped, gliding with a smirk to the earth. As the hat disappeared behind the speeding guns, Kirkland could almost read the curses on the rider's lips.

When the battery wheeled into the rifle pits vacated by the Washington Artillery, the relieved spectators at the wall, and on the hills, applauded in balloon-popping glee.

With a belly full of renewed faith, the Carolinians returned their attention to the killing fields in front.

But Kirkland's stomach gyrated again as he remembered another glaring need. He sought out Alex.

"Were you able to find many rounds?"

"Nail and I gave out what we could find," replied Alex, "but we are still very limited. The Yankees… It seems that for every man we shoot down, there are three ready to take his place. And with every charge, they are getting closer to our lines.

"Do you think we can hold?"

"What choice do we have?" mused Kirkland. "We still have this fine wall."

He wondered if he was trying to reassure Alex or himself.

"Sergeant."

The confident voice came from behind him and Kirkland turned.

It was Cunningham. A hint of a smile greeted Kirkland and mirrored the captain's tone.

"Sergeant," Cunningham repeated, "we were able to reach our supplies and get down the hill unscathed. It seems our friends in the artillery captured most of the enemy's attention. Please distribute as you see fit."

"Yes, Sir. Thank you, Sir."

Relieved, Kirkland turned and shouted.

"Nail! Alex!"

But the two of them had been leaning in to hear the good news and Kirkland nearly spit in their faces.

Feeling slightly embarrassed, he composed himself.

"You heard the captain."

He looked down at the box of ammunition that had just arrived at his feet, labeled:

1000 CARTG ENFIELD RIFLE MUSKET CAL 577

"You know what to do. Pass out the majority and leave the rest protected behind the wall."

It was now after 5 PM and the sun was falling rapidly. But the moon's companion was still uncomfortably distant and dawdling. Kirkland wished to shove the embers of sky away and pull in the cricket's song, before the enemy used its superior numbers to greet them in lunging proximity.

Night would be no savior, he mused, at least not for a good while. The Yankee lines were moving closer and seemingly with greater numbers than ever before.

Having watched Alex and Nail distribute the ammunition, he knew it was futile to do anything more except to load, pass forward and pray.

And give a little encouragement.

Walking back and forth behind his company, he gathered whatever strength he could ingest from the putrid air, stopping to load when given a rifle.

"Men, we must hold at all costs," Kirkland yelled, in his most resolute voice. "Kershaw is counting on you. Make him proud. Make Carolina proud."

The Yankees were now within a hundred and fifty yards, marching proudly without firing a shot. When a man would fall, they closed the gap as if brushing off a minor inconvenience. The men lying down in the fairgrounds were much less confident, grabbing pant legs and pleading for them to go no further. These gestures were ignored, and the Yankees continued on, rushing toward their destiny.

"Fire at will. Fire at will!" Kennedy and Cunningham, as well as McMillan and every officer with a voice left, were screaming with saliva projections.

The acrid clouds were thicker than ever, and the men fired at any sign of movement, whether true flesh or shadow illusion. Occasionally, through a window, they could pick out a target and see the effect of a Federal stopped cold in his tracks. But this was an oddity. And when they saw him, he was close, real close. Within 50 yards close.

The artillery on the heights were throwing canister, and the ground fairly shook with the combined defense.

His ears ringing a flatlined hum, Kirkland felt nothing and his hands loaded as if detached, out of his control. The sulfur clogged his nose and invaded his mouth, causing a weird sensation as if munching on gravel. And it failed to bother him in the least, for Kirkland had again been overcome by the battle shroud, fully awake yet medicated. All that remained was purity of duty.

His latest rifle loaded, Kirkland moved right to find a shooter. Spotting Fain ambling backward from the wall, he held out his gun with outstretched arms. As Fain was about to receive the new charge, a bullet creased his chest, sending a button up Marye's Heights. Momentarily stunned, Fain soon recovered. Laughing away his close call, he seized the weapon from Kirkland's hands. Returning to his place in the firing line, Kirkland heard him exclaim, "Is that all you got? That was my favorite button, you…"

The final oath was lost in the upheaval, and Kirkland couldn't help but smile.

God Bless that heathen fighter.

Somewhat revived from his semi-comatose head cloud, he attempted to gauge the distance of the enemy to the wall. And he was floored at how unhindered and crystal his view of the enemy was revealed.

They were severely weakened in numbers, clumped in groups around their flags. With every step of the quaking line, a brave man fell, grimacing as if knocked down by a hammered fist. Still they came on, driven by a motivation they would take to the grave. It was becoming obvious this would soon be their destination. While the most courageous had come within thirty yards of the wall, they were few in number, and easy targets.

The man farthest ahead was only a corporal with double chevrons. Yet as he ran, he glanced backward, gesturing wildly for those to follow. When he finally turned to face the wall, he stopped suddenly, his jaw stretched wide in a fearless roar. As the bluecoat leveled his rifle, a bullet ripped through his throat. Dropping the weapon, the man fell to his knees, clenching his neck, as blood poured between his fingers. The fire in his eyes had been extinguished yet he dropped slowly in a composed kneeling, awaiting death. When it came, the soldier pitched forward, and Kirkland detected a faint smile on his lips, as if proud to meet his end face to face with his enemy.

★　　★　　★

7 PM

"What in the hell is that?" said Joe, his eyes skyward and incredulous.

Kirkland was equally astonished at the dancing lights of mid-sky.

"It's the mirrie dancers on a frolic," said Alex. "They must have approved of our overwhelming victory."

Joe nodded, but retained his dumbfounded expression.

"The aurora borealis, you simpleton," said Alex. "It's a natural phenomenon, though quite rare this far south."

"What could cause such a display?" said Kirkland, unable to detach from the otherworldly exhibition.

287

"No one knows for sure. There are theories. . ." Alex stopped midsentence. "It's a complete mystery, really."

Kirkland couldn't determine whether Alex believed his two country friends were too uneducated to understand the science, or if Alex was speaking the truth about a puzzle among the enlightened.

He decided on the latter.

Together, the three pals stood silently mesmerized at the irregular patterns of ghoulish yet seductive lights. For thirty minutes they said nothing to each other, mouths agape, heads tilted to the heavens as the green swirls and bold spikes flaunted against the blackness. The cloud curls rippled, like swaying rows of candles, burning so bright they extinguished in only a flicker. Yet as soon as one blew out, another was lit, as if attended by a firesmith drawing inspiration from the stars.

If this was indeed some form of congratulatory message from the Creator, as some of his peers would later voice (without Alex's sarcasm), Kirkland was baffled by the intent. Surely, it was too beautiful and majestic to have anything in common with the killing fields below.

No, this was either a coincidence of the most severe, or a sign from the Creator that man, at his most ugly and destructive, would not have the final brush stroke on this day, December the thirteenth, eighteen hundred and sixty-two.

Surely, it had no connection to Flat Rock, and Kirkland soon tired of the deeper questions in this mystical display. He reached for Susan, framing her in a stroll within the light. For the first time in many months, Kirkland saw her in accurate proportions, in a detail he long believed was tarnished with distance and time.

Cradling the image as if in atlas-bending embrace, Kirkland felt relaxed for the first time in weeks. His shoulders were again in proper alignment and his knees released aggregate burdens. This welcomed trance continued until the last wispy strokes dissolved into the night, and Susan went with it.

As if standing idly by with a grotesque smirk, waiting, Darkness trampled the nourishing view. At once, with brutal force, reality awoke like a brick to the cheek. Amplified groans and beseeching calls for

288

remedy swept over the protective wall, jarring Kirkland from his serene abode.

For some reason, while the Northern Lights performed their acrobatics, the pleas of the suffering were blanketed and mute. Perhaps even the wounded set aside their plight during the light show, believing the angels of the Lord were descending to greet them. Or was it conceivable that the medicinal glow formed cotton balls that lodged in Kirkland's ears?

If the latter were true, he wished for the mirrie dancers to reappear.

"It's not the Fourth of July is it?" said Joe, returning to character. "Them were *some* fireworks."

Kirkland was already beyond the event, an aural sense having taken over, and he had no response.

With Alex, they stretched out on the ground, with their backs to the wall.

"I must confess, it was the most extraordinary natural event I've ever witnessed," said Alex. "For a moment, I believed we had marched to Canada."

"As long as we hold our ground tomorrow, and Stonewall fights like I hear he did today, I'd say we've witnessed the most extraordinary defeat in American history," said Joe, in uncharacteristic perception.

The words provoked a stare from both Kirkland and Alex.

"What? Do you think all that is rattling around up there in my head is about girls?"

"Yes," said Kirkland and Alex in unison.

"Didn't see too many of them today."

Helplessly, the group burst into prolonged laughter. Apparently not wanting to be left out of the fun, Nail walked over and sat down.

"What are you jackasses goin' on about?"

"Your face," said Joe. "It's one only a mother could love."

"Well, at least my mother loves me. And she ain't no donkey."

Joe roared, until he saw Kirkland wasn't laughing.

"Sorry Rich. I can often be confused with the village idiot."

Kirkland shook him off as he had stopped paying attention to the conversation. Joe, knowing better, left it alone. The conversation continued with Kirkland's attention pulling farther away.

It wasn't his own mother that he was thinking of.

A muffled cry in the distance had shaken him, one that Kirkland had heard before. It was a dying man reverting to his childhood, begging for the comfort that only a mother could provide. Time after time, the mortally wounded soldier called out to her, getting weaker each time until he exhaled for the last time.

Kirkland said a prayer for the dead, but before he could finish, another pitiful cry arose.

And then another. And then more. The ground beyond the wall became alive with writhing agony and distress. Some called out for loved ones, others just mumbled incoherently, drifting in and out of consciousness. Still others, panicked and pleading, complained of bitter cold as the lifeblood drained from their bodies.

To a man, they craved the sustainer of life: water.

As the desperation of these Yankee wounded escalated, even Joe went silent, and he merely stared at the ground, blinking in uncommon waves. Alex was in similar distress, his face reddened with cerebral pain.

Nail, however, strove to block all sounds, and faked a yawn. He stretched his arms in exaggerated show and rolled over on his side. Slowly and with guile, Nail covered his ears with wincing hands, as the enemy's plight continued in a wide array of torment.

Joe and Alex followed his lead, pulling over blankets reeking of gun powder and attempted sleep. Before turning in, Kirkland gazed upward, hoping for another appearance by the aurora, but without such fortune. The clouds had rolled in, and even his mother's star was shrouded in darkness.

Although weary of mind and body, the dream world failed to take. Even the most muffled intonations of suffering penetrated Kirkland's soul, and battered his spirit. Closing his eyes only amplified the sounds. He tried to tell himself that these poor soldiers would be rescued, or at least comforted, by their comrades before dawn.

But the persistent pleas told otherwise. They were left to die, alone.

With his spirit freezing, Kirkland's body began to succumb to the frigid December temperatures in similar discomfort.

Longing for a fire, but knowing it would be too dangerous, he rolled over, pulling his blankets tight to his chin. Shifting into a fetal position, Kirkland attempted to preserve what warmth he had left.

In doing so, he found stern eyes reflecting in the subtle moonlight. Joe was staring directly at Kirkland, locked with concern.

"I know what you're thinking," said Joe, in a serious tone. "If you try to help them, they will shoot you. They'll think you're robbing the dead."

"I know."

"Listen. I admired their bravery today, too. They deserved a better fate and compassion is a natural sentiment. But these men dying before us came of their own accord. We did not ask them to oppose us. And believe me, they would slaughter you in your sleep if they had the chance."

Joe took a deep breath and paused, trying to find additional words that would strike a chord with his friend.

"Kirkland, try to get some sleep. You'll need your strength. It doesn't appear the Yanks are withdrawing tonight."

Waiting impatiently for some iota of response, Joe scanned the depths of each eye, hunting for traces.

Kirkland, though, merely shifted to his back and said nothing.

He didn't have to. Joe's strange eloquence was not unlike the dueling merchants on Kirkland's shoulders, screaming into opposite sides of his head. Each had powerful arguments.

On his other flank, Alex was curiously silent, yet Kirkland could feel the intensity of a mind toiling with knots.

"I'm here Reb, kill me!"

The voice from beyond the wall was angry and forceful.

"Finish me off, you hear me? I'm here. Kill me off!"

Strong enough to eradicate a few snores from those already dozing behind the wall, the Yankee waited. When no shots came, the man became more desperate.

"Please, Johnny, I beg you," his voice breaking. "Silence this life."

Still ignored, the Yankee resorted to taunts.

"Kill me, you sons a' bitches! Damn you cowards! Cowards, I say!"

A single report echoed through the frigid air, followed by a chilling hush.

Closing his eyes hard, Kirkland tried to monopolize the image of Susan and nothing else, until his mind gravitated to his body's winded rhythms. And he fell into fitful sleep. Countless times Kirkland awoke, believing his body had frozen to the ground. He would bring his knees to his chest and repeat the move until some semblance of thaw eased into his legs. Legs intact, he blew into fisted hands, opening and closing them while pain told of their survival.

Up and down his body, Kirkland flexed to regain healthy circulation, all the while listening to the groans and deliriums of the less fortunate isolated between the lines.

"Please, Johnny, just a drop o' water for an old soldier. I can't move my legs."

"Reb, I'm dyin' over here. Can you spare a drink?"

Most tormenting to Kirkland were those requesting nothing of material nature, only acceptance into the Great Unknown. Choosing their words carefully as if speaking to Peter standing before Utopia's gates, they offered a final argument, hoping their war deeds hadn't befouled their souls.

One of these earnest prayers, long after the words drifted into the nocturnal realms, would leave a permanent mark.

"Lord, I've never been much of a church-going man. I tried to stay true to your morals and righteous path, but I've had my struggles. With my limited understanding of all things sacred, I believe I followed a good flag. But I'm afraid this war is ruled by the Devil. I pray for my friends and fellow patriots who lost their lives today, or who may soon follow in the days to come. May they find eternal peace.

I do not hate those who opposed us today. I forgive them and pray for them, for in the end we are all brothers. We were all made in your image and must one day put our differences behind us.

I offer my spirit to you, knowing my time on Earth has run its course and pray that I will soon be in your glorious presence. I ask for forgiveness for all past transgressions. Please take care of my lovely wife and my four beloved children.

As I'm sure you know, we are not wealthy, so please take pity on them and provide for their needs, if you deem them worthy.

Lord, hear my prayer. Thank you for the many blessings bestowed upon me in my 21 years. In your glorious name, amen."

Well before the penitent man was done, tears without consent burned at the corners of Kirkland's spastic sockets. Despite the pressure, he refused to allow the dam to break, wrapping his arms tighter around an impaired stomach and bruised heart. Doing his best to ignore the discordant requiem echoing across the field of mortals, Kirkland spent the remainder of the night in a revolving haze, never quite awake or falling completely into dreamscapes.

Not long after he finally closed the vigilant door of mindfulness, dawn crashed through harmony's window.

The pleadings were again numerous and singular in their desire.

"Water."

Chapter 17

DECEMBER 14, 1862

Kirkland awoke to groaning, this time so close, the wind of it touched his cheek. Opening his eyes, he was inches away from a recognizable face.

"Good morning, Joe," said Kirkland, in false cheer, arising from a night where counting sheep and a myriad of other tried devices failed to induce much slumber.

"What's so good about it?" Joe retorted. "My shoulder feels like it was kicked by a mule. No, several mules."

"Ah, you big baby."

"Easy for you to say, I'm sure loading those guns and giving us commands left you mighty sore."

Before he could respond, a breath warmed the back of this neck. Kirkland rolled to see Alex, the second of the midnight creepers, huddling closer during the frigid night. Although he had noticed this upon frequent wakings, he was agreeable to the relief from the cold.

"Sir, please point me in the direction of the nearest hospital," said Alex, also rubbing his shoulder. "I believe the condition of my right arm requires amputation."

"I think you'll live."

"Where's the barbecue?" said Joe, sitting up, gingerly. "I could eat a horse."

"I'm afraid you'll have to settle for far less," said Kirkland, reaching into his haversack. "Crumbs in abundance."

"I don't even wanna look in my pokes."

Reaching for his canteen, Kirkland shook it to gauge its contents and tilted his head back. No more than a dram unloosed into his mouth. He stretched liberally and caressed his stubbled cheeks, itching with new growth. Rolling onto his knees, he took a peek over the wall and immediately regretted it.

A harvest of frozen corpses had disfigured what had been a gentle landscape only a few days before. As far as he could see, mounds of flesh lay scattered in alarming numbers. Among the muted beings and cadaverous crowd, damaged survivors writhed and contorted, bathed and revived by torturous light.

Not more than 50 yards from the wall, a long trail of blood aimed toward the city limits. Kirkland followed the gory aisle until his eyes caught up with its struggling composer. The Yankee's blue uniform had been swallowed by earthen appetite and he blended in like a shifting reptile. Much of the soldier's right leg was missing and he dragged a torn pant leg behind. With tortoise-like plodding, his movements were subtle and almost invisible. If not for the crimson groove, it would have been easy to mistake the Yankee for another stiff. Determined elbows and one courageous knee propelled him away from danger and toward the hope of a surgeon's hands.

Judging by the pace and the length of the track, Kirkland surmised that the man must have launched his quest well before sunrise. After watching the vile spectacle for a few moments, a second man drew Kirkland's receptors near.

About the same distance as the tortoise man but 20 yards to Kirkland's left, a soldier was making a heroic effort just to sit up. He was lying with his feet toward the Yankee lines and was apparently without the use of his arms. Very slowly, his head rose, straining for the apex and freedom from prostrate form. But before the warrior reached the summit of his yearning, he trembled violently and collapsed to his original position.

Kirkland believed the man had "gone up" but he underestimated the soldier's will. Between periods of brief, comatose rest, the exertion was repeated, each time in failure.

Having seen enough, Kirkland turned away and rested his back against the wall as an intense melancholy hung over him, sapping his already weary spirit.

Where are his rescuing friends?

Why aren't they helping him?

These were the same questions thrown the previous night. Yet he knew the answers all too well.

The bravest of the enemy, closest to the wall, were farthest from help. It would be suicide for any of his fellow soldiers to help him. The litter bearers wouldn't come anywhere near them. Especially now in the daylight. They would be shot and create multiple casualties instead of one. Unless there was a truce called to bury the dead and collect the wounded, Burnside's dutiful lambs would have to endure or join the KIA list, a passing mention in a newspaper column.

If the soldier was fortunate, his home paper might get an anonymous obituary from a comrade, touting his honorable death and sacrifice for his country.

Burying his head in his hands, Kirkland closed his eyes and opened the pages of his mind, shuffling back until the book opened onto a pleasant memory. He was nine and his father took him and his siblings for a weekend of fishing at the banks of the Wateree River, several miles from their home. Both afternoons were perfect, where a slight breeze drifted over easy waters and kept the summer heat at bay. He had never seen his father in a better mood, or more talkative. His father spoke of the good ole days and told inflated stories about hooking a monster sturgeon which took hours to wrestle to shore. Richard and his brothers paid less attention to their poles than to their father's lyrical tongue and glint in his eye.

Neither the catfish nor a trophy sturgeon was biting but they didn't care. It was all about dipping toes in cool water, and the art of leisure. This was a rare experience to see the elder Kirkland pull himself away from the farms, for he was ever in constant movement, obsessed with minute details to maximize the harvest. To his credit, however, he was never blind to internal strife. When the old man felt his sons and daughter were distancing, he pulled them together, taking a day or two away from his duties. And to healing sanctuaries like the Wateree River.

Here, they rekindled the joy of each other's company. As Kirkland grew older, he wondered if his mother had given a gentle nudge from her place above, whispering in his father's ear that it was again time for a sabbatical away from life's speeding tracks to feed the roots.

"Your kin is what matters," his father would often say. "When you are lost, this is your rock, the foundation you must return to. Because of this truth, you must never abandon them. You must strive always to strengthen and protect this bond. But this is true with all relationships, however trivial. And when you treat all people with respect and honor, you will never be truly lost or alone."

The words were washing the dirt from Kirkland's skull when the thud of bullets striking the ground left him uncleansed.

Kirkland opened his eyes and turned to see a soldier in gray on the wrong side of the wall, filling a canteen at the Stevens well. The man, a Georgian, had half a dozen canteens around his neck to bring water to his messmates. Bullets were striking all around him but he casually finished his task before taking flight back to the wall. With a smile on his face, the Georgian evaded the fire, which kicked up soil all around him and ricocheted off the wall in front. As the soldier rounded the gap between the Stevens house and the wall, he was struck in the back, arching in midair, before tumbling into the outstretched arms of his comrades.

"See what I mean?" said Joe. "It's no use trying to cross that wall. Damn fool."

Kirkland's silence was more than enough to worry Joe.

"You can't be thinkin'…"

Kirkland snapped out of his gaze but didn't look Joe in the eye.

"I need your ink well," said Kirkland, without emotion.

"Sure."

Joe gave him an examining look while handing him a small tin box and quill.

"Can I get a minute?" said Kirkland. "I need to write Susan."

"Of course."

Hesitating, Joe finally left his friend in relative privacy.

Kirkland pulled out some paper Susan had forwarded and set it awkwardly against the stock of his rifle. The words came freely and he forced his hand to slow down to prevent a derby of scribble.

Dear Susan,

My love, I don't have the words to express the sweeping tenderness I have for your memory. Sometimes I think that's all have left, holding on to the thin grains of our time together. This war can fill a man with regrets. Many a night I have fallen asleep with thoughts of your embrace. It has brought me comfort in weary days of homesickness and trials.

I've longed for the day when this war is over and again I could be in your gratifying presence. Though I've never lost heart or determination for the cause of our state and fledgling nation, the conclusion of our fate seems forever distant and unknown. Despite my patriotism, not wanting to desert my brothers in arms is the only thing keeping me from running to you.

He lifted his pen and paused, trying to form words that would not bring instant alarm, but at the same time be a proper sentiment for farewell.

We have won a great victory at Fredericksburg yesterday, but the future only God can predict. If the Lord calls me before I make it home, tell my father,

298

sister and brothers goodbye for me. Give my regards to your family. I will love you always.

Yours till death,

R.R. Kirkland

Before folding it, he read it over, scrutinizing every detail. Although unsatisfied at the quality and short length, he reluctantly concluded it was the best he could offer.

Reaching into his jacket, he pulled out an envelope he had been saving, and stuffed the letter into it. Taking a deep breath, he subtly called on Alex, knowing he had already distressed Joe. Seeing Joe and Nail laughing together, Kirkland saw his chance.

"Alex, I've got a letter here for Susan. Can you hold it for me?"

Alex said nothing and studied Kirkland for several moments, making him uncomfortable. Staring at the ground, Kirkland knew his actions were giving him away. Faking a smile, he finally greeted Alex's inquisitive face.

Alex wasn't buying.

Taking Kirkland's letter with one hand, he grasped Kirkland's forearm with the other.

"You saw what happened to the last man who took a stroll. You be careful, you hear?"

Kirkland nodded and escaped to find Kennedy. He found him crouched behind the wall, sipping from a dented cup.

"Good morning, Sir. Is that real coffee?"

"Good morning. No, unfortunately. It's hard to remember what that tasted like. You want some? It's chicory."

"No thank you."

Kirkland continued with the small talk, not knowing exactly how to voice his unusual request.

"Close call?" Kirkland pointed toward the colonel's cup.

"I assume so. Didn't even notice it until this morning. Most likely it took a hit as we descended the hill."

"That was a hot maneuver. No question."

"Yes it was."

While staring at his feet, a voice from beyond the wall finally gave him the impetus.

"Water. Please Johnny Rebs. May I have some water?"

Kennedy looked up from his coffee substitute and shook his head.

"Poor bastards. Their bravery deserved better."

"Sir, with your permission, I would like to bring some water over the wall."

In mid-sip, Kennedy lowered his vessel, eyes lost in the steaming beverage. But he said nothing, and didn't appear surprised. After a second sip, he spoke plain.

"Sergeant, you'll likely be killed. Any man who so much as raises a head above that wall becomes a target."

"I'm willing to take that risk."

"Kirkland, you're a good man. I can't afford to lose you."

"I can't afford to stand here and do nothing, Sir. It will be a mark on my soul."

Kennedy appeared visibly moved by Kirkland's words, but he exhaled slowly as if trying to hinge a lucid dissent. He gulped the chicory now and grew agitated, roughly pulling out some paper from his coat pocket.

"I'm sending you to General Kershaw," said Kennedy, scribbling a note. "He is at the Stevens house."

He pointed to the Swiss-cheesed house on their left.

"You must seek his permission. If Kershaw will allow it, I will not stop you. Now go, before I change my mind."

"Yes, Sir. Thank you, Sir."

Kirkland turned to walk away, but Kennedy grabbed his wrist.

"And Kirkland. God go with you."

★   ★   ★

Kirkland gave the note to a burly guard posted outside of the Stevens house.

"I'm here to see General Kershaw."

The guard read the note and sized up Kirkland, who ignored his probing eyes. Above the small porch, in the roof, was a gaping hole punched by a shell that had crashed through and exploded, its shrapnel breaking General Cobb's leg and severing the femoral artery.

"He's upstairs," said the guard in a monotone voice, before returning Kennedy's order.

"Thank you."

Ducking in under the small porch covered with snarled and climbing wisteria vines, Kirkland opened the door and scanned the open room. The furniture had been pushed against the walls to make room for the wounded and groaning. Attending these fallen was a plump woman, pushing forty, dabbing fevered brows and checking bandages. A lit pipe was gritted at the corner of her mouth, causing the words of motherly comfort to slur. Her hair had just begun to lighten, waiting for friends of white. When the woman glided in front of sun shafts poking through bullet holes on the eastern wall, they framed her in a strange halo, suggesting there was more than her rough appearance first allowed.

Mrs. Stevens, perhaps?

If this was her identity, Kirkland was amazed. Despite an apron tainted with blood, her home wrecked and commandeered, the woman floated about without a hint of concern for her well-being.

Tipping a cap to her, Kirkland took a running start up the first few steps to the second floor before composing himself. Once upstairs, he saw the general with field glasses, staring out a broken window.

Kirkland wasted no time.

"General, I can't stand this."

Ignoring him for a few moments, deep in his own observations, Kershaw eventually turned, visibly irritated at being disturbed. But before he spoke, he released the tension in his face and assumed the southern

301

gentleman. Although puffy satchels hung underneath, the signs of exhaustion had no effect on his piercing eyes.

"What is the matter, Sergeant?"

"Forgive me for intruding, but all night and all morning I've listened to the wounded suffering beyond the wall, pleading for water and can stand it no longer. With your permission, Sir, I will bring them relief."

Taken aback, the general stood for a moment and looked directly into Kirkland's determined eyes.

"I remember you. You are John Kirkland's son, are you not?"

"I am."

"How is your father?"

"Last I heard, he was well."

"I don't know him personally, only by reputation, but I'm told he is an honest man."

"I'm sure he would return the compliment, Sir."

Kershaw nodded, evidently pleased by the exchange.

"Sergeant, don't you know that you will get a bullet through your head the moment you leave the safety of the wall? They will think you are robbing the dead."

"That may be, sir, but if you will let me, I'm willing to take that chance."

The general clutched his hands behind his back and paced.

"This is an unusual request, Kirkland. I was also kept awake by their cries. And while they remain our enemy…"

He paused, stroking his mustache.

"I don't know what Burnside was thinking. Whether it be by the hands of arrogance or incompetence, men shouldn't be sacrificed so. But they must sleep in the beds they make. And when sheep come willing to the slaughter, we must give it to them, to win this war."

"I agree, Sir. We did what we had to do so our country may live. But now I must also do what my conscience demands. God made us separate from beasts."

Kershaw stopped pacing and launched himself toward Kirkland.

"Indeed. In-deed."

He smiled like a proud father and patted Kirkland on the shoulder. This grin soon faded, and the general morphed into dignified sobriety, his blue-gray eyes gathering heat.

"I ought not to allow you to run such a risk, but the sentiment which actuates you is so noble, that I will not refuse your request, trusting that God may protect you. You may go."

"Thank you, Sir."

Kirkland turned to walk down the stairs, but the gravity of the situation held him to the floorboards. Reversing himself, with angels of death whispering in his ears, he said: "Sir, I've been proud to serve under your command."

"No," Kershaw said. "It has been my honor to lead such a reputable brigade of South Carolina's finest."

They saluted each other and Kirkland descended, feeling the beasts nipping at his heels.

★   ★   ★

The sandstone layers assumed the persuasion of both needle and spur. Against Kirkland's back, they were blocks of numbing ice, medicating his resolve. Together, they formed a soothing harbor in a vicious gale. But this wall was also dreadfully cold and awkward, with an odor of guilt.

Kirkland closed his eyes, breathing heavily. He had collected more than a dozen empty canteens from approving yet skeptical Georgians. They had handed them over with eyes of farewell, for both vessel and soldier. This was unnerving, but much more digestible than protests from his friends. And so Kirkland had avoided them, quickly gathering as many canteens as he could carry before huddling at the end of the wall.

Mother, if this is my final act, I will see you shortly. Susan, forgive me if I cannot return to you.

With the mid-morning fog lifting, Kirkland peeked around the wall, gauging the distance to the wellhouse and then to nearest wounded beyond. Although the well was a mere 30 feet away, the fate of the last man running this short gauntlet attested to how perilous even this brief expanse could be.

One worry at a time.

Clearing his mind to choke any doubts from taking hold, he took one more deep breath and dashed toward the well. It was an ungraceful run, the canteens swinging in all directions, and he crossed his arms over the straps to shun their wayward movements. This slowed him down, and he was afraid he wouldn't reach the well, let alone help the wounded.

But he pressed on, and was nearly at the well before the first bullets opposed him. Fanning his torso and thumping the ground, they swarmed, eager to sting. Churning his legs in desperation, he dove behind the wellhouse as more rounds slammed into the wooden sides. Kirkland caught his breath, and then began to fill the numerous canteens. When he was finished, he scanned the ground at his front.

This is suicide.

★　　★　　★

As he neared the first wounded man, Kirkland attempted to slow down but his wheels failed to comply.

Slipping and sliding, he tried desperately to maintain his balance, to no avail. With feet above his head, his back slammed into the ground. As he raised himself up to a sitting position, he looked to his sides, expecting to see a patch of ice. Instead, what he saw sickened him to his core. It was a river of frozen, congealed blood. He was looking at his rust-colored hands when the enemy spoke.

"Hello, Reb."

With a limp body and face parallel to the wall, a man about Kirkland's age, with frost on his straggly beard, was staring at him calmly. His head was cocked at an odd angle, seemingly locked in place.

"Hello, Yank."

This was the first man from north of the Mason Dixon line that Kirkland had ever spoken to.

"I can't feel anything below my shoulders. Shot through the spine. Must have been too far ahead of the line, a perfect target. Full of vinegar, I guess."

The soldier tried to laugh, but the pain became too great and it turned to an alarming choke.

"Please, help me sit up."

Kirkland tried to do as requested but to his horror, the man was frozen to the ground, glued by his own bodily fluids. Reaching his arms around the victim to get a good grip, he pulled. And then he pulled again. But it was as if the man's back had sprouted roots. Determined, Kirkland growled as he wrenched with all of his might, and the Yankee was pried free with a repulsive note of crackling suction.

With an arm around his shoulders and supporting the man's head, Kirkland pulled one of the canteens from around his neck.

"Here, you must be thirsty."

Slowly, Kirkland poured water into the man's mouth as bullets struck the ground all around them.

"Thank you, Reb. Lucky for you, them ain't sharpshooters. Damn fools, they must think you're robbin' me."

Gazing up at the sky with a countenance of surrender, the Federal didn't seem the least bit concerned about the bullets' near misses.

"I'm a goner and I know it. Wouldn't want to live like this anyhow."

"Is there something I can do for you, soldier?" said Kirkland, ready to grant a last wish.

Unable to move his head, the man turned his eyes and looked at Kirkland peacefully.

"Thanks for the water, friend."

Perceiving that the soldier desired privacy for his last few moments, Kirkland spotted a discarded knapsack which he placed under the man's head as he laid him down.

May this man not suffer long.

A buzz near his ear told Kirkland not to linger, and he tried to block the realization that the shooters were closing in.

Now assured that his decision was just and necessary, he maneuvered to the next fallen, yielding to Fate and God's judgment. With each step, he tossed a bushel of fear behind, until he had slowed to a confident walk.

As Kirkland approached the next soldier, he wasn't sure if the man was still alive, for he was silent and motionless. Kneeling, Kirkland could see a faint rising and falling of the man's chest, but his face was caked with dried blood, sparing no wrinkle and masking his age.

A friend had wrapped a cloth around his head before leaving him to die. This bandage was soaked through, from forehead to ear, and Kirkland feared that startling the man might cause his brains to fall out of his head.

"Sir, would water bring you comfort?" asked Kirkland, barely above a whisper.

There was no response.

He tried again, this time a little louder, but the gravely wounded man was unconscious. Considering his options, he decided to give the Yankee a drink, against long odds that the man might revive.

Putting his hand behind the soldier's head, Kirkland slowly brought it forward to prevent him from choking. Carefully opening the man's mouth, he dripped water down his throat in small doses. It had no effect, and he gently returned the soldier to his place of rest.

As he pivoted to stand and leave, the soldier gripped Kirkland's forearm with such force that it nearly toppled him from shock. Leaning in, Kirkland perceived a subtle movement in the man's lips. While they were barely noticeable spasms, without the backing of words or even sounds, he sensed an intelligence trying to assume control over a broken vessel.

Inching closer until his ear was nearly touching the Yankee's mouth, he waited. At first, only jerking gasps were audible, followed by tongue-between-teeth wind bursts. Closing his eyes, Kirkland focused hard to understand something, anything. But all he could perceive were incoherent mumbles, circling in an abyss, and prevented from binding.

A single tear escaped from the Yankee's shuttered eye, cutting a groove through a reddened cheek. Distraught and with a feeling of total helplessness, Kirkland's chin dropped to his breast. But as Kirkland was about to give up any hope of communication, the soldier inhaled deeply, and whispered in a clear tone: "Thank you."

As soon as the words drove into Kirkland's ears with a profound echo, the grip on Kirkland's arm went limp and the man breathed his last. Initially stunned, Kirkland recovered enough to fold the man's arms at his breast, and moved on.

Seeing the largest number of bodies to the northeast, Kirkland headed in the direction of the Stratton farm. Crossing through the wrecked fairground fence and into Mercer Square, the majority he encountered were cold and stiff. They were strewn about in alarming numbers, twisted at unnatural angles, and engraved on the landscape in gnarled throes of death. These murals of flesh on a wintered Virginia canvas were each unique in their poses of departing breath. While disturbing, Kirkland kept the images on the periphery, away from sinking in, and he held his mission close.

Only Medusa would enjoy this show.

The categories of this morbid spectacle were three, and Kirkland mused about all of them.

Easiest to accept were the pale faces of bowing serenity, arms relaxed and accepting. No doubt, these men had ample time for reflection before succumbing to their wounds. Quite possibly they had religion, firm in their belief that in their breast pocket lay a ticket to a paradise beyond description. Or maybe, this type of man was content with a knightly death, face to his enemy, giving his life for flag and country.

In the second category, were those of instant death. These men were crumpled at fate's fancy, as if lifted and thrown, their souls ripped from their chests in mid breath. Without recognizing their end, their faces expressed nothing, like dolls never gifted with animation.

By far the worst of the mortified were those of eternal anguish. These men did not go into the night silently or with dignity. With jaws set wide in screams, their eyes bulged, their arms contorted and reaching. Clawing at the descending curtain, they held onto the mortal rope to the very end.

Certainly, the three categories had exceptions and were bound by rules Kirkland could not fathom. Or perhaps the tintype of death was ruled by nothing more than differing shades of rigor mortis. Kirkland wasn't sure, but he was convinced of one truth. He had seen enough of it. Yet he was surrounded and the corpses were everywhere. Some were little more than boys, barely removed from the umbilicus of overprotective mothers.

On the opposite end of the spectrum, a few had been blessed with the longevity of graying hair and their death masks were easier to accept.

Betwixt were the majority, twenty-odds, moored enough to have young children at home, their wives praying nightly for a safe return that would go unanswered.

Kirkland wondered how many of these men passed away during the night, their cries for sustenance ignored, without wounds properly dressed. More specifically, did the Yankee whose last testament had affected him so, lay cold among them? Deciding against taking that hallway, Kirkland pulled himself together, and looked for another with lungs still employed.

Noticing a peculiar fort, Kirkland peered over the top. In the center, a startled man lurched backward in fear. The soldier had piled a wall of bodies three high on all sides, evidently taking no chances. No more than seventeen, with a beard more peach fuzz than grizzly, the boy pointed his rifle at Kirkland but did not fire. He didn't appear to be wounded, at least not seriously.

Kirkland raised his hands slightly, avoiding any sudden movements. While in this pause, a bullet from the Yankee rear kicked the canteen from his grip. Calmly and blindly, Kirkland reached down to retrieve the damaged vessel, maintaining eye contact with the trembling soldier. When he scooped up the canteen, the liquid was in retreat, hastily diving from the large bullet hole on each side.

"Would you like some water?"

The soldier eyed Kirkland nervously as if he was in the company of a lunatic, an escaped mad man.

"Um, I have more," said Kirkland, as the dual waterfall from the pierced canteen slowed to a trickle.

308

Finally, the Yankee's thirst became mightier than his tremors and he dropped his weapon. As Kirkland dangled a fresh canteen over the wall of carcasses, the young man pounced, emptying the contents in hurried gulps. When the soldier had bled it dry, he shook it with mouth still agape, letting every drop count.

"Here, take one more." Kirkland tossed him a second canteen, tipped his cap and moved on.

A bullet tore through Kirkland's coat, just below his right wrist and he hit the dirt. Raising his head slightly, he noticed another wounded man less than twenty feet away. He started crawling but realized he was an open target, whether standing or prostrate, and forged ahead with a brisk walk.

As he reached the man's side, he noticed the bluecoat's left leg was severed below the knee and a cloth tourniquet tied above it, no doubt saving his life. At least for now. But he would need a surgeon, and soon.

"How do ya do, Johnny?" said the soldier, a tall, thin man with a large Roman nose and extended jaw.

"Fair. How are you?"

The man looked at his grisly leg.

"Not so well. But the devil ain't takin' me yet."

Kirkland nodded, surprised by the man's good humor. "I imagine you could use some water?"

"A latrine would taste good right now. You must be an angel."

"Hardly."

Kirkland handed him a canteen and the man took a few long, savory gulps.

"You may be a soldier, but not like me. Well, if you ain't from heaven, where did you come from?"

"South Carolina."

"Well, Johnny from South Carolina. I won't fire another shot against your kind. If I live, of course."

Kirkland nodded uncomfortably, and the Yankee quickly changed the subject.

"I fought with the 11th New Hampshire Volunteers. This was our first battle, if you can believe that. Our regiment was only formed this past August. The elephant was not as I expected."

"You men fought like veterans," said Kirkland, noticing that his uniform was not black as it had appeared from a distance, just new blue.

Voices began to emanate from the direction of the town. At first it was a slow rumble, no more than a weak huzzah. But it spread like a hungry fire riding the wind. Confused, Kirkland looked nervously in the thunder's direction, as the huzzahs amped to shouts, which morphed into a groundswell of cheers.

"They have finally realized your mission. I do believe, you are now safe to walk amongst the enemy."

Kirkland turned toward the stranger in disbelief. Behind them, the wall melted, and Lee's warriors joined in the spirited applause. For a brief interlude, the enemies raised their voices as one, celebrating the wanderer.

Kirkland rose and surveyed his place between two bloodthirsty, American armies. Certainly this commotion wasn't all about him. It couldn't be. As the waves of goodwill from each side bellowed in, Kirkland just stood there, the turbulent emotions dueling in his head.

All that is human was present: love, hate, anger, compassion, joy, fear, embarrassment, awe, condemnation and pride. In the last twenty-four hours, Kirkland had felt them all, in various doses. Drawn together in a mind of chipping bedrock, the most prevailing was now—bewilderment.

The ovation from both camps ended as abruptly as it started, saving Kirkland from himself.

And then the work really began as the frantic, discordant chimes sprang forth from all directions. Unsure of his next move among the pleading masses and aware that he couldn't possibly reach them all, Kirkland hesitated.

"Go on, leave me," said the man from New Hampshire, grinning. "Do what you can. And God bless you."

He held out his hand, and Kirkland took it.

Amidst the swirl of imploring voices, Kirkland went to the closest outstretched hand.

He knelt beside the heavily bearded form, noticing the man's other arm was twisted at an angle beyond what its structure should allow. Fractured just below the elbow by a minié, the bone had poked through the skin, and fresh blood told of recent hemorrhaging.

"Good morning," said Kirkland.

"It is *now*," said the wounded, in heavy Irish brogue.

A sprig of boxwood was tucked into his forage cap, given to the men of the Irish Brigade by their general to compensate for retired brigade flags, shredded from previous hostilities.

"The way you men fought yesterday, it was a sight to behold."

"Aye, but over such terrible ground."

Kirkland nodded, scanning for materials that could be used as a tourniquet.

Nearby lay a hideously torn Yankee, barely recognizable as human. His head was missing and his right arm was a detached pile of flesh next to his body. With nauseated hands, Kirkland tore a strip from the mangled sleeve and returned to the living.

"Forgive me."

Straightening the Irishman's limb, Kirkland wrapped the cloth above his elbow and proceeded to tighten it. The soldier winced and cried out in agony.

"I'm afraid this is the best I can do," said Kirkland, lifting the man's head for a drink which he poured liberally down the man's throat.

"Thank you. Two shorten the road, if I may call you a friend."

"For the moment."

The Yankee smiled.

"Aye, for the moment."

With a shaking hand, he reached into his coat pocket and handed Kirkland a pocket watch, a Waltham, housed in a silver hunter case.

"Please, keep this as a token of my gratitude."

"I cannot accept this…"

"Please, I insist. Do me this honor. Besides, I won it in a game of euchre."

Kirkland reluctantly assented, his throat clenching as he accepted the gift.

"Here, we'll trade." He handed the man a canteen.

"The bargain of a lifetime. Now don't mind me any longer, there are plenty of others worse for the wear."

For the next hour, Kirkland continued his merciful rounds, attending to all who called or raised a quivering hand. He also did not ignore the population without strength or voice to summon him. Whether by bandaging a Mainer's ankle or quenching a Bostonian's thirst, Kirkland was compelled to offer simple acts of decency.

As he moved among the dead and wounded, the palisade between North and South began to crumble. With each conversation and moment shared, this barrier was whittled away to mere sticks with blunted edges, and further until all that remained was an impression in the earth where the foundation once stood. In this hour, they were no longer enemies.

Before the war, Michigan or Pennsylvania might as well have been the North Pole, a remote outpost, exotic and alien. Slanted, home newspapers had fostered a disdain for the people who lived in the North. But up close, these Northerners didn't seem to be shaped from a different cloth. Politics and strange tongues aside, these men Kirkland encountered were parallel beings, two feet thrusting forward, with the wind in their faces. And their fighting spirit? He had stepped around the pools of their blood and brains on this day, and would never question the Yankee's resolve again.

During this time with the enemy, the pinprick of light, dormant for so long in his chest, now radiated outward with increasing power into his ministering hands. Although there were no miraculous recoveries, no raising of the dead, a genuine healing was taking place. It was not absolution Kirkland desired and he did not seek forgiveness. He knew the goodwill shared between rivals was temporary.

Yet, as he succored each individual, collecting letters from those with no hope for survival and binding the wounds of men with a fighting chance, the nourishment reached his own belly and satisfied his own thirst. It was not an intentional, selfish benefit. It was a chance to be human again, an affirmation that the best qualities within could still survive and even flourish.

Above all, there was hope that he could return to Flat Rock without arteries clogged with death and despair. There was hope that he could return to Susan without a bricked up heart. And there was hope that when the killing finally ended, whether in truce or subjugation, the differences between North and South could eventually be reconciled.

When Kirkland had handed out the last of his canteens, he gathered up more from the dead and picked up empties from the wounded, refilling them at the Stevens' well.

On his return to the fairgrounds, he came upon the turtle man, whose crawling struggle had affected Kirkland with a large pint of melancholy. He was still now, face buried in the mud. Kirkland estimated that the man had crawled a hundred yards before succumbing to his wounds.

"Poor soul. He didn't have a chance."

Kirkland turned to see to who had spoken and was initially taken aback by what appeared to be an animated head without a connected body. Fearing he had lost his sanity, Kirkland soon realized the Yankee merely had a muddy blanket pulled up tightly under his chin. Caused by wounds hidden underneath, he was both feverish and chilled, sweating profusely.

"Sir, may I have some water?"

"Of course."

He administered the cool liquid until an entire canteen was dry.

"Thank you. I had about given up. My name is Pratt, Edward Pratt, 57th New York," said the man. "What outfit you with?"

"Second South Carolina. My name is Richard Kirkland."

"South Carolina? We are both so far from home. Sometimes I wonder how I got here."

The New Yorker closed his eyes, and reopened them with cavernous dimensions.

"Of course I volunteered. I thought it would be a grand adventure. Men by nature crave what they do not have, I suppose."

He shook his head.

"I love the Union. Don't get me wrong. And I'm sure you have your reasons for taking up arms against us. I don't pretend to understand the politics. We Americans love a good war. When we can't smell blood in the air, we must create it."

As if in sudden awareness that he might be offending his guest, the man stammered.

"I, I have a bad habit, of, of throwing my opinions to the wind, and for that I apologize."

"No need," said Kirkland. "I, too, was corrupted by the hoisting of flags and the desire for glory. That doesn't mean my patriotism for the Southern cause has lessened in any way."

He paused.

"But I may have bitten off more than I can chew."

Kirkland inflected at his own brutal honesty, and the company at which it was nakedly flung. Realizing that to stem the flow at the bursting point would only foster torment, Kirkland continued.

"Yesterday we had the high ground and a protective wall. Tomorrow may be different and we could be running up under your guns. With every day the blood hunger multiplies. I fear my stomach is growing accustomed to it."

Kirkland studied his blackened fingernails.

"I'm just a simple farm boy."

Astonished at Kirkland's words, Pratt opened his mouth and closed it twice, unsure of how to respond. But this enemy soldier impressed him.

"I come from a farm myself. But you are not simple, far from it. We are caretakers of the land, you and I. Our wisdom is in the soil, in the seed, battling Nature and all Her calamities to raise a good crop. In this war, all we do is gorge ourselves on destruction. Everything in the path of an army is stripped away, bled dry. Perhaps, in an ideal world... well, that is quite a stretch. I know the hunger you speak of. My stomach has been taken over in spells, and, I dread, twisted beyond repair.

They stared into the distance, far removed from each other, yet with equal torment.

"I do wish that your ideal world will come to pass," said Kirkland, after a long silence. "But I'm acutely aware that we'll be shooting at each other for a good while."

"Yes, it is a foregone conclusion. If I'm able to stand on two feet again, I will not forget the Johnny Reb who came to my aid. Take care of yourself, Richard Kirkland of South Carolina."

The man wriggled an arm free from his cocoon and saluted the angel of Marye's Heights.

Interlude

JULY 5, 1952
ORISKANY FALLS, NY

L ooking left and then right, with ears perked like a barn tabby, Edward
Pratt gently set the chair down in the middle of the upstair's hallway.

Careful not to make any noise, he stepped on the seat and reached for
the attic handle, pausing once again.

The clanking sounds of his mother washing dishes echoed from the
downstairs kitchen, and he could faintly hear his two younger sisters
squealing as they chased each other outside.

Now confident he was in the clear for his mission, he pulled. As the
attic stairs descended, it groaned and shivered, as if annoyed at the
disturbance from rest. Stopping its descent halfway, Edward squinted and
his face cringed, half-expecting his mother to call out with interrogation.

He opened one eye and then the other, exhaling a frozen breath when
his name was not hollered. Slowly, Edward pulled again and brought the
irritated steps to full extension.

Ten years old, with an unregulated curiosity, he had waited almost a
full 12 hours after Grandfather John had revealed a profound family secret,
hidden away within the walls of his own home.

For reasons Edward could not yet understand, the relationship between
his father and Grandpa had always been strained. As a result, Easter and

Christmas, with a few scattered dates in between, were the only annual reunions between father and son. And when they did meet, a few beers consumed by each would often end the affair badly, where one or both would storm off in a tirade.

The notable exception was the Fourth of July. On this day, father and grandpa buried the proverbial hatchet and refrained from the arguing and bickering. To accomplish this feat meant avoidance in close quarters. They walked a tightrope with eyeballs ducking and weaving like over-the-hill boxers. With the usual venom sheathed, a sidestepping, colorless language emerged, as if each were afraid to violate the patriotic Sabbath.

Of course, Edward had learned in school of the day's importance in American history, but it had always taken a back seat to the family's barbecue, fireworks and suspension of the usual bedtime.

Now old enough to perceive the fantastic absence of usual argument on this one special day, he wondered at its origin.

With his father busy in discussion with an uncle that carried outdoors, the strange elder approached him.

Out of respect, Grandfather John had always kept his distance from Edward, but the few words exchanged were polite and genuinely warm. Tonight, however, grandpa seemed to be on a mission. Though his face was weathered and ancient, his eyes appeared decades younger. Centering on Edward, they sparked like a match to kindling. He shoved smalltalk aside and got right to the point.

"As I'm sure you are aware, your father and I have had our differences," he said, without a hint of malice. "Sometimes adults grow apart for no apparent reason. He considers me old fashioned and I suppose he is right in that regard. You see, when I was nineteen, I joined the army and ended up in France, fighting the Germans."

He paused, and shuddered slightly, as if a daymare had presented itself from the distant past.

"When I came back from the war, I was not myself. I tried to put it behind me, but the horrible things I witnessed..."

He looked away, closed his eyes and clenched his fists.

317

"Well, I was not a good father or husband after that. I crawled into a bottle of whiskey for years, afraid to face the demons."

He shuffled his feet uncomfortably before taking his grandson by the shoulders.

"I don't know how long I have left in this world, and I need you to do something for me. In the attic of your home there's a large trunk. Inside you will find our family's treasure, more valuable than pirate's gold. They are your birthright. It is of the greatest importance. Do you understand, son?"

Edward had no awareness of what his grandfather was talking about, but he was more than intrigued.

Treasure? In our house?

"Yes, Sir."

"Good boy."

Puzzled but excited, Edward had waiting patiently until the next day, well aware of his father's forbiddance to explore the attic.

It was the one room in the farmhouse that he had yet to explore. Having been in the family for generations, the house had witnessed modest development encroach on the once rural landscape. Although the Pratts still owned a few dozen acres, they were now rented out for agriculture. Edward's father Jacob had inherited the place, which had become a money pit of repairs that threatened the family's loyalty to tradition. But to Edward, the large structure was an exotic playground of nooks and crannies, and the land, a mystical realm of fortresses and moats challenged by dragons. Yet he obeyed the order to stay away from the loftiest space, knowing that some day he would get his chance. And that chance was today.

Moments before, his father had left for work after a hurried breakfast, having spent too much time with the morning newspaper.

Toeing upward, he surveyed the kingdom of mysterious clutter and the darkness only added to the questing mystique. While blindly grasping for the chain of the naked, single-bulb light, he slammed into an unseen piece of furniture, which grinded a few inches across the floor.

318

He stopped in his tracks and listened, heart bulging in his chest. Hearing no rebukes or changes in background noise, he breathed easier. As his eyes adjusted to the darkness, he found the chain and pulled. In a click, the treasure room awoke.

And he was disappointed.

Much of it was mundane: old suitcases and file cabinets, racks full of outdated and outgrown clothing, more racks of Halloween costumes, including his third-grade ode to the land of Oz—a faded-cloth Scarecrow, hand-sewn by his mother.

Where is the pirate gold?

But then he saw it.

In the center of the room was an enormous rosewood trunk, seemingly out of place and beckoning. He rushed to it and placed his hands on the dusty handles. Lifting the growling lid, he peered inside.

"Find any buried treasure?"

Cringing at the recognized voice, he slowly turned.

"I…I…"

His father waived away his excuses with a calloused hand, weathered by long hours in Utica factories, most recently at the Chicago Pneumatic Tool Company.

"So your grandfather told you. I was getting around to it, but now's as good a time as any."

Edward relaxed his tightened chest, but was still not completely convinced.

Is he really not angry? What did he forget?

Dropping to a knee, his father rummaged through the trunk, finally pulling out a seemingly ancient, leather-bound notebook.

As his father thumbed through the pages, Edward was a statue. Additional chores or banishment to his room occupied a good portion of his mind.

"Ah, here it is."

He handed the diary to his son.

319

"You may find this interesting. Start here." He pointed to the yellowed page. "Put everything away when you're done and be careful up here. Well, I gotta go. Late for work."

He turned to descend the stairs.

"And mind your mother."

"Yes, Sir."

Relieved at the truancy of punishment, Edward pushed the heavy trunk so it was under the light. He closed the lid and sat on it, barely able to contain himself.

This was different from the tired black and white photographs of relatives on display in the living room, blank in expression and boring. Even the tintype of the bearded soldier, gripping a menacing rifle, had not aroused much more than flyby notice. For some reason, this was something more tangible.

Having burrowed a finger to mark his father's designated page, he opened the diary. The penmanship was perfect and unlike any style he had ever seen.

January 15, 1863
Washington

I keep proving them doctors wrong. My wound, just above the right nipple, is healing and I kept the bullet as a souvenir. Still a little feverish and weak, but holding up. The nurses have been very kind, changing my bandages and seeing to my every need.

If I survive this, and it looks like I will, I will never again point my rifle at these sons of the South. Sometimes I lie awake at night, thinking on the soldier in gray who came to my aid on the bloody fields of Fredericksburg. He risked his life to bring me water, which surely saved me from the beyond.

He said his name was Kirkland. I'll never forget that name, from South Carolina. Or was he an Angel from Heaven?

The more I think on it, I believe the latter.

Edward flipped back to the inside cover.

Edward A Pratt, 57th NY Volunteers, Co. B
1861

Jumping up and closing the book between his hands, Edward was fascinated yet a bit mystified.

We share the same name!

Starting to piece together what his grandfather was speaking of the day before, he wasted no time raising the chest's lid once again, and dove for further treasure.

Noticing a small, wooden jewelry box, he threw it open. Inside was a distorted, crumpled piece of lead—a minié ball—which was accompanied by a faded card that read:

Fredericksburg, Va., Dec 13, 1862. Plucked from my chest.

He dug further.

Hoisting a blue sack coat with a jagged hole in the right breast, he let out an audible "whoa" when he saw what was underneath: a rifle. He picked it up, surprised at how heavy it was, and turned it over until he had inspected every inch. Nearly five feet long, almost as high as Edward, the lock plate clearly showed the year, 1861, with an Eagle with wings spread and the words:

U S
Springfield

When he came to the steel buttplate, a scratched inscription was faintly visible.

E Pratt
Co B

Peering in further, he encountered a weathered kepi. Crowning the hat on his head, Edward did a pirouette as it fell over his ears.

The distant chords were playing now, their harmony resonating deep within the young scion, even if he couldn't grasp all its significance. There was no turning back. He had to find out more about this soldier with a shared name.

With the stifling July heat closing in and the sweat running from his brow, Edward put the items away and closed the chest of ancestral memories. But he kept the diary, eagerly running off to the shade of his favorite climbing tree, where he would spend the afternoon among its supporting limbs, devouring his namesake's every word.

Chapter 18

DECEMBER 16
FREDERICKSBURG, VA
5:30 PM

"**G**old!"

Joe was staring into a hole in the floor where he had just removed a curiously loose floorboard to add wood to the fire. They had run out of materials to burn, having exhausted a good supply of tobacco crates, tossed into the Rappahannock by the fleeing Virginians but rescued from the depths by weed-craving Yankees.

"Come over here," Joe yelled again.

Alex, Kirkland and Nail took their time removing their stances in front of the warm fireplace. The others simply ignored him, believing the residence had been picked clean of all valuables by the enemy.

"Quiet, or Gaillard might hear you," said Nail, the joke involving the respected major never getting old. It had become well known in the regiment that Gaillard had ventured west to California during the gold rush of the late '40s, only to come up empty. He had taken the good-natured teasing in stride, which only heightened his standing among the men. But it also encouraged more of the same. Whenever the regiment was forced to cross a shallow creek, someone would call out, ordinary rock in hand, shouting they had struck it rich with a large nugget.

And since his wounds from Marye's Heights were not serious, he was fair game again for jokes, even while he was away on furlough.

This time, though, Joe wasn't kidding.

Smiling, he pointed below. A gold locket with chain and plenty of silver—pitchers, fruit dishes and goblets—along with bone china, were packed haphazardly within the crevices. But what they were bundled with was just as exciting, and more useful. Overcoats, heavy wool shirts and scarves were in abundance. Although they were old-fashioned relics, since all were severely lacking in winter wear, they eagerly divided up the clothes.

Nail reached to pluck the locket, but Kirkland grabbed his arm.

"We have taken enough from this family," he said, releasing Nail's hand, and offering a black, tailored suit with velvet trim. "Do not forget where we are. I believe this will bring you more comfort in the days ahead."

Nail initially gave Kirkland a befuddled stare before accepting the more pragmatic prize. He held up the jacket, turning it over front and back, and shrugged his shoulders.

"Will this make me a gentleman?" joked Nail.

"It will take much more than *that*," said Joe, wrapping a scarf around his neck. "Such as the ability to speak of more genteel subjects rather than the quality of manure. Right, Alex?"

"Your complete lack of manners and social graces will not fool anyone, no matter your evening wear, my good friend," Alex replied. "You are without hope."

"You take for granted the wisdom of manure. I rather enjoy the odor of a good pile."

They all indulged in a good laugh.

"Sophistication is overrated, is it not?" said Nail.

"Well, try not to get shit on that jacket. It's quite nice," said Joe with a straight face, which made the others giggle.

324

Kirkland followed up on his plea for leaving the family's valuables behind.

"So are we in agreement? We take what we must, but leave the heirlooms untouched?"

Gauging each face more than their words, Kirkland knew the temptation but hoped for a consensus.

Alex spoke first.

"Yes, this family has suffered enough. If we can leave even a pittance to enable the family to rebuild, I'm all in favor."

Nail gave his blessing, but looked unconvinced, a feeling Kirkland shared.

The enemy had retreated across the Rappahannock the night previous, leaving the town in ruins.

While Yankee artillery had ravaged most of the buildings, the foot soldiers completed the utter destruction. During their short occupation, the men had mutated into a looting, vandalizing mob, and the streets were filled with their plunder. Upon entering the town, Kirkland was shocked at every smoldering corner. The remains of bashed pianos and fine furniture exhaled blackened ashes that fluttered in terminal sparks. A rocking horse, roller hoops and wooden penny dolls, left behind by fleeing children, lay discarded in alleyways. Books by the dozens and ladies undergarments were tossed aside in random piles. Large, heavy mirrors were thrown through windows, carpeting the ground with glistening shards, next to walls soiled with urine. Fredericksburg's businesses were treated no better than the private homes, with their stores cast out or consumed, and banks burglarized. And when they had found the liquor, the ransackers really went to work, trashing all within hand's reach.

Some of these hands (and feet), no doubt, never left the town, and were stacked in grisly mounds beneath windows, where they were tossed from the surgeon's table. The even less fortunate were buried in the many shallow graves freshly dug in every yard.

The composition was overwhelming. Wandering the streets, Kirkland was devastated, feeling great sorrow for the townspeople.

He was angry, livid even, and the hours since, waiting to go on picket duty at the river's edge, had not diminished his outrage. At an abandoned, formerly exquisite house on Caroline Street, the drawing room where the men huddled to get warm was a constant reminder. Slashed paintings and graffiti adorned the walls. Beaten and overturned, a grandfather clock lay in pieces in one corner, while bayoneted sofas sat wounded in another. Tasseled silk curtains had been ripped and piled beneath the windows. And this was all that was left behind. The rest of the furnishings were either stolen or tossed into the street.

Although shells had punched a few holes in the roof and scattered a few bricks from the chimney, compared to others in the vicinity, damage to the house was slight. It had been fortunate to escape a worse fate.

Joe looked at the hole in the floorboards and back at Kirkland.

"I admire your empathy, but we won't be here forever to protect this home. How do we keep others from stealing this cache?"

"Yes," Kirkland said. "I've been pondering that. We could bury it on the property, but the disturbed ground will give it away. It's always possible that this house will not be occupied by the pickets again. I'm afraid the best we can do is to stash the valuables and cover them where we found it. The end result is out of our hands. Agreed?"

It was unanimous and Kirkland polled the rest of the company for a total accord.

As Joe was replacing the flooring, there was a knock at the door. A shivering lieutenant entered with orders.

"Okay, men. Unfortunately it's your turn in the deep freeze."

★　　★　　★

JANUARY 26, 1863

SIX MILES SOUTHWEST OF FREDERICKSBURG

The fiddle barebacked the voice, fusing with it, as if to share in its lyrical sorrow.

The wailing of the duo was ancient and sympathetic, haunting yet familiar. Like a long-lost friend who had returned with a nourishing smile, the song's intrinsic pulse was a window to a place all in earshot held dear.

It had been among the Carolina pines and sipped from its gentle creeks. Under the tutelage of backcountry roads and resonant hills, it had been fertilized. It reminisced of rocking chairs at simple porch gatherings, where conversation began and ended with the crops and the weather. But this was different from a brass band launching into patriotic airs or even a lone bugle reminding listeners of loved ones far away.

This fiddle and voice were, in essence, the vibrations of home. And the troubadour, especially, seemed to be there, possessed by its bearing.

When the mystical traveler sang, he levitated somewhere between the compasses of earth and stratosphere. To be sure, there were many more gifted and polished, but it was doubtful the elder songmasters of Kershaw District had this extra layer, born of war. The acrid smoke and rifle kicks seasoned the throat and tongue. Under this awakening, the lyrics were almost inconsequential, for you could feel in this voice the dusty roads and blistered feet, the hunger pains and merciless rain.

Around the fire, the men joined in their own way. A few slapped a warming knee, while others mouthed the words with barely moving lips, but the majority just stared absently at destinations unseen.

A lone man sat outside the minimalist fire's glow with legs crossed, rocking back and forth as if in a primordial trance. His head bobbed to the song's meter. As Kirkland watched, the man closed his eyes and raised his palms to the sky as if channeling the Holy Spirit. With fingers slowly fanning out, he let his hands linger for several seconds, before they dropped heavily like dead weights. His head followed his hands, his chin dropping to his chest as if lulled by the music into a catatonic sleep.

Kirkland had occasionally seen him where the music called, always alone and seemingly deep in meditation.

The Army of Northern Virginia had again settled in for the long winter, waiting for the spring thaw before getting a chance to whip the Yankees again. In early January, Kershaw's Brigade began to hibernate in the pine woods north of Massaponax Creek, a tributary to the Rappahannock. The men, now well-acquainted with the Virginia cold months, built even larger cabins than the previous winter. Predictably, Kirkland had bunked with Joe and Alex, and they had invited Nail to join them. Christmas and New Year's passed with little fanfare. January brought more of the same, until late in the month, when Burnside ordered his army into action.

This offensive was foiled by Mother Nature, as heavy rains turned the roads into impassable quagmires, and the Yankees retreated back to their camps, exhausted and caked with mud. After this brief activity, it wasn't long before boredom was again rampant.

Kirkland, either through desire to escape the tedium or from actual yearning for song, had often been drawn to whatever campsite had the night's acoustic companion. Frequently, Joe and Alex would join him at these respites, which could materialize as a rousing party of brass favorites or a downhome stomp of the Georgia backwoods. But tonight Kirkland was wandering solo with an ambition for an atmosphere more serene and less a grand spectacle.

While strolling on this nibbling cold but comfortable evening, he came upon a quaint huddle. From a distance Kirkland first heard the song, which his bones recalled but his mind stumbled on in a wordless hum. While his legs moved him closer, the befuddling mist slowly dissolved into recall. Although the name remained elusive, he had heard the song as a child, and as a goofy face appeared in his mind's eye, Kirkland smiled.

The face belonged to his much older cousin, Starling, a merrymaker who would show up at the Kirkland home unannounced every few months for a visit. Starling lived as a hermit, deep in the woods along Grannies Quarter Creek in little more than a shack. At least, that's what Kirkland's father told him. To him, Starling was much of a mystery, as his questions to family elders about his eccentric cousin mostly went unanswered. All Kirkland knew was that Starling was legendary at two things: hunting and playing the fiddle, the former feeding his belly when the other, as was often the case, did not.

Through this passion for melody, Starling had an impressive catalogue of songs gathered from the mundane to the most unlikely of sources. In addition to the well-known spirituals and ethnic hand-me-downs, his arsenal included Gullah shouts from the lowcountry and Cherokee war songs. Starling put his personal stamp on them all. Though a few of his interpretations and fiddle arrangements were awkward in the translation, most were well thought out and, Kirkland believed, genius.

As a child, Richard would sit on his father's lap in front of a roaring outdoor fire and listen to his uncle blister his fingers in exuberant performances. And when it got too late, he would plead with his father to let him stay vertical for one more song. These petitions would last several songs before he would be sent to bed in chin-lowered shuffles.

While the present voice could not match Starling's otherworldly grasp of tone and vibrato he made up for it with his honest rendering. It was both intoxicating in its melancholy and a tonic for homesickness.

The opposing forces were not lost on Kirkland. Like whiskey, a song could be a crutch. Used in moderation, it could have restorative power, an umbrella that shields the rain. When relied upon and abused, it could become a beguiling elixir, pledging to keep the gray skies away while shackling a man under a leaky roof. It was fine line between euphoria and gloom, and glancing over again at the aloof and motionless man, Kirkland wondered on what side of the fence this private sat.

To what extreme and how distant is he from this Old Dominion campfire?

And then it hit him with startling clarity. He had seen this man before, and not just at musical gatherings along the Massaponax. This was the same soldier who, the day after the battle of Sharpsburg had brushed past him, wheezing and, Kirkland assumed, shot through the lung.

And he was also the same man he had startled on the eve of the Fredericksburg fight, writing in a journal while transfixed on the dawn's rise. Berating himself for not connecting the visuals earlier, Kirkland's next thought was one of amazement. After seeing the man's condition at Sharpsburg, he believed the poor soldier was walking toward a shallow grave. Yet somehow, miraculously, he had recovered, and quickly! When Kirkland had chanced upon him near the old mill on December 12, less than three months had passed since their first encounter. It didn't seem possible, but Kirkland was sure this was the same man. Was he a marvel of medicine or did he possess supernatural powers of self-healing? Desperately wanting to rush over and interrogate this enigma of flesh, Kirkland muzzled both tongue and feet. The man appeared in no condition for discourse, and so Kirkland chose not to disturb him. But until he ascertained the soldier's identity, he needed a name.

Moonbeam

★   ★   ★

JANUARY 30, 1863

Kirkland awoke to drums warning that the enemy was near.

He hesitated, snug in his bed, wondering if the rolls were beckoning from a vivid dream. Convinced the doorway was tangible, he pulled on his shoes, grabbed his overcoat and rifle from the cabin wall and ran outside. The cold air hit him like a punch to the sternum. Thrusting the butt of his rifle into the snow, he pulled on his coat and looked around.

Behind him, the door to the cabin burst open, and Nail rushed out, his head lurching from side to side. He finally noticed Kirkland staring at him and the two looked at each other in bewilderment.

Feeling a tap on his shoulder, Kirkland picked up his rifle and wheeled. Joe, with an amused grin, calmly pushed aside the rifle that Kirkland was pointing at his chest.

"Sleeping late are we?"

Joe was gorging himself on the breakfast of Kirkland's fluster and enjoying it.

"What's going on?"

"We're being attacked."

330

Kirkland shouldered his rifle, but Joe pulled it away. Still puzzled, but seeing Joe's reaction, he calmed. And then the fresh snow cover finally registered.

"Rutherford at it again?"

Joe laughed. "You catch on fast. This might be the biggest one yet. Look."

Joe pointed at the horizon.

The Army of Northern Virginia's battle flag, unfurled and screaming, were visible over a hill to the west. Its bearer was concealed by the terrain and it appeared to hover with crimson wings, waiting for its next prey to reveal itself.

Lieutenant Colonel William Rutherford of the 3rd South Carolina loved a good snowball fight. He had only returned from a severe wound in his side at Fredericksburg a week prior, and though still gimpy and sore, he was foaming for a different kind of combat. And he wasn't the only one who enjoyed a sky of white projectiles. Whenever a snow blanketed the stagnant camps, no gypsy was needed to predict what would happen next. These mock battles were carried out with an almost religious fervor. At times, regiment would hurl itself against regiment. When conditions were perfect and the snow ample, brigades would even square off, hundreds of men charging and retreating, fighting for bragging rights and winter superiority. Though at times, soldiers were wounded by overzealous play, most of the officers, from captains all the way up to Robert E. Lee, condoned or even supported this activity. After all, it was good exercise in an environment where drill was next to impossible.

"Here," said Joe, handing the rifle back to Kirkland. "Spring will come soon enough."

★   ★   ★

At the center of a large plain, which separated Kershaw's Brigade and the Georgians whom they had fought so well with behind the stone wall, Rutherford met the colonel leading the enemy brigade. While they fraternized and made a spectacle, the soldiers prepared for battle. Pyramid

331

upon pyramid of snowballs were carefully formed by hands now glazed and toughened by two harsh winters in Virginia.

Kirkland had to laugh at the oddity. Men from Georgia and South Carolina embracing the snow!

Two years ago, who would have believed it?

He reached down, gingerly, and scooped up a handful, forming it into a tight ball, pleased it was a good, sticky variety.

The leaders shook hands and Rutherford turned, a faint grin advertising his obvious giddiness. As he arrived to greet his troops, he became serious, giving a speech as if the Yankees were closing in.

"Men, the enemy is here and they wish to destroy you. I know my fellow South Carolinians will not be bullied. Wait until they get within a hundred feet and open fire."

Growling and spouting a fiendish rebel yell with as much barbarity as if facing the Irish Brigade, the Georgians charged. They began as a perfect wall of steadiness, aligned and disciplined, exhaling clouds of frigid breath. When halfway across the field, order evaporated into a discordant run, and the first snow flew, kicked upward by the advancing horde.

Kirkland crowned his pyramid with a final ball and waited.

"Looks like they have their dander up," said Joe, dancing a little jig and holding up his fists in a boxing stance. "Pity the man that arrives at my doorstep. You ready?"

"I am."

"If I should fall," Joe deadpanned, "please inform my family that I died with snowball in hand, facing the enemy."

"I shall write the *Camden Confederate*, forever preserving your brave legacy."

"Alex, pay attention. History is being made and yours truly will grab the glory."

Alex was unimpressed.

"I can see the headline already. 'Joseph Duncan, hero of the Battle of Snow Follies.'"

"That has a certain ring to it. I'll take it."

Rutherford was in front again, with his sword raised. Pointing to the foe, he encouraged the South Carolinians one more time.

"Carolina. Hold your ground and when I give the signal, fire and keep it hot."

Scrunching up his face in mock contemplation, he backpedaled.

"I digress. Keep it COLD."

Laugher filled the ranks of play.

"Remember, a hundred feet and let loose."

Directly in front, a Georgian with a long beard drafting sideways by the wind, tripped and fell ungracefully into the snow. He shook his head and immediately arose, the brim of his kepi frosted and his beard chunked with the same misery.

Joe pointed at the man and slapped a thigh, giggling loudly.

"Did you see that? A train left the tracks. That must be mighty cold."

"If he gets captured, he'll get worse."

This was often true, as the penalty for falling into the enemy's hands meant a liberal dose of winter applied in the most sensitive areas, transforming a man to a shivering icicle. And on this morn, when the mercury dipped to glacial status, it would be especially detrimental to a Southerner's constitution.

A few weeks previous, in another battle with the Georgians, Kirkland had narrowly escaped this fate, outrunning his pursuers until safely back within friendly confines. Joe wasn't so lucky and was now out for revenge, not particular of which unfortunate paid the debt.

Pacing among the lines and tracking every step, Rutherford, sensing the boundary had been breached, tossed a snowball from hand to hand. He recoiled and brought his throwing arm back. Realizing in mid-throw that he had not given the command, he paused, keeping his eyes on his target.

"Carolinians. Fire!"

Escorted by a zealous cheer, the circular arrows were unleashed toward the rapidly closing enemy.

333

Kirkland reared back and lofted a carefully placed volley, leading the target. He stopped to watch a man run straight into its path, striking him in the shoulder.

Joe, on the other hand, was pitching bullets. Not waiting to see if they hit their mark, he would toss another, and then another, in rapid succession.

Somewhere in the middle of the two techniques, Alex's throws were rhythmic and steady, aimed but not followed.

The Georgians didn't wait long to respond, and before long the snowballs brought locomotion to the lifeless sky, greeting each other in passing before slamming into a knee or breast. When within sixty feet, the Georgians stopped to reload, furiously taking up snow to keep up with the ordnance mounds of Kershaw's Brigade.

Kirkland grabbed another missile and was about to toss it when a ball hit him squarely in the throat. While the impact was minor, the snow rapidly stung, and he turned his back on the enemy. Dropping his own uncomfortable messenger, he grasped at his reddened neck, brushing the snow away.

"It's only a flesh wound," said Joe, giggling. "No furlough for you. Get back in it!"

"Are you sure?" said Kirkland, playing along. "I was convinced that would get me thirty days."

Joe laughed and underhanded a snowball to Kirkland.

Catching it, Kirkland threw the ball so hard that he lost his balance, planting a hand in the snow. He couldn't help but laugh at his own clumsiness.

"Sometimes the ugly ones are the most effective," said Joe.

"You would know."

It soon became obvious that the stockpile of weapons the Carolinians drew from was turning the tide of battle.

The Georgians began to retreat and Joe saw his chance. He took off in a run, like a lion gaining on the weakest of the herd.

"I think he may have found his calling," said Alex, who like Kirkland had paused to watch their friend streaking across the field.

"I feel sorry for the poor soul that winds up in his grasp."

As they watched, Joe closed on a slow-footed straggler and tackled him to the ground. Holding him down with one arm, he grabbed a handful of snow with the other and stuffed it down the unfortunate man's back.

Satisfied, he let the man go and jumped to his feet, fists pumping in the air.

The line of Carolinians roared.

Joe bowed and raised his arms like a victorious gladiator in an ancient stadium. But in the midst of his glory, a snowball struck him square in the back. Feigning indignation, he windmilled his arms, beckoning for the Carolinians to finish the rout. Rutherford was the first to oblige and when he reached Joe, he handed him his sword. Initially dumbstruck, Joe took the honor, and raised the blade above his head.

"Come on, you rascals!"

With a laughter-infused shout, Kershaw's Brigade charged, following their new leader.

Kirkland and Alex looked at each other and smiled.

"I believe you're right, Alex. He has indeed found his calling."

Chapter 19

K irkland held his elbows in, with his hands clenched on his chest. "I'm not fond of this time of year," he said. "And it ain't the cold. It's the whispers in the wind."

"Excuse me," said Joe. "Speak English boy. I get enough of that gibberish from Alex."

"Oh, I keep forgetting," Alex piped in. "You are comfortable in your ignorance. Proud, even."

"All right, all right. You've made your point, professor. Do continue, Kirkland."

"Thank you," said Kirkland, amused, but also feeling a bit strange waxing poetic. "But it's nothing, really. All I was saying was that we are now in our second winter away from home. And with the army idle, and little duty, a man has too much time with his own thoughts. Most of the time, all we do is sit in this little hut, waiting for spring to come, so we can get on with killing again. Sometimes when I listen to the wind at night, there's a wisdom in it, though I'm not sure I understand its meaning. Or maybe I don't like its message."

"That, I can understand," said Joe. "Other than that last part about the sky talking to you. But please refrain from joining Alex's educated camp. I need you with me in the shadows."

"Fear not, my friend. As much as I desire Alex's knowledge, I will forever remain a simple farmer."

"I'd expect nothing more," Joe teased.

"Nonsense, Rich. Your intellect is more than suited for scholarly pursuits," said Alex. "Regrettably, I can't say the same for our friend, here."

Joe, in his best caveman impression, jumped around the fire and leaned his head sideways. With a brutish grunt, he carefully placed a new log on the withering fire.

"See, practical. That's all *I* need."

Loud laughter and an evolving ruckus could be heard down by the Massaponax, and no one was ignorant of the source.

"Popskull has them chasing their tails," said Alex.

"Well at least they could've shared," said Joe, only half joking.

Nail, who'd been lying down in his bunk, perked up.

"Whiskey?"

Kirkland shook his head, knowing boredom and booze was a lethal combination, even for men of gentle disposition. But for a man like Ratcliff? A sober exchange with the feral Centaur was trouble enough.

"Come on, boys, let's pay them a visit," said Nail, enthusiastically.

"Yeah, why not?" said Joe.

Bewildered, Kirkland glared at the nonchalance of his friend.

"Have you lost your sense? The last time I checked, the three of us weren't exactly friendly."

"What have we got to lose? This conversation is running circles. I could use a little adventure."

Kirkland was about to respond, but the doldrums had gotten to the group and he knew it.

Nail took the lead as the foursome sauntered past huts populated, no doubt, with incessant card games and exaggerated yarns. By the responsive hollering at one abode, they could perceive a raconteur of spinning talent. If not inherent, Kirkland knew, a dark hut and long winter allowed for sufficient polish.

A thick blanket of clouds foiled all but the most ambitious of stars, and when outside the kinetic glow of a fire, the ground was veiled by an impenetrable darkness. With visibility lacking, at no more than an arm's length, Kirkland followed the shuffling of feet. Of course, he had often trekked to the creek in the daytime, but at night, hazards were everywhere.

At least to toes and shins.

All of the trees within the camp had been cut down and devoured by flame, but stumps large and small remained, poised to seek their revenge. On overcast nights, Kirkland and his campfire clan had often waited in silence as twilight drifted to obscurity, for the headless pines to claim another victim. When a cuss and an oath would give the prey away, they would stand and shout "huzzah," before breaking into a fit of laughter.

Kirkland hoped this time the joke wouldn't be at his expense.

As they maneuvered toward the bank, Ratcliff's voice grew sharp and dominating until the ogre and his minions were illuminated. Having reached their destination with toes and shins bereft of stubbing, Kirkland expected worse obstacles ahead.

Ratcliff had his back turned to the cautious group as they approached, and was boasting of battle exploits.

"The damn fool had both arms blown to shreds," Ratcliff recalled gleefully. "I stepped on his chest until the wind broke. I reckon the stupid boy was no more than sixteen. I thought about bringing him back for dinner but the runt woulda been small a meal."

He howled with satisfaction.

"But he had big feet."

Lifting up his right foot, he pointed, before lowering it and clicking his heels together. Noticing his audience was looking past him, Ratcliff spun.

"Well, if it ain't our lovely neighbors from Flat Rock. Couldn't resist a little rye dog? Help yourselves."

He gestured toward the barrel of whiskey.

Stepping forward, canteen in hand, Nail didn't need a second offer, but the others hesitated. Having loaded his fill from the spigot, Nail retreated to the side of his friends.

"Much obliged. Where did you find it?"

"Oh, a little farm not too far off. It was good and hidden, but we bargained with the old coot. It seems he cared more about his sow. But a couple of nights later we got that too."

He turned his attention to Joe and Alex, who were standing still, giving the barrel a good looksee.

"Go on. I ain't gonna shoot ya. My gun's all the way over there."

His laugh was sinister, but Joe pounced. Still leery, Alex handed Joe his canteen.

"Any news from home?" asked Joe, filling the vials to the brim.

Ratcliff's face changed from mischievous to downright spooky.

"Home?" he huffed. "*This* is my home. *This* is where I belong. But I do despise the winter, when my gun is silent."

Kirkland, deciding a nip or two with the boys wouldn't taint his soul too much, forged ahead to the barrel. Before he made two steps, Ratcliff lunged to block his path. With his arms away from his body, hulking, as if waiting to draw from a pistol, Ratcliff growled.

"Where do you think you're going?"

"Come on, Virgil, let the man have a drink," said Joe.

"He's a Yankee lovin' son of a bitch," said Ratcliff, staring Kirkland down. "Just what side are you on?"

"You know what side I'm on," said Kirkland, refusing to back down.

"Do I? You should have let them bastards die a slow death. Instead, you run to their aid? I say Tarleton's quarter, no mercy. Yer not a soldier. I outta drag you down to the Rappahannock and toss you across, so you can join your new friends. This here libation is for them who bleed for the South."

Joe stepped forward, causing the men behind Ratcliff, including Hux, to stand.

"Let's not get our dander up," cautioned Joe. "We all know Kirkland's reputation as a Southern Patriot."

"Patriot, hell. I say he's a damn disgrace."

"You will apologize for that statement or I…"

Kirkland grabbed Joe's arm and cut him off.

The veins in his neck were bulging rivers, and his fingers shook, lusting for double fists. It was almost painful to deny them from clenching. With his rank, he had the power to throw Ratcliff in the guard house for disrespect. And Ratcliff's whole being seemed to will it and more, begging for a harsh response. For several moments, it was a stare down, without words.

Finally, Ratcliff forced a second stab at Kirkland's honor. He was growing impatient, and getting drunker by the moment, he began to slur.

"Y' juss gonna sand 'ere, Sar-gent?"

The last two syllables were crystal in their enunciation and packing knives.

Sensing Joe was about to intervene, Kirkland spoke.

"No, Ratcliff, we're leaving. Enjoy your shindig. Come on boys."

With a pat and then a soft pull, Kirkland encouraged Joe away from his ruffled stance. It took another less-gentle wrenching until Joe finally cooled enough to follow. But not without a parting shot.

"Thanks for the drink, ladies."

★   ★   ★

FEBRUARY 11

Alex groaned, his hands resting on a head foggy and throbbing. He doubled over in his bunk, whining some more.

"What possessed me to drink that foul substance?"

Kirkland was already awake, warming himself over the coals in the fireplace. He had awoken before dawn, his insides vengeful and screaming. Though his friends had shared their whiskey with him, this was more than dehydration.

While not a teetotaler, his experience with powerful liquor was limited. He had long despised what its abuse could do to good men, the alarming change in some to loudmouth braggarts and incoherent ramblers. In others, the vice summoned even worse behaviors, a complete erosion of decency

340

and proper conduct. He'd witnessed the worst of the lot, from kin and stranger, curled up in the bottom of a jug, rarely surfacing for air. He feared losing self-control to these demons, and so he usually abstained from over-indulgence, clinging to sobriety's edge.

But Ratcliff had pushed him.

"Kirkland? You don't look so good."

"No, I most certainly am not."

"I didn't think you had that much to drink last night."

"I didn't. But the juice has never agreed with me."

He headed for the door.

"Nature calls."

Kirkland took his leave of the group, but the bodily urge was only a partial reason for his escape. His friends were used to this occasional disappearing act. Alex, who had read "Walking" in *The Atlantic* magazine, understood him better, though he was unconvinced that Thoreau and Kirkland were on identical quests.

Though infrequent and relegated to times of extended camp when his duties as first sergeant were lessened, Kirkland would sometimes feel an overwhelming sense of wanderlust. Like the previous winter, he often went away to chop and gather firewood in numbers far greater than his mess needed. Other times he left the axe behind, and just walked, away from anything resembling the human form.

On this particular occasion, the escapism was merely to digest a fragment of Susan's most recent letter, a reply to correspondence Kirkland wrote soon after the battle of Fredericksburg. It was received more than a week ago, along with a package of sweet potatoes and sorghum butter, which he and his mess had consumed in one sitting. While Kirkland had read the letter briskly and in its entirety at first, on each ensuing day he had chosen a few paragraphs to savor and memorize, as if the lines were poetry or favorite verses from the Bible. In this way, it was as if a new letter arrived with regularity, and he could converse often with his love. For in reality, the railroads were unreliable, and the mail was chronically late, or worse: lost before ever reaching its intended touch.

When letters became sparse in camp, a general trading of old material would commence. But Kirkland kept Susan's letters to himself. It didn't seem to bother his messmates, who, unlike Fain and Bury the previous winter, respected his privacy. Naturally, Joe would tease him about being a spy for the wives at home. But the Kirkland answer was always the same and accompanied by a mischievous grin: "Susan would have my hide. Her words are mine and only mine."

Kirkland made it through the camp guards with ease. Although leaving camp without a pass was risking stiff punishment, the guard was much more relaxed during the winter. When he was far enough away not to be disturbed, Kirkland sat down on a stump and pulled out Susan's letter.

He read the greeting several times.

My darling,

Looking up, he closed his eyes, and listened to her voice warming each syllable.

Then he continued reading.

I pray that you are well and have all your needs provided for. Salt and leather are becoming scarce here, as well as coffee, yet we make do with what we have. Certainly I have no cause for complaint when thinking on what you have to endure.

Often you come to me in my dreams and I wake in pursuit, wishing desperately to continue our reunion. And then I return to sleep, alone and wanting.

I can do nothing but wait for you, hoping every rider in the distance would reveal your face. I feel sorry for those who call at our home as my disappointment must be obvious to all who greet me. Will this war ever end? Forgive me for these selfish expressions. Of course, as I've told you before, the pride I have for you in defending our state cannot be measured.

Your brother, Dan, called on us recently. Though a bit thin around the edges, he looked healthy. The first words out of his mouth were to ask if I had heard from you. He had his horse shot out from under him and was home to find a replacement. He asked my father to loan him another mount. Of course my father quickly obliged as he thinks so highly of the Kirkland boys.

The letter went on in impressive length, but Kirkland stopped there and retraced the passages, absorbing each phrase as if Susan was standing before him, her lips massaging the words. Whether this image of her was accurate in its portrayal, Kirkland was unsure. But he accepted this vision as truth, resigned to the fact that, if slightly altered, the faded details were insignificant until the "reunion" Susan spoke of became reality.

When he had completed this portion of the letter to memorization, he folded it, and closed his eyes again, the words still resonating in his head.

the Kirkland boys.

The recital ended, and with shaking hands, Kirkland returned the letter to its envelope and shoved the paper gold in his breast pocket.

It was time to wander again.

The serenity of a vacant country road called him, and he stood up, aiming for no particular direction other than away from his army. When thoughts of home, of Susan, of Dan's brush with death arose, he pushed them aside and kept walking. He didn't care that the trees appeared snarled and lifeless. It mattered not that the landscape was skeletal gray and rusting brown—the color-void of winter. The weathered fence, the furrowed field, the homely barn drooping in old age. These were his pursuits. Where others in his situation would be looking for a scavenger's payday, goods to supplement meager rations, the food Kirkland was seeking could not be measured on a scale at a general store.

Noticing a trail through a patch of woods, he left the road, silent and gliding, and right into the barrel of a rifle.

343

★   ★   ★

"Move a muscle and yer done fer," said the scraggly man, with one eye closed, and a finger on the trigger. The challenger's shirt was ragged, and numerous holes that had been stitched closed were begging for a second needle. His long beard had been freed to prowl the four cardinal directions and everywhere between. He was a poor man's General Stuart, turkey feathers stuck outward from his straw hat, which was pulled down low.

Kirkland raised his arms instinctively, but froze the rest of his body, studying the gunman and his weapon. The arm was an old modified flintlock, much like the one he had first carried into battle, gifted from his brother. Seeing he was not in danger of Yankee capture, he relaxed slightly, but kept his arms high.

"I'm not foraging," said Kirkland.

The man grunted.

"And I'm supposed to believe that? You men are worse than the Yankees, nearly cleaned me out. I've got nothing left to give, you hear?"

"Of course. I'm not after your hogs. I'm just out for a walk."

The man hesitated, tapping the trigger guard, not sure of what to make of the stranger.

"Please, I know my fellow soldiers may have done you wrong," said Kirkland in a calm, but steady voice. An image of Ratcliff and his cronies flashed across his mind. "But my intentions are not to disturb you or your property."

The farmer squinted, probing hard, and Kirkland met his stare without wavering. Lowering his gun slightly, the man appeared satisfied but then raised it again, before deciding that the stranger might be trusted.

"All right then," the farmer said, resting the barrel against his shoulder. "If you come inside, my wife has some biscuits on."

"I appreciate the gesture, but…"

"Would you rather I shoot you?"

There was an uncomfortable silence, until the farmer smacked his belly and laughed heartily.

"Come on," he motioned with his free hand. "You have gentle eyes. Other than them that belong to my wife and daughter, I haven't seen the kind in quite a spell."

Kirkland tried to deny the offer, but the farmer turned and started walking away briskly in a manner that defied his age.

I must be polite. Biscuits.

Although Kirkland's manners got his feet moving, it was his stomach that caused an accelerated response. The exercise had greatly eased the rolling in his gut and the hangover's smothering blanket.

Saying nothing, the farmer headed through the woods toward a small, balloon-frame house, his blotchy, ashen hair, long and unkempt, trying to keep up.

Passing an old horse tethered to a tree with a large, heavy chain, it whinnied nervously.

"It's okay, girl. He means no harm."

Kirkland laughed inside, not because the man was reassuring his horse. It was the great care with which the man had secured the beast. The horse looked so ancient and frail that an effort to liberate it from a sapling might cause it to drop dead. And if the extra measure was meant to keep either army from conscripting the fossil, it was an unnecessary plot.

The old man arrived at the door, and gave it a gentle push. It stuttered a long, irritated groan before standing idly by.

"Come on in," said the man. "It's simple but from the looks of you, no offense, it just might be a subtle comfort."

He looked at Kirkland with alarm, hoping he didn't offend. In return, Kirkland gave him a warm smile of reassurance.

"Your home is a welcome respite from a soldier's meager dwelling. I'm honored to be your guest."

The old man lit up, obviously pleased, and stepped aside for Kirkland to enter.

"Thank you, Sir."

Once inside, the farmer racked his gun on the wall and clapped his hands.

The household appeared as if from hiding. A short, plump woman with a weary face and dirty apron stepped forward. She did not seem pleased at the intrusion to their home, but in an instant the old woman was forgotten, for behind her was a sight that caught Kirkland off guard.

Not since he left Carolina and Susan two years ago had he been in the presence of such beauty. Although the girl averted her eyes, her cinnamon curls fell gracefully onto her shoulders and framed a gilded face. A maiden of no more than seventeen, her drab, homespun clothes did not detract in any way from her radiant allure.

Initially stunned, Kirkland looked away, erasing his open jaw and hoping the stupefaction had gone unnoticed. He had seen very few examples of the fairer sex in the last two years, let alone one of such natural polish. After seeing her withered creators, Kirkland wondered how this couple could have produced such a rare specimen, or be related by blood. Even more bewildering was the fact that word had not gotten out about this jewel living so close to the army's encampment.

Did she also have a chain similar to the old mare, yet kept inside and out of sight?

"My name's Sullivan, Ethan Sullivan. This is my wife Matilda and my daughter Rose."

Kirkland tipped his cap at Ethan's wife and her daughter, who continued to stare at the floor.

"Pleasure to meet you both. My name is Richard Kirkland."

"Where you from, soldier?"

"Flat Rock, South Carolina."

"Ah, South Carolina. I have relatives that moved down there. Though we have not received a letter from them in quite some time," said Ethan.

"Are you familiar with any Sullivans in your district?"

"I'm afraid not."

"Of course. The odds would be against it that my long-lost kin would be your neighbors," said the farmer.

Matilda looked at Kirkland suspiciously and cold, making him uncomfortable in his uniform.

In an instant, however, a remarkable transformation took place in Rose. Her eyes had left the floor and ambled toward the visitor. When they met Kirkland's, her full power was revealed. The eyes were green, impossibly bright green, and it was as if they tossed a rope over his shoulders, dragging him closer. Although her grin was slight, these emerald orbs were much more telling, flirtatious even.

Matilda took a break from glaring at Kirkland, and turned it on Rose.

Averting her eyes again briefly while her mother looked on, as soon as Matilda turned her wrath back to Kirkland, the daughter followed with opposite vibes, ignoring the motherly admonishment. Now two people in the room had eyes with teeth, tearing holes in his already delicate exterior. With their biting spell, Kirkland wanted to flee, and he picked his brain for an escape plan without being rude or offending his generous host.

His impatient stomach, however, having sniffed the fresh biscuits long enough, growled mightily. Embarrassed and praying the angry call from his abdomen went unnoticed, he subtly covered his midsection with his hands.

It was too late.

"You hear that, Matilda? This boy is famished. Rose, set the table."

Both obeyed instantly.

"Please, have a seat," said Ethan, motioning to the crude dining table with a silver candelabra centerpiece adorned with three white candles. The decoration was out of place and must have been a cherished, inherited antique, for the rest of the house was sparsely decorated.

"I have yet to eat breakfast myself, as I spent the early hours hunting scavengers," said Ethan, grinning with delight at his own humor.

"Thank you Sir, but I don't mean to put you out."

"Nonsense. My Matilda knows her way around a kitchen. You'll wanna stay for this."

Seeing no way out, Kirkland followed the man's order.

"Thank you, Sir. I truly appreciate it. It does smell wonderful."

"We also have apple butter, finest in Virginia."

"I'm in your debt."

They sat down at the uneven table, where either a leg was crafted too short, or the floor had warped with age.

Brushing a thigh against Kirkland with purposeful daring, Rose put down plates and tankards for the hungry men.

"I must apologize for my earlier conduct. This area's been devastated by the presence of both armies. My hogs have been stolen. Most of my chickens, too. Even my whiskey, gone."

Kirkland tried not to squirm in body, but his mind was slithering.

"You boys sure gave the Yankees a whuppin,' though. For that, I must give rightful due."

"It was a terrible fight, Sir. But Lee had us ready."

"Indeed. God willing, a couple more victories like that will get Lincoln off our backs."

"Well, I hope you're right, but they don't seem whipped yet."

Ethan nodded, deep in thought, and the silence agitated Kirkland even more.

Rose revived her father with a serving of steaming biscuits, along with pickled eggs and cold venison sausage.

"Ah, here we are," he beamed. "We still have good ol' Clockwork, the hen. She lays an egg a day, no matter the season or the weather. Let us pray."

He folded his hands and bowed his head, and Kirkland did the same.

"Father, bless this food. For even in times like these, you have provided for us and we thank you. Please also bless our soldier guest, Mr. Kirkland, and protect him. May General Lee show us the way to victory and the end of this war. Amen."

"Amen."

His mouth watered at the plate before him, but his mind shunned the fork and knife.

"Come on now," said Ethan motioning with his utensils. "Dig in."

Kirkland picked up the fork and knife, still hesitating. But a slapping glance by the orbiting cook put his hands in motion. He sliced into the apple butter with his knife, careful not to place too much or too little on his biscuit, so not to offend. And after the first, tingling bite, it was as if a starving dog awoke from within, and he was tempted to engulf the rest of his bread, along with the egg and sausage, in one inhale. Kicking the dog away, he thanked his chef.

"This is fine butter, ma'am, the best I've had in years."

The compliment melted the edges of Matilda's frown, if only slightly, and with brevity.

Ethan smiled and nodded toward her.

"I am a truly fortunate man."

And then he grew serious, his expression turning so abruptly, that Kirkland was taken aback.

"You see, I'm tired of this war. And not just because our property, hell, all of Virginia, seems forever thrust in the middle of its highway."

Taking a gander at his family behind him, he paused, as if questioning whether to continue. Shaking his head, he continued.

"We have a son, not yet nineteen. He wanted to go off and fight and I gave him my blessing. Last we heard, he was up fighting in Maryland, but we haven't received a letter from him since September."

He sighed heavily, placing his fork and knife, tines and blade vertical, on the table.

"He ain't coming back."

"Ethan!"

Matilda crossed her arms and bit her lip, but the dams were bulging at her wrinkled corners.

"He will come back to us," she nearly shouted. "The mail's irregular. He will come back."

She burst into tears and Rose caught her in near collapse. Ethan stared into a corner, trying to remain composed. Dropping his wares, he placed his hands on the table and closed his eyes.

Kirkland searched in vain for words of comfort. Of course he suspected the worst but would not be a carrier of forlorn hope.

"I was in Maryland and you are correct in saying the mail is irregular there. It's the same throughout the army. I haven't heard from my brothers in quite some time. They're in the cavalry somewhere. But I believe they are alive and well. I must hold on to that prayer."

Ethan saw the mirage and hopped on board.

"You hear that, Matilda? It does no one any good to speculate. I was wrong to presume anything."

Striking his fist against the table, Ethan began to rise from his chair, but sank backward again.

Rose put her hands on her mother's shoulders and gently guided her out of the room.

"So tell me Sergeant, if I may be so bold. If you could go back in time, and the choice to sign up and fight was presented again before you, knowing what you now know… Would you still choose to enlist?"

Kirkland wiped his mouth with a napkin and looked Ethan straight in the eyes.

"South Carolina called and I was compelled to answer. It is my home and I hold it dear. As much as I love the flag of my grandfathers, we have been invaded. I do not pretend to understand all of the politics involved, on either side, but I do know this: everything I know and love is threatened by this war. And in its defense, I'm willing to sacrifice my life, if necessary."

Ethan's jaw solidified and his eyes called for his gun. Clenching his fists, he looked down at his hands. Turning them over, palms up, he allowed them to release their burden.

"I feel the same for Virginia, and I passed it on to Robert, my son. I was so proud when he left, with banners flying. But time and separation has led me to question my earlier resolve, I must admit. Who could have known the war would last this long? As God is my witness, if I had been more youthful, I would have joined him. I would take his place…"

"I understand," said Kirkland. "But if your son is out there, I suspect his patriotism and dedication to Virginia has not deteriorated."

Fake and high-pitched, Ethan stumbled through a laugh.

"He's a stubborn son-of-a-gun. I imagine he's the Yankee's worst enemy."

Kirkland smiled and rose to his feet.

350

"I'm sorry, but I've far extended my visit. Thank you so much for your hospitality and generosity. Please convey my sincere gratefulness to your wife for her splendid cooking. I do wish there was something I could do to prevent further disturbance on your property."

Ethan arose from his seat.

"It's the nature of war. Hungry soldiers will do as they must, just as I will do what's necessary to survive these bloody times."

Although Kirkland would have liked to soothe this dark notion, he couldn't argue with its truth. He held out his hand, which Ethan took with respect.

"I enjoyed our conversation. If all soldiers had your courtesy and honor, I wouldn't need to prowl my land with a rifle at the ready."

"Thanks again for your willingness to show courtesy to a stranger. I will keep your son Robert in my thoughts and prayers."

"We would appreciate that. By the way, he joined the 30th Virginia, Walker's Brigade. If you come across his outfit, please inquire about his fate."

"I will do so, Sir."

Ethan opened the door, and Kirkland held out his hand once more. They shook hands like old friends, but when Kirkland tried to release, Ethan held on.

Gripping with pronounced severity, Ethan's eyes flashed with blackened rays.

"Avenge my son. Kill them all."

★　　★　　★

"Rich—wander off to Carolina without telling me?" said Joe, playfully. Kirkland had strolled back into camp as the firmament sizzled with orange. He had walked all day after leaving the Sullivan farm, cleansing his burdened pores, and was weary from the effort.

"Yes, it was quite a walk. Made good time, though."

Joe laughed.

"See anything interesting?"

Kirkland tried to hold back a revealing smile, but Joe's inquisitive spell was just too seductive.

"*Do* tell of your adventures. Have a seat. It has to be more interesting than Nail's flatulence."

"Jealous," Nail called out as he left the hut, jabbing Kirkland in the stomach.

More than intrigued, Joe motioned him to a backside cushion. Sitting down, Kirkland dallied from the topic at hand.

"It was a fine day of muddy roads and barren trees. Hello, Alex, how's the professor?"

"Forced to spend my day listening to this jar of hot air." He motioned to Joe, with a look of utter boredom painted across his face.

"Heat is a blessing in this weather, don't you forget."

"He has a point there," said Alex.

Joe was getting impatient and he hovered over Kirkland.

"Enough of this small talk. I know you're stallin.' Spill it, friend."

"All right, all right. Stop your carryin' on and join us."

Joe lowered onto a carved-barrel chair, leaning in close.

"It's nothing to get your dander up about, but I did come across a family a ways off," Kirkland began. "The old man stuck in a rifle in my ear."

One sentence was all it took, and Joe was hovering again, ready for battle.

"It's okay, my friend. He turned out to be a very pleasant fellow. Unfortunately, I suspect Ratcliff and his cronies have paid him a visit or two. So I understand his less than cordial response to strangers on his land."

With both hands, Kirkland guided Joe back to his seat.

"Yes, you can't blame a man for protecting his property. Go on."

"I told him I wasn't foraging, just out for a walk."

"And he believed you?" asked Alex.

"It took a little convincing. In the end he invited me in for breakfast."

Joe took off his hat and slapped his knee.

"Please tell me there were biscuits."

"Yes, and with apple butter, eggs and venison, a meal fit for a king."

Joe's eyes went wild.

"I need to take a stroll more often."

"And that wasn't the best part."

Kirkland looked up at the tented ceiling, enjoying his friend's itchy thirst. He turned to Alex, who tried to hide his grin.

Then he stalled some more.

"What's for supper?"

"You ain't getting away with that. Well? What's this best part you're hidin'?"

"This family. They had a daughter."

"Now you're talkin'. What did she look like? And don't hold anything back."

"I don't know. If I tell you, every man in the division will know about it."

"I won't tell a soul, I swear."

Crossing his arms, Kirkland scrunched his face in disbelief.

"Hmm. I don't know. Remember when Nail told you about the mule egg? You spread it around camp like smallpox."

As a result of trusting Joe with an old story from his childhood, Nail had received a second moniker, though one less with less bite. As a child, Nail's father, in a cruel joke, had sent him into town with instructions to purchase a mule egg. Together, they would hatch it, his father had told him. To the elder's surprise, Nail returned proudly with a coconut. For weeks, Nail's family watched him do everything in his power to try to hatch a mule from the fruit before instructing him on the birthing of mammals. Ever since the story had made the rounds in camp, many had pursued a good chuckle at Nail's expense, calling him Mule Egg, Eggnail or just plain old Mule.

"Ah, that was different," said Joe, pacing. "No harm was done. Come on Kirkland, I know you want to spill it to me. Quit your stallin'."

"Sit down already. Your pacing is making me nervous."

Obeying, Joe sat down and leaned in so close, Kirkland expected him to tumble into his lap.

"She was a pure, Southern belle, the equal of any Carolina has produced."

Joe let out a whoop, enough to bring Kirkland's forefinger hush to his lips, and he almost regretted the telling.

Even Alex seemed to be riveted. Kirkland had expected the response, as the panorama of a soldier's life was almost constantly devoid of the female presence.

He was surprised, though, of how thrilling the vision of Rose struck him. This was of no disrespect to Susan, who still occupied every cell of his heart. But when a flower is dropped upon a canvas of slovenly men, it could burn a whole through the pastels.

"Kirkland, what did she look like? I must have details!"

"She was a brunette, with the face of a sculpted angel, and eyes of flashing green. She was simple but had the glow, like only the fairest ones possess."

The door opened, and a messmate returned.

"Nail, you have to hear this. Kirkland saw a beauty today."

Kirkland glared at Joe.

"You saw a woman?" Nail repeated.

Still shaking his head at Joe, Kirkland neither confirmed nor denied it.

"You saw a woman?" Nail repeated.

"Hell, yes, he did," yelled Joe. "Sounds like a celestial one, to boot. Rich, you need to tell me how to find this fair maiden."

"I wouldn't recommend it. Her father is quite protective. You're likely to get yourself a mouthful of bees."

"Might be worth it for a gander." He put his arm around Nail and squeezed him close. "Has to beat this face."

"I don't know. I clean up nice."

Joe giggled.

"Please, gentlemen," said Kirkland. "This family has suffered enough. I wouldn't be surprised if the whiskey we drank last night was stolen from that farm. They've almost been wiped out by the foraging. Please stay away, I beg you."

"Kirkland," said Joe. "You haven't even told us the location."

★　　　★　　　★

FEBRUARY 28

They hit the dirt and rolled, each man desperate to pin the other. A crowd began to gather, cheering on the scrappers and wagering on the victor.

As Fain gained the advantage, he loaded a fist and plunged it into his opponent's jaw. Recoiling, he was about to land another right when Kirkland hooked his arm. It was like trying to corral a rabid dog, but Kirkland held on as the onlookers groaned at the abbreviated version. Swearing and kicking as his friend wrenched him away, Fain demanded that he be allowed to finish the altercation.

"Save it," said Kirkland, pushing him away and standing between the two fighters. "He's on our side."

"He's a damn fool is what he is."

"Are you done?"

Fain spit on the ground, glaring at the one who escaped with only a sore jaw.

"Yeah, I'm done."

"Good. You know I have to escort you to the guardhouse."

"I know, but it was worth it." He smiled and several came over to congratulate the champ.

Turning around, Kirkland helped the object of Fain's wrath to his feet.

"You all right, private?"

"That man's a menace."

Kirkland nodded. "We know. And he'll spend the night in the guardhouse for it. But you're on his good side now."

The man gave him a confused look.

"He won't bother you anymore. You'll see," said Kirkland.

Just outside the dispersing crowd was Moonbeam, who, as others approached him, began to turn and leave.

"Say," said Kirkland to the Fain-whipped private, "you're of the Seventh Regiment, are you not?"

"That's right."

"Do you know that man?"

Kirkland pointed to the rapidly fleeing man.

"Most avoid him. He's a shirker. Won't fight. Took a wound at Sharpsburg and hasn't been the same since. Keeps to himself mostly."

"What's his…"

"If I'm not under arrest, may I be excused?" said the man, cutting the first sergeant off.

"Of course."

As he left abruptly, Kirkland looked in the direction of Moonbeam, but the soldier had disappeared into the trees.

"Come on Fain, time to answer."

He came willingly. As they arrived at the guardhouse, Kirkland spoke with the two armed soldiers out front.

A hastily constructed shack with three walls and no door, it was not a desirable place to sleep off a hangover or be thrown into for disorderly conduct. Open to the elements, most boarders learned their lesson after one night of shivering without a fire. Except for Fain, who could never seem to stay out of trouble and was often a distinguished guest.

"Put him up for the evening," said Kirkland to the guards. "One night only."

"Fain, ain't seen you for a while," said one of them. "Whattaya in for this time?"

"Oh, brawling as usual," said Kirkland.

"That's right," said Fain, proudly. "But the first sergeant saved the other fellow from a very unpleasant beating."

"It's true," said one guard to the other. "He's good with his fists."

To this, Fain beamed.

"Enjoy your quarters," said Kirkland. "I'll be back to retrieve you in the morning."

"Uh, Kirkland, I mean First Sergeant, can I have a word in private?"

"What is it?"

"Please." He motioned for Kirkland to follow him inside.

Relenting, he ducked under the roof. Fain appeared hesitant, embarrassed even.

"I, uh, was hoping you could do me a favor."

"Go on."

Picking at his fingers, he hesitated again.

"I, uh, was wondering if, uh, you could write a letter for me."

Slightly taken aback, but not completely surprised, as quite a number of the troops were illiterate, Kirkland agreed.

"Of course. It would be my pleasure."

"Thank you. If you could keep this between us, I'd appreciate it."

"You're not the only one in this camp without the ability to read and write. Far from it."

"Yes, I know. But it's always been a stick in my craw."

"I will not speak of it to anyone."

"Thank you. I know you're a trustworthy man."

"Do you have paper?"

"Oh, yes, of course."

Reaching into his coat, Fain gathered the writing material and pencil, which he handed over.

"Okay," said Kirkland, sitting down. "To whom will this be addressed?"

Putting his hands behind his back, Fain began to pace.

"Dear mother."

At his thigh, Kirkland began to transcribe the words, which soon began to flow with a polish that astonished his ears.

"Although many months have passed since I last wrote, you are ever in my thoughts and prayers. The army life is a good existence, despite what you hear to the contrary. I have a great many friends here and I would give my life for any of them. Our cause is noble and I will defend our home to the last. You need not worry about your oldest son, for I'm surrounded by the greatest army the world has ever seen. In the end, we will march home victorious.

"Please kiss Willy and Oliver for me. I'm certain that under you and Pa's care, they are growing up to be smart boys. Please write me as soon as you receive this as winter camp can be dull and we enjoy news from home. Farewell, until we meet again. G. W. Fain."

Leaning against the far wall, he sank to the floor and curled up with a dirty blanket.

"Postscript. Please send me more cider cake and applesauce cookies."

Smiling as he wrote the last line, Kirkland passed the letter.

"Your penmanship is like a woman's," Fain joked, looking it over.

"Yes, well, my teacher at the church school let the rod fall often. I do believe she enjoyed the torture."

Fain laughed. "Maybe I didn't miss out after all."

Getting up, Kirkland stretched his back.

"Good night, Fain. Don't freeze to death."

Chapter 20

Dipping the bristles into the soapy water, he lathered the brush pile long neglected on his cheek, chin and throat.

It had been several months between mowings, and as his straight razor cut through to his skin, youth began to reappear. Kirkland had surrendered this grooming habit during the harsh winter, but now it was overdue. While falling short in comparison to Farmer Sullivan's belly and sky prowler, it was remarkably thick, a new standard he hoped he would never again approach.

As he shook the fur from his razor, Kirkland gazed at the tiny pocket mirror, barely recognizing the image staring back. The cherubic velvet was long gone, replaced by hard lines and sinking eyes. He paused from shaving, and touched his cheek, wondering where that boy from Flat Rock had disappeared to. But the figure did not alarm him—much—but rather was a point of fascination and discovery. He was a man, a fact that had crept near without diagnosis.

At the ridiculousness of his denial, the first sergeant giggled. He spoke out loud, barely above a whisper.

"You old man. What has become of you?"

As he finished carving away the last scruff on his throat, Joe appeared.

Quickly, he searched for a witty rebuttal from stones he expected Joe to throw. When no words came mocking his new look, Kirkland became alarmed.

His friend's face did not soothe this worry. The usual humor and bounce in his countenance had been drained. It was not a face of melancholy, however, but one of sheepish hues with a faraway stare.

"Are you okay, Joe? You look a little peaked."

"Yes," said Joe, unable to look Kirkland in the eye. "That farm you visited, with the handsome belle. Did her father wear a straw hat with feathers?"

"Funny, I was just thinking of the man."

Kirkland went back to his mirror, alarm bells now silent.

"Why yes, I do believe he was in possession of a hat as you described."

"That's what I thought. The damn fool took a shot at me."

Kirkland laughed so hard, he dropped his mirror.

Joe was not amused.

"I'm glad you see the humor in it, especially since you sent me to him."

"I did nothing of the sort," said Kirkland, still laughing. As first sergeant, he was in charge of work details. Because enemy cavalry raids had disrupted the railroad supply line following the battle of Chancellorsville, food was in short supply, and details were sent to gather food from the countryside.

"I do not recall sending you in the direction of the Sullivan farm," said Kirkland. "You found that on your own accord. You're just mad that you missed out on biscuits and the sight of that breathtaking young woman."

"Hell yes, I am. He wasn't nearly as agreeable as on your visit."

"Perhaps you weren't very persuasive."

"Persuasive? I didn't get to within 50 yards of him before he unloosed on me."

Kirkland stopped laughing. He wondered if Sullivan's prized chicken, Clockwork, was gone and if the family was now destitute and near starvation.

"We would have paid him for the food," said Joe.

"Of course. But many others have not. I doubt he has much left to share as it is."

Standing up, Kirkland put an arm around his friend and squeezed.

"Come with me, brother. I have some rancid meat we can share."

"That sounds delightful."

Glad his friend's humor had returned, Kirkland guided Joe toward the winter shack that they'd recently reinhabited following the brilliant tactical victory at Chancellorsville. It was Lee's finest hour. Although he had dangerously split his army by sending Stonewall Jackson on a flanking march, the maneuver caught the Union forces completely by surprise.

As Kirkland was about to grab the door handle, a horseman called out to them. It was Colonel Kennedy.

"Men, I have a message to deliver from General Lee. Form ranks."

★　　★　　★

His hands shook as he pulled out General Orders No. 61 from his breast pocket. Dismounted before his men, Kennedy was pale and struggling to make sense of the words. His eyes were filled with a deep sorrow, and Kirkland held his breath. Whatever was written on that page was conceived under darkness and agony. As if aware of the occasion, the sun was muted, buried behind heavy clouds.

The colonel looked up from the message, slowly surveying his assembled men from right to left. Taking a deep breath, he cleared his throat and began to read. His voice, while not in its usual inspiring boom, was poised and reverent.

"With deep grief, the Commanding General announces to the army the death of Lieutenant General Jackson, who expired on the 10th instant at 3:15 PM."

"No!"

"That can't be."

The crowd was alive with utterings of disbelief, some with words while others could only reply with a reactive groan, as if suddenly wounded.

"Attention, men. Attention."

Gathering himself, Kennedy closed his eyes for a moment, and then continued with the astonishing message.

"The daring, skill and energy of this great and good soldier, by the decree of an all-wise Providence, are now lost to us.

"But while we mourn his death, we feel his spirit lives, and will inspire the whole army with his indomitable courage and unshaken confidence in God as our hope and strength. Let this name be a watchword to his corps who have followed him to victory on so many fields.

"Let the officers and soldiers imitate his invincible determination to do everything in defense of our beloved country."

Kennedy carefully folded the paper, staring at the ground.

"Signed, R. E. Lee, General."

An uncomfortable silence reigned, interrupted only by a few who wept openly, and by the wind blowing through a graveyard of tree stumps.

"Men, you are dismissed."

Kirkland moved through the ranks, passing several who were still frozen by the news.

Could it really be true?

Wounded in the dark by Confederate pickets who mistook his party for enemy cavalry at Chancellorsville, Jackson's arm had been amputated. Initially expected to recover, pneumonia set in, taking the life of a man who seemed immortal.

Without the leadership of Stonewall, Kirkland knew the army would never be the same. How Jackson's death would affect the army's morale, Kirkland wasn't sure. But he knew Lee's right-hand man would be impossible to replace.

★　　★　　★

JUNE 15, 1863
NEAR CULPEPER COURT HOUSE, VA

"Fooorwaaaaard…"

Kirkland looked right and then left, searching. Joe just shrugged his shoulders, unworried. As the command to embark was formed on Kennedy's lips, Alex jumped into line, breathing heavily.

362

"Here, hold my rifle, please." He handed the weapon over to Joe before he could object.

Rummaging through a stocky book, Alex found his page and held it up below his chin.

"March."

The train moved forward with Alex's nose still buried in the text.

"What in the…"

Alex cut Joe off with a raised index finger: "Sssshhh. One moment."

His mouth resting open, Joe was so shocked that he actually complied.

"Finished," said Alex, closing the book with a two-handed thud.

"I'm not carrying your gun for you."

"Of course. Kirkland, can you place this on my back?"

"You sure you want to carry that? We could be going 20 miles today."

"And I was so close to finishing when I was rudely interrupted."

Kirkland grabbed the brown-cloth book, and examined the gilt-lettered title on the spine and floral blind stamp on the cover.

"*The House of the Seven Gables*, Hawthorne. Haven't you read this ten times already?"

"Eleven, actually."

"It must be an exceptional read."

"Oh, it is a classic, with such wonderful prose."

"Here, hold this," said Kirkland, handing his rifle to Joe, who was now balancing the three weapons haphazardly to his chest.

Opening to a random page, Kirkland read from it.

Thank heaven, the night is well-nigh past! The moonbeams have no longer so silvery a gleam, nor contrast so strongly with the blackness of the shadows among which they fall. They are paler now; the shadows look gray, not black. The boisterous wind is hushed. What is the hour?

He read as long as he could, waiting for Joe to explode. He didn't have to wait long.

"You've got three seconds before I toss these to the roadside."

Before unburdening their friend, Kirkland and Alex gave each other a satisfied grin.

"A lot of good that'll do you today," said Joe. "Do you plan on hitting the Yanks over the head with it?"

"If I must."

"Forget I said anything. Can we please have a conversation about something with relevance?"

"I don't know, Joe," said Kirkland, still ganging up with Alex. "Like you said, it could be a long march."

Joe turned to the man behind him.

"Nail, you wanna talk about literature?"

"Yes, Eggnail, you fond of book-larnin'?" said a mocking voice a few rows back.

"Not in the least."

"Good. Carry on, professor and pupil. Nail and I will discuss more noble pursuits, like, uh…"

"Barbecue."

"Now you're speakin' my language."

As Nail and Joe launched into the virtues of pork, Kirkland was eager to hear about the book that had sustained Alex's interest all winter, after he'd picked up the discarded copy on the streets of Fredericksburg. Expecting to be walking all day, at least, Kirkland was ready for a long diversion from aching feet, as he regained his marching legs. Since the extraordinary victory at Chancellorsville, the army had been stagnant for a month, while Lee considered his next move. He drilled his men constantly, six days a week, and organized his force into three corps. Kershaw's brigade would stay under McLaws. Wanting to draw the enemy into the open and away from the protection of the Rappahannock, Lee decided in early June to abandon his defensive line at Fredericksburg. They would move north again, to an uncertain destination.

"Tell me about this book."

Alex dumped the first edition by the roadside.

"I hate to part with it, but it's going to be hot today."

Clearing his throat, the professor dove into his lesson.

"*The House of Seven Gables* is about magic and ridding yourself of guilt and family entanglements . . ."

★　　　★　　　★

JULY 27

MARYLAND–PENNSYLVANIA BORDER

They emerged from a corn field, with hands in prayer, as if their locked fingers were a sign that Pennsylvania was no haven for weapons or armies. Dressed in piercing black with broad-brimmed hats, they were clean, almost flawless in groom.

Although their clothes were plain and colorless, without neckties, the dozen men held themselves with the dignity of village elders called to speak in a time of crisis. Certainly, these were men of substance and weight, having earned the respect of their neighbors through years of brotherly service.

Slowly, with heads bowed, the men entered the road, blocking the path of the heavily armed invaders.

Kershaw, out front on his horse, held up his hand for the column to halt, as his subordinates vocalized the signal.

With the synchronicity of military bearing, but without a spoken command or hurried response, the men gradually lifted their chins to reveal their faces. While resolute and serious, their countenances offered no malice, no ill design. Despite having long abandoned the tender springs of youth, the wrinkles and lines were infused with a glowing, which radiated a peaceful composition. The features were different in each, by crown of nose or length of jaw, yet all had a profound virility, as if their minds were unfettered.

Kirkland gave a questioning glance toward Alex, who did not return it.

But feeling the stare, he replied, "Quakers." Though he was aware that Quakers were once prominent in the Camden area, and the cemetery in town was named in their honor, they were long gone by the time Kirkland was born.

The leader took one step forward with bold snap but conservative distance.

"Thou must not pass, for only blood will await thee."

Agitated by their odd appearance, Kershaw's horse whinnied and pawed at the strangers. Steadying his mount, the general eyeballed the leader in silence, as if unsure of how to respond to this unusual blockade. Certainly, the soldiers could easily march around these unarmed objectors, ignoring their existence. In an even more disrespectful manner, they could just plow through the Quakers, swatting them away like irksome flies.

Yet Kershaw chose to speak plainly, to acknowledge the pious men with honor.

"Gentlemen, I admire your courage, but our duty demands that we continue on this road."

The old Quaker placed his palms together and smiled.

"Please understand, we only desire peace for this land. If thou believes of a destiny in the Commonwealth of Pennsylvania, then go as thee must."

Bowing, the leader stepped backward in line with his brothers, and they departed the road as quickly as they appeared, in the same meditative gait. If they were disappointed, their faces showed no erosion from their initial, pleasant demeanors. Barely stirring an ear or leaf, they disappeared into the corn.

"They didn't put up much of a fight," said Joe with a giggle.

"They said what they had to say," Alex countered.

Kirkland looked at Alex for more, but he didn't elaborate. Instead, he was peering at a large monument at the side of the road.

"A crownstone!" he exclaimed.

"A what?" said Joe.

"An original marker imported from England to mark the Mason–Dixon line. A hundred years ago, they were placed every five miles along the Pennsylvania and Maryland border. Let's get a closer look."

Kirkland followed, but Joe was uninterested.

"An old rock? Fascinating. Ya'll go ahead and enjoy yourselves."

Leaving the column, they jogged over to the carved marker, just as the order to march was given.

"We'll catch up," said Alex.

Although weathered by a century of natural decay, a coat of arms on either side was clearly visible. Twelve feet square and four and half feet high, it dated to a time when English lords disputed the boundary.

"You see, Kirkland, facing the Pennsylvania side is the crest of William Penn, and facing Maryland is the crest of Charles Calvert, 5th Baron of Baltimore. Between 1763 and 1767, Charles Mason and Jeremiah Dixon were given the task of surveying this land, which was the final resolution of a dispute between the two British colonies."

Kirkland put his hand on top of the maker, and widened his stance, looking east. The soil beneath his right and left feet were no different, and he perceived no colliding winds. It was in fact, a rather insignificant threshold, separating North from South, Yankee from Dixie.

"If unenlightened, you could easily cross over this barrier without a notion of its significance," Alex mused.

"Perhaps, in this case, the ignorance of Plato's cave would be preferable."

Alex beamed.

"You have arrived at the great paradox of choice! But I believe this temporary shield of ignorance only delays the quest for truth, and in turn, advancement of the human race."

"What is the name of that poet you're so enamored of?"

"There are so many. To whom are you referring? Wordsworth?"

"Yes, I believe it is William Wordsworth that I've heard you recite more than others."

"That's interesting for you to say," said Alex, somewhat offended. "I was not aware that I repeat my words so often."

"No, Alex, you are free from patterns. Maybe it is this poet's imagery, which, in your *occasional* deliveries, has stuck with me somehow. Or maybe it's his name, ideal for a poet I must say."

"Yes, yes," said Alex, pondering Kirkland's answer. "I must confess, I never truly looked at his name with simple meaning."

"Are you calling me simple?"

"Far from it, my friend. It's just that sometimes we fail to capture the little things before our very eyes. Fascinating. Words Worth. As many times as I've read his lines…"

"Can you enlighten me on one of your favorite verses?"

"Hmm," said Alex, his eyebrows crossed in a brain rummage. "I may have an appropriate poem. It's rather obscure, but one of my favorites."

Clearing his throat, Alex closed his eyes. With a slight English accent, he began to recite.

Leave to the nightingale her shady wood;

A privacy of glorious light is thine,

Whence thou dost pour upon the world a flood

Of harmony, with instinct more divine;

Type of the wise who soar, but never roam;

True to the kindred points of Heaven and Home!

Alex opened his eyes as if reborn by the words.

"Of course, there is more—it's from *To the Skylark*—but you get the idea."

"No, I really don't. What is the meaning of it?"

Alex laughed.

"I'm not entirely sure, to be honest. But I like to think of the skylark as an earthly being who is equally cozy high among the heavens. He is wise in his pursuits, never straying too far, but always reaching beyond what the Earth alone can provide."

"It is indeed a wise pursuit," said Kirkland. "And splendidly written! I do believe that your exquisite taste is rubbing off on me."

"You see beauty and truth. You don't need me for that."

"Maybe. But the truth is, unless you don't want to be a skulker, we should catch up to the men."

"Right," said Alex, realizing the length of their dalliance. "To Pennsylvania!"

★   ★   ★

JULY 1, 1863
CHAMBERSBURG PIKE
CASHTOWN GAP, PA
7:30 PM

Over the downward slope, the leaves nuzzled and the branches shook hands, forming a darkened tunnel in the fading light. It was as if the trees on both sides of the pike had bonded in an arc of congratulatory shade, welcoming fair travelers who had climbed the Blue Ridge. Yet on this day, the shield was unnecessary, as the clouds above drifted slowly by in unbroken harmony. A warm, southern breeze had been pleasant for the hike, and the temperature had remained in the low 70s.

Stuck idle in the town of Fayetteville by roads choked with long wagon trains for most of the day, the Carolinians had been forced into a late start in their eastward movement. Since arriving in the area on the 28th of June, they had mostly rested their weary bones and sore feet aggravated by the long trek from Virginia. Having marched well over 100 miles in two weeks, lounging about was a bore, yet few were complaining.

Reaching the Cashtown Gap after a few hours of uneventful climbing, the men were in good spirits, knowing the worst was behind them. At least for the time being, they moved without the stop and stutter pace that had plagued them throughout the day.

Kirkland looked up at the canopy, which was growing a shade darker with each passing mile. To some, the tunnel effect at approaching dusk might appear ghostly and ominous, an Ichabod hollow where the headless horsemen might roam, but he saw only the natural beauty. His wheels lubricated by rest and bolstered by mileage, he was enjoying the day's walk.

369

"I should be used to this by now, not knowing where we are, or where we're going," said Kirkland.

"Pennsylvania," said Joe.

"Thank you for that observation." He smiled at his friend. "Master Obvious, can you enlighten us further?"

"We will end up east of where we are right now."

"Now you're on to something."

He looked up again, his head among the tree tops. But as he did so, he failed to navigate over a large mule pie. Uttering something between a groan and a wordless oath at his soiled shoes—and a few sock-covered toes—now covered with manure, the mule was not the center of his wrath. It was the shoemaker. Whether it was inferior leather, poor craftsmanship, or just the inevitability of trudging mile after mile over rough roads, the shoes just weren't up to the task. Or maybe the culprit was South Mountain itself, for it was on her back the previous year that Kirkland's brogans crumbled.

With the agony of that experience seared into his memory, the fact that his current pair was not so far gone as on Maryland Heights lessened the brutality of his ire. He soon cast aside these nagging grievances, and his head floated upward again.

"Virginia, Maryland, now Pennsylvania," said Kirkland, shaking his head. "Who knew us country boys from Flat Rock nowheresville would gaze upon these lands?"

"If you would have told me in '60, I wouldn't have believed you, I admit. In truth, I might have slapped some sense into you or deemed you unsuitable for further callings."

"Well, that second scenario might be going a bit far, but the first? I may have thanked you afterward for restoring my equilibrium."

"Yes, and I would have enjoyed giving you a slight beating."

"Of that I have no doubt. Returning to my original question—Where do you think we're headed? Alex, any ideas?"

"Not in the slightest, I'm afraid. Possibly Harrisburg, but that would be only conjecture."

"I wonder where these Yankees are, and how far away," said Kirkland.

"Judging by the amount of our men who took the road ahead of us, at least we won't be surprised," added Joe.

"You're right. Ewell's Division will have that burden."

"But the enemy could be 50 miles from here."

"Yes, or in the valley below. When was the last time we were ordered to cook three days of rations and not be in a brawl directly?"

"True, but as much as I hate the cavalry, JEB Stuart should give us good warning if the Yankees are close by."

Kirkland bristled.

"Don't you forget that my brothers are in the cavalry."

"Of course," Joe laughed. "Well, then I hate all saber-wielding fools not containing members of the Kirkland clan."

"Thank you for this exception to your blind hatred."

"You're welcome."

"I haven't heard from my brothers in more than a month."

"That would be an impossibility of late. The mail certainly won't reach us here."

"Of course, you're right. But I dream for the day when I can see them again."

"When we do get home there'll be one hell of a shindig. I can see it now, a handsome belle on each arm, asking about my grand adventures with Lee and Longstreet. Southern girls, have mercy!"

"Joe, you have a one-track mind," said Kirkland, but he was also thinking about his own hometown girl.

"Well, someone must entertain the womenfolk. I bet all they've had to court during this war is wrinkly old men and cowardly shirkers."

"Oh, yes," said Alex in jest. "I'm sure they will all swoon and fall faint to the ground in your very presence."

"Sounds good to me."

They all laughed.

A distant rumble ended their good humor, and instinct erased their smiles. For a few moments, no one spoke, as if all were measuring the distance between the flash and the boom. But they knew the outburst had not arisen from glowing clouds above. The culprits were invisible in their foreboding, and the men gripped their rifles harder, on full alert. As the cannon fire multiplied and the rage grew louder, the men quickened their pace, without orders or realization.

A flapping of heavy wings distracted Kirkland from his far-casting ears. A turkey vulture was high in a tree, its hooked, ivory beak and crimson head waiting. On an adjacent branch, a second vulture landed, much to the chagrin of the original squatter. They traded low, hissing growls that tickled Kirkland into an involuntary shiver.

Paired with the ominous sounds of battle, it was almost too spooky to fathom.

"It won't be long now," said Joe, "before we're in it."

Alex, surveying the sky through the trees, disagreed.

"No, night will prevent us today."

But what of tomorrow?

★　　★　　★

JULY 2, 1863
4:45 PM

A scream plowed through the sticky air and into the trees above the recumbent men. There was a severing crack. As Kirkland looked up, a hefty limb, 10 feet long and as thick as a man's thigh, began a hammering descent.

"Move, move!"

At the last possible second, Kirkland rolled right and the men about him scattered, as the timber-arm pounded the earth. Striking with such force that it bounced several feet, it shifted slightly on the rebound, giving Kirkland a mouthful of leaves.

In shock at the close call, he spit at the invading green, but didn't move.

"Get off me!"

It was Fain, who was not taking kindly to another man sprawled on his back.

The awkward position caused by his evasive maneuver was so ridiculous that Kirkland began to giggle.

Relishing a momentary upper hand over the diminutive fireball, he delayed his dismount, hoping a black eye wouldn't follow. The seat of power was only momentary before Fain bucked him with forceful persuasion. Landing on his back—still laughing—Kirkland offered a feathered apology.

"I'm sorry Fain, but as empty as my stomach is, I did not believe consuming this large splinter would be suitable for digestion."

Fain was not amused.

"If I wasn't saving it for the Yankees, I would frail you good, Kirkland."

"I'm pleased you are finally showing some restraint."

Muttering a few epithets finalized by a grunt, Fain turned toward the white clover field to his front. He shifted uncomfortably as another shell exploded overhead, scattering leaves and small branches, which rained down in fluttering clumps. Kirkland was feeling the strain as well, and was grateful for the brief period of light humor.

The men of the 2nd South Carolina had been crouched behind a stone wall for an hour, and were growing impatient as the artillery battle raged around them. Several batteries were in front, assailing a peach orchard 600 yards away to their left. Their guns had provoked a terrific response from the enemy, and the air grooved and shook from whistling missiles and detonating crashes.

General Hood's division had already attacked on Kershaw's right. Although the enemy had been driven from the streets of Gettysburg the day before, the Yankees now held the high ground south of town. The South Carolinians had been awoken at dawn after only two hours of nervous shuteye. The previous night, they'd marched to within two miles of Gettysburg, the unfortunate locale chosen by fate where two great armies would stumble upon each other in vicious combat. July 2 had not gone as planned. Delays and countermarches to avoid detection by the enemy had gobbled up most of the day.

Exhausted and with only a few hours of light left, Kirkland began to wonder if the rebel yell would be unleashed or muzzled.

"There will be a pause, followed by three guns fired in rapid succession," said Colonel Kennedy, passing the word along, in a sober but assured voice. "This is the signal for you to move over the wall and form on the other side."

Finally.

Lowering his eyes, a petite, slanting flower relaxed his rigid form. It was a soft, simple white variety, struggling through a crevice in the wall of farmer-cleared stones. Though far from cleansing, this purity of form untangled a few knots of dread.

"Kirkland."

He turned around to see Joe, and was startled by his appearance. The usual face of poise and cool had been replaced by austere eyes and a shaky jaw, as if Joe's spirit had been sucked from his bones. This foreign transformation spooked Kirkland, heightening his already swollen nerves. Gathering all his might just to keep from doubling over, he faked a smile.

"Kirkland, if I should fall, would you take this letter and send it to my father?"

The words sent his brittle smile running to the rear.

"Joe, you can send it yourself. Before you know it, we'll be racing stallions again back in Flat Rock."

Kirkland's reassurances failed to ease Joe's burdensome face.

"I'm afraid this will be my last battle."

He turned and beheld the clover fields to their front.

"Don't be ridiculous. You've made it this far without a scratch. You've always been the strong one, the unbreakable oak."

"No, Rich. The strong one is you. You proved that at Fredericksburg. I could not gather my nerves to help you. Or, possibly, I had no desire to. Either way, I'm ashamed because of it."

"You have nothing to prove. You walked into the fire with me time and again. It was you who kept me going. I owe you everything."

Joe put his hand on Kirkland's shoulder.

"God could not have blessed me with a better friend. Please, take this. We'll see each other again soon enough. Not too soon, I hope."

With trembling hands, Kirkland accepted the letter and placed it in his pocket.

There was a pause in the cannonade, followed by a triplet of booming.

Nodding to Kirkland, Joe leaped over the wall with the rest.

Stunned, Kirkland hesitated before regaining his bearings. His balance scarred, he jumped awkwardly, stumbling on his landing. Noticing Alex looking him over concernedly, he shook him off, swallowed hard and joined the lines forming at his front.

"Attention!" growled Kennedy. "Shoulder... arms! Right shoulder shift... arms! Guide center. At the double quick. Forwaaaard... march!"

The six regiments of Kershaw's brigade, 1,800 strong, with the 2nd near the center, dived into the field and headed toward the Emmitsburg Road which was parallel to its lines. Longstreet and Kershaw were behind them, choosing to follow on foot.

The carpet of clover was soft and inviting, and as the artillery silenced their guns to allow the brigade to pass, the smoke cleared, revealing a heavy concentration of the enemy in the peach orchard on their left.

With his senses on high alert, Kirkland noticed a climber on his right hand. Brushing the wood tick away, and attempting to do the same with Joe's premonition, he focused on his job as file closer. But in truth, Joe's words had severely rattled him. Every step was torture, and each breath was overcast with dark omens.

In previous battles, time seemed to float above his head and his mind was clear. Fear had mostly evaporated, replaced by a stillness of purpose. Now, the fear was overwhelming in its clamor, tearing away at the built up resistance. He had heard stories about ordinary men of prophecy, forecasting their last breath, as if Death had approached too close in gleeful anticipation, allowing for some kind of morbid clarity. Or maybe it was just fate, a predetermined final verse memorized deep within the soul. Whatever truth was behind these doors, Kirkland wasn't sure, but he prayed that Joe had been fooled by a trickster.

Despite the chaos within his head, Kirkland performed his duties. If a man in front ducked and paused when a shell exploded near, Kirkland was there, encouraging him to "close up" and keep going. Veterans as they were, however, most had no need for a kick in the pants or words of inspiration, and the Carolinians crossed the field with an intimidating presence, shoulder to shoulder.

Before them was a farm lane diverting from the main road, leading to a massive banked barn of the Rose family, 30 feet tall and made of stone. A similarly impressive stone house was some distance beyond.

While harassed under long range fire, casualties had been few, and the columns made it to the Emmitsburg Road with little resistance.

Longstreet, having accompanied the men as far as the fence line, waved his hat and urged his fellow Carolinians on.

"Roll them up, men!" he shouted. "Give them the bayonet!"

But there was a problem. Barksdale had not yet advanced on Kershaw's left, leaving the whole brigade exposed to the brunt of the fire in and around the peach orchard. Improvising, Kershaw decided to split his brigade into two wings. The left three regiments would turn north and drive the enemy's guns from the field, while the right wing would continue east to help Hood's push toward the Union left flank.

Crossing the post and rail fence, elevated by fearsome cheers, the men entered the road. The opposite side had a fence of similar construction, and as Kirkland climbed over, it was warm to the touch, baking in the afternoon sun. He was about to rest his Enfield on the other side to jump, when Joe appeared, his hand palm up and waiting. As he gave Joe his rifle, Kirkland was surprised to find the grim countenance gone, replaced by a face of calm serenity. The usual spark in his eyes had returned, with a depth Kirkland hadn't seen before. They were unburdened and of a lighter hue, but with a fierce resolve. Throwing his other leg over, Kirkland jumped. With a wink and a smirk usually reserved for an occasion of mischief, Joe returned Kirkland's weapon. Then, gritting his teeth like an exaggerated warrior, he slowly turned and resumed his place in the line now reforming.

Although this display sedated the outer edges of Kirkland's distress, his core was still churning and the fear remained, clawing at his throat.

Struggling against the urge to rush ahead and form a human shield for his friend, he watched as Joe entered the puzzle of shoulders. And in that moment, like a key thrust into a foggy door, something clicked and abruptly solidified. The fear burned itself out, not without coals susceptible to a quick rebirth, but dormant nonetheless. Pride settled into his pores, for Joe, for the Flat Rock boys, for all the sons of Carolina, uniting with their shoulders together and proclaiming: VICTORY OR DEATH.

Lifting his rifle, Kirkland slammed it across his torso with such force that even the adrenaline buffer couldn't mask it entirely. But it was a good pain, and he neither winced nor considered it foolish.

"Form up men! Guide center!" Kennedy bellowed. "Left wheel, march!"

They moved quickly, turning in the lane next to the imposing stone barn, to face the enemy head on. Many in passing the impressive structure, including Kirkland, couldn't help but be momentarily distracted in admiration. This farmer architect must have toiled long and carefully to assemble the stones and mortar in such perfect harmony.

While only one regiment of skirmishers could be seen in front of the peach orchard, at least 30 cannon were waiting in both the orchard and along the road that ran behind it and eastward.

Kennedy pointed to a section of these formidable guns, eerily silent 500 yards distant. It was the 9th and 5th Massachusetts batteries and their 12 Napoleons in the regiment's seething drift, pitting the will of man against the force of iron.

"There, Carolinians! Take those batteries!"

As they drove onward, a spherical case shot whistled in and exploded overhead, thumping the barn's walls and ringing the farm's bell.

The shot had not come from the batteries in front, but from the peach orchard.

As Kirkland glanced in this direction, smoke enveloped the fruited mound, as if the trees were ablaze. The orchard was receiving heavy fire from McLaws's artillery and the Federal gun crews were retaliating with stubborn ferocity. A single gun there had been aimed for Kershaw's brigade. Yet the targeted men from Massachusetts held their fire as the blackness from the orchard drifted toward them, floating in swirled patches above the road.

Moving down a slope, the men of the 2nd South Carolina entered a soupy morass. In one unfortunate step, Kirkland sunk up to his ankles, the mud squirming in between his toes. Recalling the previous night's tramping through manure piles, Kirkland didn't mind. It either covered his filth or was a welcome replacement.

For some, having wet feet was not so agreeable, and with heads down, they carefully stepped over and around the larger pools. Since these tiptoers were falling behind the advancing lines, Kirkland sloshed ahead to motivate them.

"Come on, men. Your feet are the least of your concerns. Close up. Close up, now!"

The men reluctantly obeyed, and soon the lines were together again, just in time for the Bay Staters to eradicate their silence.

In terrible succession, the Napoleons belched and disappeared behind a flashing wall of silver-gray. Iron balls of canister shot whipped through the lines, hedonistic of flesh, and desiring of bone. Their fuses glowing, spherical case detonated overhead, raining down shrapnel with lethal velocity.

One of these revolving menaces struck a man in the front rank, slicing through his shoulder and tearing a gaping hole through the guts of the man behind.

As Kirkland looked on, the second victim turned his back to the enemy, his face scalded with confusion. He took one step, rimming the bloody cavity with his hand, and fell dead without a murmur.

Frantic, Kirkland looked for Joe and was relieved to find him going forward. Again, he entertained thoughts of a human shield, but kept his composure, instead offering a quick prayer for his friend's safety.

Without control, his mind sputtered and began to reverse. Home and Susan, father and farm, an endless stream of images, convoluted and without order, danced across his vision. Closing his eyes, he attempted to squeeze and suffocate the chaos between his temples, allowing for the battle void to return.

Must not think on it now. A soldier must do his duty.

When his eyes opened, the fear had once again evaporated and he jogged forward to his place, reacquainted with the timeless atmosphere of mortal danger.

Although easy targets, the men kept their lines intact up the gentle rise toward the Yankee guns. When a man went down, they sidestepped the fallen, and threw their shoulders into a magnetic pull.

"Steady men!" Kennedy bellowed from behind them. "Hold your fire! Guide center!"

They could no longer see the guns opposing them. Only the red flashes through the smoke warned of tombstones and hospital beds. The South Carolinians were now within 200 yards and closing fast. Kirkland could smell the sulfur of their blasts now, and it ate away at his nostrils. But the fire was becoming more erratic, as if the gun crews were wavering in their defiance.

Again, Kirkland tossed his eyes at Joe.

Still there, alive and well. Two feet moving forward.

Thank you Lord.

With a short window through the smoke, Kirkland could see the enemy was breaking as several were backing away from their guns.

"Move by the right flank."

Kirkland was stunned. Had he heard this correctly? When so close to overrunning the guns ahead? It didn't make any sense to change front now.

"Move by the right flank. Do it!"

379

This time the orders were repeated all along the line, so the men conformed.

Kirkland was horrified.

Seeing the Carolinians shift from their attack, the artillerymen returned to their pieces, and soon opened with a terrific barrage of canister. Now enfilading their enemy, one iron ball could pass through four or five men with ease.

And they were torn apart.

As Kirkland marched eastward, a head rolled by and kicked upward, knocking another man senseless. Arms and legs were flung in the air, rotating in sickening flight.

One such limb, severed at the elbow, seemed to hover for an extra moment, its hand bidding adieu with a gold wedding ring flashing in the cruel sunlight.

Blood splattered Kirkland in the face, so warm and with such force, that for a moment, he thought he was gravely wounded.

Everywhere, men were screaming in their death songs or at shattered appendages soon to be victims of the surgeon's knife.

Dabbing his face with several fingers, Kirkland held them before his eyes, knowing what he would find, yet still unsure if the liquid was his. As he stared at the blood, someone crashed into his chest, throwing him to the ground. Next to him, lifeless eyes stared back.

The air went silent, as Kirkland recognized the bloody face.

Joe.

Chapter 21

In a weary daze, Kirkland and Alex stumbled through the Rose Woods, away from a failed attempt to dislodge the Yankees from a hill known as Little Round Top. They had passed by and through lands that in a few short hours had descended into Hades, every inch trampled by desperate struggle and doused by American blood.

For posterity, these places would be firebranded with heavy iron forms spelling out "Devil's Den" and "the Bloody Wheatfield." With reinforcements, the Carolinians of Kershaw's left wing had recovered from the disastrous order to turn away while at the cusp of overrunning the enemy artillery near the Peach Orchard. It had been a command for Kershaw's *right* wing that had been erroneously passed along and obeyed—with devastating consequences.

While the 2nd South Carolina had gotten its revenge against the Massachusetts batteries, driving them from the field and pushing onward through the wheatfield and under Little Round Top, it was all for nothing. All that was gained was a peach orchard of smoking trees, a stony hill and a cluster of boulders—Devil's Den. The enemy had not relinquished the high ground.

Worse, the Carolinians had been cut to pieces. Cunningham was dead, Kennedy seriously wounded. Nail and Fain had been struck down and were missing, assumed to have been taken to a hospital, but Kirkland had not learned how grievously they were hurt.

In his former company, the Camden Volunteers, which went into the fight with 40 men, only four were left to answer at the night's roll call. The Flat Rock Guards had been similarly butchered yet Kirkland and Alex had somehow escaped bodily harm.

Neither spoke as they traversed the broken landscape, stopping briefly when faint moans for water brought out their canteens to longing lips.

Passing a thumb of trees where the regiment regrouped after being shredded by artillery, the duo retraced their steps in a calculated effort to recover Joe's body.

As they neared the site of the mistaken command to turn right, the bodies were everywhere.

An imposing full moon had risen behind the enemy's lines. In this unsettling moonlight, the images appeared ghastly and medieval in number. Most of the seriously wounded had been removed to the field hospitals, leaving only twisted, broken semblances of human forms.

Kirkland didn't know which choice was preferable: the ability to see, in clear vividness, the dead and their often horrific wounds, or giving the shadows artistic license, allowing the imagination to fill in the gaps.

Curiously, however, for someone who had lost so many friends— including his best—appropriate emotions were distant. He was numb, drifting in a flat void that choked the color from his veins. The peculiar smell of evaporating rage and battle secretions was potent medicine, and Kirkland's equilibrium was off-kilter. It was a feeling similar to heavy drinking, a loss of control that throughout his life he had despised. In battle, this void was necessary to steady the nerves that were shed like snakeskin when the bullets stopped flying.

But on this day, he found it difficult to shake. The experiences were so smothering and charring, his head settled into a quiet dormancy, unable to absorb the crashing waves.

Bringing his palm to his forehead, Kirkland pressed hard as if digging in, refusing to walk the slope to total anesthesia. It was the fight of his life, holding on to the faint threads of his mother's embrace and to the granite stone of his home land. Feeling so emotionally vacant scared him more than his own death. For several minutes, he was paralyzed in his stance.

For once, Alex seemed to be equally struggling with himself and making sense of the day's events. Like his friend, he stared into nothingness, fixated on oblivion. Standing side by side, they could have been a thousand miles apart.

Beginning to panic, when all seemed lost, the creaking trees encouraged Kirkland. Slowly, a tear began to form at the corner of his left eye. It paused, as if reluctant to show itself before traversing down a powder-blackened cheek. Kirkland's hands began to shake, steadily increasing in frequency and spreading to his other limbs until his legs failed. Crashing to the ground, Kirkland landed on his back. Having conquered the void, Joe's death slapped him across the face and he sobbed uncontrollably. Writhing on the ground in both agony and release, he exorcized the War Demon's clutch.

He cried for Joe. He cried for Smith. He cried for all of his South Carolinian brothers who lost their lives that day and over the last two years of perpetual struggle. He cried for the enemy's dead and for humanity. He cried for his mother. And he cried for himself. When the tears were all used up, he wept some more until his face was a tender swamp of red folds.

And then he felt better, well enough to stand.

Through it all, Alex didn't seem to notice. He stood there, unmoved in his gaze.

Having been reborn through pain, Kirkland drew his attention to freeing his buddy. Grabbing the professor by the shoulder, he shook him firmly. Although Alex leisurely turned to eyeball Kirkland, his eyes were vacant and almost lifeless. Not having the reserve energy to confront his friend with adequate vigor, he motioned for him to follow.

After searching for a good half hour in the moonlight, peering low into chilled faces, they found Joe. His eyes were closed and he was lying on his side, curled up in a ball as if merely sleeping. For a moment, Kirkland pondered leaving him there undisturbed, allowing him to rest after a hard day's brawl, fully expecting him to rise at first light. Standing over his peaceful body, they said nothing, waiting for a sign—a snore, a shifting, anything—hoping for a miracle.

But they knew he was gone and the final acknowledgment was more an exhaled closure than a sudden bite. Lifting him by his arms and ankles, they carried him near the Rose barn where other members of the regiment were being interred. There, under an apple tree, they placed Joe in a shallow grave.

Nothing was spoken and Kirkland had no tears left to shed. They simply covered him with his blanket and Keystone dirt, next to his Carolina brothers.

★　　★　　★

Kirkland awoke with a jolt and immediately reached for his gun.

A couple of familiar faces from the Lancaster Invincibles, Company H of the regiment, stared with disengaged expressions, and he released his grip on the firearm.

Leaning against the western side of the Rose barn, Kirkland took a minute to collect his wits and noticed Alex at his side, still in nasal whispers and wrapped with dreams. He thought about waking his sleeping friend, but decided against it.

Taking a gander at the sky, Kirkland could tell the sun had only recently removed its shawl and was slowly gaining momentum on the pastoral night. He realized an unbearable thirst and a clenching stomach. Though each was irritating, he was accustomed to their voices.

Reaching into his haversack, he pulled out the remainder of the three-day rations. It was nothing but a handful of dirty cornmeal crumbs, and he palmed it all into his mouth in one savage movement. Swallowing hard with a dry mouth, Kirkland stood up and winced at his tight legs. Grabbing his canteen, he threw his head back in a lustful pose, but not even a drop would tease him.

He turned to the two soldiers next to him.

384

"I'm off for some water. Are you in need?"

"Much obliged," said the closest one. Without looking Kirkland in the eye, he handed Kirkland his canteen.

The other also handed Kirkland his empty water container, but said nothing, only nodding in meager gratitude.

With a deft hand, Kirkland carefully maneuvered Alex's canteen from his body without waking him. Then he was off, still on edge, and he caught himself marching to a silent drum.

It was almost too quiet, save for an occasional ambulance squeaking by and a random shot for a horse's mercy. At least he hoped they were for horses. But the loudest, most terrible sounds were shovels hitting dirt, and as he passed the many burial crews, they were an awful reminder of the previous day's struggle.

The mud on his shoes had dried, and Kirkland headed in the direction of their soiling, knowing the morass would lead to water. In the distance, Lee's battle standard flapped above the peach orchard, and he took small comfort in its display. While the image was not a shrine that Kirkland would hold close to his heart, so many good men had sacrificed a promising life trying to take that ground.

After all, the notion that they had all died in utter vain was too much to stomach. He still couldn't believe that Joe was gone, his indomitable spirit torn violently from a body flexing with youth.

It was a grief too fresh to be adequately absorbed, yet the hole Kirkland felt in his midsection was rapidly ascending. He was struggling to keep it lurking below. Now was not the time to curl in the fetal position with a debilitating weakness, and Kirkland knew it.

Arriving at the morass, he followed it to a small, strolling arm of Plum Run that nursed its way from the woods. The shallow stream was only a few feet wide, and Kirkland hugged the ground, removed his dusty hat and sunk his head into the water's cool bliss. The result was pure, spine-tingling pleasure. It reminded him of doing the same on many a miserably hot day at Flat Rock Creek.

Running his fingers through his hair, Kirkland could feel the layers of dirt and grease that had accumulated. He dunked his head a second time, then a third, before taking in a large swallow.

As he began to fill the canteens, he noticed something out of place in his peripheral vision. Standing, Kirkland went to investigate a clump of bushes in residence by the stream. On closer inspection, the heel of a brogan was haphazardly exposed among the green textures. Pulling the branches apart with his hands, Kirkland found the shoe was not a discarded relic, but attached to a corpse.

Face down, the man's head was inches from the water's surface. Taking hold of the dead man by the chest, Kirkland wrestled him from the muck and turned him over. Even with a mud-caked face, Kirkland recognized him.

It was Moonbeam.

Kirkland had never learned the man's real name, and now likely never would. The missed opportunity was another tortuous squeeze in his gut.

Moonbeam's leg was badly mauled, and the bone protruded slightly. A torn shirtsleeve was tied around his leg, the improvised tourniquet not enough to save his life, as he crawled for one last drink of water.

Pulling him further out into the open, Kirkland called to a nearby burial party and pointed to the body. Confident he had gotten the response he asked for, he looked down at the enigma of a man and said a short prayer. Realizing he still hadn't done this for Joe, he made a mental note to return to Joe's grave as soon as he returned with the water. He was about to head back to the Rose barn when he noticed something sticking out from inside of the man's coat.

It was a journal. Thumbing through it, it was apparent that Moonbeam had been diligent in writing for a long period of time.

"Find anything worthwhile?" Kirkland looked up to see two members of a burial party walking toward him.

"I wasn't... I know this man," said Kirkland in embarrassment, not wanting to be accused of robbing the dead.

"Well, I don't think he'll be needing anything now." The voice summoned involuntary fists.

It was Ratcliff, so filthy with battle grime that he'd gone unrecognized. His hair flared out from under his cap like sharp daggers hardened with dried sweat. As if worn like a trophy of filth, a salad of dried blood and powder mingled on his unwashed cheeks.

Ratcliff started to go through the dead man's pockets.

Outraged, Kirkland pulled his nemesis back and pushed him away forcefully.

"I said I know this man. He's from our outfit."

Ratcliff's face went sour and he puffed, "I don't care who the hell he is. He's ten minutes from being worm food. Finders keepers."

"You leave him be," said Kirkland, raising his voice.

Clenching his fists, Ratcliff took a step toward Kirkland, his hulking shoulders filled with rage.

"Private, you heard me."

"You think you're better than me? I don't care if you're a goddamn general…"

Intervening, Ratcliff's burial partner took hold of his arm. It was Hux, in a rare display of courage against his idol.

"Come on, there's plenty of other bodies to scrounge," said Hux. "No sense making trouble for yourself."

With eyes swollen with malice, Ratcliff turned on his rebellious flock of one.

"Take your goddamn hands off me…"

A buzzing wind fanned Kirkland's face, followed by a cracking thud.

Ratcliff's head exploded, showering his partner and Kirkland with blood and brains. Falling forward, the beast of man crumpled to the ground in instant death.

Shocked in an open-mouthed pose, Hux froze as the blood and gray matter slid down his face. Kirkland lunged and pulled him to the ground. The man had lost the ability to speak, although his mouth remained locked in a silent scream.

"Come on."

Kirkland helped him to his feet and they ran toward the cover of the barn. The primitive funerals of Moonbeam and Ratcliff would have to wait.

Once safe, Kirkland returned the filled canteens to their awestruck owners. With mouths wide open in gaps larger than the one on Hux, they stared at the duo covered in gore.

"Kirkland, what happened?" said Alex, jumping to his feet in a panic. "Are you all right?"

"I'm fine, Alex. It's not my blood."

Kirkland nodded toward Hux.

"Or his. A sniper got Ratcliff."

"Thank God. I mean not that he's dead, but that it wasn't you. You know what I mean."

Kirkland laughed and then regretted it, but it was amusing to see Alex stumble over words.

"God damn, Yankee bastards. God-damn sons of bitches!" Hux had recovered from his stupor and they watched him storm off in a blitz of obscenities.

"Here," said Kirkland, giving Alex his canteen.

"You must have had quite an adventure this morning. Can't go a day without saving a poor mortal's life, can you?"

Kirkland put a hand on Alex's shoulder.

"Ah, Alex, it's good to have you back."

★   ★   ★

1 PM

Boooom.

One after another, confederate cannon recoiled and spit flame from the tree line on Seminary Ridge, turning rural Pennsylvania into a smoky, trembling furnace once gain.

Listening to ruckus occurring to the north, Kirkland and Alex met each other with knowing glances. They knew the morning was only a swirling calm before the deadly storm gathered in potency. Lee's forces, far from a supply base, would have one more chance to dislodge the enemy from the high ground. Lose this day's fight, and the Confederate cause would be in serious jeopardy.

"Today, Lee will either lead us to freedom or to a traitor's infamy," said Alex, prophetically.

"He is too proud to run, that's certain."

"Yes, but I'm afraid the Yankees have a better defensive ground than we had at Fredericksburg."

"They're entrenched all right, but Lee will think of something. Have faith, my friend. When has he let us down?"

"Of course, you're right. We must not doubt him. His genius must prevail."

Although without orders, everyone in sight instinctively grabbed their hardware and prepared for day three of Gettysburg's killing fields.

The fierce cannonading continued. Not to be outdone, the enemy responded with equal gusto. Even to these veterans of the greatest battles America had ever known, it was a sight and sound to behold with unabashed awe.

In all, three hundred guns splintered the sky, crowding the air with vaulting iron and ashen murk. The explosions were a dizzying array of floating campfires, each announced with brilliant gleam, yet fizzled with the lifespan of a tumbling ash. These detonations were constant ghosts, manifesting like a legion of fireflies, blinking here and reappearing there, as if controlled by a lunatic's switch.

Observing this chaos of bursting heavens, Kirkland's mind gravitated toward the aurora seen at Fredericksburg. Although these scenes should not coexist, for reasons he could not discern, they became linked. Even as the field became a haven for impenetrable smoke, with cannons vomiting in otherworldly distress, an omen was present.

389

Though obscure, Kirkland took the strange feeling as truth. Another massacre was upon them. And he prayed that Fredericksburg would not be reincarnated, especially with the role of victor exchanged.

Suddenly, Kershaw appeared on horseback.

"Fall in men," he said with his usual force. "We're moving out."

★   ★   ★

2:55 PM

Kirkland rolled over onto his back and cupped his hands over his ears.

Yesterday, the thunderclaps, despite their intensity, had not fazed him. He had more than become used to their belligerent announcements. But this was something different entirely, approaching unbearable. The 300 cannon had been dueling for nearly two hours and the pulse of fire felt like nails being driven repeatedly into his ears. At his aural limit, Kirkland didn't care if anyone noticed his shielding efforts. A few seconds of muffling would do wonders.

Having been withdrawn to the same position from where they'd attacked the previous day, the men of Kershaw's brigade were not happy, many grumbling about retreating even an inch and giving up the ground for which they'd fought so valiantly. Relatively safe behind the stone wall, they waited, ignorant of Lee's plan, yet growing in awareness for the general's main thrust.

A sudden lull in the Confederate barrage caused Kirkland to turn over. Removing hands from ears, he noticed every man staring in the same direction—north—where troops were emerging from the shade of the treeline. As the drums rolled, a tension-clobbering growl detonated and spread southward. Its waves rolled over and swept up the Carolinians in its power, birthing their cheers and wild, manic gestures. Blasts of encouragement followed, the words and phrases unified in one ambition: the smashing of the Union line.

"Give 'em hell, Virginians!"

"Push them Yanks all the way to Washington!"

"Kill 'em all!"

Though Kirkland joined in the shouting, he formed no words. What sprang from his mouth was a primal rush, an unconscious effort to embed the attackers' hearts with vengeance. His screams were not meant for enabling death, but only as fuel for summoning victory, at whatever cost necessary to end this war. Today.

At his side, Alex was unusually animated as well, his eyes orange and his mouth spitting vulgarities at the enemy, always with fine grammar.

Everyone could now see the boldness of the attack that Lee had formulated. And they also understood what massive dangers awaited the men as they crossed the fields before them. To even reach the enemy, they would have to cross a mile-long front in the open, directly into the center of the Yankee defense.

In this charge of brute force, there would be nowhere to hide.

And if they made it across the artillery killing ground, those not struck down by canister and shells would be greeted by thousands of muskets fired from entrenched foes, desperate to avenge Fredericksburg and two years of Lee's dominance.

Yet it was a sight no American had ever seen as 15,000 of the South's finest stepped onto the canvas destined for red hues and immortal deeds. To Kirkland, the battle lines stretched into infinity, a massive force unheard of in the annals of American history.

With banners flying in confident overtures, bearing the names of Virginia, Tennessee, North Carolina and Alabama regiments, the men advanced with a steady gait and profound courage.

In astonishment, Kirkland and Alex watched the grand spectacle playing out before them. No conversation would do it justice, so they just observed and hoped, with a few prayers mixed in for garnish. Though Kirkland said a few silent ones, there was no passion behind it. This affair was entirely up to the mortals.

So taken were Kirkland and Alex by the advancing horde, when a shell screamed overhead and crashed into a neighbor tree, they barely noticed.

Their eyes were transfixed on the magnificent charge carrying the hopes of a new nation.

As the first men passed over the crest of a small hill that had shielded them temporarily, the Federal cannons grew rabid. In seconds, large clusters of men were reduced to mounds of unrecognizable flesh. Men were falling by the dozens, but the brave survivors continued on, closing the gaps as soon as they were punctured.

While the assault continued, a soup of pride and anxiety twisted Kirkland's insides into a plummeting imbalance.

The weather was getting hot, approaching 90 degrees, as if Hell was gaining a foothold. With the smoke clogging the battlefield, the Pennsylvania farmland seemed to be within moments of being torched. Greased by the humidity and internal somersaults raising havoc, Kirkland began to sweat profusely.

Taking a sip from his canteen, Kirkland took a deep breath, resigned to the fact that he could not help those making this gallant charge. Merely a witness, he stretched and bobbed his head, squinting at the small holes in the smoky arena, the roar of muskets and cacophonic shouting the only signs that the Southerners were getting close to their enemy.

In one of these lasting windows, Kirkland was drawn to one of the wounded, who was struggling mightily to find his way back to the safety of the Confederate lines. His left leg was dragging behind, obviously useless, and he was using his musket as a crutch. Several times his strength failed him and he pitched forward in dramatic tumbles to the ground. Yet each time he fell, after a brief rest, the soldier would labor to stand on his one good leg and continue. About halfway across the field, the man fell again. Kirkland waited, but this time, he did not rise to forge ahead on his pathetic retreat.

Come on, come on. Get up!

Kirkland tried to will the man back up again with projected strength, but it was a futile clenching of mind. The man could not endure.

As he continued to agonize over the soldier's grinding halt, others began to stream past him back to their lines. Some were running at full speed as if the Yankees were at their heels. As more and more came flying out of the smoke in panicked dashes, Kirkland lowered his head in despair.

Tasting victory, the Federal cannons increased their fury, sending shells careening into the fleeing troops. This was answered by Confederate artillery, and the sky was once again lit up with exploding missiles that shook the ground with finality. For a moment, Kirkland believed God had decided to swallow both sides whole and end the affair with one giant, downward thrust of a fist. But in truth, he knew exactly what had happened.

The charge was an abysmal failure.

Chapter 22

The surgeon stood in a pool of blood, high enough that it was beginning to creep over his shoes. A blade was held between his teeth, as his hands stood limp at his sides. His beardless face was fatigued and ashen, and his eyes had shrunk to mere slits of drone consciousness.

Behind the operating table—a door laid across two whiskey barrels— were the results of his latest work, a pile of hands and feet that were stacked in careless heaps. A stiff odor of burnt flesh pervaded the air, the result of cauterizing stumps with a hot iron to save time.

Politely, Kirkland asked the surgeon if he could be of service, but the man ignored the call. Louder this time, Kirkland beseeched him.

"Sir, do you need any help?"

Slowly, the surgeon turned, as if all the energy he had left was involved in the movement. He removed the amputation device from his teeth and his chin dropped heavily, scanning his apron and shirt sleeves for a clean landing. Giving up, he wiped the blade's gore on the center of his apron, adding to the red, staining layers.

"There is nothing to be done here. Only butchery."

The voice was dejected, lost, absent of all hope. All the sparks had been shed from it, leaving only a monotone drizzle.

Frozen in place, Kirkland was unsure how to respond. For in truth, the man's countenance both scared and unnerved him.

"Blood. It's all that remains," the surgeon mumbled. "Only blood."

"Sir, you need a break. Please, may I help you find some quarters? A few hours of sleep will do you some good."

But the surgeon didn't blink, and wouldn't look Kirkland in the eyes. He just stood with shoulders drooping, staring at the blade that seemed permanently attached to his fingers.

Kirkland made the decision to walk away, but not without a final diagnosis.

"Sir, you must lie down and rest. Your nerves have been taxed enough for one day. Is there someone who can relieve you?"

"Leave me," said the surgeon, stern yet without color. "Leave me. I am lost."

Reluctantly Kirkland left the man to his own devices. As he exited into the yard, he saw another surgeon, just as bloodied, leaning against a tree, and went up to him.

"Sir, the surgeon in there, he appears to be struggling with the melancholy."

"Don't you worry 'bout him," said the man, gruffly. "We are aware of his condition. No more patients will be sent his way. I will see to it."

"Thank you, Sir. Is there anything I can do to help?"

"Pray," said the surgeon abruptly, raising his blood-stained hands in front of his face. "Pray that this madness will end soon."

He took one step from the brace of the oak, and tripped over a root. Rushing in, Kirkland caught him as he fell, helping the exhausted man to relative balance.

"When this war is over, I will sleep for a year."

"I imagine you will, and it will be a well-deserved rest. Sir, I'm looking for the men of my regiment. The 2nd South Carolina?"

"I don't rightly know for sure, but I'd start with the barn yonder."

He pointed to a huge rectangular structure behind the stone tavern. Though hard to discern in the night, a yellow flag was waving over it, proclaiming the farm as a medical zone in the hope that it would be spared from the cannon's ambition. Having been designated the main hospital for McLaws's division, the old tavern and farm buildings along Marsh Creek were beyond capacity. Though most of the slightly wounded had already left on their own two feet, more than two hundred remained, tightly quartered under all available roofs, the unlucky ones forced to recuperate under the swaying branches of apple trees.

The interior reeked of sweat tossed with manure and mixed in a vat of blood.

With its limited resources, the hospital staff had done their best to make the soldiers comfortable. But it was a barn after all, in the heat of July.

The houseflies were swarming in this haven of secretion and decay, feeding on and laying eggs in the gaping wounds. Battling for air supremacy were legions of giant green horseflies chomping down on the slightest of cuts. The fortunate of the wounded, with at least one good arm to swat them with, were in constant thrashing. The smack of hand against invaded flesh, often missing the target in an unwise reflex, added thorns to those already suffering. Like a lunatic's applause, these repulsive claps encircled the barn, often sowing a violent curse. Joining in their pitiful flight were moans that hovered among the rafters, rather meek in singular voice, but in large numbers became a chant of despair.

It was dark, save for a few a lanterns in flickered illumination, scattered about the theater of broken men.

While his own physical annoyances dissipated, these sights and sounds were difficult for Kirkland to process. The void of the previous night lingered nearby, ready to pounce on a weakened soul, and he pushed it away with great difficulty.

Though he longed to escape, he knew he had to see this through with all of his faculties.

"Kirkland."

Hesitant to face whatever mangled form had called, he stalled. But it was only Alex, who had retreated to the entrance of the barn. Alex, it

396

seems, had even less remaining in his mental arsenal. His eyes were cast downward with a look of extreme nausea. It was as if he were about to keel over, like a tree cut deep and about to be felled.

"Kirkland," said Alex, slightly above a whisper. "Over here."

Lowering a mask of buoyancy over his face before pivoting, Kirkland moved with heavy step.

In a musty corner was Nail, lying on a bed of hay, his head tilted sideways. Kirkland walked swiftly over to him, the concern for his friend taking over. Raising himself to greet his comrade, Nail looked Kirkland over from head to foot.

"You look terrible, friend," said Nail.

He didn't argue. "You look wonderful yourself."

Glancing at his bandaged right bicep, Nail shrugged.

"The ball went right through, only nicking the bone. Not even a sixty-day furlough. I've had worse injuries when I was a brawler," he chuckled. "This damn surgeon wanted to amputate regardless. I told him to go to Hell."

"I'm glad to hear it's not serious."

"For certain, I won't complain that I get to keep my limb. They've been carting away arms and legs by the bushel."

Kirkland changed the subject.

"I suppose you heard that we were repulsed today."

Nail shifted his head, eying the ceiling.

"I heard."

Though Kirkland failed to elaborate on the dour situation, he was pressed.

"I hear it was quite the charge. One for the ages."

"Indeed it was. The pure definition of bravery. But it was not to be."

"It appears Old Marse Lee is mortal after all."

A few beds over, a man awoke screaming, seeing for the first time the bloody stump that used to be his leg. Or maybe it was directed at maggots squirming among the dead tissue.

"At least he's got an indefinite furlough, if he lives," said Nail, sardonically.

The man kept screaming, leaving him open to rebukes and Nail couldn't resist.

"Quit yer squakin'!" he yelled with irritation. "That ain't no rebel yell."

To the relief of all present, the poor soldier fainted back into his bed.

Nail just shook his head and continued.

"It's not over yet, this war. The Yankees will continue to have a hell of a time taking Richmond."

Kirkland could not disagree.

"That is true. A defensive campaign could save us."

"The way I figger, all we need to do is delay the war long enough until the people of the North grow tired of the fighting. Then the politicians will have no choice but to leave us be."

"So there's more to you than mule eggs, after all."

"I'm full of surprises."

He chuckled again, too liberally, and he clutched his arm in pain.

"Ah, damn Yankees," he said, grimacing.

Not wanting to venture further into the catacomb of blood, but feeling obligated, Kirkland asked about the other familiar faces sure to be nearby.

"Opposite us, over there, in one of the horse stalls, you'll find Fain. But I must warn you, it's not a pretty sight."

Kirkland took a cavernous breath, and acknowledged where Nail was pointing. He had heard Fain was badly injured, but did not know the specifics.

"Alex, you look as alive as Kirkland here," Nail called to the barn's entrance, where Alex was still cowering.

Taking short, painful steps, Alex footed over to his bedside.

"Hello, Nail. How're you feeling?"

"It's nothing to be concerned about. My Yankee killers are still intact."

Alex's face brightened. Wanting to keep it that way, Kirkland made up his mind to search out Fain alone.

"Alex, keep this vulgar brute company. I'll be right back."

★   ★   ★

With trepidation, Kirkland scooped up a lantern and wandered past the horse stalls, forcing a wincing probe in each one, searching for his old messmate.

These stalls had obviously been set aside for the most seriously wounded, men torn apart and waiting alone for the inevitable. Caged like animals marked for death, their beds offered a thin semblance of privacy for their final moments. Many were in a state beyond recognition, and to Kirkland's horror he realized that he may have passed his friend without realizing it.

As he looked into the faces of carnage, a terrible thought arose. What if he couldn't identify his friend? A chill went up his spine, and he had to apply a downward thrust of will to continue the grisly task.

Shining the cruel light into the last stall, he exhaled in fractional relief. He'd found his quarry. Although the face was untouched, the body was a mess.

Fain's right arm was amputated at the armpit and his left leg was missing below the knee. Both bandages were bloody yet seemingly fresh. A third bandage was pressed against his abdomen, crimson and alarming. Kirkland knew a gutshot usually meant a certain and excruciating end.

Sensing a visitor, Fain lifted his head.

"Kirkland," he smiled weakly. "How's my old friend?"

"Fine, just fine."

"Good. Glad to hear it."

Fain's strength failed him and he slumped backward into the hay. Rushing to his side, Kirkland propped his head up with his hands.

"Please, can you give me some water?"

Spotting a bucket with a ladle, Kirkland dunked and raised it to his lips, gently pushing Fain's head toward the liquid. Taking a few painful slurps, Fain motioned with his remaining arm that he desired no more.

"Helping one of your own for a change."

Kirkland was silent and Fain quickly recovered.

"Only teasing. I admire you for what you did. I fear God will not look upon my deeds with the same respect."

"Nonsense. You've earned your place in the Glorious Kingdom."

"Have I? I'm not so sure. My one and only motivation in this war was to kill as many of our enemies as possible."

"We're all covered in blood. Heaven cannot be denied to us all."

Fain smiled.

"I have not thought of it that way. That's why I always admired you. You have a capacity for reflection that far surpasses my ability."

"Sometimes it's more a burden than a gift."

Fain attempted to nod, but it was little more than a twitch.

"Is there anything I can do for you?"

"I'm afraid this body is broken beyond repair... I'm resigned to my fate. I've served South Carolina to the best of my ability, and in her defense I will die."

"Is this certain? Have the surgeons told you..."

"What they tell me does not matter. The end is near."

"I'm sorry to hear that."

"Don't be. I feel privileged to call you my friend."

Kirkland took a medium, concealing breath, much less than was needed to stifle the tears. And the stone face backfired, splintering into pools forming at the corners. Though contesting them with stuttered inhales, the holes were too numerous to plug and dual streams ran down his cheeks. Reluctant to allow a full breakage, he swiped at his eyes and gathered himself before responding.

"And I feel more than honored to call you the same."

With satisfaction and final approval, Fain smiled.

"Who needs the pain of old age, anyway?"

Slowly, he reached out his perspiring hand to Kirkland. As Kirkland accepted, he felt Fain's body go limp.

Go now, my friend. May you find peace and may God accept you with open arms.

Chapter 23

AUGUST 3, 1863
NEAR RAPID ANN STATION, VA
7 PM

A lex and Kirkland sat on a bluff, their feet dangling below, overlooking a wicked bend in the Rapidan River.

They had walked a mile from camp to escape the heat, and a merciful breeze greeted them, sending both into eye-shuttering head tilts. Although they'd swum in the river earlier in the day when a crossing turned into an afternoon of play, with McLaws and Kershaw as laughing spectators, they'd since dried out under a relentless sun.

As the duo sat in silent meditation, Nail came up and sat down, courteous to their distant gazing. A minute went by, then two, and Nail began to fidget. He squinted at the opposite shore, trying to find something of interest. Water. Trees. More trees. Annoying, squawking birds. Beyond that, damn Yankees, somewhere. Out of his rifle sights. To the surprise of everyone but Kirkland, he'd returned to the regiment three weeks after his wounding at Gettysburg. Much to Nail's chagrin, he wasn't sent home but to Chimborazo Hospital in Richmond.

"Too much death there," he had responded when asked about his near-miraculous return, without elaborating.

Kirkland finally spoke, though not in response to Nail's squirming.

"On this day, I was born, twenty years ago," he told them. "My father said it was an easy birth, but that I came into this world with a howling that awoke the entire district. I must not have been ready."

"Yes, I've heard your father tell this story more than once," said Alex. "He said you were inconsolable for the first hour of life."

Kirkland giggled.

"And when I finally calmed down, I slept for many hours, so long, in fact, that my father was afraid I would not awake from the trauma. My mother, he says, did not share his fears. She was convinced by my robust entrance, that I was as strong as a bear."

"Well," said Alex, grinning, "I wasn't aware of this momentous anniversary. Your mother was unequivocal in her foresight."

"I'm no bear. Not like Nail here."

Growling in mock acceptance, Nail smiled.

"I still think of my mother often, as you know," said Kirkland. "Her passing was my first experience with death. Although I was young, I remember how others grieved for her. I did not understand their sobbing, yet I felt their grief and the tears began to flow."

Picking up a small rock, Kirkland tossed it into the current, which swallowed it whole as if it never existed.

"In war, death is like a squirrel, so commonplace, we hardly notice."

"I disagree, old man. It's just that when candles are extinguished a dozen at a time, it's more than we can bear or comprehend. In this darkness we are protected."

Standing suddenly, Nail reached into his pocket.

"I almost forgot, the mail arrived. Kirkland, this is for you."

"Why, Nail, you've been holding out on us," Kirkland teased, snatching the envelope.

He recognized the writing immediately, and his heart began to race. It was the first letter received from Susan in more than two months.

"You're not going to run and hide, are you?" questioned Alex. "We could use some good news."

Running a forefinger over his lover's penmanship, he initially ignored his friend.

"Kirkland?"

Snapping out of his travels, he sighed deeply.

"I will read this letter on one condition, that you allow me to peruse it first for private endearments."

"Okay," said Alex. "We accept this condition. It's not the lovespeak that we're interested in, am I correct in speaking for you, Nail?"

"Yes, I get enough of that lovey dovey material from my wife. I don't need yours as well."

"Then, just give me a moment."

Unfolding the letter, Kirkland nosed in, as his friends watched with rabid curiosity.

Carefully, they followed his darting eyes, looking for signs of enchantment or even simple pleasures. At first, it appeared promising, but the longer he read, the darker his face became. When Kirkland had traversed to the last, his eyes failed to ascend. With a flick of the wrist, he coldly handed Alex the letter.

Ignoring the greeting and conversational springboard, Alex began to read from the meat of the letter.

I'm afraid I have bad news to share. The boy that you are so fond of, Tom, was killed by the Home Guard yesterday. The story I heard is that Tom had found an old flintlock pistol at Gum Swamp, no doubt from Revolutionary times, and kept the old relic in his cabin. And though it was rusted and not in working condition, the Guard killed Tom with the excuse that no Negro could have possession of a weapon of any kind. Your brother Sam tried to stop them but he was too late. He has since dropped out from their ranks. These men have become a curse on the land, causing disorder with their brutal tactics rather than protecting the innocent. Is there no end to this madness?

Alex folded the letter and attempted to return it, but Kirkland left it fluttering in his friend's outstretched hand.

"This is one I choose not to keep," said Kirkland, his head still bowed.

"I'm sorry, my friend," replied Alex. "I know how much you loved that boy."

"This war is hard to comprehend," said Nail, shaking his head.

"Comprehend?" said Kirkland, raising his voice. "What is there to comprehend? That God has abandoned us?"

Jumping to feet, he began to pace. His muscles were tense with rage and his hands alternated swiftly between trembling fists and wide-fingered stabs.

Exhibiting signs that he was about to blow, Alex stood up and pushed back, joining his friend on the summit.

"What is it you're asking? To make sense of war? To make sense of death?

"For these questions, I have no answer. But I know this. God is absent in war. In my eyes, the only inquiry is whether the Almighty is standing witness in a torrent of tears or in a fit of righteous anger."

Relaxing his pace, Kirkland screeched to a halt and palmed his temples, doubling over in exasperation.

"If I ever drew a breath at the entrance of this Plato's cave you speak of, I have been wrenched backward into the depths. We are simians, all of us. No better."

Standing abruptly, prepared for a heated rebuttal, Alex thought better of it. He massaged his hands while his conscience picked the brambles from his words.

"We are shackled by our circumstances, this is true. But I've never known you to be fragile and I can't bear it now. Please, friend, do not kill the horizon. Do not let this war destroy your heart."

Crossing his arms, Kirkland shook his head.

"I've seen your eyes, Alex, when they were colorless and numb. Have you been reborn?"

"I dipped my toes in Flat Rock Creek and held on to that memory. I, too, fear that permanent damage has been done. Yet all I can do, all we can do, is go on."

Snatching the letter from Alex's hand, Kirkland tore it into halves, and surrendered the pieces to the wind. As the paper glided into the river's current, he closed his eyes, exhausted with dark memories.

"Go on, you say. How do we do that?"

"You must save yourself."

Chapter 24

SEPTEMBER 14, 1863
WHITE OAK STATION
OUTSIDE OF RICHMOND, VA

As the train started to pull away from the depot, a soldier appeared, running alongside the dismantled boxcar that had been punctured by knives and axes for ventilation.

Placing his gun on the floor of the car as he ran, he was out of breath and desperate. Two hands reached out and with impressive brute strength, Bury pulled the man in. Sucking wind, he attempted to speak, but his lungs refused to share.

"Men," he gasped.

He placed his hands on his knees, panting, raised a finger and doubled over again. Finally closer to gaining his natural wind, he spoke in short spurts.

"Men, you're gonna wanna hear this," he sputtered. The corporal's name was Baskin and Kirkland knew him to be an honest fellow, neither gullible nor prone to exaggeration.

Intrigued by the visible urgency, Kirkland joined the crowd surrounding him.

"We're going to South Carolina," said Baskin, chest heaving, his head on a swivel, waiting for the car to burst.

For a moment, no one spoke, as if all were in disbelief. The idle tongues coiled quickly and at least five spoke at once. The unintelligible mixture caused Baskin to hold up his hands.

"Listen, boys, this is what I know. I overheard a dispatch and the orders were for us to go to Charleston."

His comrades pressed him for more, this time by the dozen. He attempted to shout over the growing mob of curiosity, but they were overpowering.

"Please," said Baskin. "Please, hear me."

Lessened to a slow rumble, he continued.

"Unfortunately the news isn't all good. Burnside has taken Knoxville and Bragg has been forced out of Tennessee."

All around, chins dropped a few degrees.

"I couldn't hear the entire conversation. I didn't want to appear to be eavesdropping."

"Ah, hogwash, you shoulda leaned in with pencil and paper," another shouted.

The comment sent the men into giggles.

"The damn newspapers tell us more than our own generals," said another, seconded by several.

"Yes," Baskin nodded. "Whether we will just pass through our homeland, that I cannot say. With Tennessee lost, the Carolinas and Georgia will need our defense. Lee is sending our division and Hood's to support Bragg. I'm afraid this is all I can tell you. I tried to learn more but, as usual, everything is all so hush."

While a few remained to grill Baskin for more information, the majority dispersed to smaller groups to discuss the lightning bolt.

Kirkland walked to a corner, unsure of how to react. He knew the corporal was a reliable source, but also had been conditioned to throw off such reports as phony intelligence or mere speculation.

Alex wasted little time, though, to get his reaction.

"So what do you think?" he said.

"I don't believe you've ever asked me that question," said Kirkland, legitimately surprised.

"Without a doubt I've been humbled by this war," said Alex, embarrassed. "Books can only take you so far. I know that now."

Recovering from his unintentional jab, Kirkland softened the blow.

"Alex, you will always be my teacher." He flashed a smile and sighed. "I do not know what to think. So much is out of our hands. I wish we were not so adrift in ignorance. If Charleston is truly our destination, then I hope we stay there. To put my feet on her soil only to be lifted off again—I don't know if my constitution could take it."

"You are right, Kirkland. It could be a blessing or a cruel temptation."

They sat down, watching the soldiers in animated debates.

Among one of the buoyant conversations, Kirkland pictured Joe, front and center, as he always was. There he stood, larger than life, with a mesmerized audience hanging on every word, as Kirkland had witnessed a thousand times. Gesturing with contagious energy and loaded with inexhaustible wit, he would charm them all. The topic had no bearing on this outcome, the tale irrelevant. He could make a mansion out of an outhouse. At the conclusion, when he flashed that illuminating, punch-line grin followed by a body-shaking giggle, even the most rigid had no hope of stoic survival.

An oddly placed ripple sprang from Kirkland's core, gentle at first but it quickly advanced to the surface. Before he knew what had hit him, he was laughing in uncontrolled spasms. It was a cathartic, full body release. Whether in memory or whispering beyond the grave, Joe was speaking to him.

Also succumbing to the involuntary display, Alex howled, as if under the same umbrella of healing.

Perhaps Joe wasn't so far away after all.

★　　★　　★

SEPTEMBER 12, 1863
WILMINGTON, NC
DUSK

A laughing gull coasted above the ferry in a sky dripping with gold and tangerine.

It followed the soldiers for a while, but when offered no morsel, it sped away with a high-pitched cackle. On the other side of the Cape Fear River, a train was waiting to take the regiment further south.

Kirkland watched the bird disappear into the spectacular colors. He wished to follow with a mighty leap, to be surrounded by its beauty, immersed in its warmth.

Moonbeam.

Reaching into his haversack, he pulled out the diary. His hands were reluctant and smothering. Kirkland had been here before.

Considering it a betrayal, even immoral, he had yet to read from its pages, despite being immensely curious to finally learn the mystery man's name. It was Kirkland's intention to eventually return it to soldier's family and to do this he would have to violate the diary's secrets.

But he was willing to wait. Too many names were already written on Kirkland's soul, branded and unhealed. He had no desire to add to this list, especially after Gettysburg. And so it remained in his haversack, unopened and enigmatic. As he took in the looming sunset, he flashed back to the many "almost" encounters with Moonbeam. He had waited long enough for the handshake.

Now or never.

Thumbing the diary's mouth, and shuffling the pages like a deck of cards, he vacillated once more until the voice of the inquisitive won the hand. Sitting down with his back to the fading light, Kirkland opened to the inside cover straining his eyes under the fading light.

Patrick Cairns

It was written in small, gliding script.

He recited the name out loud several times, swishing and cradling it in his mouth, until he arrived at a venerating tone.

"Patrick Cairns"

"Patrick Cairns"

Clearing his throat, he lowered his voice.

"Patrick Cairns"

Alex and several others stared at him as if he had lost his marbles but he paid no mind.

"It's a pleasure to meet you, Patrick Cairns."

Opening to the first page, he squinted again to read the words.

July 2, 1861

I do hope this war won't end before I'm able to get in a scrap with the Yankees. I couldn't bear going home without seeing the Elephant. I trust the day will come. We'll show the invaders what Carolina is all about.

He flipped to his report on the first battle of Manassas. The elephant, of course, was far from a gentle giant.

I don't know what to say tonight. The sights and sounds of the great battle we've had here today were horrible, beyond accurate description. Though we have pushed the Yankees back, it's all I can do to keep my hands from shaking as I write this. War is anything but glorious.

Remembering Cairns's awful wound, Kirkland moved ahead to a date after Sharpsburg. The words became almost unintelligible, and were garbled and disconnected. Even the penmanship had changed, from smooth strokes to jagged scribbles.

Red everywhere. The screams surround me, thirsty, so very tired, want to sleep in a tree, invisible dreaming.

From there, the entries became less frequent, until all that was described were sunsets and their coattails.

Dates became absent, though the smooth, confident style briefly returned.

Unusual meringue sky followed by a lemon wedge moon. Looks good enough to eat.

Wispy velvet, burning to turquoise and fading to black. The stars applaud.

Lilac swirls dancing around plum clouds. My shaking soul is cleansed.

Breathtaking orange, I can almost feel its heat like a campfire in the sky. Short-lived but cloudless night filled the void with diamonds.

Moving further into the diary, as the wind ruffled the pages, Kirkland could discern another change. Soon, even the stars withheld their comfort.

Cardinal heaven gone too soon. Day and night lasting forever. Wish to be absorbed by the healing light.

Spectacular gold layers and crimson hues, scaled a wall to touch them, fell back to cruel Earth. The night mocks me.

Walked a great distance to find a tall tree still standing. I climbed, she opened up with pink flares and dazzling rainbows. I reached for them, straining ever higher. It was no use.

Kirkland moved on to the last entry, dated July 1, 1863:

My soul is lost. I pray for the end.

Closing the diary forcefully, like a shutter to the storm, Kirkland gripped it with trembling hands and tears in his eyes. But he would not allow a flow of comfort. The regret was too strong, though not for reading the soldier's most personal thoughts. The pain was in the history—the failed introduction, the implosion of decency, of allowing the soldier's code to shun the weak-willed.

Kirkland's mind did somersaults, wondering if—then pleading against—the reason for his not seeking out the frail man was because he feared the rebuke of others.

Whatever the explanation, Kirkland felt guilty as charged. All of the sightings and near contact with Cairns were recalled upon his mind like swirls of vivid tintypes. The opportunities, after discovering his plight, were there. Yet he had not acted. Like most soldiers, he had despised the shirkers, those that faked illness or fell behind to avoid combat.

They were a class of worthless men not to be pitied or respected. Whether their cowardice was caused by mental instability or a weak constitution, they were treated the same. These men were outcasts, lepers shunned by all but fellow lepers. Many were given non-combat duties, such as driving the supply wagons, so the army could at least get some use out of them. Officers separated and dispersed them among trusted veterans so their disease would not spread.

Not everyone was born to be a soldier, but Kirkland wondered if some of these men like Cairns could've had their mental health restored if they hadn't been cast aside and ignored. In the end, Cairns had chosen to fight. Whether the reason for his change of heart was patriotism or wishing for his own death, it mattered little now. He had died with honor.

My sincere hope is that you are now at peace, Moonbeam.

And he said his name out loud once more as he gazed into the wilting twilight.

"Patrick Cairns."

★　　　★　　　★

SEPTEMBER 13, 1863
FLORENCE, SC
6 PM

412

With a high-trumpeting wail, the lone-note steam whistle announced that the depot was close.

The train braked, returning color to Kirkland's cheeks and rousing him from a molasses gaze. Since they crossed the border into South Carolina, he wanted to savor every field and every tree, but mile after mile of swift images had brought on a persuasive drowsiness that refused to let go. His eyes were red from the boxcar fight to stay awake, and the lids that had been creeping toward submission began to reverse. But it was slow to take. Yawning, he stretched his legs, at least as far as possible in the crowded car.

Knowing just how close the next station was to his home, the brain freeze held tightly. Maybe it was a defense mechanism, for not allowing the Carolina pines to dance in his head. This was, after all, most likely a temporary stop on a longer journey. The storms were circling in Georgia, it was rumored, and was a plausible final destination. But he could feel the vibrations of the soil, and taste its familiar wind, threatening to overwhelm. It all seemed like a dream, made worse by his traveling fatigue, and he struggled to piece together the colliding emotions.

As the train slowed to a halt, the men around Kirkland erupted into a violent cheer, so sudden it caused him to flinch. The elated, grinning faces and firm handshakes warmed him. They deserved this moment, having cheated death for so long.

Observing Nail with a fist in the air, bellowing at the top of his lungs and nearly falling out of the boxcar, he smiled. And then Kirkland joined him, slapping him hard on the back, causing a spark to reverberate up Kirkland's arm and into his heart. The fog had lifted, and he allowed himself to be carried away by the moment.

At the depot to greet them was the usual crowd of old men, coy women and flag-waving children, cheering wildly for their heroes. Among them was a large group of wounded veterans who had donned their faded uniforms for the occasion, saluting with their one good arm or waving with a crutch.

413

Kirkland turned around to share in the joy with Alex, but his friend was not smiling like the others.

Leaving Kirkland and Alex behind, the men piled out of the car and dissolved into the amoeba of greeters. Without looking at his friend, but sensing his questions, Alex opened up like only the professor could.

By road he stands with eyes o'er the trees,
The pines call and whisper sweet memories;
With zeal the owl warns of the river near;
Severed in two, though rid of mortal fear,
The man, of weary legs and rotting heart,
Seduced by dirt layers, his toes depart,
Choosing sense above honor, and color over decay.

"Wordsworth?"

Alex shook his head. "That one's mine."

He jumped from the car and moved at a steady gait.

Puzzled, Kirkland followed, trying to keep up, tipping his hat politely to the well-wishers as he passed. Finally, Alex stopped abruptly, in the center of the crossroads.

Here, the tracks went north and south, east and west. If they continued on the same track leading west, they would arrive at Manchester Junction, directly south of Camden. If they switched trains, the southern rails would take them to Charleston, and if they kept going, Savannah.

Alex pivoted counterclockwise, breathing in both views of the terrain-splitting, parallel lines of steel destiny. He seemed highly agitated and Kirkland waited for an explanation of his strange behavior. Removing his hat, Alex held it to his chest, facing west.

"If the rumors are correct, our stay here in Florence will be limited to switching trains and then we'll be heading south, to Charleston," said Alex, with his back to Kirkland. He pointed to the southern expanse of track.

414

"Florence," said Alex, gathering momentum and force. "Do you understand how close we are? Camden is but fifty miles from here."

"Don't even think on it, Alex."

"Two years, we've been gone. Two years that we'll never get back, away from our families, separated from all that we know and love."

The words were unnecessary, as Kirkland had already been flung headlong down the western track with alarming speed, thinking of his father sitting before the fire in his old, crumpled riding hat. Of Susan waiting with a kiss. He thought of his brothers and Mayberry's cooking. And he ruminated on Joe and the many others who would never return home.

The temptation was only natural, and completely unavoidable. But he disagreed with Alex on one major point.

"We didn't leave all behind that we know and love. Not all."

Kirkland turned to walk away, but Alex moved quickly to block his path.

"Richard, the war is lost," said Alex, getting close to his friend's ear, to not be overheard. He spoke softly but with a pleading desperation. Attempting to get by, Kirkland sidestepped his friend, but Alex held his ground with flaring eyes and an acute shortness of breath.

"You could be calling at Susan's door by tomorrow evening. What about Sam? Don't you want to see your brothers again? The train south leads to nothing but misery and death."

"You may be right, Alex. The war may be lost," said Kirkland, with a calm but stern answer. "But I vowed to defend my state, and I must see this to the end. No, I cannot leave now."

"You have nothing more to prove—to South Carolina, to the Confederacy, to anyone."

Smiling, Kirkland put his hands on Alex's shoulders.

"Alex, you've been a wonderful friend to me. Whatever you decide to do, I will not fault you. But my place is here, with our boys."

And then he walked away to be with his regiment.

★   ★   ★

SEPTEMBER 16, 1863
CHARLESTON, SC
9 PM

From the south, cannon fire echoed through the city, and as the train came to a stop at the Northeastern Railroad Depot, the men were wadded with somber alertness. Being at the northern limits of Charleston and far from the water's edge, they were blind to the source of their hair-raising.

Leaping out of the car, Kirkland and his company instinctively formed into line of battle, as did the rest of the 2nd South Carolina.

Anticipating this, Lieut. Colonel Gaillard stepped in front. With Colonel Kennedy still recovering from his Gettysburg wounds, he was now in charge and had already gathered intelligence about the city's current state and the regiment's orders.

"Men, I know you want to rush off in the defense of Charleston, but that is not why we are here. We are leaving in the morning."

The men groaned and began arguing in such a manner that mutiny seemed imminent. Keeping his poise, but raising his voice to be heard over the angry demonstrations, he continued.

"Men… Men, hear me now. I understand your urge to defend Charleston. I share your sentiments. Fort Sumter is under attack but they are holding their ground like true Carolina patriots. This has been going on for a month and the Yankees have gotten no closer to taking back the fort. We must practice restraint. I expect all of you to conduct yourselves with honor in our short stay here. Do not stray far from the depot as we are leaving at dawn."

The men continued to grumble, though out of respect for Gaillard, they held their tongues from further insubordination. Inspecting his men and taking great care to see if his words had dulled their bayonets, Gaillard was satisfied, if uneasy.

"All right, men, dismissed."

Grabbing Kirkland by the arm, Alex pulled his friend from a deeply-rooted stance. He had jumped on board at the very last moment when the train was leaving the Florence Depot. Never doubting that the locomotive would leave him behind, Kirkland had greeted the tardy boarder with a knowing chin. No words were exchanged, for none were needed.

"Follow me, Rich. I have a cousin who lives not far from here. He's fairly well-to-do, at least before the war. We can spend a comfortable night there, out of the cold."

Kirkland had no objection, though he wondered if he was capable of sleeping in a real bed again, and they left the depot as the other men scattered to the four cardinals.

They headed south on Alexander Street and turned right on Calhoun, passing the grounds of the Citadel. Although it was dark, they could make out the unfinished statue of the street's namesake, former Vice President John C Calhoun.

"So tell me about your cousin. What business is he in?"

"He has a large farm, and is also a merchant here in Charleston. From what I understand, he divides his time rather equally between the two enterprises."

"Ambitious."

"Yes, and talented too. Up until now he has avoided politics, though many have attempted to steer him toward some form of office. I'm told he is almost too charismatic and popular to avoid this agenda forever."

"I look forward to meeting him."

Passing the College of Charleston, they turned south again on Smith Street. The name brought a smile to Kirkland's face as he remembered the bespectacled man he first met on Morris Island beyond the town.

After walking a couple of blocks, they arrived at a spacious Charleston Single House of classical spirit, though from the street the gable end was narrow. Three stories tall with double piazzas, however, it was enormous when facing it from the garden. A wrought-iron fence surrounded the property, leaving only a small opening for a door to the first-floor porch.

"Fairly well-to-do?" said Kirkland, emphasizing the former. "I'd like to see your definition of *quite* well-to-do."

Alex opened the door and they walked in a cool breeze to the main entrance of the house.

"Okay, so I may have described his financial success with reserve."

After a knock on the door, a solid man with impeccable posture greeted them.

"Good evening, Sirs."

"Good evening," said Alex. "Please inform Mr. Cullen that his cousin, Alex Morrison, is calling."

The servant nodded and disappeared into the house.

"Are you sure riffraff like us will be welcome here?" Kirkland teased.

"Speak for yourself. I'm family, but no doubt he will look upon you with suspicion and indignation."

Kirkland smiled and gave Alex a healthy nudge to the middle of his back.

With impressive speed, the butler returned, offering an elegant bow.

"Please come in. Mr. Cullen is waiting for you in the drawing room."

As they entered the hallway, Kirkland gazed ahead at the geometric, curving staircase and upward at the alabaster and bronze chandelier. While his mouth was wide open in a beholding stare, Alex discreetly took hold of his elbow and guided him into the drawing room.

Mr. Cullen, immediately rose from a Regency caned sofa to greet them. Several years older than his guests, but perhaps only in his mid-thirties, his black tailored suit and bowtie reeked of money. Lots of it.

"Alex, what a treat it is to see you!"

He enthusiastically shook his hand.

"Charles, this is my good friend from Flat Rock, Richard Kirkland."

"It's a pleasure to meet you."

"Likewise. You have a beautiful home."

"Thank you. It has, to this point, been spared from the cannons."

Cullen laughed, although Kirkland could perceive a nagging torment below the surface.

"Please, have a seat."

Hovering over an 18th century French armchair, upholstered with blue-gray silk, Kirkland was afraid to sit down even in his new duds. Seeing Alex sit without hesitation in the matching chair, he allowed his cheeks to drop.

"Cousin, what is the state of affairs in Charleston?"

"Oh, we're holding out just fine. There are shortages, of course, just like everywhere in the South. The Yankees have lobbed some shells into the city but to this point, Fort Sumter has captured most of their attention."

A cannon boomed in the distant harbor, yet close enough for a subtle shake of the foundation.

"Damn Yankees, they keep that up at all hours. I'm so used to it now that I can sleep through it at night. Please, join me in the dining room. You must be famished."

Before they could respond, he yelled to the next room.

"Martha, please fix these boys some supper and spare nothing."

"Thank you, Cousin, but we don't want to put you out."

"Nonsense. You boys have been faithfully fighting for our cause. It's the least I can do. Besides, I just finished a later dinner and there's plenty left to offer."

"We're in your debt."

A year ago, Kirkland would have felt contempt for a man of fighting age who avoided his duty, hiding behind his wealth. When the Confederacy had instituted a draft, surely Cullen had hired a substitute who took his money to fight in his stead or was given an exemption by a powerful friend. But Kirkland had learned that forcing a man into combat did more harm than good. These men were a contaminant to unity and order, usually assuming a delicate affliction at the first sign of the enemy.

From the corner of a downward eye, attempting to conceal his gawking, Cullen gave them a thorough look-over.

"Life in the army must be difficult, I have no doubt. I've witnessed some get off that train looking much worse for wear than you two. But those are the bluest uniforms I've ever seen on our side."

He laughed nervously.

It was true. They could definitely pass among the enemy without attracting attention.

"Yes, it is a bit unusual. Governor Vance presented these to us as we passed through Wilmington. Throughout this war, we haven't been bestowed with the same uniform twice."

"Ah, Governor Vance. I'm well acquainted with him. He is truly a man of the people."

"It was a nice gesture."

"Indeed. Say, I hear you were at Gettysburg."

"Yes."

His guests both dropped their eyes to the floor, as if the word contained daggers aimed at their midsections. Mortified that the subject had turned the room cold, Cullen refrained from pressing for details and changed the subject.

"Are you staying in Charleston long?"

"No, it's a very brief visit, I'm afraid. We're leaving tomorrow."

"Pity, we could sure use you boys here, if for nothing else but your splendid company. But this is a selfish reason, of course."

"What's the status of Fort Sumter?" asked Kirkland, sensing Gaillard may have softened the details.

Cullen shook his head.

"I don't know how anybody could still be alive in that rubble. But every time a shell from Morris Island cuts down our flag, someone is there to raise it up again. And it's gone on like that for a month now. Those brave defenders refuse to give it up, God bless them."

For Kirkland, it was a strange twist of fate that Confederates were now holed up at Fort Sumter, receiving fire from Morris Island, the exact opposite of his experience two years earlier.

Can there really be anything left on that island?

"Where is the rest of your family?" asked Alex.

"I sent them to Windy Oaks, my farm north of here. I didn't want to take any chances, should our defenses fail."

Kirkland shifted uncomfortably in his chair and Alex rose abruptly. He began to pace, ready to explode.

"Carolina is our home. We should be allowed to stay here and defend her."

Alex continued to pace as a ticking silence followed, each man avoiding eye contact with the others. Martha appeared at the doorway just in time.

"Dinner is ready, Sir."

"Splendid," said Cullen, rising from his chair. "Let us adjourn to the dining room."

As they entered the room and sat down, the servants brought in food from the outdoor kitchen, the aromas of which rounded all edges and threw any remaining tensions under the mahogany table.

Wide-eyed and with saliva nearly foaming, Kirkland and Alex struggled against the urge to grab each serving tray before it was distributed. With hands clenched, they assumed proper etiquette.

Steaming collards and peppered okra, biscuits with crème and peach butter, oysters and she-crab soup. They could have kissed Martha and Mr. Cullen.

When all was served, Cullen watched them with amusement as they inhaled what to them was a king's buffet in a manner barely considered worthy of restraint. He was patient, allowing his guests to eat without interruption or idle conversation. When the forks had slowed to a more methodical pace, he finally spoke.

"I'm afraid I too must take my leave of Charleston soon and join my family on my estate. As soon as my business affairs are in order."

"How is business?" asked Alex, adding butter to a third biscuit.

"Well, the blockade has been influential to say the least, and I've been forced to drive up the prices for my wares. In times like these it is astonishing what is considered a luxury. But I don't want to bore you with my troubles. How early must you leave?"

"Before dawn."

"There are empty rooms upstairs that I keep ready for guests. I'll have Martha prepare a fine breakfast for you."

"Thank you, but that's unnecessary," said Alex.

"Nonsense. Who knows when you boys will eat again? No, I couldn't let you leave on an empty stomach."

"Again, we're in your debt."

"Yes, thank you so very much, Sir," added Kirkland, standing up to shake his host's hand.

"You're very welcome," said Cullen, following suit. "It's a pleasure to have you both in my home."

As the threesome shook hands, Cullen offered a warning.

"In the morning, be careful. The Yankees' shells seem to have a maximum range of Calhoun Street so keep your wits about you. Do you have any notion of where you are going?"

"Georgia, I suppose, to meet up with Bragg. He has lost Tennessee and we can't afford to give more ground."

"Well, may God go with you both. Before you retire, join me for a cigar on the piazza."

As they headed to the porch, Kirkland pulled Alex aside.

"Say, I don't recall seeing Hux on the train when we left Florence?"

Eying the floor, Alex sighed.

"No. When I had my shameful moment of vacillation, I saw him taking a walk. I chose not to follow."

As they stood on the piazza, mostly silent, listening to the wind, an owl landed on a railing near. It gazed at the threesome for several moments before flapping its mammoth wings and disappearing into the black.

★　　★　　★

SEPTEMBER 18, 1863
ALLATOONA PASS
NEAR CARTERSVILLE, GA
3 PM

The men were in high spirits, lining the car's edges, urging the train on in its lofty ascent through the mountain pass.

Because the first run at the crest was a failed effort, the engineer had reversed down the mountain in hopes of launching with greater momentum.

Though midday, the high, tree-covered banks aligning the route were frustrating the sun, allowing but a few sparks between the shadows. Although it was a deep cut through the rugged Appalachians, furrowed by heavy labor, the rise was substantial and daunting for a vessel burdened with troops and heavy equipment.

As the engine began the second attempt, the soldiers were ready with comical fervor, doing their utmost to encourage a successful passage. Some were kneeling at the car's opening, thrusting invisible oars forward to chest, rowing in unison. Others were stabbing at unseen waters as if fighting a heavy wind in a canoe. On the roof of the boxcar, men were lying on their stomachs, as they would on a piece of driftwood, paddling with bare hands.

"Kirkland," said Alex, chuckling. "Give me a hand."

Placing his hands against the northern wall of the car, Alex dropped his feet back and bent his knees, grunting as he pushed.

Nail interrupted his powerful stroke to cheer him on, nodding in approval.

With a playful smirk, Kirkland joined Alex against the wall, flexing with determination. He crouched lower and put his weight into it, growling louder as the train climbed ever higher.

As they neared the threshold of the mountaintop, the men strained and shouted, willing the locomotive over.

In a crescendo that matched the fiercest battle call, the pitch rose like a siren, deep at first, until morphing into a screamed falsetto.

When the train slowed its ascent, still a few hundred feet from the top, the men doubled their flails and blurred paddlings, trying to control their conjured implements over fits of laughter.

"Push, Kirkland, push!" Alex yelled. "We're almost there."

His face contorting, Kirkland dug in further, trying to keep a straight face.

"Nail, put some muscle into it."

Obeying, Nail heaved backward so hard, he knocked the two rowers behind him off their rhythm. They, in turn, rolled into the boxcar, laughing hysterically.

And the engine, despite all of their efforts, came up short again.

Creeping to a stop, the men erupted into mock condemnation, booing the lame iron horse.

Reversing again down the tracks, the soldiers fell into howling binges amid crude commentary.

"Georgia is too high," someone bellowed. "Heaven can wait."

It wasn't the first time that this journey had been delayed since the reluctant men left Charleston two days prior. Crossing rice fields and salt marshes over rickety bridges, they had made it to Savannah with little difficulty. Switching trains among the large oaks draped with Spanish moss, they had arrived at the huge Atlanta depot to find a massive buildup of troops and freight. But it was a minor inconvenience in a day where the wilted men had eaten better than they had since the war began. At each stop, enthusiastic well-wishers had showered the Carolinians with drumsticks and poundcake, baskets of fruit, and jugs of wine.

It had been one long parade, and a necessary tonic for leaving their home soil after an all-too-brief visit. Their sense of purpose had been restored, and so it was with Kirkland. He had surrendered himself to patriotic duty. While the Confederate cause was no longer a hefty motivation, it was his beloved regiment and cherished brigade, the men with whom he had bled and suffered, that he could not, and would not abandon.

Retreating further down the track this time, the locomotive stopped to take on more water, and a woodpile was raided to add fuel. They ascended again, with less humor and pleading yawns, as the men worried that a third failure could mean a long hike up the mountain.

Visualizing the engineer sweating and cursing under the pressure, Kirkland exhaled.

"I have no desire for his job," he said out loud, to no one in particular.

"Pardon?" said Alex.

"Never mind."

Kirkland smiled.

"I'm glad you're here Alex. We've seen a lot haven't we, you and I?"

"We certainly have, enough to fill several volumes."

"This reminds me of our less-than-dignified plunge down the hill at Fredericksburg. Can you recall our laughing as we descended, with the bumblebees in our ears?"

"I recall you and Joe laughing. I was terrified!"

"What was the name of that hill?"

"I believe they called it Marye's Heights."

"Yes, with your scholarly pursuits, your memory is more developed than mine."

"It was fairly beaten into us, to be honest. Yet that doesn't explain how Joe could remember the slightest conversation or trivial moment with such remarkable recall."

"He did have that talent, especially for reminding us of times when we were at our most unintentional and awkward."

Alex laughed.

"This is true. Yet we had as much ammunition directed at his faux pas to balance the arguments."

"Certainly," said Kirkland, with a giggle. "But he was always the weasel, turning the tables. He could light a room like no other."

"Yes," Alex sighed. "It's hard to believe that flame could be extinguished."

"It could not, and did not. It is here still. I can feel him sometimes, laughing in my ear."

"As can I, and I have no doubt he is enjoying our ridiculous displays."

Kirkland nodded in vigorous acceptance.

"Pray we make it over the crest this time. My feet, I'm afraid, have grown soft by this form of travel."

"Ah, they'll remember the road soon enough."

Nearing the crest again, the men went back to their antics, encouraging the train on with waving hats and vociferous whoops.

Kirkland, however, remained in a sitting position, with a slight grin on his face, watching his brothers. There was a faint glow in his eyes, hurdled from a cavern deep in his chest.

The high walls of the cut began to slow in their passing, and the men groaned at the crawling speed. But they were much closer to the top than ever before.

"Rich," said Alex, peering north from the boxcar's opening, "we just might make it."

It was going to be a close call between the locomotive and mountain, and they could feel the engine pushing to its limits. The train's vibrations escalated, and the men held their breaths. They were at the critical juncture, the train lurching forward in struggling gasps. In this tense moment, no one dared to speak, as if words would jinx the outcome and send them careening in reverse.

As they slowly rounded the top and picked up speed, the men burst into deafening cheers. Nail lifted Kirkland and shook him, before wrapping his arms in a crushing bear hug.

"Was there really any doubt?" said the giddy Nail.

"It appears Georgia isn't too high after all."

Alex was next with a handshake and a question.

"Onward to Chattanooga?"

★   ★   ★

SEPTEMBER 19, 1863
CATOOSA STATION
4 MILES SOUTH OF RINGGOLD, GA
MIDNIGHT

Alex rubbed his eyes and palmed his cheeks. He had been late and running to a college lecture on the satires of Juvenal and Persius until the deceleration of the train had slayed his nightmare.

He looked over at Kirkland, who was wide awake, unable to sleep.

"Has the engine met its match once again?" asked Alex, yawning.

"I don't think so."

The train came to a stop at a country depot no larger than a platform, and they heard the voice of Gaillard in the distance.

"This is the end of the line men. Gather your things. We will be moving out in a few minutes."

Alex eyed Kirkland suspiciously.

"Are you privy to information I'm unaware of?"

Kirkland shook his head.

"Just a notion is all."

"You must teach me this method of intuitiveness, for I am oblivious."

"I'm no fortune teller."

"No, you are not. And that is what frightens me."

Kirkland giggled.

"Do not concern yourself, my friend. I only see a long walk in our present future."

"Now that is in the realm of distinct possibility."

A burned bridge ahead had halted the ease of steam-powered movement.

After finally making it through Allatoona Pass, the engine had failed them again at a town called Dalton. It was out of water, and the men were detailed into a human chain, where for an hour they passed up splashing buckets from a nearby creek. They were delayed even further in this town by another jam of soldier-packed trains. Now less than 20 miles from Chattanooga, they were back in the realm of mortal danger, and no one could be certain just where the enemy was lurking.

Stretching his legs, Kirkland picked up his Enfield and haversack, and jumped from the boxcar. The air was prickly cold and many were grumbling at being awoken from pleasant dreams only to be tossed into a freezing night. Curses and oaths were prevalent, loud enough to annoy their commanding general.

"That is lovely language to be coming from the mouths of South Carolina gentlemen," said Kershaw sharply, before moving on.

It was all the respected commander needed to say to silence the outbursts.

Yawning again, Alex climbed down from the boxcar and looked around. The moon was snoozing under a heavy blanket of clouds, and of no help to lighten a traveler's way. It was so dark that Alex could barely make out Kirkland's features though he was standing a few feet away.

"I hope we don't have to walk too far tonight," said Alex. "We could saunter off a cliff without knowing it."

"Or stumble into a Yankee camp."

"Neither result would be a good way to end this night."

Thud!

"Get down!" someone yelled.

Hitting the dirt, Kirkland and Alex peered helplessly into the dark. They could see nothing but a black, menacing void. Something had hit the soil behind them, and close. And it was groaning.

Above them, out of the taut silence, laughter threw a tarp of confusion over the prone men. Spitting noises could be heard, which only increased the giggling hysterics, and Kirkland realized what had happened.

"Bury, how was your trip?" Silence.

"You all right, friend?" said Kirkland.

"I'm tolerable," said Bury, spitting again. "Georgia dirt ain't swell."

Blindly moving toward the voice, Kirkland helped the groggy soldier to his feet.

"Forget you were riding on top again?"

"'Fraid so."

It wasn't the first time Bury had rolled off the boxcar's roof, awakened by the train's halt, expecting the ground to be only a short leap. At Savannah, with his car in the rear and beyond the station when the train pulled in, he had rolled down a hill into a swamp. His new uniform sullied,

Bury had lumbered back up to the tracks with white eyes planted in a face of raven muck. At least on these occasions, he had correctly judged the engine's renouncement of motion. Still, it was a long fall, and Bury had avoided a broken ankle, or worse, and escaped with mere bruises and a shrug.

"The ground must have been spent," said Kirkland. "But you are a hard case."

"Naw," replied Bury. "I'm a blockhead who thinks he can fly."

"Just the same, we're gonna need you in one piece and for your sake, I'm glad our train journey is over."

★   ★   ★

SEPTEMBER 20, 1863
NEAR CRAWFISH SPRINGS, GA
ALONG CHICKAMAUGA CREEK
11:45 AM

The telling sounds of battle were humming and Kirkland could feel the tremors getting ever closer.

Now, the all-too-familiar adrenaline rush and heightened awareness rose from within his core. The butterflies had multiplied, fluttering in his fingers and toes, throat and bowels. The trials of Manassas, Antietam, Fredericksburg and Gettysburg had prepared him but did not expunge, or even dilute the anxiety of a rowdy clash in blossom.

This time, however, Kirkland felt slightly peculiar, downright strange even. He was as uncomfortable as he was at First Manassas. Sweating profusely, he struggled to unfasten the top two buttons on his coat, and in doing so he nearly dropped his rifle. With success, he was finally able to breathe again, taking large gulps of the mountain air. Though it was getting warm, the weather alone could not account for his armpit fires.

Am I feverish? Taking ill? Fatigued?

Whatever was gnawing at Kirkland had a hold of his feet. They were heavy, like anvils, but he took a page out of Joe's notebook to settle his nerves.

My feet must not be used to a complete pair of leather.

Traveling west along the Brotherton Road, the brigade turned onto what was little more than a deer trail leading northwest. General Hood's division had preceded them, and by the increasing upheaval rattling through the trees, Kirkland knew it had smashed into the Yankees. The pleasant odors of curling leaves gave way to foul, invisible smoke tickling his nostrils. Although there was little underbrush, the hardwood tree cover was heavy. What lay in wait beyond the forest or wherever they would be thrown was an uncertainty pushing down from above with a hulking weight. Yet the stutter of muskets and the roar of cannon told the men in very certain terms that the landing would be one of severe ferocity.

Perspiration stung Kirkland's eyes and bowled down his cheeks. He could not kick loose the overwhelming dread and began to wish for the bullets to deliver his calming shroud, as he expected they would.

He needed it. He craved it. Now, more than ever. Whether the strange melancholic vibrations were the result of sickness or arcane prophecy, he desperately wanted to rid them from his system.

He did not have to wait long.

With bridle reins and stirrups flapping wildly, a black stallion bolted down the trail, riderless and panicked. Like a string of ejecting firecrackers, the men dived to avoid being trampled by the Federal mount.

Kirkland, his muddied brain causing a tardy reaction, leaped at the last possible moment. Skidding on his chest, he rolled to his back.

"You still with us, Kirkland?" asked Alex.

Heart thumping in colossal chops, he dusted himself off and rose.

"No worse for the wear. I reckon this uniform needed some grease."

"That horse was sure spooked. Let's hope its owners are of the same persuasion."

"I suppose he was running at us, not away from us."

"Well, if he was out for revenge, he missed."

"Not by much."

"Yes, I saw a delay in your acknowledgement. Do I sense a thirst for peril?

Kirkland smiled.

"No, I felt compelled to admire the saddle up close. That Yankee leather is very fine indeed."

"Uh, huh," said Alex, chuckling. "I'm sure it is."

Already impatient, Kershaw ordered the men to continue at once.

"Now that you are fully awake, let's keep moving."

He raised his sword.

"Fooorwarrrrd! March."

Less than five minutes later, they exited the woods and crossed the Glenn-Kelly Road, where it became readily apparent that the brigade had arrived at an opportune moment.

Four hundred yards to the north, across a stubbled corn field, the enemy was pouring lead into Hood's men, the last remnants of which were running to the safety of the tree line. Still more Federal troops were posted further north on a knoll, along with artillery.

Maybe these western Yankees are a different breed.

Kershaw didn't hesitate, forming the brigade in a double line across the field owned by the Dyer family.

"Fix bayonets!" the general yelled with galvanizing tongue.

The Carolinians were ready to advance when riders approached their leader.

General Hood had been seriously wounded, his leg shattered. While the group conferred, comparing rank and deciding who was in command, the men continued to face north, staring across the wide-open field. Strangely, the enemy was silent. Although great clouds of smoke hung in the air, no cannon were fired and no musket balls came.

On the knoll, the flag bearers of the enemy were vigorously waving their standards.

"They think we're Yankees!" Alex exclaimed. "Thank God for these new uniforms."

"We need to get under them before they find us out," said Kirkland. "This is an imposing field."

He was right. Completely devoid of cover, and with the enemy on the high ground, a charge here had disaster written all over it. Timing was critical, and the men began to glance over their shoulders at Kershaw with pleading eyes.

"We need to move now!" said Kirkland, starting to fidget. He let the thought go with too much volume, which collected the eyes of those in earshot.

The dread had forcefully returned and sweat pooled at his temples. Taking a swig from his canteen, he buttoned his eyes and tried to center himself. After a few cavernous breaths, he said a short prayer for the safety of his friends and comrades.

"Take the fight to those men," Kershaw finally animated, pointing northward with his sword and bringing relief to Kirkland's idle anguish. The conference was over.

"Right shoulder shift. Forward. March!

As they moved, the smoke began to dissipate and beams of light tore through the cover, dancing on the ends of chosen bayonets. Still, the enemy held their fire and the Carolinians seized a collective breath. Kirkland took in his own regiment's color bearers, relieved that the wind had yet to unfurl the flags.

With every step, he expected the knoll to rupture in flame. Inhaling a modest quantity of air, he smothered it until his lungs beseeched another. Now panting with a cringe frozen on his countenance, he attempted to wipe it away with his sweat, but to no avail. The silence was too unnerving.

In the corner of his eye, he noticed Kershaw seeking out Gaillard. It was a short conversation, and Gaillard barked his order.

"2nd South Carolina, left wheel," he yelled. "At the double quick, forward!"

Unopposed, it was as clear a command as the men had ever heard on a battlefield and they moved with a precision as if at drill.

If only at Gettysburg…

It was an unfortunate musing, and Kirkland regretted that the painful memory had arisen between his ears.

As they jogged underneath the confused enemy, Kershaw's skirmishers in front now had the enemy color bearers in range. Interrupted from their wild gestures, the star spangled banners fell as if the men holding them aloft had evaporated. There was a momentary hush, as if the Yankees were shaking off an unexpected punch to the jaw. When the brief daze was over, they reached back and hurled their venom at their admitted foes.

Fortunately, the 2nd South Carolina had mostly cleared their range of fire with shielding trees between them. And they could thank Hood's men for running the artillery off the field's western ridge now before them. Their price for charging into the cannon's mouth and their infantry support, was written in blood. These men were Alabamans, "Yellow Hammers," as they were affectionately known, and the number of slain near the apex of the ridge attested to their valor.

A few were still alive, and staying put, knowing an attempt to limp across the field would be suicide. As the Carolinians passed, they summoned what strength remained in their mutilated bodies to encourage them on, knowing if the enemy retook the field, they would find themselves in a brutal Yankee prison.

One of these men caught Kirkland's attention, but not for his rousing words; for in fact, he could not speak, let alone yell. The poor soldier's lower jaw was completely gone, as was his tongue and most of his upper teeth. Yet as the soldier's approached, he raised himself onto his knees, blood pouring from the hole that an hour ago was his mouth. Slowly, he raised a defiant fist, stabbing at the heavens.

Kirkland, at first mortified, yet unable to look away, met the Hammer's eyes. Although he detected fear behind them, it was a petite slice, with the remainder glowing hot with rage. The sight of warm blood cooled Kirkland's head, and the transformation took place.

Inspired, with eyebrows sliding in and foreheads clenched, the men dashed up the slope.

433

Coming to a ravine, Gaillard pointed to it.

"This way men, let us get behind them," he said. "Column of fours, move!"

Crashing into the trees, they maneuvered to flank the enemy on the knoll, which was firing desperately to protect the high ground against the assault by the rest of Kershaw's brigade.

Here, the terrain was much more difficult, with fallen timber and scraggy underbrush, but they pushed on. Knowing that speed could save the lives of their friends charging on the plain below, they hurled themselves through vine and bush. Only the trees of prominent girth were worthy of a quick side-step and it wasn't long before they arrived at the open knoll, where they swung into attack formation prior to exiting the tree line.

They could see Kershaw's line approaching within a hundred yards of the enemy, imposing and deliberate.

"Fire on my command," yelled Gaillard, running to each company commander in order to be heard.

The flanking maneuver had worked brilliantly, and they would have the element of surprise.

Almost too easy.

While Kirkland could only see the backs of the enemy, it was obvious they were a jittery and fragile bunch. Two in particular were closing together in a slow backpedal, as if ready to waltz to the rear. Their sergeant kept shoving them forward, which would momentarily root their itchy legs. But the pattern of toe-rolling-to-heel would repeat until a gun was forced into their shoulder blades.

To their horror, Gaillard screamed the decree to fire, and as if of the same conductor, Kershaw did the same.

Ensnared in a crossfire, the Yankees responded with a half-hearted parting shot before retreating down the northern slope of the knoll. Below the slope, the enemy had also seen enough, the troops melting into a brake of oaks.

"That's it boys, we got 'em running," Gaillard exclaimed. "Fire at will."

Amidst the incessant clamor and choking smoke, Kirkland felt a curious peace waffling over him. Esoterically, he looked at each man furiously loading and firing his weapon at the panicked foe. Their faces were mostly obscured, but Kirkland could sense their connected pulse. It was as if all were linked by an invisible cord, a brotherhood of war. But Kirkland felt somehow slightly detached, an overseer of a transcendent moment. His hunger and thirst completely dissolved. His breathing, which had been concise and rampant, slowed. The air thinned and the sulfurous pungency withered. At his lower back and chest, forehead and temples, the inferno of sweat became chilled.

Even the trees seemed extra vibrant and alive, imbued with autumnal glory. Although barely above a whisper, Kirkland could detect a faint singing, as if a chickadee had landed on his shoulder. The tune was both hymn and lullaby, hauntingly close yet indistinct. He had the overwhelming notion to wrap his arms around that bird, to be enveloped by its chorus.

But as swiftly as it had arrived, the tranquility began to drift away. When it was gone, his present latitude rushed in like a speeding train, and Kirkland began to cough savagely. He did not know what had caused the gentle interlude, nor the resurgence of war's touch. But there was no time to dwell on these mysteries.

"We will wait for the brigade," said Gaillard, as the last of the enemy escaped into the trees. "Keep your wits about you."

While a few of the less-seasoned objected to the order, wishing to press the advantage, most saw the wisdom of holding their position. Kirkland was among the majority, knowing that one regiment throwing itself blindly into the woods could accomplish little.

It would be a short wait.

As the rest of the brigade climbed to the top of the knoll, they were greeted with friendly salutes and mild harassment.

"What took ya'll so long?" said Nail, to no one in particular. "Late to the party as usual."

"No, sir," said a grinning soldier of the 3rd South Carolina Battalion. "Your escorts to the ball have arrived."

★   ★   ★

1:10 PM

Kirkland gazed through the trees looking for movement, but saw nothing. The brigade had halted along a primitive road. Beyond it were three large and fairly steep hills, heavily wooded.

Not being able to see the summit through the trees made Kirkland nervous.

"What do you think, Alex?" he asked softly.

"Well," said Alex, scratching the back of his neck. "I imagine the Yankees haven't run all the way to Chattanooga just yet. They're up there all right."

"I heard some of the men say that from the top of Lookout Mountain, not far from here, you can see all the way to South Carolina. I sure would like to see her again."

"Do you mean that lovely belle of yours or the great Palmetto state?" Alex winked.

Kirkland nodded, so slight it was hardly noticeable.

"Both."

In his best British accent: "I postulate that before the New Year calls, you will be in the loving arms of both Carolina and the ravishing Susan."

"My friend, you sure know how to cheer a man."

But there was no buoyancy in Kirkland's voice and his eyes were astray.

Alex didn't need to see them to know the wounds on his face.

A single leaf, recently turned gold by nature's alchemy, seesawed in a drowsy descent, inches from Kirkland's nose. His eyes followed its silent arc to a gentle landing. Reaching down, he nudged the leaf into a pedestal palm, and held it there. He crouched, staring at its contradictions: the razor-edge, arrowed posture and pulsing veins. Its flawed and weakened shape, blemished by an insect's lunch. Yet the leaf glimmered an unspeakable warmth, absorbing beauty in its decay. To the touch, it was cool and cleansing, gentle on a weathered hand.

His gaze split from the leaf and bore a hole through the hills in front, over the mountains and found its way back to Flat Rock. Susan was there in all her radiant glory, with a teasing wink and a welcoming smile. The leaves were falling and dancing all around her, brilliant and reflective. It was as if the sun could not make up its mind which allure was more worthy of supreme illumination—foliage or belle. The vision was so real, so perfect, that for a moment Kirkland believed he was in Susan's presence, watching her laugh among the autumn spirals.

But the image disappeared in a flash, and Kirkland reached out with one hand as if to hold on, his other hand crushing the leaf with violence. When lucidity congealed, he opened his palm to reveal the disfigured muse. As he stared at it dejectedly, the slicing voice of Kershaw knocked him to attention.

"On my signal we attack, together," he growled. "The dense trees will shield us from the enemy's view. Guide on the colors. It is of utmost importance that we reach the crest as one unit."

The general set his jaw into a fearless brick as he paced, watching the brigade get into position.

"They are on the run, South Carolinians. When we break through the line, the day will be ours."

The men thundered in response to their adored leader, and in a rare occurrence, Kirkland found his rebel yell. Allowing the leaf crumbs to drop between his tingling fingers, he tossed this head back, and let out a guttural purging two years in the making. The old, trusty Enfield, massaged by suddenly virile hands, became an extension of himself as images of Joe buried in a shallow Pennsylvania grave slapped him in the face.

Uncontrolled, a dark mantra repeated in his mind.

Joseph Duncan, killed by Yankees
Joseph Duncan, killed by Yankees
Joseph Duncan, killed by Yankees

Kirkland had felt the anger before, but never like this. The usual even keel was in danger of capsizing, which both excited and terrified him. He fought against it, meekly, unsure if he desired a tourniquet to squeeze shut the electric punch coursing through his veins. In truth, he was tired of fighting the demons. Unlike the hundreds of other obsidian memories, which Kirkland was able to exorcise, or at least anchor into an abyss, Gettysburg could not be dulled. Even an image of Ratcliff had little effect. The scars were rising to the surface with a threatening clout, damaging all prior barriers.

While the battle within himself was being lost, Kershaw was ready. Studying the lines both left and right, and satisfied everyone was in place, he pulled out his sword and waved it above his head.

"This is South Carolina's day! Forward!"

The line in front of Kirkland surged across the Vittetoe Road, and into the upward-sloping ravine. When Kirkland moved, the usual battle-calm was absent, but he felt robust and charged with an immense energy. He gritted his teeth, carrying his Enfield with a murderous disposition. His chest heaved as he climbed, sending anger to his limbs, and the screams of revenge were constant at his ear.

Joseph Duncan, killed by Yankees!

As the men crashed through the brush and navigated between fallen and standing trees, the ascent became increasingly difficult and the lines almost impossible to keep intact. While Kirkland's head and feet were unburdened like never before, the steadiness was lost, and it had nothing to do with the difficult terrain. The trees seemed to frown, and even the golden leaves had atrophied to weeping gray. Glancing to the right, he

438

could not see the color bearer, but he pushed onward. As they struggled upward, they encountered no opposition other than the hill itself.

With the terrain, Kirkland could hardly keep his own bearings let alone help to keep the lines together. Stepping over a rotting log, his foot slipped in a mushy puddle, and he pitched forward, catching his fall with the butt of his rifle. As he steadied himself and continued on, he looked right for guidance.

There, through the scowling trees and unforgiving brush, the battle flag unfurled in all its magnificence. A short wind gust spread her faded but brilliant colors and reverberated in Kirkland's eyes. Pausing just for a second, Kirkland let its aura overwhelm him, as a score of its images played upon his mind. Along with her illustrious friend, the Carolina state flag with crescent moon and palmetto, and sky of mystic blue, the standard had always empowered him. Since it had been adopted by the Army of Northern Virginia after the 1st Battle of Manassas, it had been the embodiment of hope, carried into unimaginable horror, hoisted above granite shoulders by resolute hands.

The white stars, branded on a blue St. Andrew's cross and planted on crimson, was a witness to all Kirkland had experienced. His friends and comrades had died protecting its honor. Seeing it now, aloft and galvanizing this bold charge, connected the circle and renewed his spirit. The hill yonder became illuminated in a diffused grandeur. Gone from Kirkland was anger and malice, the consuming hatred. Stripped of all negativity, he stood naked with a mind smoothed of jagged edges and picked clean of debris.

Remaining was but one emotion: pride.

As Kirkland resumed his ascent, he used Kershaw's words as a breathing catalyst.

"This is Carolina's day!"

Gaillard's direction soon followed.

"Up and wheel to the left," he hollered. "Swing to the left. Swing to the left."

In the act of turning, Kirkland swiveled his head at the jumbled line. Wiping his burning eyes, he squinted for recognizable faces. Spotting Alex and Nail slightly ahead and to his right, he dug in and hiked over to them.

Gaining Alex's side, he met his friend's eyes, which were a mirror to his own. The gentle philosopher had found his soldier legs and patriotic fervor again. Like a proud father who never doubted its eventual return, Kirkland nodded in admiration. Alex returned it with the same wordless respect and they continued with matching step.

When they approached within 50 yards of the crest, the enemy revealed itself with savage fury. The summit disappeared in silver smoke as they unleashed a volley. Burrowing into the ground and slapping the trees, the bullets stampeded down the slope in alarming herds. And it would only get worse.

They had encountered the 21st Ohio Infantry, rugged frontier men armed with Colt breech-loading rifles. These Yankees could load five rounds at once AND faster than the Carolinians could arm their Enfields with a single cartridge.

As the Ohioans began to fire at will, a swarm of bumblebees descended upon the climbing travelers, filling the air with spinning death. All around, the golden leaves were sent to an early sleep, and they tumbled down in a hastened pilgrimage.

Unhurt but with miniés striking the ground all around him and buzzing his head, Kirkland was horrified to find that the trio was well ahead of the main line. Without hesitation, he leaped ahead of his comrades, shielding them from the storm.

"Seek cover! Get back!"

Not waiting to see if his friends had complied, he turned to face the enemy, leveling his rifle to cover their escape.

Before he could pull the trigger, a bullet slammed into Kirkland's chest, knocking him off his feet.

Sprawled on his back amongst the decaying leaves, his eyes followed a white oak to its upper limits and into the blue splendor above. The window to unbroken sky was eclipsed by his friends' wide-eyed terror. With vivid distress, Alex and Nail stood over him, mouthing words that he couldn't hear.

Ignoring his failing body, Kirkland summoned his last pillar of strength. He could taste a salty river invading his mouth as he gave his final words.

"Leave me. I am done for."

He choked on the blood pouring from his lips and could feel the chords of mortal life being severed.

"Save yourselves. Tell pa I died at my post. Tell Susan, I'm truly sorry."

Gasping for breath, Kirkland's mouth trembled, and his hand reached out to the sky. With a songbird's melody filling his ears, he fell backward with a countenance of gentle serenity.

Epilogue

DECEMBER 14, 2010
CAMDEN, SC

J eremy Pratt shook his head.

"He was only 20 years old when he was killed at Chickamauga," he said. "He had his whole life ahead of him. He was originally buried on his family's land with a simple wooden marker. To better honor his memory, with the family's permission, locals moved his body to this spot in 1909. While his older brothers survived the war, Richard's younger brother Sam wasn't as fortunate. He enlisted after Richard died, was wounded and captured and sent to a federal prison. While there he contracted a disease that eventually took his life after he returned home."

His 9-year-old son, Andy, stood wide-eyed at the grave before them at Camden's Quaker Cemetery. They had driven down from New York, first visiting Fredericksburg the day before. Having spent years researching Kirkland since his father took him to Fredericksburg as a boy in 1975, Jeremy wanted to take the family tradition a step further. And he wanted to show young Andy where his hero was laid to rest.

Richard Kirkland
C.S.A.
Who, at the Battle of Fredericksburg, risked his life to carry water to the wounded and dying enemies, and at

the battle of Chickamauga, laid down his life for his country
1843–1863
'If thine enemy thirst, give him drink.'

"What were they fighting for, Dad?"

Jeremy thought for a moment. He'd thought of this question often since his ancestor's diary had been passed down to him.

"Well, it was a different time, very different from what it is today. Now, the country is unified but it wasn't so back in 1861. The North and the South had different ideals, different ways of living. In that great war, you fought for whatever state you were born in. Kirkland was born in South Carolina, so he fought for South Carolina. I know I'm simplifying things but I imagine if I were born here, I would've fought for the South, too."

"You would have fought against the Yankees?"

"If I were born here, sure. Slavery was wrong and needed to be eradicated from our soil. Of course we know this now. But if I had been raised here, I imagine I would have fought with my friends and relatives. You see, people get caught up in all the things that make us different when they should really be taking notice of all the things that make us the same. You understand, son?"

"I think so," said Andy, taking a long look at Kirkland's grave and the rows surrounding it. "War is very sad."

"You're right, son. At the same time, if our forefathers hadn't fought the British, we may never have had our own country. Or if we had just let the South secede peacefully, America would have been split in half. Also, if we hadn't fought the Germans in World War II... Well, you get the point. Sometimes, war is necessary.

"But hopefully, someday, we'll become advanced enough as people that war will become a thing of the past. Someday we'll realize that killing each other in the name of religion or politics or greed is just plain foolish. I believe, at least on some level Kirkland understood this. But I'm afraid we're far from that kind of reality. As much as we think we are advanced, we have not yet left the cave."

Andy looked at his dad in puzzlement and Jeremy chuckled.

"What I mean is, humanity has a long way to go. We're still infants and we must learn from our mistakes."

Andy centered on Kirkland's year of death: 1863. He worried that not much had changed in the roughly 150 years since Kirkland was alive. America was still at war for much of it, and across the globe, people were still killing each other in alarming numbers.

"Dad, why didn't you join the military when everyone else in our family did?"

"Well, it's a personal choice. However, you must understand something. I'm very proud of our family's history. We must honor and respect those who came before us and the sacrifices they made for us. Too many people forget where they came from. And those who choose to join the military today in America—they also deserve our respect and gratitude."

Noticing the canteen resting on the shoulder of Kirkland's grave, Andy went over to examine it.

"Ah, that's the great mystery," said his father. "Whenever it gets removed or stolen, someone replaces it."

"Really?"

"Yes. And it's done anonymously, meaning no one knows who's responsible. Whoever it is must think as highly of Kirkland as our family does. Pretty cool, huh?"

"Very cool."

They stood in reverent silence for a few moments.

"Come on son, I have one more thing to show you."

Back in the car, the elder Pratt put in a CD of the Marshall Tucker Band and his son groaned.

"Again?"

"You're nine. You don't know what good music is."

As Andy rolled his eyes, they passed the section reserved for unknown Confederate soldiers, their tombstone's pale and barren, and exited the cemetery. Turning left onto Broad Street, a white-pillared mansion loomed in the distance.

"Dad, what's that?" asked Andy, impressed.

"That's the Kershaw–Cornwallis house. You know, Kirkland first enlisted in the Camden Volunteers there."

"It's huge!"

"Yes it is, son. It was rebuilt in 1977 after being torched by Sherman near the end of the Civil War."

"Sherman?"

"Let's just say that he's not a popular figure in the South."

They continued on past several antique shops and the downtown area, before taking a right on East DeKalb Street to Hampton Park.

"Here we are."

Parking, they headed straight toward a fountain in the center. Jeremy waited for his son to read the memorial tablet.

To

Richard Kirkland

C.S.A.

IN COMMEMORATION OF HIS HEROISM AT FREDERICKSBURG, DEC. 13, 1862. CHRISTLIKE COMPASSION MOVED HIM TO LEAP OVER THE STONE WALL, A MARK FOR HOSTILE GUNS, AND CARRY WATER AGAIN, AND AGAIN, TO THE SUFFERING FOE FALLEN THICK IN FRONT. 'GREATER LOVE HATH NO MAN THAN THIS.' HE FELL AT CHICKAMAUGA, AGED 20.

A Tribute from the school children of Camden

A.D. 1910

"When Kirkland was reburied," said Jeremy. "The school children collected their pennies for a year until they had enough to erect this monument."

"Wow, that must have been a lot of pennies."

His father laughed.

"I imagine so. When you become a father, I truly hope that a pilgrimage like this will become unnecessary. For that will mean that this lesson is unnecessary and peace will reign throughout the Earth. Lincoln's 'better angels of our nature' will have won out."

"That will be a good day," said Andy.

Jeremy put his arms around his son.

"Yes, and we'll remember those who advanced humanity's cause."

Arm in arm, they started to walk back to the car for the long drive back to New York, but Andy hesitated.

Reaching into his pocket, he pulled out a penny. Smiling, he took off at a gallop back to the Kirkland fountain.

Bowing, he tossed the coin into the water before jogging back to take his father's proud hand.

Acknowledgements

The American Civil War community is a great one. There are so many historians, reenactors, and enthusiasts who are so gracious and passionate about sharing their knowledge. Without them, this book would not have been possible.

I'm deeply indebted to Joseph Matheson of Camden, SC, who is the consummate supporter of Confederate history and who always went out of his way to send me information from his vast supply of files on local history. It has been a joy to go to my mailbox time and again to see what he would send on a variety of historical topics. I'm fortunate to call him my friend.

Also, I need to thank National Park Service historian (retired) Mac Wyckoff, whose knowledge of South Carolina regiments is unmatched and his books were my bibles when doing research. No one has dug into Kirkland's story more and I appreciate him always being available to help me with questions.

I want to thank my editor Carl Arnold, who gave me a different perspective and greatly improved this book.

In addition, I need to give love to the following groups and individuals:

Robert E. L. Krick, historian at Richmond National Battlefield Park

Staffs at the Manassas National Battlefield Park, Fredericksburg & Spotsylvania National Military Park, Richmond National Battlefield Park, Antietam National Battlefield, Chickamauga and Chattanooga National Military Park, Gettysburg National Military Park, Harpers Ferry National Historic Park.

Dinah Finley
Clint Ross
Darryl Sannes
The Camden, SC chapter of the Sons of Confederate Veterans
The University of South Carolina and staff at the South Caroliniana Library
The Camden Archives and Museum, and staff

I want to thank my parents, whose love and support has allowed me to follow my dreams. To my son, Tristan, you are the greatest thing that ever happened to me. When I have a bad day, you always make me smile and laugh. I am forever proud of you.

Last but not least, I want to thank my wife, Angel, for making the sacrifices to make this book possible. You allowed me to write through the night on so many weekends without complaint, getting up with our son and letting me sleep in.

If I forgot anyone, I apologize, but you know who you are.

Although it's difficult, try to see your enemies as a potential friend. The world will be a better place if we reach out with love. Fear has no place in our lives.

About the Author

Anthony J Ziebol is an accomplished journalist and writer from Minneapolis, Minnesota. After receiving a degree in print journalism from the University of Wisconsin-Eau Claire, Ziebol moved back to the Twin Cities and began writing as a staff reporter for newspapers and as a freelancer for Midwest magazines. He has given presentations on Kirkland and the 2nd South Carolina regiment throughout the United States. This is his first novel.

Made in the USA
San Bernardino, CA
05 July 2020